"CAN I ASK YOU SOMETHING, ANNA?"

Nathan spoke, his voice grave. "I want you to be honest with me. Did you palm that jack?"

Anna lifted her head from Nathan's, a smile on her face. "What do you think?"

"I think you did."

"You're right. Now can I ask you something?" She paused. "Will you marry me?"

Nathan looked up at the ceiling, then shook his head. "I don't see how I could possibly marry a woman who cheats." He kissed her gently. "Anna, you already know what my answer is. I want to marry you as soon as possible. It'll be perfect. Winter . . . Aeneva . . ."

"You're like her, Nathan, you know."

"Maybe after all this time I've finally learned from her. She taught me to be patient and if I was honorable and true of heart, what I wished most would come to me. She was right."

Nathan pulled Anna closer into his arms. "God, I love you, Kathleen Anna O'Leary," he said. "It's time for us." He kissed her, savoring the sweetness of her mouth. As he held her in his arms, he knew in his heart that they would be together for a long time.

The Great Spirit was indeed smiling on them.

FIERY ROMANCE

CALIFORNIA CARESS (2771, $3.75)
by Rebecca Sinclair

Hope Bennett was determined to save her brother's life. And if that meant paying notorious gunslinger Drake Frazier to take his place in a fight, she'd barter her last gold nugget. But Hope soon discovered she'd have to give the handsome rattlesnake more than riches if she wanted his help. His improper demands infuriated her; even as she luxuriated in the tantalizing heat of his embrace, she refused to yield to her desires.

ARIZONA CAPTIVE (2718, $3.75)
by Laree Bryant

Logan Powers had always taken his role as a lady-killer very seriously and no woman was going to change that. Not even the breathtakingly beautiful Callie Nolan with her luxuriant black hair and startling blue eyes. Logan might have considered a lusty romp with her but it was apparent she was a lady, through and through. Hard as he tried, Logan couldn't resist wanting to take her warm slender body in his arms and hold her close to his heart forever.

DECEPTION'S EMBRACE (2720, $3.75)
by Jeanne Hansen

Terrified heiress Katrina Montgomery fled Memphis with what little she could carry and headed west, hiding in a freight car. By the time she reached Kansas City, she was feeling almost safe . . . until the handsomest man she'd ever seen entered the car and swept her into his embrace. She didn't know who he was or why he refused to let her go, but when she gazed into his eyes, she somehow knew she could trust him with her life . . . and her heart.

SWEET MEDICINE'S PROPHECY #7

WINTER WOLF'S WOMAN

KAREN A. BALE

ZEBRA BOOKS
KENSINGTON PUBLISHING CORP.

ZEBRA BOOKS

are published by

Kensington Publishing Corp.
475 Park Avenue South
New York, NY 10016

First printing: November, 1990

Printed in the United States of America

*For Kathy — part of this
book belongs to you*

Chapter 1

Winter Wolf crawled silently up to the edge of the hill that overlooked the Shoshoni camp. His dark eyes quickly took in the scene: eight warriors, all of them sitting by the campfire, about twenty horses roped together near a stand of trees, and no lookouts. He squinted in the darkness, trying to see if these were the men who had raided their Cheyenne camp and stolen two of their women. There were no women with them. He shook his head. It didn't matter. They could easily have taken the women to their main camp or they could have killed them. Either way he wasn't going to leave here until he had killed as many of the Shoshonis as he could.

He rested his chin on his hands. He had walked this earth for over twenty-five winters and his tribe had fought with the Crows for all of that time. His father told him that the Cheyennes and Crows had been enemies for as long as anyone could remember and it was only getting worse between them. Many of the Crows had chosen to align themselves with the white soldiers and in many battles they fought side by side against the Cheyennes.

But the Crows weren't the only enemies of the Cheyennes. They also fought against the Pawnee and the Shoshonis. Winter Wolf could remember fighting the Shoshonis when he was still a boy, and hating them as much as he hated the Crows. It seemed that their lives were filled with hatred for many different enemies, including the white man. He heard the stories of many of the southern Cheyennes who had been placed on reservation land. It frightened him more than any evil spirit could, to think of living on land governed by a white man. He would die before he lived according to anyone's laws but those of his own tribe.

He closed his eyes and calmed himself, stilling the hatred inside, willing it to make him strong. He drew on his medicine, the wolf, and he thought of his father, who was also named after the wolf. He drew strength from knowing that he would make his father proud when he rode into camp with the scalps of these Shoshonis. It would also be good to be able to give his father their horses. Neither would make up for the loss of the women but it would help ease the pain.

He backed away from the ledge and crawled back down the hill to his horse. He patted the large paint on the nose, then grabbed the reins and swung himself up. Pulling his lance from its place alongside the horse's side, he lifted his shield. His war club and knife were in his belt. He carried no rifle. It would not be honorable to ride into this camp and slaughter these men with a repeating rifle; it would be no fight. A man was supposed to see his enemy's eyes when he killed him.

He turned his horse around and walked him down the hill. He could see the light from the campfire from where he was. He was surprised the Shoshonis hadn't picked a better place to camp, but then they were known for their arrogance, not their keen minds.

He looked up to the sky and closed his eyes. "Oh, Great Father, give me strength so that I may fight like a true Cheyenne warrior and bring pride to my people." He kneed his horse and rode full gallop toward the camp. At the edge of the camp, he uttered a shrill cry. The Shoshonis were as surprised as he thought they would be. He killed one with his lance before the man could react, then turned

8

and clubbed another on the head. Recovering quickly, the Shoshoni warriors leapt to their feet, uttering war cries that echoed his own.

He saw the glint of steel as a Shoshoni raised his rifle, but Winter Wolf was faster, and his lance flew through the air and found its target. He felt a crushing blow across his shoulders. He swung his horse around as a Shoshoni was raising his lance. Reacting instantly, Winter Wolf ducked the lance and urged his horse forward, but there was no way out. The remaining Shoshonis stood in a broad circle, surrounding him. He stopped, surveying the situation. They all held the repeating rifles. It was likely that he would die here, but at least he would die honorably. He threw his head back, baring his throat, and split the night sky with the sound of a proud warrior. He knew they would not shoot him. They would much rather take him prisoner. They would like nothing better than having a Cheyenne warrior to take back to their tribe. He was sure the torture would go on for days, and he refused to die groveling like a dog at the feet of these Shoshonis.

"Can you fight without a white man's weapon, cowards?" he shouted, issuing a challenge. One of the warriors threw down his rifle and held up his club. Winter Wolf tightened the grip on his club and rode toward the warrior. He swung the club in a high arc, but the Shoshoni dodged it and spun in a low crouch, throwing his own weapon with deadly accuracy. The force of the blow knocked the breath from Winter Wolf, and he fell forward on his horse. He tried to sit up and raise the club but it was too late. One of the Shoshonis yanked him from the horse. He fell on the ground, hitting his shoulder, and fully realized the pain in his chest when he landed. He tried to get up, but he was kicked in the ribs numerous times. They dragged him across the camp and yanked his arms behind him, knowing what pain it would cause him. They pushed him back against a rock and pulled his arms out behind him, tying him against the rock.

He looked up at them with dark, angry eyes. *"Hotameho!"*

he spat. He knew they didn't understand what he'd said. He'd simply called them "dogs."

One of the Shoshonis glared at him, then kicked him in the stomach. They spoke heatedly and pointed to him, but they didn't touch him. They walked back to the campfire and looked around at the damage this lone Cheyenne had wrought. Winter Wolf knew that he was right. They wouldn't kill him now; they would save him for their people. He closed his eyes, trying to ignore the throbbing in his chest. All Indians prided themselves on their ability to withstand pain, but he never really had been put to the test. He wondered if he would fare well and if he would bring honor to his people and to his father. He prayed that his medicine would be strong.

Nathan sat on the bouncing train and watched as Anna held his nephew. She sat next to his brother Roberto, and he was surprised that he was still jealous to see them with each other. He shook his head and looked out the dusty window. This train ride had seemed endless and it made him crazy to be confined. He heard Anna laugh as she held Robert high in the air, his small feet squirming happily. He looked at her. She was a natural beauty, one who would remain so long after she had grown old. Her dark hair and skin contrasted drastically with her deep blue eyes. Sometimes he was still surprised at her youthful beauty. They had known each other less than three years, yet it seemed as if their lives had been intertwined since they were children.

"Why are you so serious, Nate?"

Nathan looked over at his brother, his half-brother really. Roberto was the son of a Mexican father and a Cheyenne mother, and he looked every bit like both of his parents. He was tall and handsome and quite a charmer. He and Roberto had always been so different. He himself was six years older than Roberto, and he'd been raised by Roberto's mother, Aeneva, who was married to his father, Trenton. Trenton was the son of a white man and an Arapaho woman and he'd spent many of his summers in the Cheyenne camp where he met and fell in love with Aeneva. But he went into the white world and was forced into a loveless marriage with Nathan's mother, a white woman, who died giving birth to Nathan. Nathan looked like his father. He had blond hair and blue eyes but his skin was a bronze color, a gift from his Arapaho grandmother. He looked at his brother again and marveled that they were able to sit next to each other, let alone sit on the same train.

"Did you hear me, Nate?" Roberto inquired again.

"What? Oh, I'm just thinkin'." Nathan nodded absently, still watching Anna and Roberto, and seeing the obvious affection they had for each other. God, he loved her so much. He wanted nothing more than to marry her when they got back to his parents' ranch in Arizona. He wanted to see her hold their child, not Roberto's. He looked back out the window. Maybe he hadn't yet forgiven Roberto; maybe those were only foolish words he'd uttered, trying to make peace. He just knew he didn't like seeing the woman he loved with his brother. Not yet. Not so soon after he'd taken her away from him.

"Nathan?" Anna's sweet voice interrupted his reverie.

He smiled as he saw her stand. "Do you want me to walk with you?"

"No, I thought I'd take the baby for a walk. I'll be back."

He watched Anna as she clutched the baby to her bosom and walked down the aisle of the car.

"She's good with him, isn't she?" Roberto moved from his seat across the aisle to sit next to Nathan.

"Yes, she is."

"What's the matter, Nate?"

"Nothing's the matter, I just don't like trains. They make me nervous."

"It's more than that. I know you."

Nathan narrowed his eyes and looked at his brother. "How could you know me, Berto?" He looked back out the window. The monotonous clack of the train on the tracks made him tired. He looked out at the rocky countryside and squinted his eyes. He leaned forward, trying to see out beyond the rocks. He thought he saw riders off in the distance but he couldn't be sure.

"I think we'd better talk before Anna gets back." Roberto obviously wasn't ready to give up.

Nathan turned around to face his brother. "What do you want to talk about, Berto? You? Let's see, after letting us all think you were dead for ten years, you appear out of nowhere after our parents die, you force Anna to marry you and go away with you, all because you blamed me for losing you in San Francisco when we were both just boys." Nathan shrugged his shoulders. "Hell, Berto, we could even talk about the fact that you fell in love with Anna and that if I hadn't followed you two to Louisiana, you'd still be married to her."

"Again, I know I was wrong to blame you for my foolishness in San Francisco, Nate. I know it was my fault. If I hadn't run away from you and gone into that cockfight, our lives would've been totally different."

"Neither one of us would've lost ten years, Berto. We both lost time away from our parents and that's something we'll never get back."

"At least you had some time with them before they died, Nate. I never got to see them again. I only have the memories of an eleven-year-old boy to carry around with me the rest of my life."

"That was your own doing, Berto. You could've come back here once you reached Louisiana."

"We both could've done a lot of things differently, couldn't we?"

Nathan begrudgingly agreed. "I guess so."

"What matters is that Anna loves you and you love her. You two belong together. Once you're back in Arizona, you can continue your lives."

"That ranch is half yours, Berto."

"I don't want it, I've got plenty of money now."

"You're a lot richer than I am, that's for sure."

"My son is more important to me than the money. If Caroline hadn't died, maybe we could've worked things out. She still loved me."

"But you didn't love her, Berto. How could you? How could you love a woman who deceived you so badly?"

"She had her reasons, I guess. I felt sorry for her. She never had a chance living with a man like Richard Thornston."

"Well, now that Caroline has left you all of her money, what do you plan to do with it?"

"I haven't thought about it much."

"You'll never have to worry about anything again. You deserve that."

"Nate, I'm sorry for all the pain I caused you and Anna. I don't know how to make it up to you both, but I'll find a way."

"It doesn't matter anymore, Berto." He looked up when he saw Anna approach them. Even with the rocking of the train, she managed to maintain her balance. She walked erectly, her shoulders back and her head held high. She was a woman everyone noticed. She stood in front of Nathan, her blue eyes sparkling, a smile touching her lips.

"You should stand up and stretch, it'll do you good," she advised him, then handed Robert over to Roberto. "Do you mind if we trade seats, Berto?"

Roberto stood up. "Not at all. In fact, I think I'll go for a walk."

Anna sat down next to Nathan "Would you please quit staring out that window? You've been doing that all morning."

"I didn't want to interrupt you two."

Anna put her hand on his arm. "Nathan, don't do this."

"What do you want me to do, Anna? Do you expect me to forget that the last year never happened? Every time I see you and Roberto together, I think about all the times you two were alone. Sometimes it makes me crazy."

"But I told you nothing ever happened between us."

"Jesus, Anna, Roberto is in love with you. You call that

13

nothing?"

"He's not in love with me, Nathan. We spent almost a year together. We grew to care for each other, but there's nothing more than that."

Nathan turned away. He was tired and hot. He hated this damned train. "Let's talk about it later."

"No, I want to talk about it now," Anna said angrily.

Nathan looked at Anna. He knew she wouldn't let him off the hook. Strands of dark hair fell down her long, graceful neck. Her large blue eyes stared at him in expectation. He didn't want to argue with Anna; he wanted to make love to her. He leaned forward to kiss her, but the train jerked suddenly, throwing them both sideways toward the window.

"What's wrong?" Anna asked nervously, looking around the train for Roberto and his son.

"I don't know." Nathan pressed his face against the window, trying to see along the tracks. The train jerked again, but this time it screeched to a sudden stop, throwing passengers from their seats. Nathan and Anna fell against the seat in front of them, both of them landing on their knees. "Jesus . . ." Nathan muttered, getting to his feet. He looked over to Anna. "You cut your head," he said with concern, then reached into his jacket pocket and brought out a handkerchief. He wiped the blood away from her eye. "Are you all right?"

"I'm fine. Where do you suppose Berto and Robert are?"

"You sit down. I'll go check." Nathan took off his jacket and threw it on the seat. He rolled up his sleeves and walked down the center aisle of the car. He helped a woman off the floor and made sure she was seated. Belongings were scattered everywhere. Nathan reached the end of the car and slid open the heavy door. He stepped across the platform and into the next car. He saw Roberto. He looked at the baby. "Is Robert all right?"

"He's fine. But what happened?"

"I don't know, but I'm going to find out." Nathan slid open the door that connected the cars and stood between

14

them, looking out at the rocky, barren land. He jumped to the ground and strode to the front of the train. He stood beside the steaming engine to take a look, but his question was answered before he asked it. Rocks were piled on top of the tracks for a good two hundred feet. It would take them most of the day to remove them from the tracks.

"Rock slide," the engineer said lazily as he walked up next to Nathan chewing on a wad of tobacco. He chewed a few more times, then spit the dark brown liquid onto the dirt. "Damn."

Nathan crossed the tracks and bent down. He picked up pieces of rock in his hand, then tossed them aside and looked up at the hillside. Most of the rocks looked firmly embedded.

"What did you see, mister?"

Nathan didn't answer. He walked toward the rear of the train, ignoring the stares of the passengers who looked questioningly out of the windows, to a place that was easier to climb. He quickly scrambled up the rocks and walked back along the ledge toward the front of the train, where the slide had occurred. He squatted down and ran his fingers over the smooth footprints that were still visible in the fine dirt. There were no distinct heelprints, or bootprints. The prints were from moccasins. He stood up and walked back along the hill, checking the prints. Clearly, there had been at least two Indians, possibly three, and they had left their horses beyond the rocks. They had walked over to the edge, found a place where they could manage to loosen the rocks with some sort of lever, and they had caused the rockslide. But why? He shaded his eyes against the sun and looked out into the vastness beyond. He knew he'd seen riders out there. Indians? They were in northern Colorado, close to Wyoming, so numerous tribes could be out there— Pawnee, Ute, Shoshoni, Crow, Sioux, and Cheyenne. He took one more look beyond the rocks and out across the train, then slid down the bank. A group of men was waiting for him when he got down to the tracks.

"What did you see, mister?" the engineer asked again.

"This wasn't a natural rock slide. Someone forced the rocks loose and pushed them onto the tracks."

Roberto pushed his way through the Indians to his brother. "What is it, Nate?"

Nathan looked at Roberto. "This wasn't an accident, Berto. Someone intended for this slide to happen."

Roberto looked around him. He knew without asking that it was probably Indians. They had all heard about the dangers of traveling by train through Indian country when they left St. Louis, but none of them had been frightened. All three of them had the naive idea that because they had grown up with a Cheyenne mother, no Indian would hurt them. Now the stark reality was beginning to set in. To any Indian, even a Cheyenne, they were all white men, enemies. "What tribe?"

Nathan shook his head. "Don't know. Could be Crow, could be Shoshoni."

"Cheyenne?"

"I don't know, Berto. I don't think our mother's tribe would be this far south, but I don't know. The southern Cheyennes could be here."

"Well, it doesn't matter either way."

"True. They're not going to take time to ask us if we speak Cheyenne. We've got to get these tracks cleaned up and get the train moving."

"You want to tell us what's going on, mister?" one of the passengers asked.

"I think the slide was caused by some Indians. We'd be smart to clean off the tracks as quickly as possible and get out of here."

"Wait a minute," said one man, finely dressed in a brocade suit. "How do you know it was Indians? It looks to me like these rocks could've fallen by themselves."

"He knows because he's a tracker. He saw footprints up by those rocks," Berto said, pointing to the hill where Nathan had just been.

"Well, I don't want my wife scared just because you thought you saw an Indian or two."

16

"Look . . ." Nathan said, growing impatient, "I really don't care if you believe me or not, but I'm not going to be stuck out here in the middle of nowhere if a war party comes riding down on us."

"He's right." The engineer finally spoke up. "Let's get these rocks moved."

Nathan began heaving rocks over to the side of the tracks, followed by the other men in the group. Men from the other cars climbed out, joining in to help clear the debris. Roberto walked back to find Anna so she could hold Robert. He met her halfway down the train.

"You all right, Anna?"

"I'm fine. What happened?"

"Rockslide. We have to get the tracks cleared. Would you mind taking Robert back?"

"Of course not," she said, holding Robert awkwardly in her arms. "Nothing else is wrong?"

Roberto thought of telling Anna about the Indians, but he didn't want to frighten her unnecessarily. "Everything's fine. Just stay close to the train."

Anna started back toward their car. The sun was blazing down. She shielded her eyes against it and looked around her. Clumps of blue-green sagebrush and gray rock were scattered along the landscape all the way to the horizon. In the distance, the air shimmered with heat, making it impossible to tell the rock from the brush. Robert wriggled around and she gently jounced him in her arms, singing softly to him. She had no intention of going back into the hot car, so she walked toward the back of the train. People looked out at her, staring, but Anna ignored them. She wanted to stretch her legs and keep Robert distracted. She felt the sweat run down her back and between her breasts. She had always heard stories of how cold it was in Colorado and Wyoming. She didn't think, not even in the summer, that it would get this hot.

She stopped between one of the cars and propped one foot up, setting Robert on her lap. She managed to get out of her traveling jacket and slide it over his head. He imme-

17

diately tried to pull it off, but she took the baby's hand away, lifted him back into her arms, and walked to the end of the train. As she looked up at the red caboose, she noticed a man staring down at her from an open window.

"Ma'am," he said, bowing his head slightly. "Should you and the baby be back here? Shouldn't you be up in your car?"

Anna shrugged. "It looks like it'll be a while before they get the tracks cleared. I just thought I'd go for a little walk."

"I wouldn't do that if I was you, ma'am. Could be Indians out there." The man took off his blue-and-white-striped cap and drew his arm across his forehead. "I've seen 'em before."

"You've seen Indians around here before?"

"Yes, ma'am. Last time we brought the train through here I saw 'em out there waiting."

"Waiting?"

The man looked at Anna. "I think they've been waiting to attack this train for a long time."

"Who are they? What tribe?"

The man shrugged. "Could be Pawnee, could be Shoshoni. Hell, could be any of 'em the way they all roam around now."

"You said they were waiting, but waiting for what?"

"Lots of these Indians is real angry at us white folks right now, you know. They blame us for taking their land and putting them on reservations. If the truth be told, I think they hate all of us. I think they're ready to get back at us any way they can."

Anna looked at the man and then out at the rocky, open land. She hugged Robert to her. She had a strange feeling, as if she were being watched. "Do you think they're out there right now?" Anna asked without looking at the man.

"Yes, ma'am, I think they're out there somewheres."

"Well, shouldn't we be doing something?"

"We can't do nothin' until them rocks is cleared."

"What about weapons? Shouldn't someone be standing watch?"

"Ma'am, we don't have many weapons on this train. We're carrying passengers, not gold."

Anna looked at the man, her blue eyes narrowing in anger. "That is absurd. You'll pay for men to guard gold, but you won't pay to guard people?"

"It's not my doing, ma'am. I have nothing to say about it. If I did, we wouldn't even be traveling through Indian country." He wiped his forehead again. "I don't blame 'em myself. If someone was to come along and take my land away from me — land that had been in my family for hundreds of years — then tell me I had to live in a certain place or I'd be arrested or shot, I'd want to kill someone, too."

The baby cried out, and Anna patted him on the back, then leaned against the caboose, wiping the sweat from her face.

"Why don't you and the baby come on inside for a spell?" he suggested. "I got me an icebox and we could have us a nice glass of lemonade."

Anna looked up at the man and smiled. "You have your own icebox in there?"

"Was my wife's idea. She said that if I was gonna be stuck way back here by myself all day, I should at least be comfortable. So we got me an icebox, and I fill it with a block of ice every time we stop in a city. It sure comes in handy sometimes."

"What's your name?"

"Name's Emmett, Emmett Barnett." He left his seat by the open window and walked outside. Emmett was about fifty-five years old, a slight man of medium build and medium brown hair. He wore thin, wire-framed glasses. He was very ordinary-looking except for his eyes: Behind his spectacles shone the sparkling brown eyes of a man who never ceased to enjoy life.

Anna held out her hand. "My name is Anna O'Leary. I'm very pleased to meet you, Mr. Barnett."

"Please call me Emmett, all my friends do."

"I'm very pleased to meet you, Emmett." She looked down at her wrinkled dress, minus the jacket that was now

19

firmly in place on her nephew's head. Originally, it had been a simple blue linen dress with a matching jacket cut in at the waist, but now it looked more like a baby's bib with its front covered with spit-up and milk. "I'm afraid I'm not quite fit to visit."

"I myself am the father of five. I know what it's like to have a baby spit its lunch all over you." He offered Anna his hand. "I'm sure a glass of lemonade will make you feel better."

Anna held on to Emmett's hand as she navigated the bottom step. "A glass of lemonade sounds wonderful. I . . ." She broke off suddenly hearing a rumbling noise. She turned and looked behind her. There was a plume of dust rising into the air and the noise intensified. Hoofbeats! Riders were coming. Anna looked at the large cloud of dust coming toward the train. She felt Emmett's hand tighten around hers.

"I think you and the child should get up here right now, ma'am."

Anna climbed up the stairs. Emmett quickly pushed her and Robert inside.

"Go on now, ma'am."

"Emmett?" Anna tried to look out the window, but a shot rang out and Emmett collapsed against the side of the caboose. "Emmett!" Anna tried to help him up but he didn't move.

"Please, ma'am, hide yourself and the child," he whispered.

Anna clasped Robert tightly against her and started for the inside of the car. A shrill war cry made her stop, trembling. Dust swirled outside the train. Warriors flashed by, screaming, bent low over their horses. Their faces were painted, grotesque with bright colors. Their long braids trailed out behind them. Anna had never seen anything so frightening in her life. Although her birth mother was a Cheyenne, and she was raised by Nathan and Roberto's mother, who was also a Cheyenne, nothing had prepared her for this. The rumble of hooves had become thunder—

deafening, paralyzing. She forced herself to move.

The caboose was strewn with crates, cots, everything the train crew would need on their long journey. She hurried to the back of the car with Robert and looked around. There was a small desk on one side and she quickly rummaged through it. She found a letter opener but no guns. Frantically, she searched through the crates and boxes for a rifle, but she couldn't find one.

The sounds outside grew louder and Anna hurried to the rear of the car, scooting underneath a cot with Robert. Armed only with the letteropener and a small knife in her boot, she knew she had to try to fend off any attackers. She felt the vibration of the horses as they neared the caboose. Robert squirmed in her arms, but she held him tightly, clamping a hand over his mouth. She could hear the far-off screams of some of the passengers, but she forced herself to remain calm. Gunfire rang out, but she couldn't tell if anyone from the train was firing back. She wanted desperately to get to Nathan, but she knew she couldn't risk it. She had to think about Robert first.

She heard voices outside, the words coming in the strange guttural language the Indians spoke. The floor of the caboose vibrated as they entered the car, knocking everything out of their way as they searched for things that would be of value to them. She saw the moccasins of one of the Indians who stood next to the cot. She was unable to look away; the curving pattern of the beads mesmerized her. Robert began to squirm, breaking the spell. She held him tightly. The Indian who was closest to her spoke, the guttural sounds hammering at her ears. Suddenly, the cot was jerked upright. Before Anna could react, they yanked her to her feet. She lunged forward, slashing downward with the letter opener. The Indian reacted instantly, striking sideways. The letter opener clattered to the floor and Anna's wrist and hand were numb. Another warrior snatched Robert from her arms. Stunned, Anna fought uselessly as she was carried from the caboose and thrown across an Indian pony.

She tried to get down from the horse, but the man quickly swung up after her and pushed her back down. She frantically looked around her for help, but there was no one. Shots were still being fired, and the screams of the people on the train rang in her ears as the Indian rode away. Anna fought her rage and fear. The rocks and sage streamed past. It was impossible to raise her head high enough to see anything else. The horse's withers pounded into her stomach. She fought to breathe and tried to control the urge to vomit She knew her ribs would be bruised, and that walking would be hard for a few days. The dust and the smell of the animal were overwhelming.

The warrior's arm went around her waist and he dragged her upright. Reaching over her shoulder, he grabbed her thigh, forcing her to swing her right leg over the pony's neck so that she rode astride in front of him. She looked around her for the other Indian who had taken Robert and, to her relief, she saw him riding not far away. The baby seemed unhurt. She would find a way to get away, to save herself and Robert. The pain of her bruised ribs and the steel-muscled arm around her waist forced her to realize that false bravado wasn't going to save her or Robert. For an instant, fear threatened to overwhelm her, but she forced her thoughts away from her plight, closed her ears to the hoofbeats and wild screams of the Indians around her, and withdrew into her memories, looking for strength.

She thought of Aeneva and tried to draw strength from the woman who had loved her and raised her as her own daughter. She remembered Aeneva's stories about the Cheyenne's bitter fights with the Crows. She especially remembered Aeneva's story about her capture by a cruel Crow warrior named Crooked Teeth. He had tortured her, used her, and humiliated her in the worst possible ways, but Aeneva still managed to stay alive. Anna didn't know if she could be as brave.

She tried to turn her head to see if anyone was following them. The dust that rose like a brown fog behind them made it impossible to see. Were Nathan and Roberto even alive? She tried not to cry, but she felt the tears well up in her eyes. She didn't know what she would do if Nathan was dead. They had waited so long and been through so much to be together; now again, they had been torn apart.

She closed her eyes, overcome with weariness. Whatever she was going to do, she would need her strength. She forced herself to rest.

The sound of Robert's cry jerked her awake. She looked over at the Indian who was holding him in front of him, his arm around Robert's chubby body. As far as she could tell, he wasn't hurting the child. Robert was probably just hungry.

The ponies had slowed to a walk. The sun was low in the sky and they moved through the thickening sage with their heads down. Anna tried to remember landmarks in case she had a chance to escape, but the rock formations all looked the same. She looked down at the very fine, gravelly dirt ground that could easily be blown away by the wind. It wouldn't hold hoofprints for long. How would Nathan be able to track them if there weren't any signs? Hopelessness dulled Anna's thoughts and she closed her eyes again.

The horses stopped. They had reached a camp. Two Indians were tending a small campfire in the deepening dusk. Behind them, warriors kicked their weary mounts into a final gallop and circled the camp shouting their victory. The warrior who held Anna slid from his horse and pulled her after him across the camp. He pushed her down on the ground, next to a rock where another Indian was tied. Her captor pointed to her, and from his angry, heated tone, she knew he was telling her not to try to escape.

Anna looked frantically for Robert. The warrior who held him was across the camp. She expected him to carry Robert to her, but instead, he held on to the child and walked to the fire. Anna watched, too terrified to move, as the Indian grabbed a piece of dried meat from a rack and took a bite, chewing vigorously. He spit some into his fingers and shoved it into Robert's mouth. The child squirmed at first, but as the Indian kept pushing the food into his mouth, he began to accept it. The Indian laughed when Robert reached out for meat. Every muscle in Anna's body was tensed and she forced herself to relax. If they were going to kill Robert they wouldn't feed him, would they?

The Indians were talking and laughing, gesturing dramatically. She realized they were pantomiming their attack on the train. Some of them were wearing ladies' hats and shawls, others were wearing men's bowlers. Jewelry stolen from the passengers shone on necks and wrists. Anna shuddered, imagining the fate of the people she had traveled with. One warrior held a bottle of whiskey in his hand and took a long drink. When one of the others reached out for it, he brushed his hand aside. Anna watched them. What would they do to her when they were finished celebrating their victory?

There were at least twenty warriors in the camp, more than enough to guard against any escape. She looked at the Indian who was bound next to her. His long hair was adorned with only a feather and braid on one side. His eyes were dark and oval-shaped, and his nose was straight. The paint that was on his face was smeared with blood. One of his cheeks was swollen and there was a bloody, jagged wound in his dirt-caked chest. The way his arms were pulled behind him stretched the skin across his chest, making the wound gape open. But he never uttered a sound, he just continued to stare straight ahead.

Anna untied the scarf that was around her neck and reached over to clean the dirt from his wound. The Indian jerked away, and for the first time he looked directly at her, his eyes narrowed in anger. "I'm sorry," she said softly. "I only wanted to help." He seemed not to hear her as he turned his head away. She knew he couldn't understand her. She bunched her scarf up in her hand and lowered her head. She thought of Aeneva, and willed herself to be strong. *"Tsehe-shketo.* My mother," she said in Cheyenne. She couldn't believe it had just come out. She didn't speak the language fluently, but she remembered many words and phrases that Aeneva had taught her.

"*Ne-tsehese-nestse-he?* You speak Cheyenne?" the Indian asked quietly, without looking at Anna.

Anna looked at him. "*Heeheo-ohe, na-tsehese-nestse.* Yes, I talk Cheyenne a little." She stared at him. "You speak English!"

Slowly, he turned his head and stared at her. His dark eyes squinted as he looked at her. He nodded slightly.

"You are Cheyenne?"

Again, he nodded.

"My mother's people were Cheyenne," she said proudly.

"That does not make you Cheyenne," he replied coldly, turning his gaze toward the drunken Indians in the center of the camp. "You will not make it through this night."

Anna looked at him and then at the men in the camp. Her heart pounded in her chest. The Indians were working themselves into a frenzy. She searched for Robert. The Indian who had taken him was still by the fire. He had placed Robert on a robe and the child was sleeping peacefully. Angry and scared, she turned to the man next to her. "I have a knife."

He looked at her, for the first time showing a bit of interest. "Can you cut me free?"

"I can help you escape from here. Without me, you do not have a chance."

"And without me, *you* don't have a chance."

He returned his gaze to the group of men in the center of the camp. "Do not look at me." He struggled to sit up straighter. "If you cut me free, I will help you escape."

"How can I trust you?" Anna asked as she looked about her and noticed nearly half the warriors moving away from the campfire. In the darkness, Anna heard the thudding of hoofbeats and her heart leapt with hope. "What are they doing? Are they leaving?"

"They will go back to the main camp to tell of their victory there." Without turning his head, he glanced at her, his dark eyes catching hers and holding them. "The rest will stay here to guard us. They will take us back to the

25

main camp tomorrow where I will be tortured. It is unlikely they will wait that long for you."

"Will you help me?"

"I give you my word as a Cheyenne warrior," he said simply.

Anna knew how important honor was to the Cheyennes. "I have a child with me. Will you help us both?"

He nodded. "It will be a problem getting him away from the Shoshoni who has him."

"Shoshoni," Anna repeated. "These are Shoshonis?"

"Yes, and they hate Cheyennes." He turned to look at her. "They have sunk lower than any enemy of ours. Many times they have fought with the white man against their Indian brothers. It is unfortunate for you, woman, that they do not seem to care for white people on this night."

Anna held his gaze for a moment, then withdrew her eyes and looked at the men who were dancing wildly around the campfire. He didn't have to explain to her; she knew what they would do. "What about the baby? Will they harm him?"

"I do not think so. They will keep him to raise as their own."

"I can't let that happen."

"You do not have a choice, woman. Either you stay here and let them have their way with you or you come with me and try to escape."

Anna shook her head. "I can't leave him."

"*Otaha*. Listen. If we can escape, perhaps I can sneak back in later and get the child. If we both stay here, there will be no chance."

"You would do this?"

"*Haahe*. Yes. No child should be raised as a Shoshoni."

"All right, I will cut you loose."

"Where is the knife?"

"In my right boot."

"Reach down and take it out."

Anna did as she was told, then held the knife under a fold of her dress.

26

"Now move closer to me. Slowly. When you are able, put the knife behind your back and cut the rope. Just rub the blade against the rock."

Anna inched closer to the Cheyenne and put her hands behind her. The rock was to her left, so she put the knife in her left hand. She reached out until she felt the rock and the rope. She moved the blade back and forth until she felt the rope snap. "Do we try to escape now?"

"No, we wait until they are drunk."

"Is that wise? What if they . . ."

He looked at her. "You will have to trust me. I will know when the time is right. But you will have to give me the knife."

Anna looked at him. In spite of her misgivings, she knew he was her only chance. She put the knife in his hand, then moved away from him and faced the campfire again. "My mother was taken by the Crows when she was a young woman. They did unspeakable things to her. She almost died from the shame of it. But still she fought to stay alive." She fell silent. "I do not have my mother's heart. I am not as brave as she."

"If you are truly your mother's daughter, then you, too, have a brave heart."

"I thought you said I wasn't a Cheyenne."

"We shall see," he said noncommittally. "They are growing restless. Soon they will come for one of us."

"I thought you said they would come for me."

"They will also get pleasure in torturing me. It is what they have been waiting for. I killed many of their men. They wish me to suffer. They will not kill me here, but there are many ways to make a man suffer without killing him." Around the campfire, the warriors' voices rose again as they began another pantomime of their attack on the train.

"Now, take this rope and put it around your neck."

Anna took a piece of the rope that the Cheyenne had cut and wrapped it around her neck.

"Tightly. It must look like I have strangled you."

"But I thought I was going with you."

"Just do as I say, woman."

Anna pulled the ends tightly around her neck. "Now what are you going to do?"

"As soon as I am able, I will slip behind the rocks. You fall onto the ground. Do not move, no matter what they say or do. Still even your breathing."

"What good will that do? You can't fight all of them by yourself."

He looked at her, a glimmer of a smile on his mouth. "Nothing is impossible when you are a Cheyenne. Didn't your mothers people teach you that?"

Anna started to say something but stopped when she saw the Cheyenne moving. He rolled onto his belly and crawled behind the rock. Then he was gone. She dropped to the ground, closing her eyes. The Shoshonis were still laughing and drinking and she was all alone. She had placed her trust in a man whom she didn't know, and her life now depended on him.

Chapter 2

Winter Wolf watched the Shoshonis as they celebrated their attack on the train. He recognized the arrogance of victory, and he also recognized that men got careless when they felt invincible.

He looked across the camp at the prone form of the white woman. If they thought she was dead or dying, they would look for him. It would give him time to move around in the darkness, which would give him the advantage. Somehow he had to find a way to get her and the child out of the camp alive and try to slow the Shoshonis down.

He sat silently among the rocks that surrounded the camp and watched with the patience of a hawk. He was in no hurry; he could wait as long as it took. Soon, he knew, they would discover he was gone. In their arrogance, they never tied the woman up, nor had they suspected that she might be carrying a weapon, or that she would help him to escape.

He watched as one of the Shoshonis got up and danced. The others laughed as he stumbled. He grew angry and tried to get their attention, but they ignored him and he staggered off in the direction of the woman. Winter Wolf quickly worked his way back around the camp to the rocks behind the woman, waiting for the Shoshoni to get to her.

When the Shoshoni did reach her, he knelt and shoved her with his hand. She didn't move. He pushed her onto her back and started to say something, but before he could utter a sound, Winter Wolf emerged silently from the rocks and pulled the Shoshoni into the brush, choking off any sound he might make with an arm around his throat. He dragged him farther into the darkness, and waited until he no longer struggled. He dropped the man's limp body onto the ground, quickly gathering his large hunting knife and war club. He put the woman's smaller knife in his moccasin, the hunting knife into the empty sheath he wore on his thigh, and shoved the war club into the waist of his breeches.

He moved close enough to see the woman. She had not moved. He hoped more of the Shoshonis would be as foolish as this one. There was no way he could fight all of them at once. He was brave and he was strong, but, as he had recently learned, one man did not make an entire army.

A sudden shout jerked his eyes back to the campfire. The Shoshonis were running toward him. He stepped back into the brush where he could watch without being seen. One of them knelt over the woman to see if she was alive. She lay perfectly still as he pushed and prodded her. The Shoshoni straightened and shook his head, then they all scattered, looking into the darkness around the camp. They wouldn't find him, he knew that.

He squatted behind a large boulder and watched as they placed guards around the camp. The woman was ignored and the baby still slept.

The horses were tethered on the far side of the camp. If he could just get to them, it would be easy enough to stampede all but the two he would need.

He looked at the men in the camp. His hatred had made him foolish the first time he had tried to fight them. He had not used his instinct or his senses. That was what he had to do now. This had nothing to do with honor; this had to do with survival.

He worked his way through the darkness, careful not to

dislodge a single stone or snap the dry twigs of the sage-brush. Luck was with him. He was upwind, so the ponies would not scent him. He reached down and worked several small stones loose, then stood up, edging closer so he could see into the camp. The Shoshonis were no longer peering into the darkness. It was as he had hoped. They thought he had run away, and they knew there was nothing they could do until daylight.

One man was supposed to guard the horses, but his back was to them as he watched his friends in the camp. There was another guard on the other side near the woman. The rest of the men were again sitting down at the fire.

He moved along the rocks, his fingers feeling the curves and edges of each one until he was close to the horses. He threw one of the rocks among them. They whickered and stamped, drawing the guard's attention. Winter Wolf got down low and skimmed several more stones in quick succession around the nervous horses. Sensing danger on the ground, the ponies reacted as they would react to a rattler, half rearing and beating the earth with their hooves. Quickly, the guard walked among them, eyes on the ground. He grasped his rifle by the barrel, raising it to use it as a club. Winter Wolf moved forward among the horses, positioning himself as the guard came closer. At the perfect instant, Winter Wolf slammed his war club into the man's forearm, making him drop the rifle. Before the guard could cry out, he had him around the neck and was moving back into the brush. With a quick, jerking movement, Winter Wolf snapped the man's neck. In three quick steps he had retrieved the rifle and hidden it in the rocks. For an instant, Winter Wolf stood still, looking over the backs of the ponies into the camp. The disturbance had gone unnoticed.

He crouched low and went to the first horse. Patting the animal reassuringly, he cut the rope, leaving one thin strip of rawhide intact. Murmuring to calm the horses, he worked his way from one to the next, always leaving one strand of rawhide to hold them. Two that looked like strong

31

runners, tied close to the rocks, he left. When every tether had been weakened so that a single jerk would snap it, he took the two horses he had chosen and led them into the brush. The river of time was running against him now, he knew that. He tied the horses and glanced back into the camp. So far, the warriors were unaware of his movement.

He circled the camp again until he was near the woman, then looked at the man who was supposed to be guarding her. He sat on the rock that he himself had been tied to, holding a repeating rifle lazily in his hands. Periodically, he looked back into the brush, but most of the time he looked across the camp.

He crawled along the ground, the cool earth touching his belly, the rocks and twigs scratching him as he moved silently along like a creature of the night. The wound in his chest was painful, but he chose to ignore it. He was now behind the rock that had helped to imprison him. The guard sat staring across the camp, hearing nothing. Winter Wolf sprang quickly to his feet and pulled the Shoshoni backward, his forearm across the man's throat. The Shoshoni struggled in vain as Winter Wolf quickly embedded the huge hunting knife into the man's chest in the area of his heart. The man's body went limp in seconds. Winter Wolf took the Shoshoni's hunting knife and went back to the rock, picking up the repeating rifle.

"Come this way, woman. Now."

Anna obeyed, quickly following Winter Wolf. When she was outside the camp, he pulled her to her feet and dragged her back around the boulders to the horses. He untethered the animals and handed the reins to Anna. "Get up on the horse and wait for me," he ordered.

The rifle felt unfamiliar in his hands, but he knew this dishonorable weapon was his only hope. The arrogance of the Shoshonis combined with their drinking had made the task of getting the child possible, but it was still dangerous. He moved around until he found a place high enough to give him a view of the entire rock-shielded camp. He aimed the rifle at the circle of men and began shooting.

The first shot missed but brought all the Shoshonis to their feet and frightened the already nervous horses. His second shot and his third found their targets. Crouching low, Winter Wolf changed his position. The white man's whiskey had dulled the Shoshonis' senses, but he knew that they would recover quickly. Several of the warriors had run into the darkness on the far side of the camp, but three stood with raised rifles, firing into the rocks where he had been. The ponies tethered closest to the camp reared, snapping the single strips of rawhide that held them.

Winter Wolf aimed carefully as the warriors fired. He killed two of them and wounded the third. Then he began to run. He skirted the edge of the camp, his eyes fixed on the child, who was crying in confusion and fear. Shots rang out from the darkness on the far side of camp and ricocheted off the rocks where he had been a moment before. More horses broke their tethers as they began to mill in a slow circle of panic. A bay mare suddenly plunged away from the others, galloping, terror-stricken, into the camp. Wheeling, the others followed her, spreading out, wild-eyed and screaming.

Bent nearly double, Winter Wolf darted into the camp. Shots rang out overhead and the horses turned, thundering through the camp again. In the dust and confusion, Winter Wolf snatched up the crying child and ran back toward the safety of darkness.

"Over here!" Anna called when she heard him coming.

Winter Wolf ran toward the sound of Anna's voice, handing Robert over to her. He swung himself up on his horse and took the reins from her hand.

"It will be difficult to see at night," he explained. "I am more accustomed to traveling in the darkness."

Anna held Robert close to her, grateful that he was unharmed. He wriggled for a while in her arms, but soon fell asleep, unable to fight the darkness and the rhythm of the horse's gait for long. Anna kissed him on the top of the head and held him tightly. Wherever the Cheyenne warrior was leading her, she had no choice but to follow.

33

The night sky was giving way to the gray and rose of dawn before she had the courage to speak. "What is your name?"

Winter Wolf slowed his horse until he was almost next to Anna. "It is Winter Wolf. Is the child unharmed?"

"He is well. Thank you. We owe you our lives."

"As I owe you mine," Winter Wolf replied gravely. "We will have to ride without stopping until we put some distance between us and the Shoshonis."

"What will we do when it's daylight?"

"We will ride until we find a good shelter. It will be tiring but we have no choice."

"I have nothing to feed the baby."

"When it is light, perhaps we can find wild berries or fruit. I will hunt when we camp for the day."

Under the lightening sky, Anna could begin to make out the outlines of the different rock formations as they passed them. Ever-present and looming on her left side like giants touching the sky were the Rocky Mountains. In the night, even the shapes of the mountains had been invisible to her. How had Winter Wolf led them over the dangerous ground? Anna barely managed to stay astride her horse, wanting desperately to give in to sleep. She glanced at Winter Wolf. He had been wounded and his exhaustion must surely surpass her own, yet he sat his horse proudly, his eyes alert, always moving. She wondered how he managed to stay awake.

"Look to the west," Winter Wolf said softly. "The sleeping giant awakens."

Anna looked westward to the Rockies and she could see the first rays of dawn turning the snowcapped peaks gold and pink. Turning eastward, she could see the sun rising. "What do you call these mountains in Cheyenne?"

Winter Wolf looked at the magnificent mountains. "Hooh-oh-honaae-vo-oh-ohomeeoh-ohe."

"What does it mean?" Anna knew from Aeneva's teachings that most Cheyenne words had literal translations.

"It means, 'rock which is on the horizon.'"

Anna looked again at the mountains, unable to imagine what it would be like to cross them. Robert started to move in her arms, but she hefted him up to her chest, patting him on the back. Her right arm was asleep from holding him all night, but at least he had slept.

"We will stop to rest soon. I know of a place that has a stream. It also has trees for shelter. We should be able to find some food for the infant."

"Thank you," Anna said. When Winter Wolf gave her a strange look, she repeated the words in Cheyenne. *"Ne-aoh-oheshe."*

He nodded his head slightly but didn't reply, only handed Anna her reins and started to gallop. Anna dropped Robert down into her lap and took the reins with her left hand, easing them between her fingers. She had no trouble keeping up with Winter Wolf, even though he rode at a fast pace.

They rode for what seemed like most of the morning until Anna saw subtle changes in the land. The endless level expanse of the plains was broken by low, rolling hills. Dry, rocky streambeds traced the bottoms of the small valleys they crossed, and ancient cottonwoods grew, solitary testimony that water sometimes flowed here. It wasn't long before they reached a small stream that seemed to flow cheerfully through the empty land.

Winter Wolf walked his horse into the water and rode carefully upstream. Anna followed, not sure what he was doing. They rode up the shallow stream for quite a while. The horses nickered with delight. Anna knew how good the cool water must feel on their hooves after their long night's ride and she patted her horse's head in appreciation.

They were riding straight into overhanging branches, but Winter Wolf simply ducked his head and Anna did the same, making sure to cover Robert's face with her hand. She longed to stop and drink the pure, clear water but she dared not try, knowing Winter Wolf would leave her. He was her only chance for survival.

Winter Wolf stopped suddenly and dismounted, leading

his horse up the northern bank of the stream. Anna started to follow him, but Winter Wolf spoke. "Wait for me. I will return."

Anna stopped her horse in the river. She held Robert close to her and kissed his head. Cottonwoods grew all around her, their branches hanging over the stream. Wild grass grew along the banks of the river and she could imagine how it would feel to lie down on it and sleep. Before long, Winter Wolf jumped down the bank and walked to Anna's horse.

"Give me the child and get down," he commanded.

Anna did as she was told. When she was standing in the middle of the cool stream, Winter Wolf handed Robert back to her and took the reins of her horse. He led it up the same bank he had gone and Anna followed. Though it was not a steep bank, it was very slippery, and she was careful not to lose her footing as she climbed. She followed Winter Wolf back into the trees to a slight clearing. The horses were loosely tethered to a low-hanging branch so that they could graze on the wild grass.

"Did you know of this place before?" Anna asked.

Winter Wolf gave her a strange look, as if wondering how it was possible for a woman of Cheyenne blood to know so little. "Sometimes if you ride upstream you will find places like this," he explained. "Trees and plants grow in abundance around rivers. We should be able to find food."

"And we rode in the stream so the Shoshonis couldn't track us?"

Winter Wolf nodded. "Even if they do follow us, we will hear them in the water before they get close. We will be able to ride out of the trees before they can harm us."

Anna sat down on the grass, feeling totally exhausted. Robert got up immediately, and with uneven steps, began to run in the grass. She started to get up, but Winter Wolf held up his hand. He grabbed Robert and held him high in the air. Robert laughed loudly and Anna smiled. "Shall I go look for food?" she asked lamely, feeling she should contribute in some way.

"No, you rest. I will take the boy and we will look for food."

"What about your wound? You should clean it. I'll look for food."

"You can help later when you are more rested."

Anna nodded as she watched Winter Wolf and Robert go off into the woods together. She lay down in the long, soft grass, resting her head on her hands. Small rays of sunshine filtered through the branches of the cottonwoods, just enough to warm her body and make her sleepy. Before she knew it, she closed her eyes. She couldn't stop her mind from running wild. What if Nathan was dead? She didn't know what she would do without him. What about Roberto? Was he also dead? She didn't want to think about the two of them no longer being a part of her life, but she couldn't help but think of it. If Nathan and Roberto were dead, no one would come for her and Robert. She felt in her heart that both men were alive and they would rescue her, but what if they were dead and she had to stay with Winter Wolf? How could she and Robert exist in a strange and hostile land?

She closed her eyes again and tried to relax. It would do her no good to worry now. She had to try to rest. She didn't want to think about life without Nathan. She had to believe he was alive and that he would come for her. Right now, she had to remain strong and brave, and she had to try to be as helpful as possible to Winter Wolf. She knew that without him she would probably be dead and Robert would be with the Shoshonis. There was nothing to do now but be patient and pray that Nathan would soon find her.

Anna woke up with a start when she heard Robert scream. She sat up and looked around her. He was scampering back and forth chasing a bird that had flown into the clearing. Every time Robert ran toward it, it flew up and over his head, only to land in another place. Winter

Wolf sat and watched Robert, a smile on his face. Anna walked over to Winter Wolf.

"I was frightened when I heard him scream," she said, sitting down next to him. "I see I was silly to worry."

"He has been chasing this bird for a long time now. He refuses to give up. This is a good quality, even in one so young. He would make a good warrior."

Anna wanted to scream that this boy would never be raised as a Cheyenne, but she didn't want to antagonize Winter Wolf. "He is a smart child."

"He does not look like you."

"He is not mine. He is my nephew."

"And your husband?"

Anna didn't want to say that she wasn't married. She needed the protection of a marriage, even if it was a lie. "I'm sure he will be following us. He's probably right behind us now."

Winter Wolf laughed loudly. "No white man could follow the Shoshonis and then us."

"You don't know my husband."

"What makes this white man so special that you think he can track Indians who have grown up in this country?"

"He is a tracker."

Winter Wolf shrugged, obviously unimpressed with that piece of information. "I have seen many white men who were supposed 'trackers,' and they could not find their way out of a circle."

"My husband is a tracker and he was taught by his father, who was one of the best." Anna looked at Winter Wolf, suddenly irritated. "He also spent his summers with a group of northern Cheyennes."

"How is that possible?"

"His grandmother was an Arapaho and many times their band would meet with the Cheyenne band."

"So, this white man who is your husband, he has Indian blood in him."

"Yes, but he would say he feels he is more Cheyenne. His father married a Cheyenne woman after his wife died.

She raised my husband as her own son. She often told him that she couldn't have loved him more if she had given birth to him herself."

"He loved this woman as his mother?"

"Very much," Anna said wistfully, thinking about Aeneva and how much they had all loved her.

"This husband of yours grew up in a Cheyenne camp?"

"No, his mother and father left when he was a young boy. He was raised on a ranch."

Winter Wolf laughed derisively. "So, he is not a true Cheyenne. No Cheyenne would leave his home to live in the white man's world."

Anna thought of Aeneva, and she glared at Winter Wolf. "He may not be of Cheyenne blood, but his heart will always be part Cheyenne. His mother did not want him to die a young man in this land, full of hatred for the Crows or Shoshonis."

"You do not realize who you are talking to, do you?"

Anna shook her head in exasperation. "I don't care who you are, Winter Wolf. In the white world, some people are not concerned with who is a chief and who is not."

"And in the white world, are women allowed to do anything they please?"

"Women have more freedom."

"Is this in all places?"

Anna thought back to the stage stop where she and Roberto had once stopped, and the woman who was virtually a slave to her husband and his grown sons.

"No, it is not the same in all places," she answered.

"Do your men protect your women as well as we protect ours?"

Winter Wolf didn't let Anna answer. "They do not, for if they did, you would not be here with me."

"Women have been stolen from your people, have they not, Winter Wolf?"

Winter Wolf grunted his assent.

"And some Cheyenne women are different. My husband's mother was a warrior when she was a young

39

woman. She fought many battles."

Winter Wolf looked interested. "This is so?"

"Yes. She was strong and beautiful, but she was also very stubborn. Her grandfather and her brothers could never make her change her mind when she had decided upon something."

"You talk about her as if you know her well."

"I did know her well, and I loved her very much. She was the most honorable person I have ever known." Anna glared at him, daring him to say something, but he merely continued to watch as Robert raced around the clearing.

"Here are some berries. They will have to do until I can hunt. I won't take the chance of shooting this rifle until I know we are far away from the Shoshonis."

Anna nodded silently, greedily eating the tart, sweet berries. She suddenly realized that she hadn't eaten since the day before and the berries only served to make her hungrier. But she wouldn't complain.

Winter Wolf stood up. "It is time to go. We must not stay here too long."

"Wouldn't it be safer to stay here until it's night? They won't follow us at night, will they?"

"Why must I always explain myself to you, woman? You do what you will, I am leaving." He walked to one of the horses and untied it, taking the reins and leading it out of the clearing.

Anna quickly jumped to her feet and grabbed Robert. He started to kick and scream; he wasn't ready to sit still on a horse for an entire day. Anna untied the reins of the other horse and followed Winter Wolf out of the clearing. Branches hit her in the face as she walked through the trees, and her horse nickered anxiously, but soon they were through the dense growth and well beyond the stream. It now lay behind them, and as she could see ruefully, Winter Wolf was already well ahead of them.

She put Robert up on the horse, trying to hold him there with her left hand, while attempting to swing up onto the horse. The horse stepped forward nervously, not enjoying the sound of the crying child on its back. Anna looked for Winter Wolf. He was quickly becoming smaller and smaller as he rode away from them. "Hold still, Robert!" she said angrily, and the child sat still. Anna managed to swing herself halfway up on the horse's back and she held on, pulling herself the rest of the way until she was centered. She dug her heels into the horse's sides. He rode off in the same direction as Winter Wolf.

Anna managed to keep Winter Wolf in sight as she attempted to catch up with him, but she knew it would be impossible to do so. She couldn't ride as carelessly or as fast as she did when she was alone. She had to think of Robert. Still, she kept up a good pace and soon she was gaining on the Cheyenne warrior.

She looked up at the clear blue sky and the sun that was now fully overhead. It was already hot and she tried to cover Robert's head with her hand, but it did little good. He already had a slight burn from the previous day in the sun and she was afraid that his skin would blister. She reached down under her legs and pulled up the skirt of her dress, making sure her slip was still covering her legs. She put the skirt over Robert's head and back, making a kind of tent. He tried to wriggle out of it at first, but when he saw he couldn't win, he gave in and leaned against Anna, the blue fabric of the dress protecting him from the sun.

Winter Wolf was now well within Anna's sight and she slowed her horse slightly. As tough as he appeared to be, Anna sensed that he would never leave a woman and child alone in a hostile country. She looked behind her, making sure no one was following them. She didn't see anyone. She wondered again if Nathan would find a way to track her and Robert, and she knew that if he was alive, he would find her. They had made so many plans together and it seemed that they were finally going to come true. But again, fate forced them apart. What frightened her more than anything was the thought that this time it would be forever.

She had finally caught up with Winter Wolf. It was obvious that he wasn't used to women riding alongside him, but she was stubborn enough to keep trying. She knew that their lives depended on this man, yet she didn't forget that without her help, he would never have escaped. She couldn't stand the silence anymore, nor could she still the one thought that kept pounding in her brain.

"Winter Wolf?"

Winter Wolf didn't slow down and didn't even acknowledge that he had heard her.

"Where are we going?"

He slowed until his horse was even with hers. "I am trying to find my band. Since the women in my band were kidnapped, my people will have moved to a different camp."

Anna knew that Cheyenne country was far away, and it frightened her. It might be impossible for Nathan ever to find her again. "If there is a ranch along the way, the child and I will stay there. We will wait for my husband to come for us."

"We will pass no ranches," Winter Wolf said, a coldness in his voice.

"But I can't go with you to your people. I must find a way to get back to my husband."

"I told you before, woman—do as you wish, but I am going to find my people." He started to ride on ahead, but Anna's voice stopped him.

"Winter Wolf, please stop." She pulled up on her horse until she was even with him. "Will I be a captive in your camp?" She tried to keep the fear out of her eyes, but it was unmistakable.

Winter Wolf shrugged. "It is possible. There are many Cheyennes who like women with eyes the color of a winter stream. I might sell you and get many horses."

"But you can't do that."

"I can do whatever I wish. Will you stop me?" His dark eyes challenged hers.

Anna shook her head, looking down at her sleeping nephew. "No."

"You can choose to go on your own. I will not stop you."

"You know that I have no chance out here alone with a child and no weapons. I have no choice but to go with you."

"What is it you want from me, woman? You and the child have slowed me down enough already."

"I don't want anything from you. I will go with you to your camp and I will do what I must to stay alive so that I can care for this child."

"The child will not be harmed."

"The same cannot be said for me, I think." She looked at him with steady eyes. "Do you have a wife, Winter Wolf?"

"I have no wife."

Anna swallowed, trying to still the rising fear inside her. "I can be your wife. I can learn to do all the things that the Cheyenne women do."

"I do not want a wife."

"But—"

"I will hear no more of this. If you come with me, you must understand that I will sell you to another man. I have no need of a woman in my life."

Anna nodded silently. She had made her decision. "Will you at least give me a weapon? I want a weapon if I am going to be out here alone with this child. You still have my knife, don't you?"

Winter Wolf looked puzzled. "I thought you were going to come with me."

"I have been a captive once before. I will not be one again." She looked at him, her resolve firm. "Will you give me the knife?"

Winter Wolf looked at Anna for a few moments and pulled out the large hunting knife from the sheath on his thigh. "Take this. It will serve you better."

Anna took the large, unwieldy knife. "I would rather have the other."

"The other will do you no good if you are in trouble."

Anna nodded. "Thank you."

"Always keep the mountains on your right as you ride.

Try to stay close to rocks and trees when you camp. Perhaps you will be lucky."

Anna felt like crying, but she merely looked at Winter Wolf and turned her horse. She wasn't sure she was doing the right thing; all she knew was that she could never be anyone's captive again. She hoped that her pride did not wind up costing her and Robert their lives.

Anna huddled in the small shelter of the trees. It was so dark she couldn't even see across the stream. She went back to the clearing they had stayed at earlier in the day. She had spent the day futilely trying to find food for her and Robert. She had no means of carrying water and no means of building a fire. She felt totally helpless.

A rustle in the bushes made her jump, and she held the knife in front of her. She had the horse blanket wrapped around her and Robert and, as usual, Robert slept soundly. The rustling continued for a few moments and then stopped. She tried to listen and then realized that it had probably only been an animal, for if it had been something threatening, the horse would have reacted.

She was still surprised that Winter Wolf had let her and Robert go off by themselves. Perhaps Cheyennes were not as honorable as she had heard. Perhaps Aeneva was the exception.

An owl hooted in a tree and then took flight. She looked around her. Coyotes yipped frantically as they attacked their prey, and the sound sent a chill up her back. She had never before been alone in the night like this. This was a different kind of fear. This was a fear that was hard to fight.

She pulled the blanket closer around her shoulders. Even though it was summer, there was a chill in the night air and she found herself shivering. Robert slept soundly on her lap and the warmth from his small body touched her thighs. She smiled to herself, wondering how such a small thing could give her such comfort.

She thought about the next day. She wasn't sure what to do. There was still a good chance that she would run into the Shoshonis, especially if they had caught their horses. There was an even better chance she would run into another hostile tribe. She wondered how she would ever get them to a safe place.

Leaning back against the trunk of a cottonwood, she tried to relax. There was nothing she could do now. She needed rest more than anything else. Perhaps in the morning she could figure out a way to procure some food and a means to carry water.

She closed her eyes, trying to picture what Nathan would do in her place. But try as she would, she couldn't imagine him ever being as frightened as she was now. Still, she tried to think of all of the things she had learned from him and from Aeneva. She remembered Aeneva saying she used to make baskets out of reeds when she was a little girl, weaving them together tightly. Anna had watched her do it once and she thought she might be able to figure it out again.

She had no gun and no bow and arrow with which to catch animals and she had to think of a way to hunt or fish. If nothing else, perhaps she could carve a spear and try to snare a fish with it. But how would they eat it? She had no way of making a fire.

The coyotes sounded closer now, and she hunched against the tree, hoping no predator would happen by in the night. She was used to the coyotes from Arizona, but their sounds had never frightened her then, when she was living on the ranch with Nathan's parents. It was different now that she was on her own. She forced herself to be strong. She didn't want to die and she didn't want to be responsible for Robert's death. She had the blood of her Cheyenne mother running through her, and she had the strength of the Cheyenne mother and white father who had raised her.

She sat up, her back straight, and began to rock slowly back and forth, stroking Robert's back. She looked out into the darkness, forcing herself to confront it. "Oh, Great Father, help me to feel one with the night," she implored. "Help me to push away my fears so that I might help this child and myself. Help me to draw on the strength and knowledge of my forefathers and foremothers. Help me to be strong." She suddenly felt more relaxed. It had helped her to pray. Aeneva had done it often, and now she would learn from her husband's mother. She would not permit the fear to paralyze her. She would find a way to survive.

Anna sat on the bank of the stream, a pile of reeds next to her. Her skirt and slip were pulled up, her legs dangling over the side. Robert was running around the clearing chasing anything that moved, including leaves and branches, but she wasn't worried about him, for she had taken the reins and tied part of them around Robert's waist. The other side she had tied to a branch. He was content to run while she tried to figure out a way to feed them.

She took four reed strips, placing them so that they overlapped each other, and pulled all the ends tightly together. Then she took another strip and tried to work it along the outside, but it fell apart. This had been her fourth unsuccessful try. She dropped what was supposed to be a water container into the stream and watched as it floated away.

"You have a lot to learn, woman."

Anna turned around, startled by the sound of Winter Wolf's voice. He stood behind her, his hands on his hips, a bemused smile on his face. "I thought you would be with your people by now."

She turned away from him and pulled her skirt down over her legs.

"I thought about what you said of your husband's mother," Winter Wolf commented. "You said she was the most honorable person you have ever known."

Anna stared at him. "Yes?"

He continued. "I did not think she would leave a woman and child alone in a land that was unfamiliar to them." He

46

reached into a leather pouch on the side of his breeches and handed Anna some berries. "I thought you would be hungry."

Anna stared at the berries and shook her head. "I'm not hungry."

Winter Wolf shrugged his shoulders and popped some of the purple berries into his mouth. "They are very sweet."

"I told you, I'm not hungry."

"What did you have to eat last night?"

Anna gave Winter Wolf a disgusted look and stood up, walking over to Robert. She took the rope from around his waist and let him run freely around the clearing.

"You did not get very far. Did you plan to stay here forever?"

"I don't need to tell you anything. You went off and left us. You threatened to sell me. Did you expect me to be grateful for that?"

"You are alive. I think you should be grateful for *that*."

"I won't be a slave, Winter Wolf, not to you or to any of your people. I would rather die out here. At least I would be free."

"I cannot take you back to your people."

"I didn't ask you to take me back." She walked across the clearing, grabbing Robert's chubby little wrist before he ran into the trees. Then she picked him up and swung him around in the air, his delighted squeals of laughter making her smile. "You are a rascal, aren't you?" she scolded the boy, kissing him on the cheek and putting him on the ground. He ran toward Winter Wolf, hugging the warrior's leg when he reached him.

Winter Wolf smiled, reaching down to pick up the child. *"Ne-toneto-mohta-he?* How are you?" Robert reached out with his tiny little fingers and touched Winter Wolf's face. He made a sound similar to a crow, Winter Wolf laughed. "He is a smart boy."

"Yes, he is," Anna agreed, walking over to them. She took Robert from Winter Wolf and untied the rope from the branch. She walked to the horse and quickly fashioned a halter, slipping it over the horse's nose. Robert started to cry and tried to wriggle himself free from Anna's arms.

"I do not think the boy wants to leave," Winter Wolf observed.

"It doesn't matter what he wants," Anna countered, holding on to Robert, in spite of his protests, and walking back to the river bank to retrieve the blanket. Returning to the horse, she threw it over the animal's back, all the while feeling uncomfortable. Winter Wolf was enjoying the fact that she seemed unable to do anything on her own, but she refused to give in and beg him to take her with him. She propped Robert up on the horse, trying to get him to sit still, but he stretched himself over on the animal's back and began to scream. "Robert . . ." Anna said in a pleading tone.

"I told you he did not want to go," Winter Wolf said as he walked up next to Anna. He took Robert from the horse, swung him around in the air, and put him on the ground. "Where do you think you and the child will go?" he asked.

"I don't know, but it is not your concern."

"I did not help you to escape from the Shosonis just so you could be caught by them again."

"What is it you want from me?" Anna demanded.

"I want nothing from you, woman."

"Then why don't you leave me alone!" Anna walked back to the bank by the stream and stood there, her arms crossed on her chest.

"I will take you and the child with me," Winter Wolf said with a sudden change of heart.

Anna looked back to make sure Robert was all right. "I don't want to go with you. I don't want to be sold to another man to be his slave. I have a husband who loves me and one of these days he will find me."

"You are lying to yourself, woman. How do you know your husband is even alive?"

Anna felt the sting of tears and she struggled to keep Winter Wolf from seeing them. She turned away, wiping her eyes on her arm. "Would you please just go away and leave me alone. You aren't responsible for us."

"Maybe I am. You saved my life. I feel as if I should protect you."

"That's nonsense. You got us out of the camp. You don't owe us anything." She stared at him for a moment. "Is all this concern so you can sell me when you get me back to your camp?"

"I will not sell you."

"I don't understand."

"I cannot go south, it is too dangerous for me, but I will take you and the boy with me to my people. I will not sell you. If your husband is a good tracker, he will find you."

"What will I do there?"

"You will learn the Cheyenne ways. You are half Cheyenne."

"Will your people accept me?"

"They will have nothing to say about it. You will be my woman. No one will question me."

Anna flinched at the harsh sound of his voice. "No," she said firmly, suddenly fearful now that her idea might become a reality. "I could never be your woman. I love my husband."

Winter Wolf looked at Anna for a moment, then smiled. "You would not *really* be my woman; it would only appear so. I told you before, I have no desire for a wife."

"But I don't speak Cheyenne well."

"You will learn, just as I learned English."

It was suddenly very quiet. Anna turned around; Robert was gone. "Robert!" she screamed, running into the trees to search for him. "Robert!" Blindly, she ran through the branches, pushing her way through the path in the trees.

"Woman, he is here." Winter Wolf's voice rang out.

Anna ran back to the camp, relieved when she saw Robert in Winter Wolf's arms. She took him from the Cheyenne warrior. "Don't ever do that again," she scolded softly, crushing the boy in her arms. She kissed his head and held him against her chest, then looked over his head

49

to Winter Wolf. "Thank you," she said simply.

She sat down against a tree trunk and held Robert against her chest, rocking back and forth and humming to herself. The shade of the tree surrounded her and Robert, and she suddenly felt very relaxed and very tired. She closed her eyes as she rocked and laid her head back against the trunk of the tree. She heard movement next to her and she opened her eyes. Winter Wolf was spreading the blanket out on the ground next to her. He took Robert from her arms and put him on the blanket.

"Rest now, woman. You are tired. I will watch over you and the boy."

Anna didn't argue but lay down on the blanket next to Robert and quickly fell asleep.

She slept well into the afternoon, until the smell of roasting meat awakened her. Winter Wolf was sitting by a small fire, holding a rabbit over it. Robert was still sleeping soundly. She walked over to Winter Wolf. "You hunted? I didn't hear any shots."

Winter Wolf didn't look at her as he held the rabbit on the stick over the small flames. "I set a small snare."

"It smells wonderful." She sat down next to Winter Wolf, tucking the skirt of her dress underneath her.

Winter Wolf pulled the rabbit from the fire and let it cool over one of the rocks. "You were very tired."

"Yes. Thank you for staying with us so I could rest."

"Are you still going to take the child and go?"

"I don't have any other choice. I must get back to my husband."

"And what of the boy? How will you travel with him each day? How will you feed him? How will you carry water for him?"

"I don't know, but I'll find a way."

"There is only one way. You both must come with me."

"I don't want to be your woman, Winter Wolf."

"Do you not understand? You would not truly be my woman. I would only say that you are mine so that other warriors would not trouble you."

"What would I have to do?"

"You would cook, hunt, dig for roots, and make sure that I am comfortable."

"I will be a slave."

"How do women in the white world treat their men?" Anna was silent. "What do you mean?"

"Do they cook for them?"

"Yes."

"Do they clean for them?"

"Yes."

"So, they make their men feel comfortable?"

"I suppose so, but it's not the same thing."

"I want to help you, woman. Why do you fight me?"

"Because I'm not sure why you're doing this."

"You do not believe what I said before?"

"I don't know. Yesterday you told me you would sell me to another man for twenty horses and today you tell me you'll protect me."

"I prayed to the Great Father last night. He told me that I must care for you and the child."

"What else did he tell you?" Anna asked, the doubt obvious in her tone.

"He told me that I would not be a man if I left you and the boy out here alone to die."

"We won't die."

"You cannot be sure of that. You must not take a chance with the boy's life."

Anna lowered her head and stared at the ground. Why had Winter Wolf suddenly changed his mind? How did she know she could trust him?

Winter Wolf tore off a leg from the rabbit and offered it to Anna. "You have until nightfall to make your decision. After that, I will go and I will not come back."

Anna put the meat up to her mouth and stopped. The decision had already been made for her. "I don't have a choice. I will go with you, Winter Wolf."

Winter Wolf nodded. "Eat now. You must build up your strength."

Anna nodded, biting into the warm, tasty meat. She looked at Winter Wolf as he tore at the meat on the bones with quick, almost savage bites. He frightened her. The thought of going with him to his people frightened her even more. She looked back at Robert still asleep. He was so small, so innocent. She didn't have a choice. She had to go with Winter Wolf and hope that he was a man of his word. He was her only hope.

Chapter 3

Nathan lay under the train, holding his shooting hand steady with his other hand. He took aim at an Indian who rode by and shot at him. The man fell from his horse and rolled along the ground, lifeless. Nathan could hear the whooping sounds of the Indians in the distance as they rode away, and his body could feel the trembling of the earth. He crawled a little ways out from underneath the train and observed with horror the bodies that lay everywhere. He crawled the rest of the way out and stood up. Hearing a man moan, he saw the engineer, who was lying on his back, an arrow in his shoulder.

"I'm going to try to pull the arrow out," Nathan said to him.

The engineer nodded slightly. "Just do it, mister."

Nathan ripped open the blood-soaked shirt and overalls and pressed his hand tightly around the shaft of the arrow. He put one knee on the man's chest to hold him still, and with a quick motion, he pulled out the arrow. The man screamed loudly, beads of sweat breaking out on his face. Nathan took his bandana and pressed it against the open wound. "I'll be back when I can," Nathan said, running toward the car he and Roberto and Anna and Robert had occupied and pulled himself up into it. The cries of the women and children reached his ears before he went inside. A woman held her dead husband in her lap; a small child was tugging at her dead mother's lifeless arm. Nathan shook his head in disgust and hurriedly worked his way back to their seats. Anna wasn't there. He looked around. Her purse and bag of food was still in place under the seat. He rushed to the end of the car and looked around. She was nowhere to be seen. A woman put her hand on his arm.

"Mister, I saw your wife," she said.

"You saw Anna?" Nathan asked anxiously, squatting down next to the woman.

"She went outside with the baby. I warned her not to go out there in this heat, but she did anyway."

"Did she come back in?"

The woman shook her head. "I never saw her again."

"Thank you," Nathan said, the disappointment obvious in his voice. He walked back out of the car, jumping down on the ground, then went to the end of the train, trying to see if Anna was anywhere outside, though he knew it was a futile search. He went back down the train to the next car and went inside, helping people who wanted to go outside, trying to comfort others who had lost loved ones. He had just finished helping an elderly man when he remembered he hadn't seen Roberto since the Indians attacked. He ran to the front of the train, looking underneath it as he ran along.

"Looking for your brother, mister?"

Nathan turned toward the voice. It was one of the men who had helped move the rocks from the tracks. "Yes, have you seen him?"

"Last time I saw him was when those redskins rode in here." He motioned to the other side of the train. "I saw him run between the cars and go over there . . ."

"Thanks." Nathan ran around the engine and stood on the other side of the train. He walked down the narrow opening between the tracks and the hillside, trying to see if Roberto was anywhere around.

"Nate . . ."

Nathan looked around at the sound of Roberto's voice,

but he couldn't see him. "Where are you, Berto?"

"Back here, underneath the train."

Nathan walked toward the middle of the train and stopped when he saw a pair of boots sticking out from under one of the cars. He stooped down to get a look at Roberto. "Are you hurt?"

"Yeah. I think you're going to have to pull me out."

Nathan looked around him. There was hardly any room behind him because of the hill. "I'll have to pull you out from the other side." He walked to the end of the car and climbed between it and the next car. He got down on his stomach and crawled underneath until his head was next to Roberto's. He started to grab Roberto's shoulders but his brother moaned in protest. He wrapped his arms around Roberto's chest and pulled him out. When he got him out into the light, he could see that he'd been wounded in the shoulder and leg. Blood soaked his shirt and pants leg. He ripped the shirt away from Roberto's shoulder, wincing at the sight of the wound. It had been made by a war club and had caused an ugly, jagged wound. Roberto was still bleeding profusely. Nathan ripped the sleeve from Roberto's shirt and pressed it against the wound, trying in vain to still the bleeding.

"I didn't even see the bastard hit me. When I turned around to shoot, another one got me in the leg with an arrow."

Nathan shook his head. "You're hurt bad, little brother." He took his knife and split Roberto's pant leg so he could have a look at the leg. Roberto had already pulled out the arrow. The wound was bleeding, but it was clean. It would have to be cauterized.

"How are Anna and Robert?" Roberto asked, holding the shirt against his shoulder.

Nathan looked up, his light eyes meeting Roberto's dark ones. "I can't find them, Berto."

"What!" Roberto tried to sit up but grimaced with the effort.

Nathan pushed him gently down. "I'll find them. They're probably just on another car."

"But Anna would be out here by now trying to find us."

"Just relax, will you? I said I'll find them." Nathan ripped the other sleeve from Roberto's shirt and pressed it against the wound. "Hold that on there. I'll be back as soon as I can." Nathan got up and walked down to the first car. He climbed inside and searched for Anna and Robert, then continued the same process until he had gone through all the cars. They were nowhere to be found.

He located a water bag and went back to Roberto, trying to still the fear that was rising inside of him. As he got closer to Roberto, he could see someone kneeling over him. He heard Roberto scream and Nathan ran forward, dropping the water bag. "What're you doing?" he shouted, now seeing that the person he was holding by the shoulders was a woman dressed in man's clothing.

"It's all right, Nate. She was helping me."

Nathan walked back and got the water bag. He knelt over Roberto and held his head up as he tipped water into his mouth. "We've got to get you out of the sun."

"You need to let me finish cauterizing both of those wounds first. He'll bleed to death if you don't."

Nathan scrutinized the woman. She was slight of build, of medium height, and had nondescript brown hair. She had on men's leather pants, a blue shirt, and a buckskin jacket. A large hat covered most of her face. As she sat back on her boot heels, he could see a light sprinkling of freckles across her nose, and even though she squinted he could see her eyes were a light green in color. "Who are you?"

"My name is Rachel Foster. Dr. Rachel Foster."

"Doctor?"

"Yes, I'm a medical doctor."

Nathan looked at her clothes again. "I've never seen a woman doctor, especially one dressed like you."

"It's dangerous for a woman in this country. I find it easier for me to be dressed like this."

Nathan looked down at Roberto. "Will he be all right?"

"Eventually, yes. But he's lost a lot of blood."

Nathan looked at the wound on Roberto's shoulder. "It looks like you've already cauterized this one."

"I was trying to do it when you pulled me away." She handed Nathan her knife. "You're going to have to take this up to the engine to get it hot again. Bring it back quickly."

Nathan took the knife and ran to the engine of the train. He climbed up and went inside. He went to the furnace and opened the door. Red-hot coals still shone from inside. He stuck the knife blade on some coals and left it there until the blade shone red, then removed it and ran back to the doctor, handing her the knife.

The doctor barely looked at Nathan. "You might want to hold him down."

Nathan knelt behind Roberto and pressed his brother's shoulders to the ground while the doctor pressed one side of the blade directly onto the open wound. Roberto started to yell but turned his head away, beads of sweat pouring down his face. The doctor didn't say anything. She didn't even acknowledge Roberto's pain but quickly moved to the wound on Roberto's leg and pressed the other side of the blade to it.

"It's all right, Berto. It's over now." Nathan turned his nose away from the smell of the burning flesh. It reminded him of a story his mother had told him of his great-grandmother, Sun Dancer, and how she almost had been burned at the stake by some Utes. His great-grandfather, Stalking Horse, had rescued her, but her legs had been badly burned. Sun Dancer had been embarrassed and afraid that Stalking Horse would not want to look at her legs anymore because of the scarring, but Stalking Horse had told her he didn't see any scarring on her legs; he saw only the beauty. He thought then of Anna, and his

57

stomach tightened. He felt as if he were going to be sick.

The doctor's voice interrupted his thoughts. "Your brother will be fine, but he won't be able to travel for some time. You're going to have to get him back on the train and then find a place to stay for a while when you get to the next town."

"I'm not going anywhere until I find my son," Roberto said, trying to sit up. "I won't leave here without him."

Nathan sat down on the ground next to his brother. "I can't find him, Berto. I can't find Anna, either."

"Where are they?" Roberto tried again to sit up.

Nathan gently pushed his brother back to the ground. "I think the Shoshonis took them as captives, Berto."

"No," Berto said quietly, the pain in his eyes evident.

"Why don't we get him into the train? The sooner we get everyone back onto the train, the sooner we can get out of here."

"Thank you for your help, Doctor." Nathan shook Rachel's hand.

"There's no need to thank me. I'll check on your brother later."

Nathan nodded to Rachel as she walked away, then put one arm under Roberto's shoulders and the other under his leg and lifted him up, carrying him to their car. Two men helped him lift Roberto up and put him on the bench seat that he and Anna had shared. "I'll be back, Berto. Just rest."

"Find them," Roberto uttered, closing his eyes.

Nathan hurried out of the car and ran to the front of the train. All the surviving men were clearing the rest of the rocks from the tracks. Nathan pitched in, tossing heavy rocks to the side of the tracks like they weighed nothing.

"Shouldn't we post a guard?" one of the men asked, nervously looking around him.

"They won't be back," Nathan answered without looking at the man.

"How do you know?"

"They have everything they want." Angrily, Nathan heaved the rocks, trying desperately to block out the image of Anna being held captive by Shoshonis. It was so unfair. They had known each other for barely three years and they had spent so little of that time together. It seemed that fate had conspired to keep them apart. He loved Anna more than anything in the world and he wanted to be with her. Nothing would keep him from finding her.

"I think you better slow down. Here, drink some water."

Nathan looked up to see Rachel holding a water bag. "I'm not thirsty." He continued to pick up rocks, but Rachel's hand on his arm made him stop.

"If you want to help your brother," she said, "you're going to have to take care of yourself. You're not going to do him any good if you wear yourself out."

Nathan hesitated and took the bag from Rachel, drinking greedily from the leather bag. "Thank you. I'm fine now. Why don't you go on back to the people who really need you?"

"Are you always this friendly?"

"Look, I don't have time for small talk, lady. I just want to clear these tracks and get out of here." Again, Nathan picked up rocks and threw them with a fury. He was surprised when Rachel took off her coat and pitched in, working as hard as any of the men. "You don't have to do this," he said.

"I know that." She continued farther down the tracks, picking up the scattered pieces of the hillside.

"I'm sorry for the way I acted," Nathan said softly, following Rachel down the tracks.

"It's all right. I'm used to it."

"Why, because you're a woman?"

"Yes, and because people who've lost someone aren't always in their right mind."

"I never said I lost someone."

"You didn't have to," Rachel said, trying with all her might to budge a heavy rock.

Nathan bent down and managed to roll the rock off the tracks, then looked at her. "I think the Indians took my wife and nephew as captives." He didn't want to explain that he and Anna weren't actually married. As far as he was concerned, they were.

"If you need to hire someone to help you look for them, you could ride all the way to Fort Collins, but Deeker's Creek is closer. I've heard that sometimes—"

"I don't need to hire anyone," Nathan broke in brusquely, reapplying himself to the task at hand. He didn't feel like any more talk. He worked his way down the tracks until he couldn't find any more rocks, then started back toward the engine, but stopped when he saw Rachel sitting on one of the rocks off to the side. She had taken off a boot and was rubbing her foot. "Everything all right?"

"I just have a blister. Nothing a good soaking in a cool tub won't cure."

"Do you know how long it will take us to get to Deeker's Creek?"

"If all goes well, we should be there in a day or two."

"How long to Fort Collins?"

"Longer."

He nodded. "We're going to have to bury the bodies before we go. I don't like leaving all those people out here. It's not right."

"I know, but we don't have the time to bury everyone."

"Then we should take the bodies with us."

"Where would we put all of them?"

"We can have one car just for the bodies. There's enough room now."

Rachel nodded. "I'll organize it." She slipped her boot back on.

Nathan walked up and down, checking to make sure all of the rocks were removed from the tracks.

"Hey, mister," one of the crew said, meeting him. "I hear you're the one who knows something about Indians."

"I know a little."

"Do you think they'll come back?"

"I don't think so. They got what they wanted. You didn't have guns or anything else of value, did you?"

"No, just people."

Nathan looked at the man, trying to control the urge to punch him in the face. "The doctor is planning to have one car for all of the dead."

"We can't do that! We can't waste time on people who're already dead. We've got to get out of here."

Nathan grabbed the man by the front of the shirt. "Listen, we're not leaving here until we get all the bodies on a car. They won't be left out here to rot in the sun. Do you understand?"

"Yessir."

"Now go and help the doctor, and tell whoever's going to run this thing that we're going to leave as soon as the bodies are loaded and the tracks are cleared."

The man nodded and ran back toward the train.

Nathan shook his head angrily. "Bastard!" he mumbled to himself, then walked along the tracks, kicking smaller rocks out of his way. The other men had finished and were going back to help load the bodies onto one of the cars. Nathan joined them, trying to find comfort in the fact that Anna was not among the dead. It was hard for him to ignore the cries and pleas of relatives who prayed that their loved ones weren't dead.

When he and the others were done with their gruesome task, he returned to his car and sat down on the floor in front of Roberto. His brother was still asleep. Nathan started to cover his face with his hands, then stopped and held them up in front of him and stared at them. The smell of death was all over them.

The sound of the train's engine was a relief to all as it expelled steam and they slowly started to move along the

61

tracks. A small group of men had already volunteered to shovel coal in shifts. Everyone was tired and frightened, but it appeared that most were willing to cooperate.

Nathan laid his head back against the wooden bench seat, stretching his long legs out into the aisle. He tried not to think about Anna, but his mind continued to go back to her. He didn't know much about the Shoshonis. He didn't even know if they kept white women as captives or if they killed them. He couldn't bear it if Anna suffered, if she were murdered in some horrible way.

"Here, have some more water." Rachel sat down on the floor next to Nathan.

Nathan nodded his thanks and took the bag from Rachel, first pouring it over his hands to get some of the dirt and smell from them, then taking a long drink. He handed it back. "Thanks."

"Hungry?"

Nathan couldn't resist a smile. He turned slightly and looked at Rachel. "Are you sure you're a doctor? You remind me of my mother."

Rachel shrugged her shoulders. "I suppose that's a compliment." She rummaged through the small basket she had with her and handed Nathan part of a sandwich. "It's old and warm, but at least it's something."

Nathan took the sandwich. "Thanks again."

"I'm sorry about your wife."

"I'll find her. As soon as I find a place for my brother to stay, I'll go out after her."

"You'd better be careful. The Shoshonis are dangerous."

"You know about the Shoshonis?"

"Not much. My uncle would know more than I do."

"I'll have to have a talk with your uncle." Nathan took a bite of the sandwich, grimacing as he did so. "What is this?"

Rachel couldn't contain a smile. "Cucumbers and tomatoes. It was all I had."

Nathan continued to eat the sandwich, in spite of his

aversion to cucumbers. "Are you from around here?"

"Originally I'm from back East. When I got my degree in medicine I found out it was harder to practice than I thought it would be. I was smarter than most of the men I knew, but because I'm a woman, I wasn't given any chances to prove myself. So, I decided to come west. I figured there wouldn't be many women doctors out here. I also figured if people were hurt badly enough, they wouldn't care who tended to them."

"You live in Colorado?"

"I live with my uncle on his ranch outside of Deeker's Creek."

"And do they let you practice medicine there?"

"They're getting used to me. I suppose they don't have much choice."

Roberto moaned and Rachel looked up at him. "Why don't you trade places with me?" she suggested. "I'd better check him."

Nathan moved out into the aisle and let Rachel take his place. He watched as she deftly examined Roberto's wounds. She held his head up slightly and let him sip from the water bag. When she was through, she sat down against the seat. "He's delirious. He keeps calling for Anna. Is that his wife?"

"No," Nathan replied. He had a knot in his stomach and it wasn't from Roberto's murmuring Anna's name in his sleep but because he couldn't do anything to help her. "Do you suppose your uncle would mind talking to me about the Shoshonis?"

Rachel shrugged her shoulders. "I don't think so, but he has a friend who might be able to tell you more. He's sort of crazy. He's been living by himself for years now. My uncle says he knows more about the Indians around here than anyone. He used to be a scout for the Army."

"Would your uncle introduce me to him?"

"I suppose so, but don't expect too much. Like I said, he's pretty crazy."

"I don't care how crazy he is, as long as he can help me out."

"All right, I'll make sure you meet him. You know, I don't even know your name."

"It's Nathan Hawkins, and I already know you're Dr. Foster."

"Please call me Rachel. You're the first person close to my age that I've talked to in so long. Don't spoil it by calling me 'Doctor.' "

Nathan smiled slightly. "Thank you for all your help, Rachel."

"I told you before, there's no need to thank me. It's what I do."

"But you didn't get paid for what you did today. Just how do you make a living at being a doctor?"

"I get by. People who can, pay me, the ones who can't, pay me in other ways. You should see the jars of jam, the laying hens, and the milk goats I've acquired over the last two years. My uncle thinks it's wonderful."

Nathan couldn't resist a real smile. He liked this woman. She was genuine and she was nice. He reached up and pushed loose the large hat hanging by the cord around her neck. She looked surprised, but she didn't put it back on. She wasn't pretty like Anna was pretty, but she was pretty in an earthy, natural way. She had more freckles than he had first thought and her green eyes were rimmed by dark eyelashes. She had a small face with small features, all except her mouth, which was full and very sensual. Nathan thought it didn't quite fit with her face. Her brown hair was pulled into a knot on top of her head, but strands had fallen around her face and neck. Nathan thought she looked more like a young girl instead of a grown woman. He liked her face very much.

"So, what do you think, that I'm plain-looking, but if I dressed in the right clothes and fixed my hair, I could be pretty?"

"I wasn't going to say that. I like your face. It's honest.

64

I bet you don't hide things well."

Rachel pushed the strands of hair back from her face and took a deep breath. "No, I don't. Sometimes it hurts me as a doctor. My patients can see if something's wrong just by reading my face. That's why I wear the hat. At least I can hide behind that." The train lurched suddenly, and Rachel fell against Nathan. He put his arm around her and pushed her back up against the back of the seat.

"You look tired, Doc."

"I suppose I am."

"Why don't you get some sleep? I'm sure you'll have your hands full when this train stops."

Rachel nodded and closed her eyes, leaning back against Nathan's arm.

Nathan watched Rachel. She seemed perfectly content to lean against him, to rest her head against his arm. He was a virtual stranger, yet she had already begun to trust him. He closed his eyes and he saw Anna. Had she found someone she could lean on when she was tired, had she found someone she could trust? The thought of her being alone somewhere with Robert, trying to survive, ate at his very soul. He had to find her. No matter what it took, he had to find her.

The town was ready for the train as it rumbled to a stop. The engineer had tapped a telegraph line and sent a message ahead. People had come out with wagons and buckboards, and the closed wagon from the mortuary was waiting to take bodies out to the cemetery. Some people cried because they saw beloved survivors, other cried because they saw their loved ones dead.

Nathan helped unload the dead bodies and then helped carry the wounded to Rachel's office near the train station. She quickly administered to the ones who weren't badly hurt and sent them on their way. The ones who needed more attention were placed in a separate room with four cots, and when they were filled, the other injured people had to wait. The women of the town helped Rachel in any way they could. Rachel stitched, cauterized, and cleaned wounds, and gave morphine to the ones who were in bad pain. As soon as Rachel finished tending to patients who lived in town, their relatives took them home. She would check on them all the next morning. The others, who were just visitors, were put up at the hotel or taken in by hospitable towns people. It was well into the night when Rachel finished. Roberto was her last patient. When she finished with him, she walked to the front room to find Nathan, but he was gone. She went to the washbowl and scrubbed her hands, then wiped them clean on a fresh towel. She removed her bloodied apron and sat down in one of the chairs in the waiting room, exhausted and drained. She leaned her head back against the wall and closed her eyes.

"Are you hungry?"

Rachel opened her eyes and slowly turned her head at the smell of food. Nathan was standing at the door, a large tray in his hands.

"Dinner," he announced. "I thought you'd be hungry. Do you have a table I can put this on?"

Rachel got up and brought in one of her instrument trays. "You can set it down there. What do we have?"

"Steak, potatoes, bread, butter, peach pie, coffee, and a bottle of brandy." Nathan pulled two chairs to either side of the small makeshift table. He poured them each a cup of coffee, and took a long sip of the hot liquid. "I think this is the best cup of coffee I've ever had."

"Tastes pretty good to me, too. Thank you, Nathan."

"You worked hard today. How do you do it? How can you look at life the same way when you've seen so much death?"

"Because of that, I do look at life differently. I love life, I love every second of it. Maybe I'm a doctor because I'm so afraid to die."

"I admire your courage. I'm not sure I could do it."

"Thank you, but don't admire me too much. I'm just like any other person. I want a nice home someday, and a man to love me. Maybe even children."

"Yeah, I know what you mean," Nathan replied. Suddenly all he could see were Anna's blue eyes and her bright smile. He wasn't hungry anymore.

"I know you're worried about your wife, but you need to keep your strength up. Besides, if you don't eat that steak, I will."

Nathan smiled and took a bite of the thick, juicy steak. "Do you know a place where Roberto and I can stay for a while? The hotel is filled up. A stable or anything will do."

"How about my uncle's ranch?"

"No, I couldn't do that."

"Why not? You can help out with the chores while you're there and hopefully my uncle will introduce you to his friend."

"I'll pay you if we stay."

"I don't want your money, Nathan."

"But you'll take it if we stay there. You've done too much for us already."

"All right, I won't argue."

"When will Roberto be able to travel?"

"Not for a few weeks at least. He was pretty badly hurt."

"Then I'm going to have to go without him."

"I don't think he'll like that. He seems to be real worried about his son and that woman."

"I know, but I'll lose valuable time if I wait for him to get better."

"Just wait a week and we'll see how he does. If it looks like he's going to be laid up for a long time, then you go on ahead."

Nathan nodded his agreement. He didn't realize how hungry he was until he had finished his pie and was pouring himself and Rachel another cup of coffee. He opened the brandy bottle and emptied some into both of their cups. The sweet smell of the liqueur wafted through the room.

"I can't believe a woman like you isn't married, Rachel."

"I think you know the reason why I'm not, Nathan. I'm not as pretty as most women and I'm a helluva sight more independent than most. I suppose men don't feel comfortable around me."

"I feel real comfortable around you," Nathan countered.

"You're different from most men. Most men run as soon as they get near me."

"Maybe it's the clothes, Rachel. You're real pretty when you take off that damned hat. I bet you'd be even prettier with your hair down and wearing a dress instead of those old buckskins."

Rachel looked down into her coffee cup, obviously embarrassed. "It really doesn't matter, Nathan. I'm not out here to look for a husband."

"I'm sorry. I didn't mean to embarrass you."

"You didn't, you were just being honest." She stood up and put her chair back against the wall. "If we're going to go out to the ranch tonight, we'd better get started."

Nathan put the tray on one of the chairs and carried it back into the office. "Where's Roberto?"

"Follow me," Rachel said, leading Nathan into the next room behind a curtain. Roberto was asleep on one of the cots.

"He's out. Maybe I should leave him here."

Rachel shook her head. "I gave him some morphine. He'll sleep through the night."

"I don't want to put you and your uncle out. We'll just stay tonight. Tomorrow we'll be able to find someplace else to stay."

"Are you embarrassed, Nathan, because you asked me such a personal question? Well, don't be. I like an honest man."

"I still think it would be best if we stayed here tonight. I can take Roberto out to your ranch in the morning."

"He's not going to feel anything, if that's what you're worried about. In fact, he'll feel less tonight than he will tomorrow when the morphine wears off. It's better to move him tonight. Now, if you'll carry Roberto outside, I'll bring my wagon around."

Nathan watched Rachel as she walked out, shaking his head. She was, indeed, a very independent woman. She was also a very good woman. He liked her. He sat down on the cot next to Roberto. His brother's dark skin had a deathly pallor to it and his breathing was labored. Nathan reached over and wiped the sweat from his brother's face. They had had their share of problems, but Nathan wasn't ready to lose his little brother. He wanted to get to know him again. They both deserved that much.

He heard the wagon out in front of the office and he lifted Roberto into his arms, barely able to get him through the door. Rachel already had placed a blanket in the back of the wagon and while Nathan was putting Roberto down on it, Rachel ran back into the office to lock up her drug cabinet and turn out the lamps.

Nathan got into the back of the wagon and sat next to Roberto, leaning against the back of the wagon seat. He looked up when he saw Rachel come down the steps from the office and climb up onto the wagon.

"Aren't you going to offer to drive?" she asked.

"Why should I? You probably wouldn't let me anyway."

Rachel smiled to herself and clicked the reins. The horse moved forward. "It's a ways to the ranch. Why don't you try to rest."

Nathan wanted to argue with her, wanted to tell her he'd take over, but he was too tired. He rested his head against the wooden slat that separated the seat from the back of the wagon. The wagon wheels creaked unmercifully, as did the aged wood of the wagon, but Nathan didn't care. Nothing could keep him from closing his eyes at this moment, and the rhythmic rocking of the wagon served to make him even more drowsy. He felt his entire body relax, as he rode with the bumping of the wagon along the dirt road.

He thought of Anna as he had first seen her in San Francisco. She had been a young girl, barely eighteen years old, and he had never seen anyone so beautiful in his entire life. He had asked her to dance and she had looked up at him with the most beautiful blue eyes, eyes that bespoke of her vitality and joy of life. So much had happened since then, though they had had so little time together.

His mind began to race. How would he find her? He was a good tracker, but he would be in Indian territory, trying to find out if Anna was with the Shoshonis or if she had been traded to another tribe. Another thought slowly creeped into the back of his mind, but he pushed it out. He wouldn't allow himself to even think that Anna might not be alive.

How was the man who kidnapped Anna treating her? he wondered. Was he good to her or had he hurt her? He couldn't stand the thought of her being hurt again. It had happened too many times before. He had promised her he would take care of her this time, but again, he had failed.

The wagon came to a stop and Nathan jerked awake. He sat up, unsure of where he was. Then he heard Rachel's voice.

"Stay here and I'll go get a lantern."

Nathan moved to the back of the wagon and sat on the end, stretching his long legs out on the ground in front of him. He couldn't see much. It was a dark night, with very little moon. He could see the barn and the house and the vague outlines of mountains somewhere in the distance. He heard the nicker of horses and, from far away, a lone coyote sounded its soulful cry. A light went on in the house and then he saw Rachel come down the steps to the wagon.

"Uncle Zeb is here, Nathan. He can help you with Roberto."

"I can carry him, Rachel. Thanks."

"Oh, don't be so all-fired stubborn. I may be old, but I ain't lost my muscles yet."

Nathan watched as a man came out of the darkness. He was tall and slim and his face was completely covered with a long white beard. "It's all right, I can—"

"Don't argue with me, boy. I don't take kindly to people who argue with me."

"All right," Nathan agreed. He leaned into the wagon and pulled Roberto down by his legs until they were dangling over the edge.

"I'll take his legs," Zeb said, not waiting for an answer from Nathan.

After Zeb had taken the weight of Roberto's lower body, Nathan got behind Roberto and wrapped his arms around his brother's chest. Both men quickly carried him up the porch steps and into the house, following the lantern that Rachel held in front of them.

"In here," Rachel said, leading them to a room in the rear of the house. Rachel pulled down the comforter on the bed and Nathan and Zeb laid Roberto down, Nathan pulled off his boots, then stood next to Rachel as she wiped Roberto's face with a cool cloth from the washstand. "I'll just check him over to make sure he's all right. You go on out with Zeb."

"Are you sure?"

Rachel reached out and squeezed Nathan's arm. "It's all right. Go out with Zeb. He has some wonderful old whiskey I'm sure he'd like to share with you."

Nathan followed Zeb out of the room, looking back at Rachel and Roberto as he did so.

"Over here, boy. Sit down. You look like you been in a fight with a bear and you lost."

Nathan smiled. He liked Zeb already. He looked down

71

at himself. His shirt and pants were covered with dirt and blood and his boots were so covered with dust that it was hard to see what color they were. "I'm a mess. I'm sorry."

Zeb waved his hand in the air. "Don't care about the dirt. Just glad everyone's all right."

"You mean Rachel."

"Well, I don't know you very well, do I? Don't 'spose I can care about you very much until I get to know you. Now how about some of my whiskey? It'll wake you up and put you to sleep at the same time."

"Thanks." Nathan sat down in a large leather chair, the familiar smell of the leather bringing back thoughts of his father.

"Here you go," Zeb said, handing Nathan a cup of whiskey. "Rachel's always after me to use the crystal, but I hate that stuff. Makes me nervous."

Nathan nodded and took a swig of the strong-tasting liquor. It lit a fire in his throat and chest. He felt as if all of the muscles in those areas were constricting. He opened his mouth to say something but nothing came out.

"Makes you lose your voice for a second, don't it?"

"Yeah," Nathan agreed. "What is it?"

"It's real sour mash whiskey. Good stuff. A friend of mine makes it, name of Lyle. Some folks think he's crazy, but I know better. He's just smarter than the rest of us."

"Why do people think he's crazy?"

"He lives up in this old cabin by himself. Almost never comes to town. Lives off the land. I think folks is mostly afraid of him because the Indians don't bother him."

Nathan sat up, suddenly more interested. "He knows about Indians?"

"Yeah, I'd say he knows about most tribes around here."

"What about the Shoshonis?"

"Probably. Why, was they the ones that hit the train?"

"Yes. I know about the Cheyennes and Crows, but I don't know about the Shoshonis."

"Well, they're as fierce as any of the other tribes and

they and the Cheyennes have been warring with each other for quite a few years now."

"Where would they go?"

Zeb shrugged his shoulders. "Who knows? They could be anywhere by now. Lyle will probably know."

"Can I meet him?"

"I don't know. Lyle's not real friendly to outsiders. Likes his privacy."

"I need his help, Zeb. My wife and nephew were taken from that train."

"I'm real sorry about that, boy, but Lyle's heard those stories before. People don't speak to him until they need his help. He's real tired of that."

"Will you at least take me to see him?"

Zeb took a long drink of his whiskey. "I guess it wouldn't hurt none to go up to see him tomorrow. But don't count on nothing, boy."

Nathan lowered his head and sipped at the whiskey, feeling it help him relax. He looked up as Rachel came into the room and he suddenly felt much better. She had taken her hat and jacket off and pulled her shirt out of her pants. She looked like a little girl dressed up in her father's old work clothes.

She smiled when she came into the room. "I see Uncle Zeb gave you some of his rotgut."

Nathan smiled in return. "It's strong stuff."

"Stronger than anything you've ever had, I'll venture to say."

"Uncle Zeb, have you eaten anything tonight?"

"I had me a bowl of beans and some bread. What more could a man ask for than a good bowl of beans, eh, boy?"

Nathan nodded his agreement. "I can't argue with that, Zeb."

"Uncle Zeb, can you introduce Nathan to Lyle?"

"I already told him I'd try, but I can't promise nothing. You know how Lyle is, honey."

"I also know how much he likes you. He'd do anything

73

for you, Uncle Zeb."

Zeb looked at his niece, his face visibly softening. "I'll try, honey, that's all I can do."

"Thank you, Uncle Zeb. It's very important. Nathan's wife was taken, as well as his little nephew."

"All right, all right, I said I'd talk to Lyle in the morning. Will you leave me in peace for now?"

"I hope we're not putting you out," Nathan said anxiously, leaning forward in the chair.

"Hell no, Rachel's always bringing home strays."

"Zeb!"

"Well, it's the truth, ain't it?"

"I think you've had too much whiskey tonight."

"Now you're going to start lecturing to me! I hate it when you do that."

Nathan stood up, unwilling to be in the middle of a family fight. "I'll sleep in the barn. I don't want to put anyone out."

"No, you won't sleep in the barn! You'll sleep in here." Rachel walked over to Zeb's chair and stood in front of him, her green eyes glaring. "I won't put up with your rudeness tonight!"

Zeb sat up, putting his cup down on the table in front of him. His face changed. He no longer looked like a grizzled old scoundrel. He suddenly looked much softer, much more caring. "I'm sorry, boy, I meant no harm. I was just kidding with you. Of course you're welcome to stay in the house. We have plenty of room. You can stay in the room with your brother if you want, or you can sleep out here on the couch."

"I don't want to be any trouble," Nathan reiterated.

Zeb looked from Rachel to Nathan. "You won't be no trouble. I'm glad to have the company, actually. It's good to talk to someone besides Rachel. She's always yelling at me anyway." Zeb picked up his cup from the table, he walked to Rachel and looked at her, his blue eyes twinkling. "Night, honey." He kissed her on the cheek.

74

"Good night, Uncle Zeb," she said, kissing him back.

"Night, young fella. See you in the morning."

"Good night, Zeb." Nathan watched Zeb as he left the room. He couldn't help but notice how elegantly the man walked. His long silver hair flowed down past his shoulders and his beard reached almost to his chest, encompassing a face that was at once handsome and fearsome. In his day Zeb had probably been a man to reckon with.

"He's a real character, but don't worry, he'll take you to see Lyle."

"You seem to have a lot of power over old Zeb."

"That's what you think." Rachel walked to the big leather couch and sat down, pulling the blanket from the back and covering her legs. "Zeb Foster does whatever he pleases."

"It's obvious he loves you."

"Yes, but he still does whatever he wants to do, and me and everyone else be damned."

"He's your father's brother?"

"Yes, but they never got on. When I finished college, I came out here and spent a summer with Zeb and we got along wonderfully. He invited me to live with him if I ever came out this way. So, when I settled here two years ago, I decided to move in with him. It's been quite an experience."

"He seems like an interesting person. I bet that beard hides a lot."

"He fought in the War Against the South. That's where his family is from. There's a lot he won't tell me and there's a lot my father never told me. I don't know what happened between them. Sometimes I think it had to do with my mother. I think Zeb and my mother were in love, and for some reason, my father married her. I don't think Zeb ever forgave him for that—or forgave her." Rachel smiled wanly. "You're lucky you and your brother get along so well."

Nathan shook his head. The story of Zeb Foster could

have been his story, except that now he didn't know where Anna was. If she had been married to Roberto, at least he would have known she was alive and well. He stood up, placing his unfinished cup of whiskey on the table next to the chair. "I think I'll turn in now. Thank you for everything, Rachel. I hope I can repay you somehow."

"I don't need payment, Nathan."

Nathan stepped forward, taking Rachel's hands gently in his. "You're a special lady." He bent down and kissed her on the cheek. "I'll see you in the morning."

"Nathan, why don't you take my room. You'll never fit into that bed with Roberto and the floor's going to be hard and cold. I can take the couch."

"I'll be fine. You worry too much."

"You're sure?"

"I'm sure."

"All right. Good night then."

"Good night, Rachel." Nathan walked to the rear of the house and into the room where Roberto was staying. There was a lamp on the bedside table that was turned up only slightly, just enough to illuminate the room. Roberto was sleeping peacefully. Nathan took the extra blanket from the foot of the bed and threw it on the floor. He sat on the chair by the door and took off his boots, letting them fall to the floor with a thud. He walked over to the table, turning down the light until the room was completely dark, then lay down on the floor next to the bed and wrapped himself in the blanket. He didn't feel the hardness or coldness of the floor; he felt only the pain of missing the woman he loved.

Chapter 4

Anna regarded Winter Wolf as they rode in their cloak of silence. She knew they had formed an unlikely and uneasy alliance due to the unusual circumstances. She had freed him so that he could save her life and he had saved her life so that he could free himself of any guilt he might have felt. This was a union based solely on need, not on compassion.

As the trail narrowed, she held her horse back and followed Winter Wolf through a thicket of sage that caught at the uneven hem of her dress. She felt the chill of the early-morning wind through the raggedly cut cloth. But the chill was worth it. Robert rode silently on her back in the sling Winter Wolf had made for her out of part of her skirt, leaving both her hands free to ride.

Winter Wolf was a clever man, and she forced herself to watch him, to learn from him. She didn't know what his plans were for her when they reached the Cheyenne camp, but she knew what *her* plans were. She would do whatever it took to survive, and while doing that, she would learn. She would keep her eyes and ears open. She would learn to hunt and skin an animal and make its skin into clothing. She would learn to dig for wild roots, and where to look for wild berries. She would learn the best places to camp and the best places to look for water. She would learn everything the Cheyennes could teach her about survival, and when the time was right, she would take Robert and she would escape.

She looked around her as they rode. Every morning she rose, stunned by the sameness of the horizon. It was as though every day's riding took them no farther and brought them no closer to anything. The chalky soil scattered with low-growing brush and sage stretched forever, except to the west where the immutable blue-gray wall of the Rockies rose seemingly to the sky. They were steadily veering east and it frightened her, but as long as she could see the mountains she knew she could still get back to Nathan.

She made herself be strong. She let her anger drive her to be alert. She was not angry at Winter Wolf, but angry at the circumstances that still managed to keep her and Nathan apart. But she had resolved that she would get back to Nathan and they would be together again. She was a strong woman and she was raised by strong people. She and Robert would get home, no matter how long it took.

Winter Wolf's silence unnerved her. At first she hummed to Robert as they rode, but a sharp glance from Winter Wolf stilled her voice. She had given up trying to talk to him. She understood that her safety and Robert's depended on the honor of a man who would tolerate neither delay nor interruption on a journey he would have preferred to be making alone. Knowing that her very survival depended on this quiet, fearsome man, Anna rode silently, soothed Robert the instant he cried, and even, in the darkness of a prairie night, cut the brass buckles from her boots so that they wouldn't jingle as she rode. *Invisible*, she thought to herself, as the sun woke her every morning. *I will be invisible.*

Nathan tightened the cinch on his horse as he waited for Zeb to come from the house. He took a deep breath. It was a beautiful morning, the air clear and cool. Zeb had long ago fed the barnyard animals and let the cattle and horses out to graze. It was easy to see that Zeb and Rachel were completely self-sufficient here. They had all the meat, cheese, and milk they could ever want. They had eggs and chickens and pigs, and every kind of vegetable growing in their garden, as well as fruit trees of various kinds. The only reason Zeb ever went to town, he claimed, was to check on Rachel. Rachel claimed Zeb went to visit his friends in the saloon.

Nathan leaned against his horse and looked at the house. It was a plain, two-story wooden structure with a long porch out in front, but there were soft, feminine touches of Rachel everywhere—in the white lace curtains on the insides of the windows and the perky shutters on the outside. Flowerboxes added color to the weathered wood of the house. Although the scars of the hard Colorado winters showed on the outside of the house, inside it was warm and hospitable.

He had seen this morning what he had missed the night before. The front door opened on a large room that was dominated by a fireplace on one side and a spotlessly clean window on the other. Zeb had a special piece of wood that he nailed over the window in the winter to protect the glass that had traveled all the way from St. Louis to give him a view of the mountains he considered his own. The plank floor of the living area was warmed by colorful Indian blankets. Two leather-covered chairs faced the fireplace and a long leather couch faced the window. There was a gun rack above the mantel, and along the top of it a parade of astonishingly lifelike animals attested to Zeb's skill as a whittler.

Before he had gone outside to saddle his horse, Nathan had paused in front of the bookcase next to the fireplace and smiled. The shelves reflected the appealing paradox of Rachel's personality. The lower shelves were filled with serious medical textbooks, farther up were novels from New York and England, and the uppermost shelf was stacked with fashion catalogues from the East. Nathan had been able to hear Rachel in the kitchen slamming the heavy ironwear as she cooked breakfast. He pictured the tiny woman in her workpants and flannel shirt, glanced again at the fashion catalogues, and his smile widened into a grin

Nathan heard the sound of Zeb's heavy boots on the stairs as he descended from the upstairs bedroom and crossed the living room. A second later, the screen door slammed and Zeb was on the porch. "All right, boy, I'm ready," Zeb said as he put a buckskin bag over his shoulder. He patted it as he neared Nathan. "This here's our lunch and our drink. You can't never go anywhere around here without something to eat and drink. If you get lost, you'll die just like that," he said, snapping his fingers.

Nathan smiled and waited until Zeb mounted, then he followed suit. As they left the ranch and he looked up at the Rockies, he wondered if Anna could see them, too.

Despite his age, Zeb kept his horse at a steady lope even where the ground was pitted with prairie dog holes and broken by gullies. When the sage gave way to scrub pines and the ground slanted steadily upward, he slowed his pace slightly.

They guided their horses easily across a small stream and came out in a grassy meadow on the other side. The dirt was much softer and richer. Cottonwoods lined the streambanks, and above them Nathan could see the seemingly endless pine forest. Blue jays raced by, screaming at the intruders, while a hawk screeched overhead, gliding on unseen currents of air.

As the pine trees thickened, Nathan dropped back to

follow Zeb. The old man wove a zigzag course between the rough-trunked trees. After about a mile, they crossed a small clearing. On the far side, Zeb stopped his horse and dismounted. "Wait here, boy. I'll go check and see if Lyle's here. If he sees you coming, you'll never get a chance to talk to him."

Nathan watched as Zeb disappeared into the trees. The hawk screeched again and Nathan looked upward, watching the beautiful bird as it glided up, then down, then up again, only to find another air current and swoop gently downward. It hovered for a moment, as if checking to make sure there was no prey, then flapped his wings and flew away. Nathan envied his freedom.

"Over here, boy."

Nathan quickly dismounted and tied the horses. He followed Zeb through the thick growth of pines. The pine needles snagged at his jacket. The pungent smell of the forest and a sudden, eerie darkness enveloped him. As quickly as the darkness had come, the sunlight returned, and they were standing at the edge of a small clearing. A small cabin stood in the rear of the clearing, pressed up against a stand of pines. Its chimney reached into the trees, blowing out smoke into the dark greenery. Nathan walked forward, aware of how his footsteps sounded on the bare earth of the meadow. They were louder still on the boards of the wooden porch.

"Go on in, boy. I'll be back," Zeb said as he disappeared into the trees.

Nathan nodded and knocked on the door. When there was no answer, he called out Lyle's name. Again, there was no response. Impatiently, Nathan pushed open the door and went inside.

"Shut the door. You'll let the warmth out."

Nathan shut the door, trying to focus his eyes in the semidarkness of the small cabin. "My name is Nathan Hawkins, I—"

81

"I know what you're here for." Lyle came from out of the shadows, a rifle propped on his arm. He looked like a penny postcard of a frontiersman. He was dressed in buckskins from head to toe, the fringes on the shirt and pants moving in unison as he walked. His hair was dark and long and he had it pulled back in a ponytail. He had a full beard but unlike Zeb's, his was neatly trimmed. Waving the rifle at Nathan, he motioned him to sit down on the crude, wooden bench.

"You're Lyle?"

The man walked forward, propping a foot on the bench next to Nathan, the barrel of the rifle settling close to Nathan's head. "What're you doing here, boy?"

"I already told Zeb."

"Well, tell me."

"My wife and my nephew were taken from a train just south of here by the Shoshonis. I came to find out if you know anything."

"Why would I know anything?"

"Zeb said you know everything about the Indians in these parts."

"If I did, why would I tell you?"

Nathan tried to control his anger, but he was quickly losing his patience. "Look, I'm going after my wife and nephew whether you help me or not. I just thought you might be able to give me some information."

"Maybe I can, maybe I can't," Lyle said lazily, spitting out some tobacco on the wooden floor right next to Nathan's boots.

Nathan looked down at the brown stain on the rough wood. "I need your help. I don't know anything about the Shoshonis. I'm not even sure where their territory is."

"How do you know it was Shoshonis?"

"A few people on the train said so, and I remembered some things."

"What things?"

"My mother was Cheyenne. She said the southern part of her tribe sometimes fought with the Shoshonis. She said they were awesome soldiers, brothers to the Comanches in the south."

Lyle seemed to weigh Nathan's words. "Your mother was a Cheyenne?" He stared at Nathan. "You sure don't look Indian."

Nathan wanted to lie but figured this old man was too sly for it to do any good. "My father married a Cheyenne woman when I was just a small boy. She raised me. She was the only mother I ever knew."

"Then you grew up with the Cheyennes?"

"No, my parents left when I was still a boy. I grew up in Arizona."

"Hmmm," was all Lyle said, but he laid his rifle on the rough-hewn table and took his foot down from the bench. He sat down, in an old rocking chair that was by the fire, visibly relaxing as he rocked back and forth. "The Cheyennes and Shoshonis, they been fighting for a time now. They hate each other, almost as much as the Crows and Cheyennes hate each other."

"If they kidnapped a woman and child, would they harm them?"

Lyle shrugged his shoulders. "Can't say for sure. Indians, all Indians is unpredictable. They can save your life one minute and run you through with a lance the next."

Nathan sat forward, his elbows on his knees, his head drooping forward. "I need to find out about my wife, Lyle. Is there any way you can find out if the Shoshonis have taken a white woman captive?"

"You give me too much power, boy. I don't know that much."

"That's not what I heard. I heard you know everything that goes on around here."

"I hear some things."

"God!" Nathan slammed his fist down on the bench.

"Can't you just give me a simple answer? I just want to know if you can help me find my wife. If you can't, I won't waste your time. Or mine." Nathan stood up and started toward the door.

"Just hold on, boy. Don't be so danged impatient." He waved Nathan back to the bench. "Sit down. Could be I know a few things."

Nathan walked back to the bench and stood facing Lyle. He wanted to put his hands around Lyle's throat and choke the words out of him, but he knew that wouldn't help. The old man would speak when he was good and ready.

"It was the Shoshonis that hit that train, all right. They're called Snakes, too, you know, because of living along the Snake River. There's a western band of them that lives real simple on the other side of the Rockies, then there's these ones who are warriors just like your people." Lyle shook his head. "It's strange, though. They're pretty peaceable with white folks most of the time. Been known to help them out quite a bit, more so than any other tribe I know. Can't figure why they attacked that train. Seems like all the Indians are going crazy these days."

"Is there any way I can find out if they're holding a white woman?"

"Don't see how. No telling where they could be. They might even have traded her by now."

Nathan clenched his fists. Lyle was right. How was he going to find Anna when she could be with any tribe in the northern Plains? "I don't even know where to start," he said softly to himself.

"I know me a Crow scout. He owes me a few favors. He could probably find out if them Snakes is holding any white women or if they traded her to someone else."

"I'd be grateful, Lyle." Nathan looked around and saw that Lyle probably wouldn't care about money. "I don't know how I'd repay you, but I'd find a way."

"I don't want no money."

"I wasn't talking about money. If there's anything I can do for you . . ." Nathan shook his head. "I need your help and it's that simple."

Lyle reached down on the floor and came up with a jug. He uncorked it and took a swig out of it. "Ah, that's good stuff. I don't need no payment from you, boy. Here, have a drink." He narrowed his eyes. "I don't share this jug with many men."

Nathan got up and took the proffered jug, taking a small drink from it. He forced himself not to cough as the liquid burned his throat. "Thanks."

"I guess you'll be wanting that information soon," Lyle said, taking the jug back from Nathan.

"I'd appreciate it. I'd like to start looking for her as soon as possible."

"You go on back with Zeb and I'll be in touch. Be patient, boy. It might take me some time to find that Crow."

"I don't have time, Lyle."

For the first time the old man seemed to consider what Nathan was saying. "All right, I'll get you the information soon." He stood up, indicating their talk was officially over.

Nathan held out his hand. "Thank you, Lyle."

"I ain't done nothing yet, boy. Go on back to the ranch. If you're lucky, your woman is well and you'll get her back soon."

Anna was miserable. She had tried to keep the fact she had been bleeding for two days to herself, but Winter Wolf saw the blood on her skirt. He had gotten very angry and walked away, refusing to ride near Anna or eat near her. When they crossed a stream, he motioned for her to go into it. When she refused, he pulled her from her horse, took Robert from her back, and pushed her into the stream. He ordered her to bathe and cleanse herself. He told her not to come near him as long as the bleeding continued. He even refused to let her hold Robert. On the fourth day when her bleeding had stopped, she rose in silence as usual, broke camp, and allowed Winter Wolf to ride off, carrying Robert. For the first hour after sunrise she rode behind him, but then her anger got the better of her. She kicked her horse into a canter to catch up.

"What is it I have done?" she demanded.

Winter Wolf looked at her, his dark eyes angry, and rode ahead. Anna refused to be ignored.

"Please tell me, Winter Wolf," she demanded, catching up with him. "I meant no offense."

Winter Wolf slowed his horse. "The bleeding has stopped?"

Anna felt embarrassed. "Yes."

He nodded. "You are allowed to be with your men when you are in such a condition?"

Anna was puzzled. "Yes. It is a natural thing for a woman, Winter Wolf. Surely you must know that."

Winter Wolf replied with a grunt. "Our women are not permitted to go near our men when they are like this."

"Why not?"

"It is believed they will lessen a man's power, and if he lies next to his wife before a battle, he will be wounded."

"Where do the women go?" This was something Aeneva had never included in her stories of Cheyenne life.

"There are special lodges for the women during this time. They usually stay there four days."

"I don't understand."

"There is nothing for you to understand, woman, it is our way. We believe that a woman like this should not eat boiled meat, only roasted meat, she should not touch a shield or any other weapon or sacred bundle, and she should ride a mare instead of a horse."

Anna forced herself to be quiet. Now she understood why Winter Wolf had avoided her. He had been afraid. He had been afraid of a bleeding woman. She smiled, amazed both by his fear as well as his sudden willingness to talk.

She looked over at Robert on Winter Wolf's back. The child had adapted well. He seldom complained and he seemed to accept the fact that Winter Wolf was his father for the time being. For that, she was thankful, but still it made her uneasy.

As twilight approached, Anna looked behind her. She could still see the Rockies, but they were growing smaller. They were getting farther away and that frightened her. She wondered how far Winter Wolf was planning to travel before they reached their destination.

Anna heard a strange bellowing sound and she twisted on her horse to see what it was. At first, all she could see in the fading light were clumps of sage. Then one of them moved. A bull buffalo stood facing the sunset, an answering sound in the distance seeming to summon him. As he galloped off to join the herd, the heavy thudding of its hooves startled her almost as much as its bellow had.

"*Hotovaoh-oha*. You understand?" Winter Wolf asked in the waning light.

Anna was surprised that he had spoken to her again. She nodded her head. "Buffalo."

"The Indian would not survive without the buffalo. They give us food and clothes, yet they know we are not the enemy. The enemy is the white man who hunts just for pleasure. I have seen many carcasses lying on the ground, rotting flesh that could have fed many people, but the white man took only the skin." He stopped for a moment and stared at the animals that grazed quietly in the distance. "If the buffalo dies, so the Indian will die."

Anna looked at Winter Wolf, but she couldn't see his

face clearly in the twilight. His voice had sounded sad and she looked out over the darkened land. She, too, felt sad. She had seen men shoot from the train windows for sport. This was not the way it should be. "I'm sorry" was all she could manage to say, and she knew it sounded hollow. She expected him to get angry at her again, but he said nothing. He sat on his horse in the silent night and stared out into the darkness.

"There was a man who lived long ago in our tribe. His name was Sweet Medicine. He was a hero to many. It is said that before he died he had a vision. In this vision he saw many things. He talked of a time when strange people called Earth Men would come. He said they would be light-skinned and would clip their hair short. He said they would not speak our tongue. He said their ways would be very powerful." Winter Wolf was silent for a moment. "Then he said that the buffalo would disappear and our ways would change. He said we would forget our own ways and take after those of the Earth Men. He said we would forget all of the good things of our life and be forever changed."

Anna could sense Winter Wolf's sadness, but she could say nothing because she knew that what he was saying was true. She had heard Aeneva speak often of Sweet Medicine and of his prophecy that the white man would eventually eliminate the Cheyennes and all of their brothers. Anna knew it was true because of all she had seen and heard. The whites feared the Indians because they were different, and because they were different, the whites didn't want them around anymore.

"I will not lose what I have been taught. The white man will never change me," Winter Wolf said angrily. "I will die before the white man makes me live as he does." He turned his horse and rode northward in the darkness.

Anna followed in silence, feeling a kind of sadness she had never before known. It was the first time she had felt a true connection to her mother's people and it was the first time she realized that her mother's way of life, and that of Winter Wolf and his people, could be quickly coming to an end.

Roberto angrily grabbed the bowl from Nathan. "I'm not an invalid, Nate," he insisted. "I still know how to feed myself."

"You could've fooled me," Nathan said laughing and pointing to the soup that had spilled on the bedspread.

"Dammit!" Roberto yelled.

The door to the room flew open and Rachel came in. "Is everything all right?"

"Everything's just fine," Nathan said with a huge grin. He stood up. "Berto was just telling me how well he feeds himself."

Roberto looked at Rachel and shook his head. "Why don't you get him out of here."

Rachel looked from one man to the other. "It's nice to see two brothers who get along so well." She walked over and sat down on the bed. "Why don't you go get yourself some dinner, Nathan?"

Nathan nodded and left the room. Rachel took the bowl from Roberto's hands and placed it on the bedside table. She put her hand on his forehead. "Your fever has finally broken. That's good." She pulled the bedspread down to Roberto's waist to look at his wound, but Roberto quickly pulled it back up. Rachel smiled. "You aren't embarrassed, are you?"

"I'm not used to women looking at me when I'm . . ."

"Who do you think undressed you, Roberto? It wasn't Nathan."

"You undressed me?" Roberto repeated.

"Don't worry, I kept my eyes closed the entire time," she said mockingly, pulling the bedspread back down. "Stop

89

acting like a child. I'm a doctor, and a damned good one. You're lucky I was on that train and not some barber who pretends to be a doctor." She lifted up the dressing on his chest, took a look, then pressed it back down. "It's healing nicely. Let's see your leg." Roberto stuck his leg out from underneath the bedspread and Rachel quickly examined it. When she was through, she handed him the soup bowl. "It might help if you sat up a little straighter."

Roberto tried to sit up, but the pain was obviously great and he stopped. "I'm not really hungry right now."

Rachel took the bowl and dipped in the spoon, pressing it to Roberto's mouth. "Eat."

Roberto didn't argue. He opened his mouth and took the soup. When he had finished, Rachel made him drink a glass of water. "I've never had a doctor feed me before."

"Well, don't get used to it," Rachel said, taking the soup bowl and standing up.

"When can I leave here, Doc?"

"My name is Rachel, not Doc," she told him, surprised at the angry tone of her own voice. "You can't leave here for at least three more weeks."

"I can't stay here. I've got to find my son." Again, Roberto struggled to sit up, but groaned as he did so.

Rachel rushed to him and pushed him back on the pillow. She sat on the edge of the bed. "If you leave here without mending, you'll be endangering your life. Wait until you heal, Roberto, then look for your son. You'll do him no good if you're dead."

Roberto stared up at the ceiling. "He's only a baby."

Without thinking, Rachel stroked his forehead, trying to get him to relax. "Tell me about your son, Roberto."

Roberto smiled. "He's real cute and full of the devil."

"How old is he?"

"He's just a little over a year, but he's smart. He's been walking for over two months."

"Does he look like you?"

90

Roberto looked at Rachel, his eyes narrowing. "Does he have dark skin, do you mean?"

"I didn't mean that at all. I don't care about your skin. I think you're a very attractive man." Rachel took her hand away from Roberto's forehead and put it in her lap. "I wanted to know if he looks like you or his mother."

"He looks like me, only his skin is a little lighter." He stared at Rachel. "Are you trying to ask me if I'm married, Doc?"

"Why should I care if you're married?"

"Well, I'm not. Robert's mother died. We were never married."

"I see," Rachel said softly, getting up from the bed. She walked over to the window and looked out.

"Does that make you think less of me?"

"I don't even know you."

"But I know you."

Rachel turned from the window. "How could you know me?"

"Oh, I've met you before, Doc. You're afraid to be a woman. You're a pretty little thing, but you cover it up by dressing in men's clothes and wearing a big old hat. You live way out here with your old uncle and you probably don't see many men. In fact, that's probably why you live here, because there aren't many men here. You're smart and you're a good doctor, but you're afraid to be a woman."

Rachel walked to the bedside table and picked up the bowl and glass and crossed to the door. She paused for an instant, looked over her shoulder, but the clever reply she hoped for wouldn't come. She slammed the door as she left the room. Dumping the dishes into the kitchen bucket, she went outside to the porch. Nathan was sitting on the front steps, but she ignored him as she strode by.

"I was just thinking about coming in there and doing the dishes for you," he said from behind her.

91

She hurried down the porch steps and into the yard, hearing Nathan's bootheels on the steps as he got up and followed her. When he caught up with her, she felt his hand on her arm. "What's the matter with you?"

Rachel jerked away and kept walking, her arms crossed in front of her chest, an angry expression on her face. "You try to do something nice and what do you get?" she asked angrily.

Nathan looked around. "Are you speaking to me or just to anything that will listen?"

Rachel stopped, her anger subsiding when she saw Nathan's smile. "I didn't ask you to follow me, did I? I said I'd take care of your brother, didn't I? Well I think I've done that admirably well. I haven't asked anything in return, have I? Well, have I?" she demanded, aware that she hadn't given Nathan a chance to answer any of her questions but too angry to stop.

"No, no, you haven't," Nathan agreed.

Rachel turned and continued walking. "What's the matter with that brother of yours? Did he ever have an accident where he hit his head?"

"What are you talking about?"

"He doesn't seem to know how to talk to people civilly. He doesn't seem to know what manners are."

"Oh," Nathan said thoughtfully, "Roberto's been like that since he was a boy. He doesn't much care what other people think of him and he'll say just about anything that's on his mind."

"I noticed."

"He said something that hurt you, didn't he?"

Again, Rachel stopped, dropping her arms to her sides. She looked at Nathan for a moment, wondering if she really could trust him. "Your brother is an arrogant, boorish . . ."

"Rachel . . ." Nathan said gently, reaching out to touch her shoulder. "I'm sure he didn't mean to insult you. It's

92

just his way."

"Of course he meant to insult me. He had every intention of insulting me."

"Rachel, I'm going to be honest with you."

Rachel fought the impulse to walk away.

"You don't strike me as the type of woman who gets insulted very easily. You can take care of yourself. Remember? I saw the way you handled those men on the train. If Berto said something, he said something that hurt you, not insulted you."

Rachel turned away from Nathan and started to walk again, only more slowly this time. She reached up and pulled some leaves from a low-hanging tree, crumbling the dry leaves and letting them float out behind her as she walked. When she reached the fence to the pasture, she stopped, propping a foot on the lower rung of the fence and leaning against it, her arms hanging over. She stared out into the pasture that had turned brown from the summer sun.

"It's pretty here, don't you think?" she said, staring out at the pasture, ignoring Nathan as he stood next to her.

Nathan smiled. "Yes, it's real pretty."

Rachel looked at Nathan. She couldn't resist a smile, grateful that he hadn't pursued the conversation. She felt silly that Roberto's blunt remark had upset her so much, but maybe he had been right. Nathan had leaned over the fence and was patting one of the mares on the muzzle. His hands were strong and his knuckles were covered with small scars. Sometime, somewhere in his life, he'd had to fight for what he'd wanted. For the first time in her life, Rachel found herself interested enough in a man to find out what he had fought for and why.

Before she could see anything, Anna could hear the dogs bark. She glanced at Winter Wolf, but his face was impassive. Robert stirred in the sling on her back, but the swaying motion of the horse's walk increased as they headed downhill and Robert went back to sleep. Between the cottonwoods on the far side of the river, Anna caught a glimpse of movement. Winter Wolf kicked his horse into a canter and without a backward glance splashed into the shallow river, leaving Anna on her own. She felt her mouth go dry. For weeks she had dreaded this moment and now it was finally here. For an instant, she fought an impulse to wheel her horse around and to flee, but she knew that she could never make it on her own, even if Winter Wolf didn't follow her.

Anna sat almost frozen as her horse picked its way across the river and followed Winter Wolf into the stand of cottonwoods. Small dogs darted out of the bushes and snapped at the heels of her horse. Close behind the dogs came children, their dark eyes wide with curiosity. The older boys held bows. One of them notched an arrow and aimed at Anna. She instinctively reached behind her to touch Robert, but the boy was laughing and had lowered the bow. An instant later, the children had vanished. Anna heard their laughter as they hurried ahead of her toward the village.

The lodges were bigger than she expected and there were at least a hundred of them set in a semicircle that opened onto the riverbank. The smell of wood smoke hung in the air and voices speaking the sharp and guttural Cheyenne tongue surrounded her. Women, dark and unsmiling, stepped from the trees. One of them tugged at the blue cloth of her skirt. Before Anna could react, more people appeared, staring, reaching to touch her, surrounding her horse so that it had to stop. Frantically, she searched for Winter Wolf, finally spotting him talking to a tall, dignified-looking man. If he was aware of how frightened she was, he obviously didn't care.

She endured the stares and touches of the people and

the laughter of the children who kept pointing to her eyes, but when one of the women reached up to touch Robert, she reacted angrily, and involuntarily she screamed Winter Wolf's name.

Winter Wolf turned, and for the first time seemed to remember Anna. As he strode back through the people, they willingly moved, talking to him and smiling at him as he passed. When he reached Anna, he didn't look at her but merely took the horse's rope and led it through the village.

Anna felt acutely embarrassed. She could see that Winter Wolf was angry with her for interrupting his talk with the other man. She didn't know what to say to him so she simply lowered her head and tried to ignore the stares of the people who followed the horse. She couldn't afford to make an enemy of Winter Wolf. He was her only ally.

When the horse stopped, Winter Wolf motioned for her to dismount. She quickly did as she was told and he led her inside a lodge. She stood still for a moment, trying to adjust her eyes to the semidarkness, but a rough hand on her upper arm made her turn.

"Do not speak my name in front of my people again." Winter Wolf tightened his hold on her arm so that it brought tears to her eyes.

She nodded her head. "All right," she said quietly, forcing herself not to cry in front of him.

"You will stay here. You will not move. I will take the boy." He reached for the sling but Anna pulled away.

"No!" She backed away from him. "You won't take him away from me." She looked at Winter Wolf, seeing for the first time, the power in his body. He was not tall, but he was extremely muscular. He could easily kill her just by putting one hand around her throat. But she didn't care. She didn't want him to take Robert away from her, for she knew if it came to that, he would probably keep the boy for himself and give her to the people of the tribe.

Winter Wolf moved forward. "Why do you always defy me?" He stood so close to her, Anna could feel his breath on her face. "Do you know what I can do to you here? There is no one to save you, woman. There is no one to care for you. You are alone."

Anna bit her lower lip to keep from crying. She could taste the salty blood as she broke the skin. "I don't care what you do to me, I don't want you to hurt the boy." She put her arms behind her, trying to shield Robert from him.

Winter Wolf reached up and Anna flinched, sure he was going to hit her. His hand went to her mouth and wiped the blood away. "You know I will not harm the boy. I wish to get him some food."

"I can feed him here," Anna said unconvincingly, frightened by the nearness of this man. Again his hand touched her mouth. She tried to turn her head away, but his other hand came up behind her head.

He held up the hand stained with her blood. "Why do you do this? Is this a punishment?"

Anna shook her head. "I was frightened."

"Have I ever harmed you?"

"No, but you are with your people now. I don't—"

"You think I will turn you over to my people so that they may torture you?" he interrupted.

"I don't know what to think."

"If I had gone with you into the white world, what would you have done? Would you have turned me over to the white man so he could torture and kill me?"

"Of course not," Anna replied disdainfully.

"Then you must trust me, woman." He held out his arms. "Give me the boy."

Anna tentatively pulled the sling around and removed Robert from it. She held him in her arms for a moment, kissed him on the cheek, then gave him to Winter Wolf. "Please, Winter Wolf, I trust you with his life."

Winter Wolf took the child in his arms. He looked at Anna once more, nodded, then left the lodge. Anna reached up and wiped the blood from her lip. She held her hands out in front of her. They were shaking. He had never frightened her more than he had at that moment, yet he was right. She had no choice but to trust him.

She took a deep breath and forced herself to relax. She walked to the fire that had been built in the middle of the lodge, in a hole that was about a foot deeper than the floor of the rest of the lodge. There was a pot of stew cooking over the fire and the smell made Anna's stomach churn. She hadn't eaten a good meal in so long. She walked around. There was a backrest on the opposite of the lodge flap, in the back of the tipi, and in front of it, there was a woven mat covered with a thick buffalo robe. Other robes lay folded to the side of the backrest. She noticed that the area on which the mat and robes lay was a few inches higher than the rest of the ground. The lining from the tipi extended in a few feet into the lodge floor and was used as a place to put things on. There were weapons, baskets, and clothes all around the lodge. She shook her head. So this was how Aeneva had grown up.

The lodge flap opened and a young woman walked in holding a bowl. She walked to the fire and dished some of the stew into the bowl and handing it to Anna, turned to leave.

"Thank you," Anna said in English, then remembered her Cheyenne. *"Ne-aoh-oheshe."*

The girl stopped, looking as if she might say something. But she merely nodded her head slightly, then left the lodge.

Anna sat on the floor, afraid to sit on any of the robes. She held the bowl to her mouth and sipped at the broth of the stew. It tasted warm and spicy. She quickly drank all of the broth and then ate the pieces of meat and vegetables that were at the bottom. She wanted more, but she didn't know if she should help herself. She decided against it, not knowing what the Cheyenne rules were for eating.

She felt alone and frightened, and suddenly very tired. She crossed her legs in front of her and rested her hands on her knees and began to rock back and forth. Closing her eyes, she thought of Nathan and wondered what he was doing. She knew he was alive. She had always known in her heart that she would know if he was dead, and she knew that he was not. But where was he? Would he be able to track her? They had crossed many streams and rivers. Would it be possible for him to pick up the trail? She pictured him in her mind and she could see him clearly, standing tall and straight, his blond hair grown longer, his skin dark from the sun, and his blue eyes reflecting the clear sky. She missed his smile and his warmth, but most of all she missed someone with whom she could share her feelings. She could honestly say that Winter Wolf had not treated her badly, yet he acted as if she weren't a person at all. She couldn't stand it anymore.

She felt her head begin to drop when the flap to the lodge awakened her. She opened her eyes. Winter Wolf had come back. He was carrying Robert easily in one arm, and in the other he was carrying a blanket and a basket. He motioned for Anna to come to him. She quickly went to Winter Wolf, gratefully taking Robert from his arms.

"Here is water," he said, setting down the willow basket, "and here is a blanket. You can use this to carry the boy around in." He dropped it on the ground next to Anna.

"Thank you," she said, taking the blanket from the ground.

Winter Wolf walked to the back of the lodge and sat down on his robe, leaning against the backrest. "You have eaten?"

Anna turned. "Yes. Thank you."

"Come here," he commanded.

Anna obeyed, and sat next to Winter Wolf. She held Robert in her arms and kissed him on the head. He seemed very contented.

"Tomorrow you will learn some of our ways. You are with the Cheyenne now. You must not question what we do. Do you understand?"

"Yes," Anna said, involuntarily biting at her lower lip again.

"Woman, do not do that!" Winter Wolf said angrily. "I will not hurt you unless you do something to make me distrust you."

Anna stopped biting her lip. "I'm sorry." She lowered her head. She hated the way she sounded. She had resolved to be strong, but now it seemed that all of her resolve had vanished.

"You must listen to the women who teach you. You must try to speak our language. You must not speak to any of the men in the village. Do you understand?"

"Yes."

"You must learn our ways, woman. I will not take you back to your people."

Anna raised her eyes, trying to still the tears that threatened to flow. "I know that you cannot take me back to my people, Winter Wolf. I ask only that you treat me fairly and that you take care of me and the baby. In return, I will do whatever a Cheyenne woman does for her man." She grimaced as she said the words. She didn't want him to think she was willing to bed with him, but she did want him to know that she was willing to try to fit in with his way of life.

"I told you before I am in no need of a wife. I do not need you to care for me."

"Winter Wolf, please do not sell me to another. I can make myself useful. I will—"

Winter Wolf held up his hand. "That is enough. You

speak too much. I will sleep now." He lay down on his robe and pulled another robe over him.

Anna didn't know where to sleep. He had said nothing to her. She looked around her. There were other robes next to Winter Wolf, but she didn't want to use any of them. Instead, she lay down on the cool earth and wrapped the blanket around herself and Robert. She didn't know what Winter Wolf had in mind for her, but she would not give up. She would learn his ways and she would find a way back to Nathan.

Chapter 5

Nathan was helping Zeb bring in the livestock when he saw Lyle. His first instinct was to ride straight to the man, but he resisted it and waited for Lyle to find him. He sat on his horse, following the cows with his eyes as they ambled their way down the pasture in the yard.

Lyle finally came through the fence. "I got some news for you, boy," he announced.

Nathan forced himself to contain his excitement as he propelled his horse into motion. "What is it, Lyle?" he asked, riding by the old man.

"For a man who wants to find his woman so badly, you sure don't seem excited."

Nathan kept on riding into the yard and dismounted by the corral, opening the gate. He stood behind, waiting for Lyle to ride up. "I figure if you have something to tell me, Lyle, you'll tell me."

Lyle cocked his head to one side and shook his finger at Nathan. "You're quick, boy. I like that. I'll be sitting on the porch when you're done."

Nathan waited until all of the cattle were in the corral and then closed the gate. He looked back. Zeb was still up in the pasture checking on a fence. He led his horse to the barn, took the saddle and blanket off, and gave him a feed bag. Then he walked to the water pump. He took off his bandana, wet it, and wiped off his face with it. Taking the cup from the back of the pump he filled it with water, then took a big gulp and hung it back up. He walked to the porch steps and sat down. "So, what news do you have?" he asked Lyle, while leaning back against the railing along the stairs.

"The Shoshonis don't have no white women."

Nathan looked at Lyle and then quickly looked away, out into the pasture. "You're sure?"

"I'm pretty sure. My Crow friend knows what goes on."

Nathan nodded his head, trying to still the rising fear and anger that was growing inside him. "Thanks anyway, Lyle."

Lyle got up from the rocking chair and sat down on the step next to Nathan. "This is a real nice place if you want to settle down. Then again, if you got someplace to go, I suppose it ain't so nice."

Nathan looked over at Lyle, a puzzled expression on his face. "What?"

"I hear tell the Cheyennes got themselves a white woman and a baby," he said nonchalantly, as if this information would mean nothing to Nathan.

"You're sure?" Nathan looked at Lyle in shock.

"That's what I hear."

"Northern or southern Cheyennes?"

"Northern, from what I hear. 'Course, they're not moving about in the same area anymore. There's a group of them up in southern Wyoming. Been on the warpath. Real angry at the whites."

"The Cheyennes," Nathan repeated to himself. He wasn't sure if this was good or bad. Even if they let him into their camp, he wasn't sure they'd listen to him.

"This could be good for you, boy, seeing as how the Cheyennes is your people."

"It doesn't really help me, Lyle. I haven't seen my

mother's people since I was a kid. No one will remember me. And my hair and eyes aren't going to help me out much, either."

"Well, it's up to you to find a way in there. I got a name for you . . . Winter Wolf. The man who might have your woman. He is the son of Brave Wolf, a Cheyenne war chief."

Nathan turned, unable to contain the shock on his face. "Brave Wolf?"

"You've heard of him?"

"If it's the same Brave Wolf, he's my mother's brother. That means that the man who has my wife is my cousin."

Lyle gave out a whistle. "I sure don't envy you, boy, having to go in there and confront family. Indians is real sticky about their captives."

Nathan shook his head. He couldn't believe this was happening. His cousin had Anna, and for the time being, there was nothing he could do about it. He could only hope that Winter Wolf was as honorable as his aunt had been. He stood up and extended his hand to Lyle. "Thank you, you've been a great help. I don't think I could've found all this out by myself."

Lyle stood up, spitting the brown tobacco juice onto the ground. "I wish you luck, boy. You're gonna need it."

Nathan went into the house. Roberto was sitting up in one of the chairs in the living room, reading one of Rachel's books. He was healing nicely, but Nathan wasn't sure if he was ready to travel yet.

Nathan stood in front of his brother. "I'm going to look for Anna and Robert. I can't wait any longer."

Roberto dropped the book in his lap. "If you're going, I'm going."

"You can't. You're not well enough yet."

"He's my son, Nate."

"I know that, Berto, but we can't wait until you're

103

completely well. I have to go now."

"You've heard something from that old man, haven't you?"

Nathan walked over to the big window and looked out at the Rockies. It was a beautiful sight, but its beauty eluded him at this moment. "Lyle told me Anna and the baby are with some Cheyennes." He didn't face Roberto as he spoke.

"Cheyennes? I thought Shoshonis hit that train."

"They did, but they must have traded Anna and Robert."

"Why would they trade with the Cheyennes when they've been fighting with them for years?"

Nathan whirled around, an angry expression on his face. "How am I supposed to know why they're with the Cheyennes, Berto?"

"What is it, Nate? There's something you're not telling me."

Nathan turned back to the window, staring out at the dark mountains. "Lyle thinks that the band of Cheyennes who has Anna is headed by a war chief named Brave Wolf." He turned around. "Do you remember that name, Berto?"

"My God, he's our uncle."

Nathan nodded. "And it's his son who has Anna and Robert."

"This could cause some big problems for us," Roberto said slowly.

Nathan sat in the other chair. "Brave Wolf might let us take Robert because he's your son, but he might not let me take Anna back. What do I do then? Do I try to get help from soldiers and fight against my mother's people?" He ran his fingers through his hair. "God, I wish Aeneva was here. She'd know what to do."

"*You* know what to do, Nate. You have to get Anna. She's not Cheyenne. She'll never make it there."

104

"But she *is* Cheyenne, Berto, remember? They might just think she fits in fine."

"I'm going with you."

"I'm not going to argue with you, Berto. If you think you can keep up with me, come along, but I swear, I'm not going to slow down for you. I have to find that band of Cheyennes as quickly as possible. Anna's life may depend upon it." Nathan got up and went to his room. He took the blanket he had been using and folded it in half lengthwise and laid it on the bed. He rummaged through his suitcase and found an extra pair of socks, a shirt, his jacket, and some money. He rolled everything up in the blanket and laid the roll on the end of the bed. He went back to his suitcase and pulled out his gun and holster and laid them on top of the roll. When he was through, he went out to the kitchen.

Rachel was in the living room talking to Roberto, but when she saw Nathan, she followed him into the kitchen.

"There's been news of your wife?" she asked.

"Lyle told me she's being held by some Cheyennes, by my uncle's band, in fact."

"That's good, isn't it?"

"Rachel, I haven't seen my uncle since I was a small boy. Even if he does remember me, it doesn't mean he's going to let me take my wife away from his son."

"His son? Your cousin has your wife?"

Nathan shook his head. "It's strange, isn't it? If my father and Aeneva had stayed in the Cheyenne camp, I would've been brought up with my cousin. But now, he's as much a stranger to me as I am to him. In fact, he probably sees me as an enemy."

Rachel touched Nathan's arm. "When are you leaving?"

"In the morning."

"That soon? Don't you have to make preparations?"

"No, I'll just need some food, if you don't mind."

"I'll get some together for you tonight." Rachel was obviously disconcerted. "I'm sorry you'll be leaving so soon, Nathan. I was just getting to know you."

"Don't worry, I'll be back. Roberto will be staying."

"What?" Rachel's cheeks flushed crimson.

"He's not ready to travel yet, is he? I know he thinks he is, but he can't even get up and down from a chair without it causing him pain."

"No, he shouldn't be traveling." Rachel walked to the counter, her back to Nathan.

Nathan went up behind her. "Will it be an inconvenience for you if Berto stays here, Rachel? If it is—"

"No," Rachel said softly, turning to look at Nathan. "He's welcome to stay here as long as he likes." She shrugged her shoulders. "I just seem to get along better with you, that's all."

Nathan smiled, and put his hand on Rachel's cheek. "You are quite a lady, Dr. Foster. I'm really glad we had this chance to get to know each other."

"Me, too," Rachel said, her eyes lowered. "I hope you find your wife, Nathan. I wish you the best of luck."

"Don't worry. I'll be back to get my brother. Besides, I want Anna to meet you. I think you two will like each other."

"I'm sure we will," Rachel replied, her tone indicating her discomfort.

Nathan gently kissed Rachel on the cheek. "Thank you for everything, Rachel. I'll never forget what you've done." Nathan saw the tears well up in Rachel's eyes, but he didn't want to find out why they were there. He couldn't let himself get involved with another woman. He needed to find Anna, and he needed to find her soon.

Nathan sat in one of the chairs by the fire, Zeb in the

other, both drinking Zeb's brew. Nathan had gradually acquired a taste for it and had really gotten to enjoy Zeb. The old man was full of stories and tales and he made everything sound like an adventure. Rain pattered against the window, and at the flash of lightning, Nathan looked out toward the mountains.

"Something, ain't it? That's why I ordered that window and put it there. Get to watch all kinds of things like that."

"Rachel won't try to come home in this rain, will she?"

"Naw, I don't expect so. Baby probably won't be born till the morning anyhow. Don't worry about her, boy. She's real used to taking care of herself."

A clap of thunder in the distance made Nathan look out the window again, and a bright flash soon followed. He worried about Rachel. She'd been gone since dinner to help a woman deliver her baby. Zeb was probably right that Rachel was just fine. Still, he was worried about her. She was just stubborn enough to try to bring the wagon back in a storm.

"Did you even hear what I said, boy? Why are you so interested in that storm?"

"Sorry, Zeb, I was just thinking that Rachel's the kind of woman who'd try to ride in a storm like this."

"Stop that now, or you'll have me worrying all over the place. She'll be fine. Even if the baby is born early, she'll stay the night there. She's not foolish enough to try to get home in this weather."

"You're sure?"

"Damnation, no I'm not sure, and if you hadn't gone and got me all riled up, I woulda been fine." Zeb slammed his cup on the table. "Maybe I should ride out to the McCauleys' and make sure she's all right."

Nathan stood up. "Why don't I do it?"

"You crazy, boy? You're leaving here the first crack of dawn, or did you forget that?"

"No, I didn't forget that, but I also can't forget every-thing Rachel did for us. Why don't you tell me how to get there, Zeb?"

Zeb shook his head and muttered to himself. "I thought my niece was stubborn, but I think you're worse than she is." He looked at the flash outside the window. "I won't argue with you anymore, boy. My eyes ain't good enough to see in this stuff, and you're a lot younger and stronger than I am. Go get yourself a jacket and I'll tell you how to get there."

Rachel tried to calm her horse, but the thunder and lightning frightened him and he bolted. She wrapped the reins around her hands as the lightning flashed again, closer. The horse took the bit in his teeth and galloped on, senseless with terror. The wagon slewed and pitched as the wheels slid across the flooded ruts in the road. Rachel braced her feet against the wooden footrest, put-ting her entire weight into pulling back on the reins, but it did no good.

The lightning flashed again, changing the road to an eerie imitation of daylight. Rachel hauled harder on the reins, wrapping the slippery leather around her hands a second time. If the wagon shafts broke, there would be no way to free herself in time—the horse would probably drag her to death. But she had no choice. It wasn't that far from the road to the ranch. If she could just keep the horse on the road, she'd make it.

The sky flashed again, and this time the light was blinding. The road, for an instant, became a splintered mirror, every puddle reflecting the unnatural light. Al-most simultaneously, the shattering crack of thunder split the night. Rachel flinched, feeling the sound as much as she heard it.

The horse veered suddenly, and the wagon wheels slid

into a deep rut. The wagon tilted, tipped, and Rachel desperately freed her hands from the reins, but it was too late to jump. For an instant, the wagon rolled on at an impossible angle. Then Rachel was falling, helpless, as the wagon crashed onto its side. The motion stopped and Rachel felt a searing pain across both legs.

For a moment she lay still, feeling the cold mud seeping into her clothing. The rain stung her face. She forced herself to sit up and clawed at the rough wood that pinned her legs. *I'm in shock,* she thought. *Both my legs are probably broken. Zeb won't come looking for me. How many times have I insisted he respect my ability to take care of myself? Less than a mile. Less than a mile from home and I'll probably die here.*

Nathan rode slowly, reins tight, one hand reassuringly on his horse's neck. With every lightning flash, he squinted through the cascade of water pouring from his hat brim. The storm had gotten worse over the last hour. If Rachel hadn't started home earlier, he couldn't believe that she would try the trip now. Lightning flashed again, and he leaned forward straining to see. There was a shape on the road. Maybe it was only a big rock, but he urged his horse forward a little faster. The next lightning flash confirmed his fear. Rachel's wagon lay on its side. Her horse stood trembling, its head down against the driving rain.

"Rachel!" he screamed. But if there was an answer, it was lost in the sound of the rain. He slid off his horse and looped his reins over the upturned wheel. He felt his way around the wagon, calling her name. Lightning flashed again, and he finally saw Rachel. She was lying in the mud, her legs pinned underneath the wagon.

"Rachel, can you hear me?"

Rachel lifted her head slightly. "Yes."

"It's Nathan. I'm going to get you out of here."

"I think my legs are broken, Nathan," she said, her voice choked with pain.

Nathan stood, quickly surveying the situation. He had to get her out from underneath the wagon. Her horse was standing calmly now, but if it bolted, it could easily drag the wagon forward and crush her. The next flash of lightning allowed him to find two rocks of a useful size. He carried each separately to the wagon, putting one on either side of Rachel. Then he squatted, his back against the rough wood, and dug his bootheels into the mud. He strained to lift the wagon. When it was high enough, he worked the rock into place with his boot, then eased the weight of the wagon onto it carefully, making sure it would hold. Then he repeated the process with the second rock on the other end of the wagon. Almost shaking with relief, he pulled Rachel back and out of danger.

He ran back to the wagon, sliding his muddy hands along the axles and wheel spokes. It would hurt Rachel much less if he could right the wagon and use it to take her to the ranch. Next, he checked the harness. Rachel's horse still stood quietly. He straightened the collar and tightened the girth strap. Everything looked all right. He got his lariat from his saddle and secured it to the side of the wagon. Dallying the lariat around his saddlehorn, he backed his horse slowly and steadily, feeling the increasing pull as the lariat grew taut. The wagon creaked and groaned as the pull increased, then shifted and righted itself, the wheels sinking deeply into the soft mud.

Nathan tied his horse to the back of the wagon and ran to Rachel. He lifted her carefully, tensing against her moan of pain. He laid her gently in the wagon, then took off his jacket and wrapped it around her.

"My bag," Rachel said, her voice strained. "You have to find my bag."

Nathan turned as lightning flashed. The bag was close to where Rachel had lain, half buried in the soft mud. He wrenched it free and put it over the side of the wagon.

Rachel's horse was exhausted and still terrified, but when Nathan urged it forward, it pulled the wagon steadily toward the ranch. When the horse stopped in the yard, Nathan quickly leapt from the wagon and lifted Rachel into his arms. He carried her up the steps and kicked at the front door until Zeb opened it.

"Good God, what happened?"

"Show me her room, Zeb," Nathan commanded, and followed Zeb up the stairs. While Zeb turned up the lamp, Nathan laid Rachel on the bed, unbuttoning her muddy shirt.

"I'll do that," Zeb said angrily, stepping in front of Nathan.

Nathan deferred to the old man and stepped aside. "I think both of her legs are broken, Zeb. Do you know what to do?"

Zeb shook his head. "Hell, she's the doctor. She's always helping everybody else. Now she's hurt and I can't do nothing for her."

Nathan noticed that the old man's hands were shaking. Gently, he put his hand on Zeb's arm. "Why don't you let me take over. Go down and see to the horses. Bring up some of your brew. And don't forget Rachel's bag."

Zeb didn't argue and hurried out of the room.

Nathan quickly stripped Rachel and was shocked by the chill of her skin. He wrapped her in a blanket, then covered her with the heavy feather comforter. He looked down at her lying in the bed. Her hair was soaked and lay in strands around her head. Her normally light skin looked extremely pale, and the tiny freckles on her face stood out against her deathly pallor. She muttered something, but Nathan couldn't understand what she'd said.

111

He put his face close to hers.

"Rachel, can you hear me? It's Nathan."

Rachel spoke again, this time opening her eyes. "You'll have to set my legs, Nathan."

Nathan swallowed. "How do I do that?"

"First you'll have to pull each one to make sure none of the bones are crooked."

Nathan looked down at the petite woman in the bed, and he knew there was no way he could inflict such pain on her. And what if he did it wrong? "I can't do it, Rachel. I'll go find another doctor somewhere who can help you."

"I am the only doctor around here, Nathan. You'll have to do it. Uncle Zeb can't stand pain." She closed her eyes and her head fell to one side. "Will you get my bag? I'm going to need something for the pain."

Nathan ran downstairs. Zeb was standing just inside the door holding Rachel's bag. Nathan took it from him and ran back up, taking the stairs two at a time. He heard Zeb's bootheels on the stairs, and a moment later, the old man was standing next to him, visibly shaken. Nathan knelt next to the bed. "Rachel, I have your bag."

Rachel opened her eyes, smiling weakly. "There's a bottle of laudanum . . ."

Nathan rummaged through the black bag and came out with the blue bottle. He put his hand behind Rachel's head and lifted it slightly, holding the bottle to her lips. She sipped from it and lay her head back against Nathan's arm. "Is Roberto all right?"

"Can't you stop being a doctor for even a minute?" Nathan asked gently. He held the bottle to her lips again. When she was done drinking, she closed her eyes, and Nathan put the cork back on the bottle. "You're going to have to tell me what to do, Rachel."

Rachel opened her eyes, looking behind Nathan to Zeb. "Uncle Zeb, don't worry, I'll be all right. I need you to do something for me."

Zeb leaned closer to the bed. "Anything, darlin'."

"I'll need splints for both legs, back and front. Good flat pieces of wood."

"Okay, Rachel darlin', I'll do that. I'll do that right now."

Rachel's eyes followed her uncle as he left the room. Then she looked at Nathan. "You'll have to do it while he's out of the room, Nathan. He couldn't stand it if he saw me in such pain."

"Rachel, I—"

"In my bag you'll find some gauze. Wrap that around the splints to keep my legs immobile. Stand at the foot of the bed, Nathan."

Nathan did as she commanded, then loosened the covers so that both of Rachel's legs were exposed. They were streaked with mud, but worse than that, they were swollen and bruised beyond belief. And there was an odd crookedness to them that scared him. Would she ever walk again? "What do I do?"

"Take my foot and lift it slightly. Get a good hold around the ankle, then with one, swift movement, pull toward you. You should hear a cracking sound. Do the same thing with the other leg. When Zeb gets back, splint them. The pain should knock me out, but if it doesn't, give me some more laudanum. Don't worry, I'll probably have a fever for a day or two. Try to keep the fever down." She closed her eyes and swallowed. "Thank you, Nathan. I know this isn't easy for you. Good luck finding your wife." Rachel took the pillow from underneath her head and pressed it against her mouth.

Nathan threw off his hat and wiped his sweaty palms on the bedspread. Slowly, he lifted Rachel's left foot. He was amazed at how small and dainty it was. For some reason, it made him smile. Then he looked farther up and saw the ugly discoloration and swelling of the leg

113

and set his mind on what he had to do. He put his left hand underneath her leg, right above the ankle, the other hand on top of the ankle. He took a deep breath and pulled firmly on the leg. He heard a cracking sound and, above that, he heard Rachel screaming into the pillow. Sweat poured down his face and he wiped his wet shirtsleeve against it. He took her right foot and did the same thing. Again, Rachel muffled her scream with the pillow. When he was finished, he moved to the bedside and took the pillow from her face. She was deathly pale. He put his hand on her cheek. As much as he wanted to search for Anna, he knew he could never leave Rachel now. Neither Zeb nor Roberto could care for her. He couldn't leave until he was sure she was able to take care of herself. He owed her that much at least.

Anna followed the women around the riverbank gathering sticks and twigs for fires. She did whatever they told her to do, and they told her to do a lot. She felt like a slave. She seldom saw Winter Wolf except at night when he came into the lodge to sleep. He didn't speak to her. The only thing he did do was take Robert for a time each day and there was nothing she could do about it.

As she knelt on the ground to gather twigs, she felt something hit her head. At first she thought something had fallen out of the tree, but the second time she got hit, she realized someone was throwing something at her. She turned around to find the women giggling. One of the women was standing in front of the others, pointing to Anna and gesturing obscenely. While Anna glanced at her, the woman picked up another twig and threw it at Anna.

"*Ne-veoh-oh-nehesheve!* Don't do that!" Anna commanded in Cheyenne. She stood up, dropping the bundle of twigs she had placed in her sling.

The woman sauntered toward Anna, laughing loudly. When she was only about a foot away, she reached over and shoved Anna backward. Anna stumbled but did not fall. She walked back toward the woman and stared at her, her blue eyes full of hatred. One Cheyenne word immediately came to mind.

"*Eshkoseese-hotame.* Sow," Anna said in a voice loud enough for all the women to hear.

The women were suddenly silent, shocked by the nerve of the white woman.

The Cheyenne woman screamed loudly and shoved Anna so hard that she fell backward, hitting a branch. It ripped her dress and poked into her back. Before she could do anything about it, the woman was on her, hitting her on the face and chest with her fists. Anna tried to roll away, but the Indian woman was much heavier and she held Anna pinned to the ground. Anna reached up and grabbed one of the woman's braids and pulled as hard as she could. The woman screamed and Anna pulled even harder. Then the woman reached up with her hands to grab her hair, and Anna seized the opportunity. She closed her other hand into a fist and hit the woman on the side of the head, knocking her over. Anna quickly rolled away and scrambled to her feet. She looked around for a stick and picked one up, holding it menacingly in her hand. The woman got up, holding her head, but stopped suddenly.

"*Na-naoh-ohsooh-ohenoho!* That is enough!" Winter Wolf stood behind Anna. The woman who had attacked Anna lowered her head and ran away. Anna turned around, the stick still held defensively in her hand. "What is it you plan to do with that stick, woman?" he asked.

Anna looked down at the stick in her hand and suddenly realized how feeble it looked. She felt very embarrassed and dropped the stick on the ground and turned around, walking back to the pile of sticks she had dropped. She knew that Winter Wolf would probably punish her but she didn't intend to stand around and wait for it. She knelt on the ground and began piling the wood into the front of her sling. She flinched when she felt Winter Wolf's hand on her back.

"You are bleeding."

She turned her head slightly to acknowledge him, but she didn't look at him. "It is nothing." She went back to gathering the wood.

She felt Winter Wolf's hands on her shoulders as he pulled her up and turned her to face him. "She could have killed you. Did you not know that she carries a knife?"

"No."

"And you were not afraid?"

"I didn't have time to be afraid." Anna felt for the first time the bruise on her mouth as she spoke. Her whole face felt sore.

"This will not happen again."

"If you are going to punish me, Winter Wolf, please do it now." She looked at him defiantly.

"Is that what you wish?"

Anna ran her hands through her tangled hair. "You will do what you wish anyway. I don't care anymore." Anna started to turn away, but Winter Wolf's hand on her shoulder stopped her.

"You are a stubborn woman. I should have let the Shoshonis deal with you. It would have been their punishment." He shook his head in exasperation and put his hand on her arm. "Come."

Anna didn't know where Winter Wolf was leading her, but she suddenly didn't care. She was so tired she could barely walk, and her body had never been so sore. She hated sleeping on the hard ground night after night, but she refused to ask Winter Wolf if she could use one of his robes.

Winter Wolf led Anna upstream through the cottonwoods until they reached a fairly remote part of the river. Then he stopped. "Take off those silly shoes," he said, pointing to her boots.

Anna didn't know what he intended, but she sat down and took off her boots and stockings, rubbing her tired and blistered feet. "I swear I'll never complain about anything again if you'll just let me go home."

"Take off the dress," Winter Wolf commanded.

Anna turned and looked at Winter Wolf. "I will not!"

"Take of the dress or *I* will take it off."

Anna looked at Winter Wolf's cold eyes and she complied. She unbuttoned the front of the dress and slipped it down to her waist, then pushed it underneath her and pulled it off her legs. She held the dirty, ragged blue remains of what had once been a lovely blue traveling suit. Sitting on the riverbank in her slip, she felt very naked. If Winter Wolf asked her to take off her slip, she didn't know what she'd do.

"Now, get into the water and bathe. I will be back." Winter Wolf bent down and picked up the boots and dress and disappeared into the trees. Anna was so relieved that he didn't ask her to take off the rest of her clothing that she didn't question where he was going.

She slipped down the edge of the bank until her feet touched the cool water. She had longed to do this since they had arrived. She felt filthy, and she knew that she must smell horrible. She waded into the cool water and began washing the dirt from her legs. Then she sat slowly down in the middle of the river until the water came up to her neck. It was much colder than she had thought it would be, but she didn't care. She washed her arms and neck and then tilted her head back until her hair was wet. She ran her fingers through it to try to untangle it, and then rinsed it again. She scrubbed her face with her fingers until it ached, but at least it felt

117

clean. She stood up and looked down at her torn and stained slip. She took the skirt of the slip between her fingers and began to rub the edges together, trying to get out as much dirt as she could. When she was through, she sat back down in the water and put her head back. She felt her hair float out behind her on the water and closed her eyes. For a moment she could imagine that she was back on the ranch in Arizona with Nathan, taking a swim in the lake. She wondered if she would ever see that beloved place again.

"Come, woman, it is time."

Anna sat up and opened her eyes. Winter Wolf stood on the bank, his long black hair hanging down his bare chest and shoulders, his face, as usual, showing no emotion. Anna pulled her hair tightly in the back to rinse out the excess water and then walked toward the bank. She was aware that her wet slip clung to her body and that Winter Wolf could see through it, but she refused to be embarrassed. She waded to the bank and realized that it was too steep to climb up. She would either have to crawl up it and get dirty again, or she would have to walk downstream until she found a shallower place in which to get out.

"Give me your hand," Winter Wolf said.

Anna took his outstretched hand, amazed at how easily he pulled her up the bank. She stood before him, feeling completely naked, but he seemed to take no notice. He shoved a bundle into her arms.

"These will be your clothes," he said. "There are also moccasins. Dress quickly."

Anna decided to take off her slip because she was beginning to shiver. She turned her back to Winter Wolf and quickly pulled the slip off over her head and, just as quickly, pulled the soft deerskin dress over her head. It fell to her knees and was decorated with brightly colored beads and quills. She walked to a nearby tree and leaned against it while she pulled on one moccasin, then the other. She couldn't believe how comfortable they felt. She bent over to pick up her slip, but Winter Wolf took it from her hands.

"What about my sling? I need it to carry Robert and to collect wood."

"You will have another. Come."

Anna nodded and followed Winter Wolf back into camp. She noticed that many people stared at her, but she held her head high, unwilling to give them the satisfaction of knowing how frightened she really was. When they got to Winter Wolf's lodge, she started inside, but Winter Wolf stopped her. "Sit here. I will return with the boy."

Anna did as she was told, not quite sure why Winter Wolf had suddenly changed his mind. Normally he didn't want her outside of the lodge unless she was with the women. Now, he wanted her to sit outside. People walked by, some carrying water, others carrying pots of food to share with neighbors. As Anna observed the people in their routine, she realized that they really weren't all that different from people anywhere. They laughed and talked and ate and slept, the same as everyone else in the world. The only difference was, they did it outside, under the open sky.

Anna heard a child's cry and looked up to see Robert running ahead of Winter Wolf. She saw by the look on the child's face that he was crying with excitement, trying to outrun his larger pursuer. When Robert saw Anna he ran into her arms and buried his head in her chest, assuming, as children do, that Winter Wolf wouldn't be able to find him if he didn't see Winter Wolf.

Winter Wolf sat next to Anna, looking over at Robert. "The boy grows quickly. Soon he will need a name."

"He already has a name," Anna snapped.

"He needs a Cheyenne name." He looked at Anna a

moment. "You, too, need a name."

"I also have a name, Winter Wolf. It is Anna."

"I do not like that name. I will think of another for you."

Anna looked at him in frustration. The man did whatever he wanted to do and he always thought he was right. "I like my name."

"It does not matter. You will have a new name."

Anna knew it was no use arguing with Winter Wolf when he had made up his mind. She started to get up, but he put his hand on her arm. "I was going to get you your meal."

"Sit. It is good to sit and look sometimes."

Anna still couldn't figure out why he wanted her to sit in front of the lodge but, again, she didn't argue. She tickled Robert and held him high in the air, pretending that he was a bird that could fly. The child's delighted laughter rang loudly and people stopped and smiled.

"See how people look at this boy. They like him."

"He's a likable child," Anna said, pulling Robert to her and kissing him on the head. "You don't have children of your own, Winter Wolf?"

Winter Wolf didn't look at Anna. "I have no children."

Anna looked at him. She had the distinct feeling that he was hiding something, but she was not about to pry. Robert crawled from her lap to Winter Wolf's, and immediately the man smiled, picking Robert up in his arms. *"Hahkota,"* he said endearingly.

"Hahkota?" What does it mean?"

Winter Wolf held Robert in front of him, letting him play with his long hair. "It means the bug that cannot stay still, the one that jumps from one thing to the next."

"You mean a grasshopper?" Anna laughed.

"You do not think it is a good name for this one?"

"It's a very good name for him. *Hahkota,*" Anna repeated.

"Tonight you will meet my parents," Winter Wolf said casually.

Anna didn't know what this meant. "Is it wise for you to do that?" She looked at him.

"What do you mean?"

"Your people do not like me, Winter Wolf. I would not want any of them, especially your parents, to think less of you because of me."

"My parents would only think less of me if I behaved less than honorably. They would like to meet the woman who saved my life."

"I didn't save your life. I only cut you loose."

"And what do you suppose would have happened if you had not cut me loose? Do you think the Shoshonis would have let me go?" Winter Wolf shook his head. "I think not. You saved my life, woman."

"Just as you saved mine," she said thoughtfully. "I am grateful, Winter Wolf. I know I have been difficult at times—"

"Yes, you are a difficult woman," Winter Wolf eagerly agreed.

"It's just that I miss my husband and my people."

"Look at me, woman."

Anna looked at Winter Wolf, unable to resist his commanding tone.

"I told you before, I cannot take you back to your people. Do you truly understand this?"

"Yes, I understand."

"It seems then, that you do not have a choice but to stay here with my people."

"My husband will come for me," Anna said adamantly.

"No white man will come into our village. He would be killed before he could enter."

"No, you can't do that. What if someone needed your help, what if—"

"He will not come for you, woman. You must accept

121

this."

"Then I will try to get back to my people on my own."

"I will not stop you," he said, lifting Robert high into the air, "but you will not take Hahkota with you."

"He is my nephew. You cannot keep him from me."

"I will not let the boy go with you. He would not have a chance."

Anna stood up, her cheeks flushed in anger. "But you would let me go alone? Perhaps it would've been better if I had never cut you loose. Perhaps the Shoshonis would've been kinder to me than you are." Anna strode past the front of the lodge and out through the trees. She stood amid the branches of the cottonwoods, the tears rolling down her cheeks. She pulled a piece of the bark from a tree and threw it on the ground, then crushed it with her foot. She clenched her fist and looked at it, then slammed it against the bark of the tree. "No!" she screamed, her voice echoing among the trees. Then, resting her head against the trunk of the tree, she cried for the first time, great sobs wracking her body. She hung on to the trunk of the tree and fell slowly to the ground. She had never thought it was possible that she would have to stay with the Cheyennes the rest of her life, but now it seemed likely. Even if she thought she was strong enough to make it on her own through Cheyenne country, Winter Wolf would never let her take Robert. It was clear that he now thought of the boy as his own. She sat on the ground, her hand bleeding and throbbing with pain, but nothing mattered to her. She felt as if her life were over and she would never be free again. She looked at her hand and tried to make it into a fist, but she could not. She was afraid she had broken it in her rage.

She looked up when she saw some children playing in the river. They were so young, yet their parents didn't seem to worry about them being alone. One thing she had already learned from the Cheyennes was that they believed in making their children independent at a very early age. The young boys were already walking around with small bows and arrows and the girls helped their mothers skin animals and tan hides.

She heard the children squeal as they played and splashed each other in the shallows of the river. The sound of their laughter brought a smile to Anna's lips. She had already ceased to be an enemy to the children, and many of them had walked with her and helped her to gather wood. They were much more accepting than their parents.

She heard a child's scream, but it wasn't the high-pitched, carefree sound she was used to. She whirled and ran to the river's edge, where she could see the children. Three young boys, no older than six years of age, were running through ankle-deep water, headed for the deep channel in the middle of the river. A child lay floating facedown in the deep water. Without thinking, Anna began to run, kicking her moccasins off as she entered the water. She ran until the water was deep enough and then began to swim. At first she was grateful that the current pushed her, but when she paused to breathe, she saw that that same current was taking the child away from her. She redoubled her efforts. The channel curved with the river, deeper in some places than others, but always so deep that she had to swim. The riverbed was strewn with rocks left there by spring floods, and it was impossible to avoid hitting them. The sharp, scraping pains in her legs were numbed by the cold water and she ignored them, trying to watch the child as she swam.

The river narrowed. Huge boulders jutted into the river from both sides. The channel deepened and the current became swifter. Anna gave in to the racing water, raising her forearms to protect her face when the current pushed her against the rocks. When she could, she swam hard, trying desperately to close the distance between her and the child. The river became even narrower, and Anna saw the rising walls of a canyon ahead. She was closer to the child and she knew that she had to reach him now. Ahead, the river churned, almost white. The child would almost certainly be killed against the rocks and for her to try to swim the white water would be certain death.

The river swept her around a boulder. On the other side, the water ebbed and swirled and the child floated close to shore. In seconds, Anna knew, the current would sweep them both into the mountainous canyon. She forced her aching arms and legs to move, swimming faster. An instant before the current swept them up again, her cold, stiffened fingers grasped the child's wrist. She fought to keep their heads above water as the current carried them toward the canyon. Swimming frantically, she worked her way to the edge of the channel. In the shallower water, the current was less strong. Ahead of her she saw a fallen tree that jutted into the water, held there by rocks. She strained to swim toward it, to free herself from the pull of the current. The moment her shoulder struck the log, she knew she would live. But the child? She raised the child out of the water and saw for the first time that it was a little boy. Using the log to steady herself and him, she pounded on his back, willing him to take a breath. When she had almost lost hope, the boy began to cough, ridding his lungs of water.

She tried to maneuver herself toward the bank, one arm holding the boy, the other arm sliding along the rough bark of the tree. The boy began to cry and Anna stopped for a moment. She held him tightly, kissing the top of his head. "It's all right. You're safe now." Her arms began to shake. She still had to get them to shore, and it seemed so far away.

"Woman!"

Anna turned and looked toward the bank. It was Winter Wolf standing on the bank by his horse, a rope in his hands. He threw the rope in a high circular arc and out toward her. It fell short the first time and he had to throw it again. She was able to grab it the second time. It was already in a noose, and Anna slipped it over her head and tightened it around her waist. She raised her hand, and Winter Wolf pulled the boy and her toward the bank. Even when she was in water shallow enough to stand, her legs wouldn't support her. Winter Wolf waded into the cold water, took the boy from her, and circled her waist with his arm. The fear and exhaustion she had held at bay overcame her and she leaned heavily against him, feeling the impossible warmth of his skin through her sodden clothing. He had saved her, and she knew that for a while at least she didn't have to be brave or strong.

Chapter 6

Nathan sat on Rachel's window seat staring out into the trees. It had been two weeks since Rachel's accident and she seemed to be getting stronger. At first, her legs had swollen up to twice the normal size and they had turned varying shades of purple and blue. He was sure he had crippled her for life by his ministrations. But within the first week, Rachel was wiggling her toes, and she discovered that her right leg wasn't as bad as the left. She said it would take months until she was fully healed, possibly longer. From what she could tell, they weren't as badly broken as she had originally thought.

Nathan continued to stare out the window. Two weeks. A lot could have happened to Anna in two weeks. She could have been traded, she could have been hurt, she could have béen killed. He looked back at Rachel sleeping on the bed, and he knew it was time to go. He could see that she was beginning to depend on him too much and he couldn't let that happen. She was confusing gratitude with love.

There was a knock on the door and Roberto entered the room. "Thought you might be hungry," he said, handing a food-ladened tray to Nathan.

Nathan nodded his thanks and picked up the sandwich. "How are you feeling?" he asked his brother.

"I'm getting stronger every day. How about you?" Robert took the chair from Rachel's desk and sat next to Nathan.

"I'm fine. There's nothing wrong with me."

"Nothing finding Anna won't cure."

Nathan put the rest of the sandwich on the tray and took a drink of milk. He looked over at Rachel before he spoke. "I'm leaving tomorrow, Berto. I can't wait any longer."

"I've wondered why you waited this long." He, too, glanced at Rachel. "I didn't realize your feelings for her were that strong."

"She saved your life and she took us both into her home. We both owe her, Berto, or have you forgotten?"

"No, I haven't forgotten. But I think I'm strong enough to look after her now."

"Good, because I have to go. I don't think Rachel will understand."

"Why should it matter if she understands, Nate? Why is that so important to you?"

"I told you why."

"No, you told me what you wanted me to hear. But I know you. You wouldn't be here if you didn't care about her."

"Of course I care about her." Nathan looked over at Rachel and smiled. She looked so young in her flowered nightgown, her brown hair spread all over the pillow. It was hard to believe she was such a competent woman. "She's a nice woman. I didn't want to leave her when she was in such pain. I wanted her to know that someone besides her uncle cares about her."

"I think she knows that now."

Nathan shot Roberto an angry look. "What's that supposed to mean?"

"That means the woman is crazy in love with you,

Nate. It's written all over her face."

Nathan stood up. "You're out of your mind, Berto," he said as he left the room and went downstairs. Standing in front of the window, he stared out at the mountains as he had so many times before. He heard Roberto follow him down the stairs and across the living room but he didn't turn.

"Get out of here tomorrow, Nate. You don't owe Rachel anything more. You saved her life and you helped her get better. Now it's time for your own life. You have a woman somewhere out there who's waiting for you to find her. She probably needs you a hell of a sight more than Rachel does." Roberto pressed his hand into Nathan's shoulder. "You know I'm right, Nate."

Nathan nodded. "It's not just Rachel. I'm afraid what I'm going to find out there." He turned back to the window.

"We both know Anna is a tough woman. She'll survive as long as she knows you'll find her."

"But what if she's given up? What if she thinks I'm not coming for her?"

"Anna will never give up. She needs you, Nate, and so do I. I need you to find my son and bring him back to me."

"God, I hope she's all right, Berto. I don't think I could take it if she weren't."

Roberto turned Nathan around, staring into his older brother's blue eyes. He loved this man more than anything in the world except for his son. Nathan had always fought for him, had always been willing to do anything for him. He couldn't expect that strength to go on forever. He put his arms around Nathan and was surprised when Nathan hugged him back.

"It'll be all right, Nate. Trust in Anna and trust in yourself. You'll be together again."

Anna moved her face away from the pungent smell, but a hand forced it to the steam. She began to cough and her chest felt as if a ton of rocks were on it. She opened her eyes, but she couldn't see anything; she heard voices in the background but couldn't understand what they were saying. She closed her eyes again.

Winter Wolf stood behind his mother, Little Deer. "How is she, Mother? She does not seem to want to wake up."

Little Deer tucked the heavy robe around Anna's chest and stood up. "She does not want to live, my son."

"She wants to go back to her people," Winter Wolf stated.

"If you were to be taken to the white man's world, would you not want to come back here to your people?" She looked at Anna. "It makes me sad to look at her."

"Is there anything I can do, Mother?"

"There is nothing any of us can do. We cannot will her to live. That must come from her."

Winter Wolf watched his mother as she continued to fan the fire next to Anna, hoping that the smoke from the leaves would help her to breathe easier.

Winter Wolf walked to the back of the lodge. "Haahe, Father. May I sit with you?" he asked.

Brave Wolf gestured to the robe next to him. "Sit, my son. What is it that troubles you about this white woman?"

"This is a woman of great spirit, Father, a woman of great courage."

"Yes, the little ones told me that she did not hesitate to save Little Bird. She shows no fear."

"Her heart breaks to see her people again, Father."

"What are you saying, my son?"

129

Winter Wolf looked at his father. "I am going to take her back."

Brave Wolf showed no emotion. "You cannot do that, Winter Wolf. It would be too dangerous. Think. An Indian, a white woman, and a child traveling through Indian country and white man's country. It is a wonder that you three made it here alive."

"She will die if she stays here, Father. She risked her life to save me."

"As you risked yours to save her from the Shoshonis."

"I do not want her to die, Father."

"You cannot take her back, my son, but you can take care of her here."

Winter Wolf looked at his father in the dim firelight of the lodge. "What are you saying, Father?"

"Do you care for this woman?"

"I do not know."

"Do you respect her?"

"Yes."

"And you admire her courage."

"Yes."

"Then take her for your wife. You will learn to care for her."

"No, I cannot do that."

"It is all you can do for her, Winter Wolf. If she is your wife, she will be treated with great respect in this band. No one will think to speak against her."

Winter Wolf looked away from his father. "She would never consent to such a union."

"Perhaps if you were to treat her with more respect, she would consider it."

Winter Wolf looked across the lodge at Anna. She lay fighting for her life. "I never thought I would take another wife," he said absently.

"Your wife has been dead for over two winters now. How long must you grieve?"

"I loved Rain Woman, Father. I do not think I could ever be a husband to another woman."

"It is time, my son." He pointed to Anna. "Why not this woman? The blood of our people runs through her veins, she is part of us. She has the heart of a warrior."

"I tell you, Father, she will not have me."

"You have been too long without a woman, Winter Wolf. You have forgotten the ways in which a woman likes to be courted. Perhaps you should talk to your mother."

"I do not know, Father. I do not know if this is the right thing to do. I must think on it."

"You do what you must, my son."

Winter Wolf walked to Anna, squatting next to her, staring at her flushed face. She mumbled words that he couldn't understand. He reached out and touched her cheek. It felt soft and warm. He didn't know how to act with her. His father was right; he had been too long without a woman. Rain Woman had been so gentle and sweet, and she had loved him since they were children. It would be different with this woman. She was from a world that was totally unlike his. It would be hard for them to make a life together.

"She is very pretty, is she not?" Little Deer asked from behind him.

Winter Wolf couldn't resist a smile. "Yes, Mother, she is pretty for a white woman."

"She is strong also. She would be able to bear a man many children."

Winter Wolf removed his hand from Anna's face and sat back on his haunches. "Mother, you do not want me to marry a white woman, do you?"

"She is only half white. The Cheyenne blood in her is strong. It is easy to see."

"But she was raised in the white world, Mother. She is more white than Cheyenne."

131

"If she cannot go back to her world, perhaps she could find it in her heart to stay here."

"I do not think so. She will never stay here." Winter Wolf looked at Little Deer. "She is married to a white man, Mother. This man must have a great love for her."

"If his love is great, he will find her, my son."

"It will be impossible for him to find us. I feel as if he does not have a fair chance."

"When have you ever cared about a white man, Winter Wolf?"

"I know how much I loved Rain Woman. If she had been taken into the white world, I know how I would have felt. I would not have known where to look," he stated as he left the lodge. He walked out of the village and stood in the trees, listening to the river as it flowed past. He didn't know the right thing to do. If he took this woman for his wife, then he had to care for her for the rest of his life. That meant, if her husband ever did come for her, he could never let her go.

Nathan had been riding for days, following trail after trail and not knowing where to go. He had no idea where Brave Wolf's band was located, knew it would be pure luck if he found them at all.

He stopped and reached for his water bag, taking a long drink. He'd already run into a hunting party of Crows, but with his rifle raised and his ability to converse in Crow, they didn't bother him. He asked them if they knew of any Cheyennes, and they told him what they could. The only Cheyenne band that they had seen had summered along the winding river the previous year; perhaps they were there again this year. It was hard for Nathan to believe that the Crows didn't know where the Cheyennes were, but he had heard that the hostilities between the two tribes were beginning to die down after almost seventy years of fighting.

He rode in the direction that the Crows had suggested, riding mile after lonely mile along the sage-covered, rocky terrain, with only an occasional buffalo to keep him company. He knew that this was just the beginning of his journey and he must be patient. He held on to the fact that Anna was a strong woman, a woman who loved him with all her heart.

Roberto carried Rachel down the stairs, placing her on a chair. "I still think you should use my room. Then you wouldn't have to worry about the stairs."

"I like my room, thank you," Rachel replied curtly.

Roberto had noticed that ever since Rachel had awakened and discovered Nathan was gone, she had been in a foul temper. He sat down in the chair next to her. "Zeb and I are making you some crutches for when you're able to put weight on your feet." Rachel didn't answer, merely stared out the window. "I think I'm dying, Rachel. I've just stuck a knife in my heart and I can see the blood spurting out of my chest."

"What did you say?" Rachel asked absently, still staring out the window.

"Never mind." Roberto walked over to the window. "Are you still angry with me for what I said that day?"

"I don't know what you are talking about."

"That day in my room when I insulted you and you ran out."

"I don't even remember what it was you said."

"Oh, you remember, all right, and I figure since I've already insulted you once, I might as well go ahead and do it twice."

"What are you talking about?" Rachel asked angrily.

"Nathan won't be back without Anna. He loves her

133

more than anything in this world. So, if you think he'll come back for you, don't count on it. He'll search for her for the rest of his life if he has to." Roberto expected Rachel to pick something up and throw it at him, but she didn't. She simply continued to stare out of the window.

"I know he loves his wife, Roberto. I'm not as stupid as you think I am."

"I never thought you were stupid, Doc."

Rachel looked up at him for the first time. "Your brother is the kind of man every woman dreams about. He's kind, handsome, gentle, and very much a gentleman."

"He's everything I'm not."

"If you expect me to argue with that statement, I won't."

"I didn't expect you to argue, Doc. But I still think I'm right. You're afraid of something. Nathan looked good to you because he's married and you knew he couldn't fall in love with you."

"That's nonsense!" Rachel replied angrily, looking away from Roberto.

Roberto stood in front of Rachel. "I bet under all those men's clothes, you're a real exciting woman, Rachel. It's too bad you don't let it show once in a while."

Roberto walked to the front door, hearing the crash of something against it as he walked outside. He liked Rachel and was glad he was going to be stuck here for a while.

Anna sat against the backrest, sipping broth out of a bowl. When she was finished, she handed it to Little Deer with a gesture of gratitude.

"You are feeling better today?" the Indian woman asked.

"Yes, much better. Thank you for everything you've done for me. You're very kind."

"You were very brave to do what you did for Little Bird. You put yourself in great danger."

"He's just a boy. He couldn't save himself."

Little Deer smiled. "You have a good heart."

"The boy, is he well?"

"Yes, he is fine. He will think before he tries to go to the middle of the river again."

Anna looked around. "Where is Robert? Is he all right?"

"He is fine. He is with Winter Wolf."

"Winter Wolf is good with him."

"He is beginning to think of Robert as a son. It is good to see him with a child again."

"Again?"

"Winter Wolf was once married and had a son. Rain Woman and her family were hunting buffalo. They were attacked and killed by white hunters."

"My God," Anna said, shaking her head. "They even killed his son?"

"No, my grandson was trampled by buffalo when he tried to run away." Little Deer's eyes filled with tears. "I thought Winter Wolf would die from the grief. He and Rain Woman had known each other all of their lives."

"No wonder he hates white people so."

"He has been a bitter man since he lost his wife and son. I want him to forget his bitterness and go on with life." She looked up and smiled when Winter Wolf came through the lodge flap. "My son, will you sit with Hevavahkema while I go and dig for roots? The women will be waiting for me."

Winter Wolf walked to his mother and took her hands. It was obvious he had great love for her. "I will watch her, Mother. Visit with your friends." He smiled. "I know they will have many questions to ask about the white woman."

Anna watched as Little Deer left the lodge. She was amazed at the youthful grace of this woman who was a grandmother. She reminded her of Aeneva. She looked up at Winter Wolf. "What did your mother call me?"

Winter Wolf sat down cross-legged on the robe next to Anna. "She called you 'butterfly.' I told her that I thought your eyes reminded me of the blue circles on the wings of butterflies."

"It's a lovely name. Your mother is kind, Winter Wolf. I like her very much."

"She is a good woman."

Anna looked down at her hands. "I want to thank you for saving my life. I think I was getting ready to die when you found me in the river."

"I do not think so. You are much too strong for that. You would have found a way to live."

"It was frightening."

"It is something that my people do not fear enough. Many times the children are allowed to play alone in the river. When the current is strong, they can be taken away easily."

"Perhaps you should talk to your people and tell them that the children shouldn't be permitted to swim in the river alone."

"I have already spoken to my father about it."

Anna looked at Winter Wolf and back down at her hands. She felt acutely uncomfortable with him this close to her. "You don't have to stay here. I'm fine."

"We must talk, Heva." Winter Wolf had used only part of the word. Anna found she liked the sound.

"What must we talk about? You're going to tell me that you won't take me back to my people, and if I want to go alone, I can't take Robert with me. You don't have to tell me again."

"That is not what I intend to say."

136

"What then?" Anna looked at Winter Wolf and noticed that he seemed uncomfortable.

"I want to take you for my wife, Heva."

Anna felt her mouth go dry. She attempted to speak, but nothing would come out. A thousand things raced through her mind, but foremost was the thought that if she married Winter Wolf, she could never leave this village.

"I don't know what to say, Winter Wolf. I'm unprepared for this."

"I, too, am unprepared. I did not think I would ever marry again. I had a wife and son who were killed by white hunters over two summers ago and I have been filled with hatred ever since."

"Then why would you want to marry me, knowing that I'm white."

"You are also part Cheyenne. My people are also your people. And I like the boy. Hahkota has become like a son to me."

"Winter Wolf, I'm honored that you would ask such a thing of me. I'm sure many women would be honored to be your wife, but I'm already married. You know that."

"And you believe this man will come for you?"

"I have to believe he will come for me."

"And if he does not?"

Anna lowered her eyes. "I don't know what I'll do. I can't imagine my life without him."

Winter Wolf reached out and touched Anna's hand. "You must imagine your life without him, Heva, for I do not think he will come."

Anna pulled her hand away from Winter Wolf's touch. "Please, I don't want to talk about this right now."

"We must talk, Heva. I want to take you for my wife."

"But why? You have seldom even spoken to me."

"I did not think I could ever care for another woman again, but as I grew to know you, I found that I respected you greatly. I admired you when you fought Buffalo Woman, and I admired your courage when you saved the boy from the river. You are the kind of woman I could live with and respect."

"People need more than respect to be together, Winter Wolf. You loved your wife greatly, didn't you?"

"Yes."

"That's how I feel about my husband. You and I cannot be together just out of respect."

"Love can grow from respect."

Anna looked at Winter Wolf. She couldn't believe this was the same man who had always been so distant. "I cannot marry you, Winter Wolf."

"You will change your mind, Heva."

"I will not change my mind."

"Then I will make you." Winter Wolf stood up. "Rest now. I will be back later."

Anna shook her head as he left the lodge. She couldn't understand why he suddenly wanted to marry her. Was it because she had saved the boy's life? It made no sense to her. She tried not to think about it. She just wanted to rest.

When Anna awakened, she saw the wildflowers scattered around the robe. She smiled, picking one up, putting it to her nose, and breathing deeply. It smelled like lilac. She was beginning to have a real affection for Little Deer. She was so thoughtful. She looked up when Little Deer came into the lodge.

"How are you, Hevavahkema? You have more color in your cheeks."

"I am well, Little Deer. Thank you for the beautiful

flowers."

"I did not bring you the flowers. You must thank Winter Wolf for those."

"Winter Wolf?"

"Yes, it seems my son and Hahkota picked wildflowers this afternoon and then scattered them on your robes."

Anna shook her head in wonder. "I can't imagine Winter Wolf picking flowers." She held another flower to her nose.

"There are many things about my son that would surprise you."

"Winter Wolf has asked me to be his wife, Little Deer."

"I knew that he would, and it pleases me. You would make a good wife for my son."

"I already have a husband, Little Deer."

"As I said before, if you think your husband will come for you, then you must wait. But if you think he will not, you should marry Winter Wolf. He would be a good husband to you. He can be a gentle man. You would command great respect as his wife."

Anna twirled the purple flower between her fingers. "Do you love Brave Wolf?"

Little Deer fussed around the pot on the fire before answering. "I thought my heart would burst the first time I saw Brave Wolf ride by on his horse. He was so handsome. Every girl in the band wanted to become his wife."

"So you loved him very much?"

"Yes, and my heart grows more full of that love the older I get."

"That is how I feel about my husband, Little Deer." Anna stopped as Little Deer turned from the fire to listen. "I could never love your son in that way. Never. I wouldn't be doing an honorable thing if I married

139

him."

"You are a good woman, Heva. I like your honesty."

"Winter Wolf deserves to have a wife who will love him and give him children. I'm sure there are many women in this band who would like to become his wife."

"It is true, there are many, but Winter Wolf would not marry just any woman, Heva. The woman he marries must have a good heart, she must be strong of mind, and she must be honorable. Can you not see that you are all of those things? You are the woman for my son."

Anna shook her head in exasperation. "Please, Little Deer, I'm grateful for all you've done for me, but I can't marry Winter Wolf. It wouldn't be fair to either one of us."

"It is your decision to make, Hevavahkema . . . Are you hungry?"

"No, thank you. When can I get up?"

"It would be best if you rested for another day, then I will let you walk."

Anna nodded. "Was Rain Woman pretty?"

Little Deer looked at Anna. "She was very small and very delicate. She had a pretty smile that made you feel good. She was very pretty and she made my son very happy."

Anna laid her head against the backrest and closed her eyes. What would it be like to be the wife of Winter Wolf? He was so obviously well loved and respected that she, too, would be treated with great respect. He had shown her that he could care for her. He was a good man, she was certain of that, but he was not the man she wanted to spend the rest of her life with. She knew that Nathan would come for her, yet he wasn't here. She realized how difficult it would be for him to find her. She couldn't even remember the many different trails they had taken and the many streams they had crossed to get here.

"Heva." Winter Wolf's voice startled Anna from her rest. "Will you walk with me?"

"She should not be walking, Winter Wolf," Little Deer said. "She is yet too weak."

"It will only be a short walk, Mother."

Anna quickly pushed the heavy robe from her legs, anxious to get out of the lodge. "I will walk with you, Winter Wolf."

Winter Wolf bent down and slipped Anna's moccasins onto her feet. She felt her cheeks flush as his hands touched her feet and ankles. It was such a thoughtful thing for him to do, yet it seemed so intimate.

Winter Wolf offered his hand to Anna. She took it and stood up, her legs feeling shaky. He put Anna's arm through his and guided her out of the lodge. She squinted at the bright daylight, reaching up to cover her eyes. The air smelled so clear and fresh and the sounds of people made her feel good. She smiled at Winter Wolf as he led her through the village to a corral where the band kept their most valuable horses. During one of their few conversations, Anna had asked him why the Cheyenne kept some horses in the corral and why they let some roam free. He told her that their most valuable horses, usually their war horses, were kept in the corral so they couldn't be run off or easily stolen.

They went to the corral and Anna leaned against the railing, reveling in the sight of the horses. She had always loved to ride and Trenton and Aeneva had taught her the beauty and freedom of riding a horse.

"Look, there . . ." Winter Wolf pointed to a large Appaloosa.

"She's beautiful." Tears came to Anna's eyes. The mare reminded her of Trenton's beloved Appaloosa, a horse no one could ride but Trenton and then Anna.

"Look, do you see on the other side of her?"

Anna strained her neck futilely to see, but she heard the tiny nicker of a colt and saw the Appaloosa as he tried to keep pace with his mother. He had two black spots on his rump, four black socks, and black spots on his nose. He couldn't have been more than a few days old, his long, spindly legs looking as though they could barely hold his weight. He tried desperately to drink some milk from his mother, but she kept moving around and he whinnied in frustration.

"He's so beautiful," Anna said, a smile covering her face.

"Look at his legs. He will be a big one. At least twenty hands high, I think."

"His mother is so beautiful, too."

"She is the offspring of a stallion that was in our tribe. We were lucky to get this horse."

"She's yours?"

"Yes, but I do not use her for war. I knew that she would have foals someday. I just didn't know if they would turn out to look like her."

"You're lucky. This one will grow up to be magnificent."

"He is yours, Heva. I want you to have him."

Anna looked at Winter Wolf. "I can't take him, Winter Wolf, he is much too valuable a horse." She shook her head adamantly. "No."

"He already belongs to you. It is up to you to train him."

"I won't be here long enough to train him." Anna turned away from the corral and started back toward the village.

Winter Wolf grabbed her by the shoulders, pressing his fingers into her flesh. "Listen to me, Heva. If your husband does not come in one full moon, I want you to be my wife. You cannot stay here forever. The people of my village frown upon women who are alone. You must make a decision."

"It might take longer than that for my husband to find me, but he'll be here eventually."

"It has already been a long time. Think, Heva . . . everyone on that train knows it was attacked by Shoshonis. Why would he come looking for you here?"

Anna felt as if a knife had just been put through her heart. Winter Wolf was right. She knew now that Nathan would never find her. It wasn't possible. Her only option was to marry Winter Wolf.

"What if I were to become your wife and then my husband came for me? Would you let me go?"

Anna could feel Winter Wolf's fingers dig into her shoulders. "If you did consent to become my wife, I would never let you go."

Anna pulled away. "I could not be a true wife to you, Winter Wolf. You will want children and I . . ." Anna couldn't complete her thought. How could she tell this man that she could never make love to him?

"You will share my robe, Heva, but I will not force you to do what you do not wish to do. I would hope that you would willingly come to me."

Anna couldn't look at Winter Wolf. "You ask too much of me, Winter Wolf. Right now, my heart aches to see my husband. I want to be with him. I want to share his bed." She looked at him. "Why do you want a woman who does not want you?"

"You will learn to want me. I am a patient man, Heva."

Anna ran her fingers through her hair. "Please, leave me alone."

"I will say nothing for a full moon. If your husband is not here by then, I will take you for my wife."

Anna knew that there was nothing she could do now.

143

She couldn't go back alone, and she couldn't wait here forever, hoping against hope that Nathan would come. Her only chance would be to live with Winter Wolf and become his wife and the mother to his children. She closed her eyes against the sting of tears. She had always dreamed of having Nathan's children, children with light hair and light eyes, children who would grow up around the ranch in Arizona. Instead, she would have dark-haired, dark-eyed children, children who would grow up in an Indian camp and who would live with the fear of the white man coming to get them. She suddenly felt weak and stumbled against Winter Wolf.

She didn't open her eyes as she felt him pick her up in his arms and carry her back through the village. She turned her face to his chest, unwilling to let the women of the village look at her. He took her inside the lodge and placed her on the robe, gently covering her. She heard him speak to his mother, but she couldn't understand what they were saying. The strength that had always guided her, had always provided her with the courage to get through any situation, was slowly eroding, and with it, pieces of her heart were being chipped away. Soon, she would be married to a man she did not love and forced to bear his children. Life had never seemed more unbearable than it did at this moment.

Nathan looked back at the small band of Cheyennes. They had been friendly to him, had even invited him to share food and spend the night. They had almost killed him when he had ridden into the camp, but when he spoke their tongue so fluently and talked of his great-grandmother, Sun Dancer, people listened and were impressed. They had also heard of his mother,

Aeneva, and they wanted to know about this warrior woman. He had hoped that they would know something about Anna, but they did not. They had not seen Brave Wolf's band since the summer before and could only guess where he might be now. So Nathan was riding in a new direction, northeast, ever mindful that his journey might be fruitless, and that he might never again see Anna.

"I hate these damned things!" Rachel shouted angrily, trying to get down the porch steps on her new crutches. Roberto sat in one of the rocking chairs, a smile on his face.

"Well, you could always throw the crutches away and start walking."

Rachel stumbled on the second step and Roberto jumped up, catching her so she wouldn't fall. "Leave me alone! I can do this myself."

Roberto held his hands up in the air. "Sorry, I'll let you be. You should be glad you're not one of your own patients," he said smugly, hopping down the steps and walking into the yard.

"Wait!" Rachel called, leaning against the railing.

Roberto stopped and turned around. "I'll only wait if you'll be civil. I'm getting tired of being insulted by you, Doc."

Rachel's mouth turned down at the corners. "Will you please help me? I can't take being in that house for another second."

Roberto walked back to Rachel. He put his hands under her arms and easily lifted her to the bottom steps, ignoring the look of surprise on her face. "You hardly weigh a thing. You're going to waste away if you don't start eating something, Doc." He reached for the fallen crutches and placed one under each arm.

145

"There, try it now."

Rachel put the crutches in front of her and swung her legs forward. Roberto could see that she was still in a great deal of pain, but she had sworn that occasional exercise would be good for her. He watched her as she virtually willed herself across the yard to the pasture fence. When they reached the fence, he could see the tiny beads of sweat that had broken out over her face from the effort.

"I think you should go back to the house," Roberto suggested. "You're not as strong as you think."

"What do you know?" she exclaimed angrily. She turned on her crutches and started back but lost her balance and fell to the ground. As she landed on her injured legs, she cried out in pain.

Roberto quickly and gently picked her up in his arms and started toward the house. "No, please, I don't want to go back there," she said, burying her face in his chest.

He carried her to her special place behind the house. He'd never seen it until the week before when he'd gone exploring. The little stream that ran by the house was lined with cottonwoods and wildflowers. On the bank closest to the house, there was a small area where Rachel had planted rosebushes. She had built herself a bench to sit on so she could smell the roses as she sat and read. It was her own special place.

Roberto sat her down on the bench and stood in front of her. "I'll leave you alone, then come back for you in a bit."

"Don't leave, Roberto. I'd like some company."

"Do you mind if I sit down, then?" he asked.

"No." Rachel stared at the lovely pink roses in front of her. "These are my favorites. I love them. But in a few months they'll be dead and I'll have to plant new ones."

"Why don't you find some kind of flower that won't freeze?"

"I like roses. It's worth the effort of replanting them every year just to see them bloom and smell their glorious fragrance."

"You're a strange woman, Doc. I don't think I've ever known anyone like you."

"That doesn't sound like a compliment."

"You seem to make things hard for yourself," he observed. "A woman with your experience and your brains could be a doctor anywhere, but you chose this place." He gestured to the roses. "You plant flowers that you know will die just so you can see them bloom for a few weeks in the summer." He looked at her. "And you let yourself fall in love with a man who you know can never love you." He could see the crimson flush in her cheeks, but he didn't stop. "I can't figure out why you're so hard on yourself."

Rachel took a deep breath, staring at her pink roses. "I was the only child of a man who would've given anything to have a son. He was so disappointed in me. He loved me as much as he could, I suppose, but he always reminded me that I was only a woman and could never amount to much. So I suppose I spent most of my life trying to prove to him that I would and could amount to something." She shook her head, tears rolling down her cheeks. "The bastard died before I became a doctor. Do you know what he said to me before he died? He told me to give it up. He told me that no man would ever let a woman doctor treat him. He told me I had wasted my time trying to become something that only a man could be. I think I hated him for that."

Robert touched her shoulder gently. "I'm sorry, I guess I've been too hard on you."

Rachel wiped the tears from her face, smiling grimly.

"But you were right. I have been afraid to be a woman because I was always told that I was a failure at it by the man I loved the most in this world."

"You're not a failure Rachel. You're anything but that."

"Now you feel sorry for me."

"I don't feel sorry for you, I'd just like to see you enjoy life a little more."

"Why does it matter so much to you, Roberto?"

"Because I wouldn't let myself live for a long time. I let hate guide me for so long that I wasn't even sure what love meant. Anna helped show me."

"You love her, too." It was a simple statement, not an accusation.

"I guess that's something you and I have in common." He met Rachel's eyes. "We both love people we can't have. I must admit, it does make things easier. We know we can't have those people so we're safe. We don't have to be with anyone. We can just feel sorry for ourselves."

"That sounds horribly grim." She tried to stretch out her legs but grimaced.

"Let me carry you back to the house," Roberto offered.

"Not yet, I like it out here. It's so peaceful."

"Are you sure you're going to be all right? You'll be able to walk again, won't you?"

Rachel smiled broadly. "You sound concerned."

"I *am* concerned. The people around here need a good doctor," Roberto said with a straight face.

Rachel playfully hit Roberto on the shoulder and laughed. "You're a strange man."

"I'm not all that strange. I want to be loved, just like any other man." He leaned forward, rubbing his hands back and forth on his legs. "And I want my son back. I hope he's all right. I love him so much." Roberto felt

148

Rachel's hand on his shoulder, and he looked at her. He was surprised to see her green eyes were so gentle and that her face wore such a look of concern. He reached up and touched her face, moving his hand softly over her lips. "You're a pretty woman, Doc." He leaned forward and barely touched his lips to hers. He felt a tentative response from her, but he pulled back and looked at her again. "Am I allowed to pick one of your roses?"

"I suppose so."

Roberto got up and walked to the rosebush, looking for the perfect flower. He found one, the petals just beginning to open and burst with beauty. He broke it off and took out his knife, scraping the thorns from the stem, then returned and handed the rose to Rachel. "It's time you started getting back a little bit of what you give, Doc."

Rachel took the rose and put it to her nose. She breathed deeply, closing her eyes as she did so. When she opened them, Roberto was startled by the look in her eyes. It wasn't one of anger, and it wasn't one of disgust. Rachel Foster looked like a woman who was ready to be loved.

Chapter 7

Anna stood completely still as Little Deer dressed her in a fine dress made of soft deerskin that was decorated with long fringes, blue, red, and yellow beads and quills, and a belt of silver coins. Little Deer had arranged Anna's long black hair in one single braid which she had draped over Anna's shoulder. A single white feather hung from the end of the braid. Little Deer had tied a thin, beaded strip of leather around Anna's forehead. Except for her blue eyes, Anna looked as much like a Cheyenne as any other woman in the tribe.

"You are truly lovely, Hevavahkema. Winter Wolf will be so proud when we take you to his lodge."

"Thank you, Little Deer," Anna said softly, unable to bring herself to feel any excitement about her marriage. She had prayed every day for the last month that Nathan would come, but he had not. Now, she had no choice but to marry Winter Wolf.

Little Deer stood in front of Anna, a small pot in her hands. "I will paint your face now."

"I don't want that, Little Deer."

"But it is traditional. All brides have their faces painted."

"This is not a traditional wedding, Little Deer. Please, I do not want it."

150

"As you wish," Little Deer said, obviously disappointed.

Anna touched Little Deer's arm. "I did not mean to offend you, Little Deer. Please understand that this is difficult for me."

"I understand, Hevavahkema. You are putting on a brave face."

"Little Deer, I must ask you something in confidence."

Little Deer put her bowl down and faced Anna. "What do you wish to ask me?"

"I know in my heart that my husband will come for me one day. I have spoken of this to Winter Wolf. He says he will never let me go once I become his wife." Anna shook her head in frustration. "Please try to understand, Little Deer. In my world, when a woman marries a man, it is for life. My husband will always be my husband, even if I marry Winter Wolf."

"What is it you ask of me, Hevavahkema?"

"Will Winter Wolf let me go if my husband comes for me?"

Little Deer lowered her eyes and turned away. "What you ask is a very difficult question."

"Please, I need you to be honest with me, Little Deer."

Little Deer turned back to face Anna. "I know my son. Once he has taken you for his wife, he will die before he will give you up to another man."

"But he's my husband, Little Deer."

"You must understand, Hevavahkema, your ways are not like our ways. Perhaps you are married in your world, but once Winter Wolf has taken you for his wife, that is the only marriage that he will respect."

Anna walked across the lodge, still not able to believe she was going to become Winter Wolf's wife on this morning. She was so filled with fear that she had thought of packing a horse and leaving early that morning. But she didn't. Though she knew Winter Wolf

151

wouldn't have stopped her, she was afraid. She was afraid of the unknown and she was afraid to leave Robert with Winter Wolf.

"What is it you wish to do, Hevavahkema?"

"You know what I wish to do, Little Deer, yet I am unable to do it."

Anna felt Little Deer's hands on her shoulders, but she didn't face her. "My heart aches for you, Heva, but there is nothing I can do. I can only help you in your new life with my son. I will make it as easy for you as I can."

Anna nodded. "May I have some time alone? Please, just a few minutes."

"I will return shortly."

Anna walked around Little Deer and Brave Wolf's lodge. It was large, and weapons of war hung all around it. Baskets filled with dried flowers, herbs, roots, fruits, and vegetables were stacked on one side. There were backrests, willow mats for sleeping, and various robes on the mats. This was how Aeneva had grown up and these were the things that had helped mold her.

She picked up the bowl Little Deer had set on the ledge. It was filled with a deep blue paint. Anna dipped the first two fingers of her right hand in the paint and drew them in a diagonal line across each cheek. She also put a small horizontal line on her chin, then wiped her fingers on the edge of the bowl and set it down. She waited.

She had forgone all the traditional ceremonies of the Cheyenne wedding except for letting herself be escorted to her husband's lodge. Normally, she would have been led on one of the best horses by another woman to the lodge of her husband, or her husband's father. Young men related to the man would come out and lift the bride from the horse onto a blanket, then carry her into the lodge in silence. Traditionally, when the bride entered her mother-in-law's lodge, she would take off her new clothes and be dressed again by the women relatives of the man. They would dress her in clothing that they had made especially for her, they would comb and re-braid her hair and they would give her various pieces of jewelry to wear. Then she would sit by her new husband and they would eat a meal prepared by the girl's mother-in-law.

But no traditional ceremony would be done on this day. Little Deer would simply walk Anna to Winter Wolf's lodge, she would enter, Little Deer would serve them a meal, and they would be married. It was so simple, yet it meant so much to these people.

When Little Deer reentered the lodge, her face broke into a smile when she saw Anna. She took the young woman's hands in hers. "I will be like a mother to you, Hevavahkema. I will help you adjust to your new life."

"Thank you, Little Deer. I think I am ready now."

Little Deer led the way out of the lodge. Anna looked straight ahead, purposely not looking at any of the people who stood by to watch as she became Winter Wolf's wife. She was determined to show them how strong she could be.

Winter Wolf's lodge was close to his parents' lodge so Anna didn't have far to walk. A boy ran in front of her and she stopped, recognizing Little Bird, the boy she had saved in the river. She smiled and he smiled back, handing her a small bunch of flowers. She bent down and hugged him, happy to see his smiling face. When she looked up, she could see his mother, an approving look on her face.

Anna stood up and walked to the flap of the lodge, waiting as Little Deer held it open for her. She entered it and walked to the rear of the lodge. Winter Wolf was already sitting at his backrest. She barely looked at him as she sat down. She felt his eyes on her but she refused to look at him.

Little Deer quickly entered the lodge with bowls of food. Other women followed, carrying more dishes. When they were through, Little Deer stood in front of them.

"I wish you both a long and prosperous life together," she toasted, "and I hope that your children are strong and honorable." Then she lowered her head and left.

Brave Wolf then entered the lodge and walked to the rear, his eyes passing from Winter Wolf to Anna. Anna thought he was a very handsome man, but he frightened her. He seldom smiled and always seemed angry.

"It is a fine day for a wedding. I hope that this is a good thing for you, Winter Wolf, and for you, Hevavahkema. I hope you have many sons and daughters, and I hope you will always honor and respect each other." He nodded his approval and then left the lodge.

Anna stared after him. It was the first time Brave Wolf had ever spoken to her or even acknowledged her presence.

"Eat," Winter Wolf said, handing a bowl to Anna.

Taking it from him and sipping at the steaming broth of the stew, she stared straight ahead, afraid to meet Winter Wolf's eyes, afraid what she might see there.

They ate in total silence, and when they were through, Winter Wolf moved the bowls away. He sat down on his robe facing Anna, his back as straight as if he were still sitting against the backrest. "You look lovely, Hevavahkema."

Anna looked down at her hands. "Thank you."

"You are frightened?"

"Yes," she answered nervously.

"I am also frightened."

Anna looked at him then, surprised at his gentle tone. "I didn't think you were afraid of anything."

"I am afraid that I will grow to care for you too much and then I will lose you as I did Rain Woman."

154

Anna didn't know what to say. She played with the fringe on her skirt, avoiding Winter Wolf's eyes.

"What do you call it in your language when a man and woman are together?" he asked, his voice low.

"What do you mean?"

"When they share a robe."

Anna still couldn't look at Winter Wolf. "We call it many things in my language, but if you truly love someone, it is called 'making love.'"

"That is a strange thing, is it not? One *feels* love, one does not *make* love."

Anna laughed, finally looking at Winter Wolf. "If you love someone, you make love to them."

Winter Wolf shook his head. "It makes no sense to me. In our language we say that we desire a person. It is that simple."

"But love and desire are different things."

"Not in my world."

"This will never work between us, Winter Wolf. We are too different."

"You are here in my lodge, are you not?"

"I had no choice. You knew I could not find my way home alone. You knew that." Anna pulled a piece of fringe from her dress. "I may be part Cheyenne, but I am also part white. I will always be part white. You will never change that, Winter Wolf."

"We have been married only minutes and already you order me about. If my friends hear of this, I will lose all respect in this band."

Anna couldn't keep from smiling. Winter Wolf sounded so light-hearted, and when he smiled, it changed his entire face. He looked almost handsome. "I will not order you about in front of your friends."

Anna forced herself not to move when Winter Wolf reached up and touched her face. "Blue, do you know what it means?"

"No."

"It symbolizes the cloudless sky and means peace and serenity."

"Your mother didn't tell me."

"You must watch out for my mother. Some say she is a witch. She learned many things from my father's sister, who was a healer. She knows many strange mixtures. She probably put something in our food to make us do unspeakable things to each other."

Anna's eyes widened, looking at the bowls. "Your mother would do that?"

Winter Wolf laughed loudly. "I did not realize you were so easy to trick, Heva."

"I didn't know it was a trick. For all I know, your mother truly might have put something strange in my food."

"To make you do what?"

"To make me fall in love with you."

"I would not want any mixture to make you do that, Heva. I would want you to love me on your own."

Anna's eyes met Winter Wolf's, and suddenly she wasn't frightened anymore. She had spent much time with this man, and he had never harmed her in any way. He was a good man, an honorable man, and one, whom she was now finding out, could be pleasant as well. "You must be patient with me, Winter Wolf. I have so much to learn."

Winter Wolf reached out and took Anna's hand in his. "I will be patient, Heva. You are my wife. It is my job to make you happy."

"I'm not sure I can ever be truly happy, Winter Wolf. But I will try to be a good wife to you. I will try."

"I cannot ask for more, Heva."

She forced herself to smile at her new husband. This was her life now, but inside, she could never ever give up the hope that Nathan would come for her. She also planned to keep learning from the Cheyennes, and maybe if she learned enough, she and Robert could leave. But she remembered Winter Wolf's words: once he had taken her for his wife, he would never let her go.

"What do you wish to do?"

"Do?" Anna asked warily.

"We have the rest of the day and night. What do you wish to do?"

"Can't we go outside and go for a walk or a ride?"

"It would not look good for us to come out of our lodge before tomorrow. People would wonder. They would think we do not desire each other."

"Oh" was all Anna could manage to say. She knew that Winter Wolf had said he wouldn't force her to do anything, but would he keep his promise?

"Do you wish to sleep?"

"Sleep? No, I'm not tired."

"Then we must use this time to get to know each other."

"What do you mean?" Anna asked anxiously.

"We should ask questions of each other."

Anna relaxed. "What would you like to ask me?"

"Tell me about your family."

"I don't really have a family."

"What of your mother, your Cheyenne mother?"

"She died when I was very young, and my father took me and traveled from city to city. He drank whiskey all day, so I was left alone much of the time. He decided to go west and we joined a wagon train. When we got to Arizona, the train was hit by the cholera. My father and I both got ill and an Indian woman found us and took care of us. She and her white husband took us into their home."

"This is the woman you call your mother?"

"Yes, she was my mother in every respect. When my real father decided to leave me, she and her husband raised me as their own daughter."

"Your father left you? Why would he do such a thing?"

"He was a slave to his whiskey and he knew that his life was not the life for a young girl. It was a wonderful thing he did leaving me with Aeneva and Trenton."

"Aeneva?" Winter Wolf's body tensed immediately. "That is a Cheyenne word. It means 'winter.' "

"Yes, I know. She was born during a blizzard and she was strong and healthy, so her parents named her Aeneva."

"You did not tell me that this woman was also Cheyenne, Heva. I thought you spoke of your birth mother when you spoke of your Cheyenne blood."

"What does it matter, Winter Wolf? My birth mother gave me the Cheyenne blood, but Aeneva taught me about family, honor, and respect."

Winter Wolf stood up, his face a mask of anger. "Why did you not tell me this before?" he demanded.

"Tell you what? Why are you so angry?" Anna stood up. "Please, Winter Wolf, you wanted to know about my family."

"Tell me of Aeneva's husband. He was a white man?"

"Yes, Trenton was a white man, but he was also part Arapaho."

"He was a light-haired man?"

"Yes, Aeneva used to say Trenton had hair the color of corn and eyes as blue as the sky."

Winter Wolf paced around the lodge. "Did Aeneva have children of her own?"

"Two sons, Nathan and Roberto."

"These were her children by blood?"

"No, only Roberto was her blood son. But she raised Nathan as her own son, and I truly felt like her daughter."

"Where are these sons now?"

"I don't know. They were on the train with me when it got attacked by the Shoshonis." She stared at Winter Wolf. "Nathan is my husband and Robert, Hahkota, is Roberto's son."

"You would marry your own brother?" Winter Wolf demanded angrily.

Anna smiled. "He is not my brother, Winter Wolf. I was not even raised with Nathan and Roberto. When Aeneva and Trenton found me and took me in, Nathan and Roberto were lost and presumed dead. When I finally met Nathan, we were both grown up."

"And what of your mother, Aeneva?"

Anna turned, her eyes filling with tears. "Both Aeneva and Trenton are dead. I loved them with all my heart and I wasn't there to help them when they died."

Anna half expected Winter Wolf to comfort her in some way, but instead he walked to the flap of the lodge. "You should have told me about this before, woman."

"Told you what?" Anna asked in puzzlement, walking across the lodge to talk to Winter Wolf, but he left abruptly. She wanted to follow him, but she didn't want to embarrass him in front of his people. She didn't know what had made him so angry, but whatever it was, it had driven him from the lodge on their marriage day.

Winter Wolf went to his father's lodge, but he wasn't there. Little Deer was shocked to see her son so angry on his wedding day, but Winter Wolf refused to speak to her. He walked around the camp until he found his father sitting with some of his friends, gambling and telling stories.

"Ah, Winter Wolf, has your new wife tired of you already?" one of the men asked, laughing heartily.

"May I speak to you, Father?"

Brave Wolf looked at his son. "What is so important

that it would take you from your wife on this day?"

"Perhaps he has forgotten what to do, Brave Wolf," another of the men chimed in, and they all laughed.

Brave Wolf smiled. "Is it so important, my son? Your wife is waiting for you."

Winter Wolf steadfastly ignored the others who laughed and taunted him. "It cannot wait, Father."

Brave Wolf nodded and stood up. "Let us go to the river so we do not have to listen to the laughter of the coyotes."

They walked through the trees and along the riverbank. "What is it, Winter Wolf?" he asked. "I do not like the look on your face."

"I found out something about my wife, Father." He lowered his head, looking ashamed. "She is the daughter of your sister, Aeneva."

Brave Wolf stopped, his face a myriad of emotions. "The woman you have taken for your wife is my niece?"

"Yes," Winter Wolf replied angrily.

"How can this be? She looks nothing like my sister."

"She is not her blood daughter. Aeneva and her white husband adopted her when she was a child."

"What of Trenton's son, Nathan?" Brave Wolf shook his head and smiled. "That child was more Cheyenne than most of our children. He was beloved by many. They liked his light hair and light eyes, but more than anything, they liked his spirit. He was a fine boy. I truly thought of him as my nephew. Did Heva say what has become of him."

Winter Wolf's eyes narrowed. "He is Heva's husband, Father."

Brave Wolf shook his head. "No, Aeneva would never allow—"

"They were not raised together," Winter Wolf broke in. "When Aeneva and her husband found Heva, she was a young girl. Aeneva's two boys were gone. Heva did not

160

meet her husband until she was grown."

"Two sons? Aeneva has another son?"

"Heva says he is a blood son, but I do not know if the white man is the father."

"This is unbelievable. To find out about my beloved sister after all of these years." He smiled and shook his head. "It is a miracle."

Winter Wolf clamped a hand firmly on Brave Wolf's shoulder. "Father—"

"Did Heva say how Aeneva is doing? Is she well?"

"Father, Aeneva is dead."

"No, that cannot be. She is younger than I, and she was always so strong." Brave Wolf's eyes filled with tears. "I cannot imagine that my sister is dead. How did it happen?"

"I do not know. Perhaps you should speak to Heva."

"Yes, I will do that. I am sorry about this, my son, but it cannot be helped. We must find a way to get Heva back to her husband."

"No!" Winter Wolf replied emphatically.

"Winter Wolf, this is not right. She is the daughter of my sister. Aeneva would not want it this way."

"She is my wife, Father. I will not give her up."

"She is your cousin."

"She is not my cousin by blood."

"But she is the wife of your cousin. It is not right."

"I am not related to any white man. He was not your sister's son. He was the son of the white man she married," he said bitterly.

"Be careful, Winter Wolf, or you will find just how angry your father can get." He stepped close to his son, staring into his dark, angry eyes. "Nathan was as much of a son to my sister as if she had borne him herself. Sometimes I would watch the two of them together and I would stare in awe at the love that was between them. He was her son, Winter Wolf, and what you are doing is

161

wrong. I do not approve."

"I do not need your approval, Father. Heva is my wife. She will stay with me. As I recall, you wanted me to marry her. It was not my intention."

"That was before I knew she was married to my nephew. Think, Winter Wolf. This is a cruel thing you are doing. How can you keep this woman from the man she loves?"

"Do you want me to go into the white world, Father? Do you want me to take Heva and Hahkota and travel many miles through Indian country and white country? Is that what you want, Father?"

"He will come for her, Winter Wolf. I know this man, he will come for his wife."

"How can you know him, Father? He was only a boy when you last saw him."

"But I remember him well. He was like his father, and he was like Aeneva. That would not change after all these years. Mark my words, Winter Wolf. He will come for his wife."

"Let him come. I will be waiting for him."

"You will not harm him, Winter Wolf. Do you understand me?"

"Why do you care so much for this man, Father? He is just a white man."

"Listen to me, boy," Brave Wolf said, his jaw clenching tightly. "That white man's father was also the white man who saved my sister's life many times. Trenton was like a brother to me. No, he *was* my brother." He stepped closer to his son. "You are too consumed with hatred to understand, Winter Wolf. We had white men in this band at a time when few white men came to our land. My uncle was a white trapper. I loved him, just as I loved Trenton. I also love Nathan. He is my blood, Winter Wolf, just as you are my blood. I will welcome him into this camp. Do you understand?"

162

"Will you also hand Heva over to him?"

"The decision will have to be Heva's. I will not lose either you or Nathan because you cannot agree on this woman. When he comes here, you will let her decide. Do you understand, Winter Wolf? Nathan will not meet with any accidents while he is in this camp. He is family."

"He is not family to me, Father," Winter Wolf spat. He paced angrily about, but stopped when he saw the look on his father's face. He had never known Brave Wolf to show such anger. "But I will not threaten him in any way. I will respect your wishes."

"It is the right thing to do, Winter Wolf. You cannot force Heva to stay with you if she is in love with another man."

"I do not wish to talk any longer, Father," Winter Wolf said angrily, walking away.

"Winter Wolf . . ." Brave Wolf called after his son. "I will talk to Heva now. She must know the truth."

"Do what you must, Father," Winter Wolf responded without turning.

Brave Wolf strode back into camp, ignoring the taunts and jeers of his friends. He held his hand up to Little Deer to silence her as he passed by their lodge, and he went directly to Winter Wolf's lodge. "Haahe, Heva. May I enter? It is Brave Wolf."

"Please enter, Brave Wolf."

Brave Wolf went into the lodge and motioned Anna to sit down on her robe. "I have something of great importance to tell you, Heva." He sat down opposite her.

"What is it, Brave Wolf? Is Winter Wolf all right? He is angry at me. I think I offended him in some way."

"You offended no one child," Brave Wolf said gently, reaching out to touch Anna's cheek. Even though this young woman was not his sister's blood daughter, she had been raised by Aeneva and had assumed many of

163

the Indian woman's qualities. "Did you ever hear your mother speak of her brothers?"

"Yes, she spoke often of them. Why do you ask?"

"Did she ever call them by name?"

Anna shrugged her shoulders. "I do not recall. She said that her oldest brother was her favorite. She said he spoiled her. I know she loved him very much."

"I am Aeneva's oldest brother, Heva."

Anna started to shake her head, but stopped as she studied Brave Wolf's face. She could see the resemblance between him and Aeneva. "But how could that be . . ." She turned away, her hands covering her face.

"I know this is a shock to you—"

"Nathan is Winter Wolf's cousin!"

Brave Wolf put his hands on Anna's shoulders, trying to calm her. "I have spoken to Winter Wolf. I have asked him to give you up. He will not."

"Can't he take me back, Brave Wolf?"

"It would be too dangerous for all of you. It is not possible. You must wait for Nathan. That is all you can do."

"You speak as if you know he's coming."

"He is my sister's son. He will come for you."

"Winter Wolf said he would never let me go."

"He has given me his word that he would not harm Nathan. I said it must be your decision whether you go or stay."

"This is so strange. Aeneva would have given anything to see you again."

"Tell me about my sister, Heva. Was she happy?"

"She was very happy, Brave Wolf. Trenton loved her very much. They had a good life together."

"How did they die?"

"It was a sickness, some kind of fever. I was not with them at the time. Nathan tried everything he could to save them. He almost died from the fever himself. He blamed himself for not being able to save them. He loved them both so much." She smiled sadly. "He thought of Aeneva as his blood mother and she thought of him the same way. Her face lit up whenever she was with him."

"It is good to know that she and Swiftly Running Deer were happy together."

"That was Trenton's name?"

"Yes. He could run faster than any boy in the village. He was like my brother." He stopped, his brows furrowing. "Tell me of Aeneva's other son."

"Aeneva had another son, but Trenton was not the father."

"How is that possible? She would never leave Trenton."

"She was taken captive by some Comancheros. She was injured and lost her memory and this man took advantage of that. She said that she came to depend on him and love him in a different way. He took her to Mexico and that is where she had Roberto."

"Roberto," Brave Wolf repeated the name. "What is he like?"

"He is very much like you were in your youth, I think. He is strong and willful and will say whatever is on his mind. And he is very handsome. He looks very much like Aeneva."

"He is a good person?"

"Yes, he is a good person. He loves his son very much."

"So, little Hahkota is really my great-nephew. My sister's blood runs strongly through him. It is easy to see that."

"I need to be with Nathan, Brave Wolf. Do you understand that?"

"I understand, Heva, but there is nothing I can do."

"What if Robert and I went alone? You could tell me which direction to go," Anna pleaded.

165

"No, I could not let you go. You saw what happened to Winter Wolf, and he is a Cheyenne warrior."

"He tried to attack a war party of Shoshonis by himself. I will not do that."

"That does not mean you will not see any Shoshonis. Do you feel they treated you well? Do you think they would have treated you as well as Winter Wolf has?"

"I know Winter Wolf has treated me well, and for that I am grateful, but I have another life."

"I will not let you go, Heva, but if Nathan comes to this village to get you, I will let you decide which man you want to be with."

"Why would you let me go with Nathan and you won't let Winter Wolf take me back?"

"Because Nathan can be a white man or he can be an Indian. Winter Wolf can only be a Cheyenne; he cannot be anything else. You and Nathan would have a better chance together."

"What do I do until he comes for me?"

"You are still Winter Wolf's wife. He gave me his word that he would not hurt Nathan when he comes to this village, but he also said that he would not give you up. You will have to live as his wife, Heva. There is no other way. Winter Wolf is my son, but he is no longer a boy. He is a fine warrior and well respected in this village. I cannot humiliate him in front of the people here. He has to have a chance to fight for you. Do you understand?"

"I understand I have no choice," Anna said bitterly, standing up and walking across the lodge.

Brave Wolf went to her. "I am sorry, child. I wish it did not have to be this way. I wish I could take you back myself, but I must think of my people. And I would never forgive myself if something happened to you or to Hahkota. If Nathan is truly the man you love and want to be with, you must trust in your heart that he will

166

come for you."

Anna nodded. "Thank you, Brave Wolf. I am glad I got to meet my mother's brother. She would be happy to see us together."

"Yes, I believe she would." Brave Wolf took Anna's hands in his. "I must go now, child. Be patient, but also remember that Winter Wolf is not a bad person. He is a man who carries great sorrow around with him wherever he goes."

"Can I leave the lodge, Winter Wolf?"

"It would not be a good thing."

"I want to talk to Winter Wolf. I don't think he should be alone right now."

Brave Wolf thought for a moment, then nodded. "I will simply tell my people that this is a new custom. The wife must search for her new husband. Come with me. We will find Winter Wolf."

Nathan watched, huddled in the rocks, as the white hunters slaughtered the buffalo. They rode around them, shooting them like bottles off of a fence. The herd was wild with fear, but the constant rifle fire and shouting forced them to keep running in a wide circle. When the group of men was done, there were at least fifty carcasses lying on the ground.

Nathan remembered going on the buffalo hunts with the Cheyennes. They had always been exciting times because the Cheyennes depended so heavily on the buffalo for everything. Not only did they use them as a primary source of food, they used their fur for robes, their bones for weapons, tools, and ornaments, and they even used their sinew for thread. They had killed what they needed and left very little for the buzzards.

It was different with these men. They slaughtered for the fun of it. They took the fur and left the rest to rot or to be eaten by wolves, coyotes, and buzzards. It made him sick to think of how many Indians could have eaten, clothed themselves, and made weapons from all of the buffalo that were lying dead. The men quickly skinned the animals and threw them in piles on wagons. They seemed to enjoy what they were doing.

When they had finished skinning the animals, they mounted their horses, others their wagons, and they headed south to sell their skins. Nathan heard their laughter as they rode away and, once again, he was ashamed to be a white man. No Indian would ever think of wasting an animal that was so highly respected.

Already, buzzards gathered in circles overhead, and it gave Nathan an ominous feeling. He hoped this was not a sign of something bad to come. He led his horse from the rocks and down to the land below. He stared at the ravage and waste, and shook his head. He looked up at the clear sky.

"Oh, Great Father, I am sorry for this waste. I wish more white men could live as the Indian does, and learn about the land and the creatures that inhabit it." He stopped, forcing himself to continue. "Please help me to find my way back to Anna. I need this woman and I love her. If I cannot have her, let her be safe." Nathan looked once more at the ravaged carcasses and mounted his horse. It had been a long time since he had prayed to the Great Father. It had made him feel strong. It had given him hope.

Anna found Winter Wolf downstream, sitting on the bank where he had pulled her and the boy out of the water. She sat next to him, looking out at the water. "I did not mean to hurt you, Winter Wolf."

"Why did you not tell me before today?"

"Because I didn't know. I swear I didn't know that

Brave Wolf was Aeneva's brother."

"In all the years you lived with her, she did not speak of her own brother's name? That is difficult to believe, Heva."

"I am not lying to you. She spoke often of her two brothers, but she used Cheyenne words to speak of them. I didn't understand what she was saying."

"This will change nothing. You are still my wife."

"I know that." Anna tried to pick her words carefully. "I will be your wife, Winter Wolf, as long as you give me your word you won't hurt Nathan if he comes here."

"Why do you and my father worry so much about this white man? Is he so weak that he cannot fight his own battles?"

Anna forced herself to remain calm. "I just don't want anything to happen to him."

Winter Wolf's dark eyes narrowed in the expression that Anna had come to be wary of. "I will give you my word that I will not harm the white man if you will give me *your* word that you will stay with me, even if he comes for you."

"That's not fair, Winter Wolf. Your father said it would be my decision."

"My father will not go against me on this, Heva. We are bound by blood. He will choose me over the white man."

Anna felt her heart pound in her chest. She knew that Winter Wolf spoke the truth. Brave Wolf would never go against his own son, even for Nathan. "Why do you want me for your wife? You never wanted me before."

"You are the right woman. It is that simple."

"It doesn't bother you that I don't love you?"

"I don't require love. I require a wife, and a woman to give me children."

"Is that all you want?" Anna asked angrily. She stood up. "If all you want is a brood mare, I am not the

169

woman for you, Winter Wolf. I will fight you. Every time you want me, you'll have to fight me. I will never love you. Never."

Winter Wolf jumped to his feet and ran after Anna, roughly pulling her around to face him. "Understand, woman. It does not matter what you want. You are in the Cheyenne world now, not the white world. You have no choice anymore. You will do as I say because I am your husband."

"You aren't my husband. You have no heart. I would rather be a captive of the Crows or the Shoshonis than be your wife."

Winter Wolf's hand shot out and struck Anna solidly across the face. She stumbled slightly, but she stared into his eyes, resolving not to cry. "Hit me again if it will make you feel like more of a man, but you will never break my spirit." Anna felt her cheek throb from the blow, but she didn't move. "Why are you punishing me for your wife's death, Winter Wolf? I was not there. I did nothing to her."

"You are white," he spat out.

"I thought you had learned by now that not all white people are like those hunters."

"All white people hate all Indians."

"That's not true."

"You hate me, do you not?"

"Only because you are forcing me to. You're angry with me because of what you've learned. It's not my fault, Winter Wolf. I didn't know Brave Wolf was Aeneva's brother."

"You speak well, Heva, but I will not believe your lies like my father has chosen to do." He grabbed her upper arm and yanked her forward. "We will go back to the lodge now."

"No," Anna said stubbornly, knowing that she would suffer for it.

"I will drag you through the camp if I must."

"Then drag me, because I'll never go willingly with you."

Winter Wolf's fingers closed like a steel trap on her upper arm and he jerked her forward. People lined up to stare, but Anna held her head high and looked back at them. When they reached the lodge, Brave Wolf was waiting for them.

"Winter Wolf, this is not right."

"Do not stand in my way, Father. If you do, I will take her and leave this band forever."

Brave Wolf looked from his son to Anna and stood aside. Anna's eyes met his, and she could see the pain that was there.

Winter Wolf pulled her into the lodge and threw her down on the robes. He looked enormous, impossibly remote, a dark nightmare of a man. His eyes locked on hers as he pulled off his buckskin shirt and pants until he wore nothing but his breechcloth. He took the large hunting knife from his sheath and dropped to his knees in front of Anna, his dark and angry eyes still boring into hers.

Anna felt herself tremble. He was going to kill her. She stared back at him, terrified that her courage would fail her, that she would give him the satisfaction of pleading for her life.

Snakelike, his brown fingers closed over her forearm. Slowly, inevitably, his greater strength forced her to extend her arm palm-up. Like a snake striking a second time, he sliced into the delicate skin halfway up the arm. Anna flinched from the pain, but she remained still, unable to move even her eyes until the bright flash of the knife jerked her gaze upward. Winter Wolf had cut his own arm. Anna glanced at his face, but his eyes were down, watching. He seemed to be waiting. Waiting for what? Anna heard the thought in her confused mind, but had no answer. Slowly, deliberately, he put their arms together. There was little pain from the cut. All Anna could feel was the warm stickiness of their blood as it ran down her arm and dripped onto the robe. "Now you are a part of me," he said softly, his voice barely audible. "Can you feel my blood flow in your veins, Heva?"

Winter Wolf, she heard herself think. The man is contained in his name. Like a cornered wolf, he was unpredictable and erratic. But what was making him feel so trapped? She had seen the kindness in him, but just under its surface was the ever-present threat of violence. She continued to stare into his eyes, unmoving. He sat back on his heels, slowly taking his arm from hers. Anna cradled her wounded arm. The cut wasn't that deep and the flow of blood slowed to a trickle.

"You are frightened of me, Heva?"

Anna nodded her head. She knew that fear was written all over her face.

"Then you must learn not to make me angry. I can kill very easily. Is that what you want? Do you want me to kill you?"

Anna took a breath, her voice shaking. "Is that what you want?"

Winter Wolf was up on his knees again, towering over Anna. "I want a woman who knows how to be a wife to me. If you cannot be a wife to me, then you will be my slave." He shrugged his shoulders. "Perhaps I will even give you to some of the men. Most have never known what it is like to have a white woman."

"I hate you!" Anna said deliberately. Winter Wolf took Anna's chin in his tight grasp. "Good, Heva, let that hatred drive you as it has driven me. It will make you strong."

Anna saw something in Winter Wolf's eyes that she'd never seen before. Behind the anger and wounded pride lay a crushing anguish. She understood. The violence came not from cruelty but from a hurt so deep it might never heal. Tentatively, she reached out to touch his face, unsure of what his reaction might be. Her hand trembled uncontrollably, but still she gently touched his cheek. He didn't move and in his eyes she saw that she had touched that deep wound. He was afraid that she might hurt him. Anna leaned forward, not knowing why she needed to comfort him but unwilling to let him suffer any longer. She put her other hand on his shoulder and slowly leaned her body into his. She felt the warmth of his chest as she pressed against him and the strength of his shoulders as she wrapped her arms around them. "I'm sorry, Winter Wolf," she said tearfully. "I am truly sorry."

Her body trembled and she was frightened that he would push her away, but he did not. Instead, slowly, he lifted his arms and put them around her waist. Anna couldn't make sense of her feelings and she began to cry. Her body shook with her sobs and she felt Winter Wolf's arms tighten around her. She knew he was a good man, her heart had told her that, but he was also a man who had suffered greatly. He had risked his life to save her and Robert and now she knew she must help him.

Anna felt her body relax in his arms and she felt safe. She didn't want to move. She didn't want to remember the hateful things they had said to each other. She wanted this moment to last. But Winter Wolf slowly pushed her away. He reached his hand up and she flinched, thinking he might hit her again. Instead, he wiped the tears from her cheeks.

"You make me feel again, Heva. It frightens me."

Anna nodded. "Yes, I know. It would be so much easier to hate you, but I don't."

"Will you lie next to me, Heva?"

Anna lay down next to Winter Wolf, hoping that he wouldn't hurt her. They lay on their backs, looking up at the sky through the top of the lodge.

"I cannot undo what I have done. I have never hit a woman before."

"I made you angry," Anna said, hoping to make things easier for him.

"It does not matter. My father has always said that I let my anger control me. He is right. You suffered for it."

"I will watch my tongue. I speak without thinking."

"Perhaps we have done enough talking on this day. Let us rest. When our minds are clear we can talk again." His hand reached out for Anna's, and she gratefully accepted it, entwining her fingers in his. She needed Winter Wolf, but she now knew that he also needed her. She closed her eyes. For the first time since she and Winter Wolf had escaped from the Shoshonis, she felt herself at peace. Whatever happened, she knew she would survive and that Winter Wolf would help her.

Chapter 8

Nathan saw movement across the river and pulled up on his horse. At first he thought it was an animal but then realized that it was a group of Indian children.

He rode upstream until he found a shallow place in which to cross. Before he had reached the other side, two riders came into the river, rifles aimed at him.

Nathan held up his hand. *"Haahe.* I am the son of Aeneva, sister to Brave Wolf. I have come to see my uncle." When the men didn't say anything, he repeated what he'd just said in Cheyenne. If the men were surprised, they didn't show it. They motioned him forward. One led the way and the other followed.

They rode up the bank and through a stand of cottonwoods until they came into the camp. Nathan's nostrils flared at the familiar smell of wood smoke and roasting meat. Women giggled as they pointed to the blond-haired, blue-eyed stranger who showed no fear as he rode into their village.

Nathan looked around him as he rode, searching for any sign of Anna. He was surprised how easily they had let him enter the camp. He wondered if something was wrong.

The lead rider stopped in front of a lodge painted with the sun, moon, and a large wolf. The man spoke through the lodge flap and soon a tall man emerged, a man who was very familiar to Nathan. Nathan couldn't resist a smile as he saw Brave Wolf. He jumped down from his horse and went to him, extending his arm in greeting. *"Haahe, naxane."*

Brave Wolf grasped Nathan's arm tightly. *"Haahe, natse."* Brave Wolf then pulled Nathan into his arms, clapping him firmly on the back. He pulled away and stared at Nathan, shaking his head. "It is good to see you, Nathan."

"And you also, Uncle."

"I knew you would come. You are my sister's son." Brave Wolf looked around at the gathering crowd and pulled Nathan with him into the large lodge. "Come in here with me. We will have more privacy."

Nathan followed Brave Wolf to the rear of the lodge and sat down on one of the mats. "Is there a white woman in your village, Uncle? She has dark hair and—"

"She is here," Brave Wolf said curtly, cutting Nathan off.

"Is she well? She's not hurt?"

"She is well."

"May I see her? I have traveled long and far to find her, Uncle. It is a great weight from my heart to know that she is safe."

"There is something you must know, Nephew."

"What is it?"

"She is married."

"What? But she's already married to me." Nathan knew he couldn't tell his uncle that he and Anna weren't really married, for then, he might never have a chance of getting her back. He forced himself to be calm. He knew that the Cheyennes had different customs and he couldn't afford to make an enemy of his uncle.

"We did not know of this until after the marriage took place."

176

"Is she married to the man who took her from the Shoshonis?"

"Yes. He is called Winter Wolf. He is my son."

Nathan shook his head. "My cousin is married to Anna."

"None of us knew, Nephew. You must believe that."

"I believe you, Uncle. But it doesn't matter now. I'm here, and I want to take Anna back with me."

"It will not be that simple, Nephew."

"Why not? You are respectful of marriage, Uncle. Surely you must understand that if this woman was married to me first, then that is the true marriage."

"And you must know, Nephew, that we only respect the Cheyenne marriage."

"I won't leave without her, Brave Wolf," Nathan said finally, eliminating the familiar term with his uncle.

"Winter Wolf will not let her go." He shook his head. "I told him you would come for her. He would not listen to me."

"And what about Anna? Are you going to go against her wishes when she wants to come with me?"

"What if she does not wish to go with you, Nathan? What if she wishes to stay here? Will you respect her decision?"

"She would never want to stay here. I know her, Brave Wolf. We are as much in love as my mother and father were. Nothing can keep us apart."

"It appears you are wrong, Nathan. My son can keep you apart."

"And you will allow this, Brave Wolf? You are the leader in this village."

"Yes, I am the leader, but Winter Wolf is my son. If I defy him, he will take Heva and go."

"Heva?"

"It is her Cheyenne name. It means—"

"I know what it means, and I don't care. I know Anna

177

and I know she wouldn't stay here willingly." He calmed himself, thinking for a moment how his father or Aeneva might have handled the situation.

"Aeneva would never have approved of this, Brave Wolf. You are taking away the rights of the woman Aeneva raised as her own daughter." Nathan watched Brave Wolf's eyes, and he could see by the Indian's expression that he had reached him. He softened his voice as he spoke. "You are my uncle, Brave Wolf. I will not defy you. I respect you. It is what my mother taught me." He leaned forward, his eyes narrowing with determination. "But know this, as long as I live and breathe, I will not leave the woman I love here with another man."

Brave Wolf continued to stare at Nathan and finally averted his eyes. He thought for a moment. "You are a good man, *natse*. You are the man I thought you would be."

Nathan wasn't sure what Brave Wolf was trying to say, but he was patient, nodding as Brave Wolf spoke.

"I cannot send you away from my village without your woman, but I also cannot take her away from my son. I will think on this matter and I will be fair. Will you allow me some time?"

"Of course, Uncle. I know you will be fair."

Again, Brave Wolf reached out and clasped Nathan's shoulder. "I look at you and I see your father, Swiftly Running Deer, and I remember what an honorable man he was. You must have given him great joy."

"He taught me many things, Uncle. He taught me always to be fair and respect the rights of others, but he also taught me to fight for whatever I believed in. Do you understand?"

"I understand completely." Brave Wolf stood up. "You will stay in my lodge."

"Thank you, Uncle." Nathan watched as Brave Wolf

left the lodge. He took a deep breath and exhaled. He didn't know what to do next. He wanted more than anything to go and find Anna, but he decided against it. He needed Brave Wolf on his side. He had to be patient. As long as he knew Anna was safe, he could wait a while longer.

Roberto heard the creek of the old rocking chair out on the porch as Zeb and Lyle drank and talked. He felt as if he'd been listening to that old rocking chair for years, when in fact it had only been a couple of months.

Rachel was sitting in one of the chairs by the fireplace going over one of her medical books. She had seen a woman earlier in the day whose symptoms she wasn't familiar with. Rachel, Roberto had quickly discovered, was not one to let things go without exhausting every possible effort.

He glanced over at Rachel as he set the table. He liked her. She was such an honest woman it was hard not to like her. But he also found a vulnerable side to her as well. She'd tried so hard to act like a man all of her life that she never really learned what it was like to be a woman. Although their relationship was still somewhat strained, it was getting better. He even got the feeling Rachel was beginning to care about him a bit.

Soon after Nathan left to look for Anna and Robert, he decided to go after Nathan. His mind had begun to conjure up horrible pictures of the Cheyennes and what they might do to his son and Anna. But when he decided to go, Rachel practically pleaded with him to stay. She told him he wasn't completely healed and she told him she and Zeb needed him to help around the ranch until she was completely well. Although she had gotten skilled with her crutches and was able to put some weight on her legs, it still would be a while before she

179

would regain full use of her legs. It had surprised him that she had wanted him to stay.

"Dinner's ready, Rachel," Roberto said, standing by the old oak table, watching Rachel as she stubbornly refused help.

She smiled, managing to get to her feet with her crutches, and walked to the table. "I'm not sure I'll ever be able to get used to a man who not only cooks, but sets the table."

"My mother made both of us do it. She said she didn't want her boys to grow up thinking they were too good to help a woman."

"I would have liked your mother."

Roberto pulled out Rachel's chair for her and took her crutches as she sat down. "Yes, you would have liked her. You have a lot in common with her. She was a woman warrior in her tribe. Many of the men didn't want her, but her grandfather and brothers supported her. She was a good warrior."

"How lucky you were to grow up with a mother like that. I never knew my mother."

Roberto was enjoying their conversation. He didn't want it interrupted by Zeb and Lyle. "I suppose I should call those two in from the porch," he said grudgingly.

Rachel shook her head. "Not yet. This is nice."

"Yes, it is." Roberto took Rachel's plate and put a piece of ham on it. "Would you be willing to go for a ride with me later?" he asked nonchalantly, handing her plate back to her.

"I probably shouldn't. I have a lot of reading to do."

Roberto could see the flush come over Rachel's face. She really wasn't sure how to act around a man when she wasn't in control. She was afraid to enjoy herself. "I like you, Rachel, and I think you like me, too." He waited, hoping she would look at him. When she finally looked up, he continued. "We're two adults. We're not children. It's all right if we're attracted to each other."

Rachel took a sip of her wine. "I never said I was attracted to you."

"You never said you weren't. I'm only asking you to go for a ride with me. It's the least you can do."

"What does that mean?"

"Who's been doing the cooking, cleaning, and most of the work around the ranch for the last month?"

"And who saved your life?" she countered. "If I hadn't been on that train, you'd be buried in our little graveyard outside of town."

"All right, then, we both have helped each other. So, will you go for a ride with me?"

"Why is it so important to you?"

"I want to be alone with you, away from this place. Maybe I'm going a little crazy around here."

"Why don't you go into town?"

"What's in town besides a saloon and some stores and restaurants?"

"I don't know what you want from me, Roberto," Rachel said in a bored tone.

"I don't want anything from you, Rachel. Haven't you figured that out yet?" Robert replied angrily. Quickly, he stood up, his chair falling backward onto the floor. He strode out of the house and down the porch, ignoring the slamming screen door and the snide comments from the two old men. He walked over to the fence by the pasture, kicking at one of the poles. "Stubborn damned woman. What did she think I was going to do?" he asked himself. He followed the fence up the hill, dragging his hand along the rough wood. He was feeling restless. If Nathan didn't come back soon, he was going after him.

"Roberto?"

Roberto turned around. Rachel was walking after him, slow and steady, measuring each step carefully. He wanted to run to her, to make sure she was all right, but he decided not to. She was a grown woman, and a doctor to boot. She knew her limitations.

"Will you please wait up?"

"I don't need any lectures, Doc," he replied sarcastically, walking slowly away from her.

"Roberto, please."

Roberto turned around. Rachel was standing under one of the cottonwoods, leaning on the trunk. She looked so tiny and frail in her pants and shirt. He walked back down the hill. "Are you all right?"

"My legs are a little sore, but I'm all right. Can I have your arm?"

Roberto held out his arm and Rachel put hers through it. She leaned against him as they walked. "I'm sorry. I'm not good at this."

"Good at what?"

She stopped. He felt her hand tighten on his arm. "I'm not good at being with men, except when they're my patients."

"You don't have to act any special way, Rachel. Just be yourself. You don't even realize how charming you are."

She was obviously embarrassed by the compliment. "I know what I look like in these clothes, and I also know that I'm not the prettiest woman in these parts."

"But you *are* pretty, Rachel." Roberto's hand tightly touched her cheek, pushing the wisps of hair that hung in her eyes. "You have pretty eyes, but you always hide them with that stupid hat. And I bet if you wore a dress once in a while, it would make you feel good. You have a nice figure."

"Why would I want to start wearing dresses?" She turned her head, trying to remove her face from Roberto's touch.

"Even I like to dress up once in a while, Rachel. There's nothing wrong with it."

"But it all seems so silly. Women only dress seductively

and fix their hair in certain styles so they can get a man. I figure either a man will like me for who I am or he won't."

"And you're not willing to compromise?"

"What do you mean?"

"Why not dress up once in a while? Just because you're a doctor doesn't mean you can't be a woman."

Rachel took her arm from Roberto's. "There's no reason for us to talk. We can't seem to agree on anything." She started slowly down the hill.

Roberto reached out and stopped Rachel from going any farther. Her legs were still shaky enough that she didn't have her balance. She fell against Roberto and he wrapped his arms around her, her arms pinned to her sides. "You really are pretty," he said, lowering his mouth to hers. He fully expected Rachel to turn away, but she didn't. He felt the softness of her lips as he moved his mouth against them. He could feel her body tremble and he pulled away, looking into her eyes. "I don't want to hurt or frighten you."

Rachel struggled against his arms but was unsuccessful. "What do you want? You want to take me to bed?" She shrugged her shoulders. "Take me. I can't fight you. I'm not strong enough."

Roberto dropped his arms, shaking his head in disgust. "No, thank you. I won't force myself on any woman." He walked down the hill toward the ranch.

"Where are you going?" Rachel demanded angrily.

"I'm going into town where I can find myself a woman who is not only willing, but one who knows what being a woman is all about." Roberto didn't turn to see the expression on Rachel's face. He only hoped he had gotten to her in some way. He wanted this woman, and he wasn't going to give up until he got her.

* * *

Nathan had waited patiently for three days while his uncle decided what to do, going out only at night when the village camp was quiet. He'd wanted desperately to see Anna, but he knew he couldn't risk it. He had to wait for Brave Wolf's decision. He paced nervously, trying to think of ways to get Anna and Robert out of the camp. Each plan he thought of turned out to be dangerous. Even if he managed to get out of Brave Wolf's lodge, he would have to get into Winter Wolf's lodge without waking him and get Anna and Robert out. It seemed impossible.

He wondered what his uncle was going to say. He understood Brave Wolf's position. Winter Wolf was his son and he didn't want to hurt him. Yet Nathan knew by the look in Brave Wolf's eyes that he had felt torn. Nathan was a connection to Aeneva, and that was something Brave Wolf couldn't forget.

And there was Winter Wolf himself. Nathan didn't know how powerful he was, but he suspected that he would follow through on his threat to take Anna away from the camp if Brave Wolf persisted in making his son give her up. Brave Wolf would never put his son in a position where he would have to choose between his people and Anna.

He willed himself to be patient. He sat down, closed his eyes, and tried to picture what his life would be like once he left here with Anna. He heard the lodge flap open, and he knew it was Brave Wolf. From the look on his uncle's face, he could see that Brave Wolf had made his decision. Nathan stood up, waiting for his uncle to speak first.

"I have thought long and hard on this, Nephew. It is a hard decision to make. I do not want to lose my son, for he will live out his years with me. You, I will probably never see again."

Nathan felt his heart sink, but he remained still.

"However, you are my sister's son, a son she loved beyond all else. She would never forgive me if I hurt you. She would want me to be fair. That is what she would do." Brave Wolf's expression became less intense. It was plain to see that he cared greatly for Nathan. "Heva will remain with Winter Wolf in his lodge. According to our ways, she is now his wife."

Nathan stared into Brave Wolf's eyes, hoping this wasn't the complete answer. Still, he said nothing.

"But, according to your ways," Brave Wolf continued, "she was your woman first. I must also be fair to you. So I have decided that you will stay in this camp until the first snow. You will live as we do, eat as we do, sleep as we do, and hunt and fight as we do. You will have your own lodge. Heva will visit you for seven days, and she will visit with Winter Wolf the next seven days. When the first snow comes, I will let Heva decide which man she wishes to stay with. If," he stepped closer to Nathan, "she decides to stay with Winter Wolf, you will leave and never return. But if she decides to be with you, I will allow you both to leave and I will send some of my warriors to help guide you safely."

Nathan tried to hide his shock. He hadn't expected this from Brave Wolf. He had assumed that Brave Wolf would side in favor of his son. Nathan knew he had given up much by trying to be fair to him. "I do not know what to say, *naxane*. You have been very fair. I will live by your laws and I will help in any way I can. If Anna decides to stay with Winter Wolf, I will leave in peace. I will cause no trouble for you or your people." Nathan meant what he said.

Brave Wolf nodded. "I did not expect that you would cause trouble, Nephew."

"I know this is not easy for you, *naxane*. I do not want Winter Wolf to be angry with you."

"I am still the chief of this band. If my son wishes to

defy me, he may do so. But he will not take Heva with him. Guards will be placed around the camp. Neither you nor my son will be permitted to leave alone with Heva."

Nathan nodded. "I understand. It has been a long time since I have lived in a Cheyenne camp, Uncle. I have forgotten many things."

"I will guide you, Nephew. I am not happy about this which is happening between you and my son, but I am glad that you are here. You can learn some of our ways and take them back with you. Perhaps you can teach other white people that not all Indians are bad."

"I will do that, Uncle." Nathan walked around the lodge, trying to think of a way to ask Brave Wolf a favor.

"What is it, boy?"

Nathan smiled as he looked at the handsome man. In that moment, he had sounded like Aeneva. She had always known when something was wrong. "May I see Anna once? I just want to talk to her. Then I will abide by your rules."

Brave Wolf thought for a moment. "I will talk to Winter Wolf now and tell him my decision. Go through the cottonwoods and wait by the riverbank. I will send her to you. Speak only for a short time, Nephew. There is no need to anger my son further. He will be angry enough."

"*Neshe-pevaoh-ohe, naxane*. Thank you, Uncle."

"No!" Winter Wolf kicked his backrest, knocking it across the lodge. "I will not give her up."

"It is no longer your decision, Winter Wolf."

"Why do you do this to me, Father? Why?"

"I am not trying to hurt you, my son. I am trying to do what is best for everyone."

"Why do you even consider the feelings of a white

186

man?"

"I told you before. He is my sister's son, as much a son to her as if he had grown in her womb. He is a good man, an honorable man. He will abide by my rules, Winter Wolf. I would expect the same of you."

"She is my woman, Father."

"She is also his woman. Can you not put yourself in his place for even one moment?"

"How could I ever put myself in the place of a white man, father? White men do not care about us. They only want to kill us and take our land. And if they don't kill us, they put us on land of their choosing, treating us like animals."

"I understand your anger, Winter Wolf. Many of my family and friends have been killed by whites, but many have also been killed by other Indians. We are not perfect, Winter Wolf. We, too, have killed whites who were guilty of nothing but getting in our way."

"They should not be on our land. It is *our* land!" he shouted.

"I will not argue with you. You have heard my decision. If you cannot abide by it, you will leave this band without Heva. If you cannot listen to your father, your chief, then perhaps we are better off without you."

Winter Wolf looked at his father. He could see the anguish in his eyes. "I am sorry, Father. I know this has been difficult for you. I will do as you say."

Brave Wolf embraced Winter Wolf. "I am proud of you, my son."

Winter Wolf pulled away from Brave Wolf, nodding approvingly as he looked into his eyes. "And I am proud to be the son of a warrior and a man such as you, *tseheheto*."

"I have told Heva to meet with Nathan by the river. I will give them some time to talk, then I will send her back to you. At the end of seven days, she will go to

Nathan."

"I understand."

"If you truly love this woman, Winter Wolf, then control your anger. You will never win her with threats. You will only drive her away. Show her that you have the courage to be gentle."

"I will try, Father. I will try."

Anna walked through the village. Brave Wolf had told her to go through the trees and to the riverbank where the river formed a pond. She didn't know why he was sending her there. Perhaps to give him and Winter Wolf time to talk.

She had heard rumors of a white man who had ridden into camp, and her heart had been filled with excitement thinking that it might be Nathan, but no one had seen him since he'd arrived. Besides, if it had been Nathan, he would have found her. He would never have left without her.

She stopped for a moment by a cottonwood, peeling the dry bark from the tree. She felt strangely calm. Ever since the day Winter Wolf and she had fought, he had been extremely kind to her. He had been gentle and he had never forced her to do anything. At night, she had felt him move closer to her, but he had never hurt her. He had only pulled her close to him and wrapped his arms around her. She had begun to find it quite comforting.

During the days, he had spent a lot of time showing her how to use a knife and bow and arrow. He had also taught her how to skin a small animal and utilize every part of it so that nothing went to waste. He had taught her many things. She knew that the men made fun of him for spending time with her, but he didn't seem to mind. She had a new respect for Winter Wolf. He had treated her well, and she would not forget it. Nor would she forget the look in his eyes the night she had touched him and he had taken her into his arms. He had needed to be cared for, just like anyone else.

She tore off another piece of bark and crumbled it into smaller pieces as she walked through the trees. She could hear the crack of branches as she stepped. She came through the trees and walked upstream, toward the pond. There was no one there. She shrugged her shoulders.

"Anna?"

She froze at the sound of the familiar voice, the voice that brought so many memories flooding back to her. She turned. Nathan was standing in the trees, looking tall and lean, dressed in a blue shirt and pants, his hat covering his eyes, his blond hair grown long, almost to his shoulders. He stepped out of the trees and walked toward her with long strides until he stood in front of her. She felt as if she were in a dream, and if she spoke or moved, it would all go away.

"Are you all right, Anna?" Nathan asked, his voice filled with concern.

"Yes" was all she could manage. She couldn't believe he had actually come for her. "Nathan," she then said, her voice filled with emotion. She stepped forward, wrapping her arms around his waist, laying her face against his chest. She felt his arms go around her. It was such a familiar feeling. She closed her eyes as his hand stroked her hair.

"I was so worried about you, Anna." His voice was filled with emotion.

She looked up at him. "I knew you'd come."

Nathan lowered his mouth and kissed her. She moved her mouth against his. It felt so right to be with Nathan. They had fought so hard to be together.

Nathan pulled away, pushing his hat back. His eyes

189

seemed to reflect the color of the clear sky. She had forgotten how truly blue they were. "We don't have much time."

"What do you mean? Now that you're here, you can take me away."

"I can't do that, Anna. I have to abide by Brave Wolf's decision."

"What decision?"

"When I rode in here three days ago, I was ready to take you right then and leave. But Brave Wolf made it clear that if I did that, I'd never make it out alive, or Winter Wolf would take you and I'd never see you again. So I pleaded with him to understand how I felt about you. I asked him to be fair."

Anna dropped her arms, then shook her head, her face filled with sadness. "He said I had to stay with Winter Wolf."

"No, he said I could stay here until the first snow. He said you will stay one week with Winter Wolf, and the next week with me. At the end of that time, if you want to go with me, he'll let you. If you want to stay with Winter Wolf, I will leave and not make any trouble."

"But I want to go with you, Nathan. I want to go now." She wrapped her arms around him again.

"Listen to me, Anna. We don't have a choice. It doesn't matter that you want to go with me now—he wants to give Winter Wolf a chance to win you. But he's being fair to me, too. He could have sent me away that first night."

"I won't be able to stand it, knowing you're so close to me and I can't be with you."

"But you *will* be with me, every other week. But during the times you're with Winter Wolf, you must act like his wife. I don't want you to do anything to make him or Brave Wolf angry. We just have to be patient a little longer, Anna. We can do this."

190

"He scares me, Nathan."

"Has he hurt you?"

"No, not really. I just never know what he's thinking. I'm afraid that he'll never agree to his father's wishes and he'll try to kill you and take me away from here."

"He won't be able to do that. Brave Wolf will have guards around the camp. Neither Winter Wolf nor I can leave this camp with you."

Anna turned away and looked out at the river. "When will we be together, Nathan?" She felt his arms wrap around her and felt the warmth of his body behind her. She closed her eyes and laid her head back against his chest.

"It won't be long, Anna. We'll be together soon."

"Heva!" Winter Wolf's angry voice commanded Anna from behind them.

Anna turned and looked at Winter Wolf and then at Nathan. "I don't want to go with him, Nathan. Please don't make me go with him," she said, her voice pleading.

"We don't have any other choice, Anna. There's no way I can get you out of here. This is our only chance."

"He'll make me suffer for this," she said softly, looking at Winter Wolf's imposing figure standing by the trees.

"I'll be nearby. If you need me, call for me. Do you understand?" Nathan put his hands on her arms.

Anna jerked away. "Don't do that in front of him. He has a horrible temper, Nathan. Please don't do anything to anger him."

"I'll be careful, Anna. And I'll be watching you. I love you."

Anna looked at Nathan and couldn't resist a wan smile. She reached out to touch him, but Winter Wolf's voice made her stop. She looked at Nathan again and headed off toward the trees, her head lowered. She didn't look at Winter Wolf as she approached him, merely walked past him and through the trees. She hurried into the camp, rushing to the lodge. She didn't want to be humiliated in front of everyone again. If Winter Wolf was going to punish her, she preferred that he do it in his lodge.

Inside the lodge she went to the cookpot and stirred the rabbit stew. She knew Winter Wolf was behind her, but she didn't know what to expect from him.

"Look at me, Heva," his voice commanded.

Anna stood up and looked at Winter Wolf. "You are angry with me."

"I am angry because I might lose you to this white man. You do not make me angry."

Anna relaxed. He was constantly surprising her. "I don't know what to say to you, Winter Wolf."

"I want you to say nothing. I only require that you be my wife while you are with me. When you are with him, I want to hear nothing about it." He walked past her and sat down on his mat.

Anna followed him, sitting down next to him. "Where is Robert?"

"Hahkota is with my mother. Why do you worry about him so?"

"I . . ." Anna shook her head. "He's just so young."

"You think that I will take the boy away from you?"

"You said that you would. You also said that you would never let me leave here."

Winter Wolf's expression didn't change, but his eyes grew darker. "I will abide by my father's decision. If you wish to leave with this white man when the time comes, I will not stop you."

Anna studied Winter Wolf for a moment. She couldn't understand why he was so calm. It was almost as frightening as if he had gotten angry. "You are not angry with your father for his decision?"

"I have no choice. I will do as he says."

192

"I'm sorry I've put you in this position, Winter Wolf."

"It is not your fault, Heva." Winter Wolf reached out and ran his hand along a strand of Anna's hair. "You are very pleasing to the eye, Heva. Sometimes I wonder if you are not a witch."

"I'm no witch, Winter Wolf. Just as you are no monster."

"You are a woman worth fighting for, Heva. Yet, I wonder. Am I fighting for nothing? Have you already made up your mind to go with the white man?"

Anna couldn't meet Winter Wolf's eyes. She looked past him. Should she tell him the truth or should she lie? She felt Winter Wolf's hand on her chin, forcing her to look at him. "I don't know." Anna met Winter Wolf's dark eyes. She felt as if she were being pulled into a darkness from which she might never emerge.

"Do you care for me, Heva?"

Anna continued to stare into Winter Wolf's eyes. She remembered the things they had shared and the many nights he had held her close. "Yes."

"If this man had never come for you, would you have stayed with me and been content?"

Anna started to look away, but Winter Wolf forced her to look at him. "I . . ." Anna was confused. She was not used to such tenderness from Winter Wolf.

"Truth, Heva."

"Yes, I would have been content to stay with you, Winter Wolf." She swallowed, trying to gain some control over her emotions. Winter Wolf took his hand away from her chin.

"Then I must make you never want to leave me. I must bind you to me."

Anna couldn't look at him. She knew what he was saying. She heard a pounding in her ears. Winter Wolf wanted her to be with child. Then, he knew, she would never leave him. How could she fight him? She was his wife as long as she was in his lodge. He could make her do whatever he wished. She would have no choice in the matter. "You are stronger than I, Winter Wolf. I cannot fight you. You will do whatever you wish with me and I will have no say."

"I know this to be true, Heva."

She looked at him, trying to be brave. "I must also live by your father's rules. I am your wife while I live in this lodge. I will do whatever you say."

"And what of your wishes, Heva?"

"What?"

"Do I just forget that you have a mind of your own?"

"I don't understand."

"I care for you, Heva. I grow more fond of you every day. I will not force you to do something which will make you hate me."

"Then what do you wish of me, Winter Wolf? I have been honest with you from the beginning. You know that I love my husband from the white world. I have never lied to you about my feelings for him. Do you think that you can make me fall out of love with him?"

"I think that I can make you care more for me, Heva. I think you already do care for me more than you will say. You are a part of me, Heva. Whether you want to believe it or not."

Anna felt his black eyes burn into her. There was something about this man that could not be explained. It was as if he were weaving a delicate, invisible web around her, a web that would keep her bound to him. She didn't look away. His hand touched her cheek and slowly caressed her neck and shoulder. She felt it move behind her head and gently pull her toward him until her face was only inches away from his. She could feel his warm breath on her face, and as she rested her hands against his chest, she could feel the pounding of his heart as clearly as if it were her own. She tried to

194

think of Nathan, but it was as if Winter Wolf silently commanded her to think of nothing but him.

"I am a part of you, Heva. I will always be a part of you," he said, his voice deep with emotion.

Anna's breath caught in her throat. She was unable to speak. He pulled her close to his body until their cheeks touched. She felt his arm go around her and she rested her head on his shoulder. Again, she felt that strange intimacy with him. Yet, it was different from anything she had experienced before. Winter Wolf was forcing her to acknowledge her need for him only through emotions, not through a physical act. She now knew that Winter Wolf would only make love to her if she was willing. He would continue to touch her and to look at her until he wore her down. She closed her eyes and refused to think that that would happen. Nathan was here now and she would never give in to Winter Wolf, no matter how gentle and patient he was with her.

"I feel your body relax, Heva. You grow accustomed to my touch." It was a simple statement, not a boast.

"You are a smart man, Winter Wolf. You have learned that your anger will not endear you to me." She leaned back and looked at him. "But you have not yet learned that I love only one man."

Winter Wolf smiled, an expression that looked odd on this man who seldom showed any emotion. "I never thought I could love again, Heva. The heart is a strange thing. It can play tricks on you."

Anna couldn't believe that he had used the word "love." He couldn't actually be in love with her, could he? She thought it was a game to him, a game of possession. Now he was saying something else. "My heart has always been true."

"But it can be torn in half. Be careful, Heva, for if that happens, it will be difficult to put it back together again."

Anna looked down, picking at a piece of the mat. She didn't like what Winter Wolf was saying. She felt his eyes on her and continued to ignore him. He lay down on the mat next to her, his head resting on his hand. He stared up at her. "What do you want from me?" she demanded angrily.

"You must watch your anger, Heva. Do not let it control you."

Confused, Anna started to get up, but Winter Wolf took her hand and pulled her back down on the mat. He moved close to her, his head next to her knee. "Come lie with me, Heva. Let me feel your body next to mine."

"It's still daylight. What if—"

Winter Wolf pulled Anna down on the mat next to him. She lay on her back, while he still lay on his side, head propped on hand, staring at her. She looked up at him. "Why don't you take me and get it over with?"

Winter Wolf reached over and wrapped a piece of her hair around his finger. "I could have done that many times. That is not my wish."

"Then what is? Please tell me."

"I told you before. I want you completely with me when you are here. If, indeed, this is to be fair, then you must devote all your time to me when you are here in this lodge. I want to know that your mind is here, not in the lodge of the white man."

"I can't control my thoughts."

"You can always control your thoughts, Heva. If you wish to make yourself think of the white man, you will. But if you wish to make yourself think of me, you will."

"I already told you I'd be your wife. I'll do whatever you want me to do."

"You are not listening to me, Heva. All I want from you is a chance. I want no more." Winter Wolf lowered his head to Anna's chest.

Anna gasped as she felt Winter Wolf rest his head on

her breasts, but he did no more. Tentatively, she reached up to touch his head. Somehow, it felt right that she should be comforting him. She closed her eyes.

"*Ne-mehotatse*, Hevavahkema." Winter Wolf spoke the words softly.

Anna opened her eyes. She didn't know what the words meant and she didn't want to know. She didn't want to be bound any closer to this man than she already was.

Chapter 9

Nathan studiously ignored Anna and Winter Wolf as he walked past them. As much as he wanted to see Anna and talk to her, he knew the only way he could get her out of this camp was to honor Brave Wolf's wishes. It was especially important that he not anger Winter Wolf in any way. When Anna was with Winter Wolf, he had to respect the fact that she was his wife for that time.

He felt Winter Wolf's eyes on him as he walked by his lodge. Nathan didn't look at him. He wanted to confront the Indian, but he knew it wouldn't accomplish anything. He had to be patient. He had to learn the Cheyenne ways and help his uncle in any way he could.

He began by taking off his gun and clothes and changing into the buckskin pants Brave Wolf had given him. He put on a pair of Brave Wolf's moccasins and tied his knife sheath around his thigh. He was visible enough as it was with his light hair; he needed to at least dress like the Cheyennes. He slept in his own small lodge that Little Deer had erected for him near the trees. He had expected Winter Wolf's mother to be resentful of his presence, but she had been gracious. She had known him when he was a small boy and had helped to care for him when their band was being chased by Comancheros. She had loved Aeneva and had wanted to know about her life with Trenton.

He headed to the circle where his uncle was sitting with many men. Brave Wolf had told him to come to the circle after he had eaten. He said it was important for the men to get to know him or they would constantly distrust him. Nathan asked permission to sit in the circle, and Brave Wolf gestured at him to sit down. Nathan felt the dark eyes staring at him, scrutinizing him. His uncle had told him to remain quiet unless he was asked to speak.

"This is my nephew, the son of my sister Aeneva, the great grandson of Sun Dancer and Stalking Horse."

The men looked at one another, puzzled at how a Cheyenne could be so light of hair and eyes.

"I have asked my nephew to stay with us until the first snow. Then he will return to his people."

"Why is your nephew here, Brave Wolf?" one of the men asked.

Brave Wolf sat tall, his pride evident. "He is here for Hevavahkema. They were married in the white world."

"Then why not let him take the woman and go back, Brave Wolf? Why let this woman cause so much trouble?"

"She is not the cause of the trouble, Yellow Bear. She was merely a victim of circumstance. Now she is desired by two men of two different worlds. It was up to me to be fair to all three people."

"What is your decision, Brave Wolf?"

"She will be with Winter Wolf for seven days, then she will be with my nephew for seven days. By the time of the first snow, she will decide which man she wants to stay with."

"If she chooses to stay with Winter Wolf, will this white man leave peacefully?"

Nathan looked at Brave Wolf, who nodded his assent. "I have given my word of honor to my uncle that if the woman, Hevavahkema, chooses to stay with Winter Wolf, I will leave in peace and never return to my mother's people." He looked again at Brave Wolf, his expression one of respect and admiration. "I would never do anything to disgrace my uncle or my mother's people."

Brave Wolf didn't wait for anyone to object. "You have heard my nephew speak. Do any of you disagree with my decision?" He waited a moment and continued. "I would like to teach my nephew some of our ways while he is here. He is smart and quick. He was like one of us as a boy, he can be again. Let us teach him about us so that he can return to the white world and teach others about us." The men nodded their assent. The meeting was over. Some of the men began to talk about other things, while others took out bones with which to gamble. Brave Wolf stood up. "Walk with me, Nephew."

Nathan followed his uncle through the village, returning the looks of the village people who had never before seen a white man, especially not a white man with such fair hair and eyes. "I will have to work hard for them to accept me, Uncle. They don't think they can trust me. I must prove them wrong."

"Yes, they are distrustful of outsiders, especially white men. You must make them see that you will fit in."

"I will not let you down, Uncle."

Brave Wolf stopped, staring at Nathan. "When you were young and Swiftly Running Deer first brought you to our people, my grandmother, Sun Dancer, loved you from the first. She would stroke your hair in wonder, for then it was white. None of us had ever seen a person with such light hair. She said you reminded her of the snowbird, the bird with soft white feathers that came out in the winter. So she called you 'Shehe.' But you have grown. You are no longer a snowbird. You observe and you see. You remind me of the hawk. That is what I will call you. Aenohe."

"Thank you, Uncle. It is a good name. I will try to live up to it."

"We will go to the corral. There are horses that must

be broken. Now would be a good time to prove your worth, Aenohe."

Nathan walked with his uncle, wanting to show his worth in any way he could. The corral was a round enclosure made from tree limbs and rope. The animals could easily knock it down.

"There, look at that colt." Brave Wolf pointed to the Appaloosa colt.

Nathan couldn't believe his eyes. The colt had almost the identical markings of his father's Appaloosa, a horse that only Trenton and Anna could ride. He told Brave Wolf of the similarity. "He was a wild animal, but when my father was around, he calmed down. He did the same thing when Anna rode him."

"I knew the animal well. It was I who gave him the stallion."

Nathan looked at Brave Wolf and smiled. "Yes, I remember now. My father said that after he found my mother in Mexico, they tried to take your horse back to you, but you wouldn't take it." He looked out at the corral. "Where did this colt come from?"

"From the same place as your father's horse. That stallion sired many foals. They are all descended from the horse my grandfather gave my grandmother on their wedding day."

"And do you now ride an Appaloosa, Uncle?"

"Who do you think sired this fine colt?" He walked to a group of men who were holding on to a horse, waiting for another man to mount him.

Nathan was intrigued. He had vague memories of watching some of the Cheyenne men break horses in the river, where the water would tire the horses so they would quit bucking. But this day the men were breaking them on land. The horse was blindfolded. A man stood on either side of him, shoulders braced along the horse's neck. One of the men grasped the horse's ear, twisting it. A third warrior vaulted to the horse's back, and the men holding it stepped clear. The horse reared, came down, and gathered itself for a second lunge. The warrior riding it whooped loudly and the horse broke into an uneven gallop, arching its back to kick repeatedly. The warrior lashed it with the rawhide reins and it began to run instead of buck. The warrior guided it in a huge circle across the rocky ground. By the time he rode the horse back toward the group of warriors, it had almost stopped fighting him.

"These men are very skilled," Nathan observed.

Brave Wolf smiled. "That is true, but this man is not the only one who has ridden that horse. There have been many before him. They each ride him until they are thrown or the horse gives up."

"It makes more sense than the way we do it. Usually one man will stay with one horse until he is broken. Sometimes it can take days just to break one horse."

"Would you like to try, Nephew?"

Nathan knew that Brave Wolf wanted him to prove himself. "Yes, I will try, Uncle."

Brave Wolf walked to the group of men and spoke to them in rapid Cheyenne. They turned and looked at Nathan. One of them said something and the rest of them began to laugh. Nathan knew the Cheyennes were some of the best horsemen on the Plains, and he could see by their expressions that they not only expected him to make a fool of himself, they were going to enjoy it. He walked over to Brave Wolf when he saw his uncle motion.

"They'd like to see me break my neck," Nathan said in a low voice.

Brave Wolf laughed loudly. Everyone looked at him, but he ignored them. "Yes, you are probably right. You will have to prove them wrong."

Nathan watched as the warriors entered the corral and used a long rope to lasso a large paint stallion. The animal reared proudly and defiantly, his white mane and tail flashing in the sun as he tossed his head. Even once one of the warriors had managed to get his lasso around the stallion's neck, it took four of them to bring him from the corral to where Nathan would mount him.

Low, approving, laughter ran through the watching men as they saw the white man approach the horse none of them had been able to ride. Nathan stood back as they fought the tall, muscled horse to a standstill.

"*Ne-naestse, veho.* Come here, white man," one of the Cheyennes called to Nathan.

Nathan ignored the Cheyenne and walked through the group of men to the horse. He attempted to stroke the animal's neck and to calm him, but the jeers of the men made it impossible. "*Heoh-ohkotoo-oh-ohestse!* Be quiet!" Nathan shouted loudly in Cheyenne.

The men quieted immediately, startled more at Nathan's command of the language than by the fact that he would dare order them to do anything. Abruptly, the warrior holding the rawhide lasso slapped it into Nathan's hand, and all four men quickly stepped backward. In the instant before the stallion realized it was free, Winter Wolf stepped forward and held the big animal motionless so that Nathan could vault onto its back. Startled that Winter Wolf had helped him, Nathan was very nearly thrown when the stallion exploded into a series of twisting leaps that jarred his spine.

Before he could regain his seat, the big stallion slid to a stop and reared, springing off his hind legs to land with his muzzle almost brushing the ground. Nathan saved himself from pitching forward over the horse's neck by grabbing its mane. Only the sheer strength of his hands and arms saved him from sliding backward when the powerful animal reared a second time and sprang into another series of bone-shattering maneuvers. Nathan was astounded at the power and agility of the horse. If anyone ever did manage to break him, he would be the kind of horse men hoped to own.

For the next few minutes, Nathan fought to keep his balance, to find the rhythm of the horse's movements. Beneath his knees, the stallion's muscles knotted and released, foam flecked his shoulders and flanks, and his shrill screams punctuated the drumming of his hooves on the hard ground. As if he realized the futility of trying to throw the rider who clung so skillfully to his back, the stallion reared yet again. Nathan leaned forward, shortening the rein and bracing himself for the violent explosion he knew could come the instant the horse's front hooves touched the ground again. The stallion screamed in frustration and fury, pawing at the air. Nathan leaned farther forward, throwing his weight against the stallion's neck. The horse screamed again, and Nathan felt the premonition of fear run through him. The stallion was arching himself backward, throwing his muzzle into the air. He was doing what only one horse in a thousand has the courage to do. Following an instinct as old as the equine race, he was going to throw himself backward, he was going to try to crush the enemy on his back!

Nathan jerked his hands free of the stallion's mane and flipped the reins away. For an instant of time that seemed to stretch into hours, he could only cling to the horse's back, feeling the crushing weight of the stallion start its inexorable backward fall. Then he threw himself sideways, kicking and clawing to gain every possible inch of distance. The horse could fall sideways, could pin and crush his legs, if he didn't manage to throw himself completely clear.

Nathan hit the ground and rolled to break his fall. He scrambled to his feet and, ignoring the pain in his shoulders and back, grabbed the reins of the stallion before it could regain its footing. Nathan spoke reassuringly as the stallion clambered to stand up, then patted its sweat-soaked neck as it stood trembling.

"Too bad, white man."

Nathan looked at Winter Wolf. The Indian wasn't tall,

but he was extremely muscular. His chest and arms were enormous, and he looked like he could knock the horse into submission. He didn't want to think what he could do to a woman. "I'm afraid I didn't honor your father very well. He was expecting me to show your people I could break a horse."

"No one told you that this horse has not been ridden by any man yet. Not even by me."

Nathan was puzzled by the man's air of cordiality. "Why don't you ride him, Winter Wolf? Maybe between us, we can break him." The stallion had lifted his head. His nostrils were flared, but the fear had gone out of his eyes and he was no longer trembling. Nathan extended the reins, but Winter Wolf didn't take them.

"What do you think of my father's decision?" he asked simply.

"I think it's fair. I won't do anything to break the rules."

"That is good to hear."

"You did well, Aenohe," Brave Wolf said from behind.

Nathan turned. "It seems I'm not as good as I thought I was, Uncle."

"No man has yet to even ride that horse. The only person who could do as well as you would be Winter Wolf."

Nathan looked at his cousin. "Yes, I think Winter Wolf could break him." The stallion pawed the ground and danced sideways. Nathan tightened his grip on the reins.

"Why do you not ride the horse, my son?"

Winter Wolf looked from his father to Nathan. "I do this not to dishonor you, white man. I do this because you and my father have asked me."

"I want you to break him, Winter Wolf," Nathan said sincerely. "I'll hold him for you."

The moment Winter Wolf's weight settled on the stallion's back, the animal leapt into the air. Nathan

205

watched in admiration as Winter Wolf's muscular body shifted, following the movements of the horse without overbalancing or fighting the natural rhythm of the powerful lunges. Slowly, gradually, the stallion bucked less, settling into an uneven gallop. As much as he admired Winter Wolf's ability to ride, Nathan marveled at the strength and endurance of the stallion. Long after most horses would have collapsed from exhaustion, the stallion kept running. Finally, Winter Wolf pulled the stallion to a stop near the corral as cheers rose from the other warriors. He slid from the stallion's back and raised his hands into the air.

"Hear me." Winter Wolf's voice carried. The men became silent. "If the white man had not ridden him first, I could not have broken him." Winter Wolf walked to Nathan. "The horse is yours."

Nathan tried to see what was really behind Winter Wolf's dark, inscrutable eyes. "I can't take him, Winter Wolf."

"I give him to you as a gift. You have earned him."

Nathan knew that to refuse Winter Wolf's gift would be an insult not only to him, but to Brave Wolf as well. He took the reins in his hands. "Thank you. He is a valued gift."

"I must go now. We will talk again, white man."

Nathan watched Winter Wolf as he walked away, puzzled by the Indian's generosity. He walked to Brave Wolf. "Winter Wolf has given me the horse."

"It is a good thing."

"Why would he do that, Uncle? I don't understand."

"You may be his enemy because you are white and because Heva loves you, but he still respects what you did here today. You would do well to remember that, Aenohe. Try to make Winter Wolf your friend, not your enemy."

"Yes, Uncle, I will try." Nathan walked away from the men and headed toward the river. He walked upstream to the pond he had Anna seen the day before. He quickly stripped and waded into the shallow pond, rinsing off the dirt. He stepped out of the water and pulled on the buckskins. They stuck to his wet legs. He sat down on the wild grass that grew by the edge of the bank. He pulled a piece of grass out of the ground and stuck it in his mouth, chewing absently on it as he lay back on the grass, staring up at the sky. He wondered if his coming here would prove fruitless. Until Nathan had actually seen Winter Wolf, it had never occurred to him that Anna might stay with the Indian. The man was not ordinary. He had never met anyone who was so powerful in body and spirit. If he had made such an impression on him, he could imagine how Anna had been affected!

"Hello."

Nathan sat up as he heard Anna's voice. "What are you doing here?"

"I come here often to swim or just to be alone."

"Where is Winter Wolf? Does he know you're here?"

"I haven't seen him."

"We can't risk being seen together, Anna. You have to go."

"I just wanted to see you, Nathan."

Nathan heard the fear in Anna's voice. "What is it? Has he hurt you?"

"No, he hasn't hurt me. But he frightens me just the same. It's as if . . ."

"What? Tell me, Anna."

"It's as if he's controlling my thoughts. He's determined to make me fall in love with him."

"I know."

Anna stooped down next to Nathan, her voice low. "Why can't we leave here? There are no guards watching us now. I know many ways we could escape."

"How far would we get with Robert? He's still so young, Anna. We couldn't ride hard. It wouldn't work."

"I'm scared, Nathan."

"Are you falling in love with him, Anna?"

"No, but he makes me feel things. He looks at me and he—"

"I don't want to hear anymore. I don't want to hear what you and Winter Wolf do in his lodge."

"Nathan, I—"

Nathan stood up. "I'm going to leave. He can't find us together." Nathan walked away without looking at Anna. He knew he'd hurt her, but it was better than Winter Wolf finding out they'd been together. He'd seen the man's power and he didn't want him to hurt Anna. Nathan knew he would just have to wait until Anna came to him. As much as Winter Wolf tried to make Anna fall in love with him, Nathan would try that much harder to make sure it would never happen.

It was the seventh night, and Anna paced nervously around the lodge waiting for Winter Wolf to return. Tomorrow she would go to Nathan and she couldn't wait. She rubbed her hands together. The nights were beginning to get cool. Autumn had set in. Winter Wolf had said that in a few weeks they would break camp and go to their winter camp grounds. Anna wanted to be gone by then.

The camp was quiet. Everyone was asleep. She heard the wild yipping of coyotes in the trees as they eagerly devoured their night's meal. Where was Winter Wolf? Had he gone on a hunt and not told her? Had he gone on a raid and been taken captive or been hurt? He was always in the lodge by the time the sun set, and if he went out again, he always told Anna where he was going. But she hadn't seen him since early this morning when she'd gone to the woods to dig for roots. She'd heard voices and had seen Winter Wolf talking to a beautiful young woman. She was called Bright Leaf, and it was obvious that she was eager to become one of Winter Wolf's wives.

Anna continued to pace around the lodge. Was it possible that Winter Wolf was with Bright Leaf? She was unmarried, Anna knew, and therefore her chastity would be honored. But what if they were talking about marriage? What if Winter Wolf brought her into this lodge?

She heard footsteps outside and she hurried to her mat, quickly pulling her robe up over her. She turned on her side, away from the flap, unwilling to look at Winter Wolf as he came inside. She heard him walk to the rear of the lodge and sit on the mat. He said nothing.

Anna wanted to talk to him. She wanted to ask him where he'd been, if he'd been with Bright Leaf, but she was embarrassed. She was in love with Nathan, after all, so what did it matter what Winter Wolf did? Finally, she turned over, unable to keep quiet. "Are you well, Winter Wolf?"

Winter Wolf lay on his back, his arms folded underneath his head. "I am very well, Heva."

"I had not seen you all day. I was worried."

"Why would you worry about me, Heva?"

"I thought something might have happened to you."

"My day was full. There was no need to worry."

Anna twisted her mouth in frustration. The man said nothing that he didn't want to. "I will go to Nathan tomorrow."

"Yes, I know."

"I thought we would talk this evening."

"What did you think we would talk about, Heva?"

Anna couldn't believe this. He was staring up at the sky through the smoke hole, exhibiting no interest in the conversation. "I thought you didn't want me to be with him."

"Ultimately, it will be your choice, Heva. It will do no good to worry about it." He closed his eyes. "I am weary. I will sleep now."

Anna stared at Winter Wolf in the waning firelight.

What had happened to make him change so much during the course of the day? She shivered slightly and realized that she wasn't used to the cool nights. She looked at Winter Wolf and she moved close to him. "May I lie next to you? I am cold."

"If you wish," Winter Wolf said lazily.

Anna lay close to Winter Wolf, feeling the warmth from his body. She moved so that her head lay on his chest. The rhythmic beating of his heart sounded in her ear like the steady swing of a pendulum. "What will you do while I am gone?"

"I will keep busy. Why do you suddenly worry about me, Heva?"

"I'm not worried, I just know how angry you were with me."

"I am no longer angry. I am glad this white man is here."

Anna looked up at Winter Wolf as he stared at the sky. "Why are you glad, Winter Wolf? Just a while ago you wanted to kill him."

"I no longer feel that way. Now I look at the white man and I feel strong. He makes me be strong."

"I don't understand what you're saying, Winter Wolf."

Winter Wolf's eyes stared at Anna's. "I find that this white man is not weak as I had thought he would be. He is *notse.*"

"What does that mean?"

"He is my enemy, yet I do not hate him. He is alien to me, from another tribe. I do not understand him, but perhaps I can learn to respect him."

"What made you change your mind about him?"

"I did not say I changed my mind." His hand stroked Anna's neck. "I am pleased that he appears to be a worthy opponent. It will make all this more enjoyable." He moved suddenly, pushing Anna to the mat, crushing her with his weight. She felt as if she would suffocate. His eyes seemed to look through hers as he pressed her

210

hands to the mat. His body stilled hers. "You are not strong, Heva. I could take you anytime I wish. Do you know that?"

Anna could barely breathe. "Yes" was all she managed to say.

"I want you to remember that," he said, moving his face closer to hers, brushing his mouth against hers.

Anna was surprised at his tenderness. It occurred to her that she hadn't seen any of the Indians kiss. Perhaps it was not one of their customs. Perhaps Winter Wolf was unsure of himself. But just as she thought this, his mouth covered hers, moving in a slow and caressing manner. She didn't resist him. She enjoyed the soft and gentle kiss of this strong man.

Winter Wolf rolled away, leaning on his side, surprising Anna by his sudden movement. She looked at him, her eyes questioning. "I want you to remember something else, Heva. I did not take you. I was gentle with you." He stroked her cheek. "Do you wish to lie with me?"

"Yes."

"Will you remove your dress? I wish to feel the warmth of your body against mine."

Anna sat up, feeling her heart pounding in her chest. She had never taken her clothes off at night. She looked at Winter Wolf and she knew she couldn't deny his request. He was asking her to trust him and she had no choice. She removed her moccasins and got to her knees, quickly pulling her dress over her head, then covering herself with her hands. She couldn't meet Winter Wolf's eyes. She saw him move and she held her breath, afraid of what he was going to do. He got onto his knees behind her, picking up her long braid. He untied the leather strip that held the mane of hair and quickly set it loose. He ran his hands through her long hair, then turned her around to look at him.

"Never have I seen a woman as lovely as you, Heva."

He took her hands from her breasts. "I would like to slit the white man's throat and take you away from here. I would like to take you and put my seed inside you, I would like you to bear my children. But," his hand touched her bare shoulder, "I will do none of those things." He lay back down on the mat and pulled Anna next to him. He put his arm around her and Anna rested her head on his chest. She felt his hand stroke her hair and she closed her eyes.

"I don't understand you, Winter Wolf," she said almost to herself.

"Do not forget me when you are with the white man, Heva. Think of me at night. Think of what it is like to lie next to me."

Anna closed her eyes, trying to still her trembling body. She would have expected anything from Winter Wolf but this. Anything. She felt her body relax and, with it, her mind. She wondered what would have happened if Nathan had not come for her. Would she have been content to be Winter Wolf's wife and bear his children? She didn't know the answer. But she did know one thing: Winter Wolf was becoming more and more important to her.

Anna took her few belongings and moved into Nathan's lodge the next day, but when she got there, he was gone. She felt strange, somehow and was beginning to wonder if she fit anywhere in this world. She sat for a moment in the small lodge, on the mat where Nathan slept. His clothes were rolled and placed behind the mat. She unrolled them and grabbed his shirt, holding it to her face. She closed her eyes and breathed in his familiar smell. She recalled the first time she had seen him at a ball in San Francisco. She was only eighteen years old and she didn't know who he was, but unbeknownst to them, they had been raised by the same people. They had danced one simple dance, but it was a dance that had changed Anna's life. She had fallen in love with Nathan the moment he had taken her into his arms and waltzed her around the floor.

She rolled out her mat next to his, put down her few baskets, and left the lodge. She had promised Little Deer that she would spend time with her today. She went to Brave Wolf's lodge and stood at the flap.

"*Hahee*, Little Deer. It is Heva."

Little Deer quickly appeared at the flap, a large basket in her arms. "Come, Heva, we will dig for roots."

Anna said nothing. She followed Little Deer into the woods and tried to listen to what she was saying. She pointed out several plants, telling Anna the medicinal properties of each, but Anna merely stared and nodded.

"Have you heard anything I have said, Heva?"

"I'm sorry, Little Deer. My mind is elsewhere today."

"I am sorry for you, Heva. I could not live with two men. I have trouble enough pleasing one man."

Anna smiled. "I feel like I am a prize in a contest, Little Deer, nothing more. Winter Wolf seems pleased to have an opponent as worthy as Nathan, and Nathan probably feels the same way. I'm beginning to feel I don't belong with either one of them."

"But you will have to choose, Heva, and you will have to choose carefully."

Anna bent down, taking the root-digger from Little Deer's hand. She pushed it down into the soft ground, and worked it around the plant until it was loose, then she pulled the plant from the ground, the root intact. She handed it to Little Deer.

"That is good, Heva. This we call 'witanots.' We dry it, pound it up, and boil it in water. We use it as a drink to relieve the ache in the stomach."

"My mother used to have many plants." Anna shared the memory with Little Deer. "She had a special medicine that she always carried in a pouch around her neck.

She said it was a mixture of many plants and would cure almost anything. When she and my father got the fever, Nathan didn't think to use this medicine and he blamed himself for their deaths."

"I am sorry, Heva."

Heva looked up at Little Deer, a sad smile on her face. "But it saved Nathan's life. He got the fever soon after Trenton and Aeneva got it and he almost died. I remembered Aeneva's medicine bag. Roberto helped me to make a medicine from it."

"If Aeneva were here, none of this would be happening."

"I thought you wanted me to stay with Winter Wolf."

"I want what is best for you, Heva. You are right. You are being dangled between these two men like a piece of meat. It can do no good. One will eventually kill the other. You will always blame yourself if that happens."

"I am quickly tiring of this game, Little Deer."

"Your mother was a warrior, Heva. She was considered an equal among the men. She would never allow herself to be treated as you are being treated."

Anna stood up. "It's different for me, Little Deer. These were Aeneva's people. Her grandfather was a chief and her grandmother a healer, and her brothers were brave warriors. I have no connection to this tribe. I have no power."

"You are wrong, Heva. You have what Aeneva has given you." She took Anna's hand and led her out of the woods to a place where flowers grew wild and grass grew tall. "Sit, Heva. Let me tell you a story."

Anna sat down, watching Little Deer as she put her basket down and gracefully sat on a patch of grass. "This is my place. Not many know of it. I come here often when I tire of the chatter of the women or the boastings of the men."

Anna smiled. Little Deer reminded her a lot of

214

Aeneva.

"Your mother was a warrior, a good warrior. She was better than many of the men. When she thought Trenton was not coming back from the white world, she became reckless. She thought nothing of riding into a group of Crows by herself. She had gone on a raid with the men to try to get some of our women and children back from the Crows. Aeneva showed no fear. But she was taken captive by a horrible Crow chief named Crooked Teeth. He kept her for a long time. It is said he did unspeakable things to her. He led her around on a rope that was tied around her neck, he beat her, and if she fought him at night, he punished her in the worst way."

Anna had heard the story of Aeneva's capture by the Crows and Trenton's subsequent rescue, but she had never heard the details. She had no idea that Aeneva had suffered so much. "But Trenton found her."

"Yes, he found her but she was not the same. She was a broken woman. She was afraid to look at him. She did not speak for a long time. He decided not to take her back to the band. Instead, he took her to the mountains, to the dwelling of the white trapper who was blood brother to Stalking Horse. Trenton took her there and cared for her. He bathed her, fed her, and he was patient with her in every way, but still she did not respond. He was afraid that her will and spirit had been broken. Slowly, Aeneva showed signs of her old self and she began to talk to Trenton of her horrible captivity. She even began to laugh. But Crooked Teeth came for her again. He followed them to the cabin. They tried to fight him off, but Trenton got hurt. It was up to Aeneva to fight her old enemy alone."

"Why didn't she tell me this?"

"Aeneva would never tell of her own bravery. Perhaps it was a memory that still frightened her."

"What happened then, Little Deer?"

"Her fear almost overcame her. When she saw

215

Crooked Teeth again she was reminded of his strength and power and brutality. But she did not back down. She fought him with a knife and she overcame him."

"She killed him?"

"Yes, and after that she finally realized her strength."

"I wish I had known." Anna stopped. "What are you trying to tell me, Little Deer?"

"Aenohe loves you very much. It is obvious. Winter Wolf cares for you in his own way. They are both men, and they are both strong. But you, Heva," Little Deer leaned forward, her brown eyes looking intently at Anna, "are the one with the true power. You must learn to use it."

Anna lowered her eyes, thinking about what Little Deer had just said. "It's confusing, Little Deer. When I'm with Winter Wolf, I care for him. But I know when I'm with Nathan, I won't want to leave him."

"It is what they both want you to feel. But you must not give them so much power. It is time you wielded the power, Heva. Like your mother, the warrior, you can be an equal to these men in many ways. Do not let them make you feel like less of a person because you are a woman."

Anna shook her head and smiled. "You sound very much like Aeneva. She would have been proud that you spoke this way to me, Little Deer."

"I loved Aeneva like a sister. She taught me many things about courage and honor. Do not let your heart be torn apart by either of these two men, Heva. Be honorable to yourself."

Anna took Little Deer's hands in hers. "Thank you, Little Deer. I know this has not been easy for you. Please believe me when I say I don't wish to make your son unhappy. He has been good to me in his own way. I do care for him."

"But your heart is with Aenohe, is it not?"

"My heart has always been with Nathan. It would be

best for everyone if we could leave today."

"Why do you say that, Heva?"

"I'm afraid if I spend more time with Winter Wolf, I will learn to care for him in a different way. We will all suffer if that happens, Little Deer."

"Then do what you must, Heva. Do what you must to save your heart."

Winter Wolf held the knife point in his fingers. He glanced at Nathan, a sly smile on his face. He turned back to the tree, ignoring the yells of the other man, and threw the knife. It hit the center of the mark in the tree that had been carved for the purpose of the game. Everyone ran to the tree, nodding their heads and smiling. They at once turned to look at Nathan, who also examined the mark.

"*E-pevaoh-ohe, na-vesesone,*" Nathan said in a low voice, his eyes never leaving Winter Wolf's. It was obvious from Winter Wolf's expression that the words had surprised him. "You have done well, my cousin," Nathan said.

Winter Wolf said nothing. He pulled his knife from the tree and handed it to Nathan. "Do you wish to try, *veho?*" Winter Wolf still used the derogatory term "white man."

Nathan shook his head. "I have my own knife." He walked back to the line where Winter Wolf had stood. Many of the Cheyennes were betting horses, weapons, jewelry, and some were even betting wives. Nathan knew that most were betting against him, but he didn't mind. He knew he had a long way to go to prove himself to these men. He pulled the knife from its sheath and held it by the sharp point. He brought his arm back and squinted his eyes, staring at the target. He remembered what his father had always taught him about games of skill, that much of the skill came from luck, and sometimes you made your own luck. He smiled lightly as he thought of that, and it calmed him. He brought his arm back, and with a quick movement, the knife went sailing through the air to stick in the tree. All of the Cheyennes went running over to check. Nathan didn't move.

"You are so sure you missed that you are afraid to check, *veho?*"

Nathan heard the sarcasm in Winter Wolf's voice. "No, I'm so sure it hit the target that I don't have to check."

"Look here, Winter Wolf. His knife has landed next to your mark in the center."

Winter Wolf walked forward and checked the knife. It had landed in precisely the same place as his own, actually cutting into his mark. "Yes, it is also in the center." He pulled the knife out and walked back to Nathan, handing him the weapon. "You did well, *veho*. Luck was with you."

"It wasn't luck, Winter Wolf. There's no such thing as luck in games of skill." Nathan could barely keep a straight face as he spoke. He put the knife back in its sheath. "I'd like to ride the stallion. Would you like to ride with me?"

Winter Wolf didn't hesitate. "I will ride with you, *veho*. But are you not worried that I may stab you in the back as you ride?"

"You're so sure that I'll be in front of you?" Nathan asked mockingly. He could see the glimmer of a smile on Winter Wolf's face.

"Only if I let you be. Come."

Nathan followed Winter Wolf to the corral. Winter Wolf threw Nathan a rope halter, and Nathan slipped it over the stallion's head and nose, leading him out of the enclosure. Winter Wolf led an Appaloosa stallion out of the enclosure.

"Is he the father of the colt?"

"Yes, he is descended from a horse my great-grandfather, Stalking Horse—"

"Gave to Sun Dancer on their marriage day," Nathan interrupted. "I may have lived in the white world, Winter Wolf, but my mother was a Cheyenne at heart. She told me all the stories of this band and she wanted me to be proud that I had lived here when I was younger and that I used to sit in Sun Dancer's lap."

Winter Wolf seemed surprised. "You knew Sun Dancer?"

"Yes, I remember her well. Even though she was older when I met her, she was still one of the most beautiful women I had ever seen. She was very tall, and her face had a certain quality about it." He looked at Winter Wolf, suddenly feeling self-conscious. "Anyone who knew her would tell you the same thing. When you were with Sun Dancer, you felt as if nothing could hurt you." He led the stallion away from the corral, ignoring the curious stares of the men who watched them. "My father took her to her final resting place."

"Why did she not have my father or your mother take her?"

"They didn't want her to go. They loved her so much they were hoping she would die with them."

"But your father felt differently?"

"My father loved and respected Sun Dancer very much. He saw how unhappy she was. He told her he would take her to where Stalking Horse lay. She was overjoyed. She said good-bye to her grandchildren and left with my father." Nathan's clear blue eyes looked at Winter Wolf. "When my father told me this part of the story, tears rolled down his face. He said that he and Sun Dancer traveled for many days until they found Stalking Horse's scaffolding. My father said Sun Dancer changed into a beautiful dress and braided her hair with beads and feathers. Then she put on her most beautiful quilled robe and took her most prized possessions, placing them beside her. Then she said good-bye to my father. She took off her silver necklace and gave it to him."

"I have heard of this necklace," Winter Wolf said thoughtfully, leaning against his horse. "It has something to do with your father, does it not?"

"When Sun Dancer was a young woman, she was kidnapped by a white trapper. He stopped at a small farm and tied her in the barn while he looked for food. A small boy watched her from a hiding place in the barn. He had light hair and blue eyes. He had never seen an Indian and Sun Dancer had never seen such a fair child. The boy thought she was an Indian princess because she was so beautiful and Sun Dancer thought the boy was a blessing sent from the great Spirit. The boy cut her loose and helped her to escape. The only thing Sun Dancer had to give him in return was a silver necklace that her mother had given her. She gave it to the boy and he kept it."

"The boy was your father."

"No, he was my grandfather. He gave the necklace to my father. My father gave it to Sun Dancer when he found her. When Sun Dancer was ready to go to Seyan, she gave the necklace back to my father to give to Aeneva."

"And where is the necklace now?"

"My mother gave it to me to give to Anna."

"But she wears no necklace."

"Someday she will," Nathan said confidently. He regarded his cousin for a moment. "You and I are connected, Winter Wolf, and not just through Anna. Have you ever wondered what it would have been like if I had stayed here and grown up with you?"

Winter Wolf's eyes seemed to cloud over for a second, but they soon cleared. "No, I have never wondered such a thing. You are a white man, I am Cheyenne."

"Yet I know things about your family that you do not. Our families have been intertwined for four generations. I think we were destined to meet, Winter Wolf. There is a reason that we were thrown together like this."

It was obvious that Winter Wolf didn't like the turn the conversation was taking. Without speaking, he swung up onto his stallion and galloped away from the camp.

Nathan watched, fascinated by his cousin. He really did wonder how differently things might have turned out if they'd grown up together as his father and Brave Wolf had grown up together. He swung up onto his horse. The stallion was still skittish, and he took off in a wild gallop in Winter Wolf's direction. Nathan let the horse have his lead, and he naturally followed the other horse. Winter Wolf drove his horse hard, managing to keep ahead of Nathan. Nathan smiled to himself. This reminded him of when he was younger and he and Roberto would race. He always beat Roberto because he was older, but it was fun racing with him. He was also reminded of the times he had raced with his father and Aeneva. His father was a strong rider, one who could ride all day withowt tiring, and Nathan had always enjoyed racing against him because he seldom won. But he also loved to race against Aeneva. She was so naturally skilled with a horse that it was beautiful to watch. It was as if the horse knew what to do without any commands.

He pulled up on his horse, slowing him to a canter and finally, a walk. Nathan looked around him at the sage- and rock-covered ground and the river that wound its way southeast. Tall cottonwoods grew along the banks of the river and rock formations that had withstood the test of time dotted the riverbanks and the horizon. Nathan had vague memories of what it had been like to live with the Cheyennes. They had spoiled him, he remembered, and treated him as if he were a little god. He had run and played all day long until he had been exhausted and fallen asleep in soft, warm robes. He recalled the smell of the wood and sage fires, and he remembered sitting in Sun Dancer's lap while she told him stories from times past. He had a special feeling for these people. They were his people, too. He didn't want to cause them any problems.

"What is it, white man? Am I too fast for you?"

Nathan hadn't realized that Winter Wolf had also slowed down, waiting for Nathan to catch up. "What if you had grown up in the white world, Winter Wolf?" Nathan shook his head. "Things are so strange. What if Aeneva had taken you with us? You would have grown up in our world and felt differently about white men."

"I think not, *veho*. Nothing will make me change my mind about white men."

"What if I leave and let Anna stay with you? How would you feel about me then?"

Winter Wolf pulled his horse to a stop. "I would wonder why you would do such a thing."

Nathan swung one leg over his horse, looking out at the horizon. "I'm tired of trying to make a life with Anna and having it never happen. Maybe we were never meant to be together. If I go back to my world, you two can make a life for yourselves."

Winter Wolf studied Nathan for a moment. "You are serious about this?"

"Yes, I'm serious."

"You have not even spent a day with Heva. Why would you make such a decision now?"

"Because if I spend any time with her at all, I will fall more in love with her. And what if she decides to stay with you? What do I do then?"

"You go back to your world and your life there."

"I think I'll make it easy on myself and leave now." Nathan turned his horse around and started toward the village. He could hear the footfall of Winter Wolf's horse, but he didn't care. Something strange had happened, something unexplainable. Suddenly, he just wanted to go home.

"This does not seem like something you would do, *veho*. You surprise me."

"You don't know me well enough for me to surprise

you, Winter Wolf. You don't know me at all."

"But I do. I have heard all about you from my father and Heva. My father said that you would do anything to get Heva back. What has changed your mind?"

"I don't want to talk about it anymore. I'll send her to your lodge when I get back."

"No!" Winter Wolf said angrily. "Stop, Aenohe. Listen to me!"

Nathan stopped his horse. "What's the matter, are you afraid I'm lying or are you going to miss our competition?"

"I am afraid of neither. I am bothered that the son of Aeneva would give up so easily."

Nathan looked at Winter Wolf. It was the first time Winter Wolf had openly conceded that Aeneva was his mother. "She wouldn't want me to cause problems for her people. I'm making it easy for you."

"What about Heva?"

"What about her?"

"What if she truly loves you and wants to go with you?"

"I think she cares enough for you. She could be happy here."

"I do not understand this. I would have expected you to try to kill me and take her away. What has changed your mind?"

"Maybe it's being here, with my mother's people. I don't want to cause trouble for anyone. She would have wanted me to do the honorable thing. So I'll do that. I'll walk away."

Winter Wolf leaned over and grabbed Nathan's arm before he could ride away. "You cannot. It is not honorable to walk away from someone you love. Heva is a good woman. She deserves to have a man who will fight for her."

"You'll fight for her."

"But she loves you. I know this to be true."

223

Nathan also knew it was true, but he wasn't swayed by Winter Wolf's argument. "I'm tired of fighting, Winter Wolf. I've already lost my mother and father. I've lost Anna several times, and I didn't see my brother for over ten years. I just want to live in peace on my ranch."

"And will you find yourself a woman on this ranch?"

"I don't know, and right now I don't care. I just want to go home."

"And what of your people? What will you tell your people about us?"

Nathan thought for a moment before he spoke. "I'll tell them that the Cheyennes are a good and honorable people who are fighting for their lives. I'll speak of the kindness and generosity that was shown to me, and I'll speak of Brave Wolf and his son, Winter Wolf." Nathan smiled weakly at Winter Wolf and urged his horse into a gallop. He rode back to the village, not understanding his feelings. It wasn't like him to give up so easily, nor was he willing to try anymore.

He rode to his lodge by the trees and went inside, lying down on the mat. He felt tired. He wanted to rest a few days then head on back to Rachel's ranch. Once there, he would give Robert back to Roberto, and he would head on home. He closed his eyes and dreamed of the ranch, but when he saw it, he saw Anna, riding his father's Appaloosa. He couldn't live on that ranch without being reminded of Anna.

The flap to the lodge opened and he heard Anna come in, but he didn't open his eyes. He heard her walk across the lodge and sit down next to him. He could smell the scent of lilac on her.

"Nathan?"

He wanted to ignore her, but he couldn't. He opened his eyes. She was smiling. A piece of lilac was tucked in the braid that was draped over her shoulder. She looked so young and pretty. It would be hard to leave her. "You need to pack your things," he said to her.

224

"Why? Are we leaving? Is Brave Wolf letting us go?"

"No, you're going back to Winter Wolf."

"That's not possible. I'm supposed to stay with you for seven days."

"You're going back to Winter Wolf."

"I don't understand, Nathan."

"I'm leaving here in a few days. I'll be taking Robert with me. You'll be staying with Winter Wolf." He couldn't look at her face as he spoke.

"You don't mean this!"

"I do, Anna. You'll stay here, and I'll go. You care for Winter Wolf, I know you do. In time, you'll forget me and you'll build a good life with him."

"Don't you even care about what I want?"

Nathan felt her fingers on his shoulder. "I want to leave here now, Anna, and I can't take you with me."

"Why are you doing this, Nathan? I don't understand. What have I done?"

"You haven't done anything, I'm just tired of fighting every other man in the world for your love."

"That's not fair. I haven't asked for all of these things to happen to me. Why are you punishing me?"

"I'm not punishing you. I just want to go home."

"I can't believe you're saying this. I thought you loved me."

"I do love you, but I'm tired of loving you. I don't have the energy for it anymore."

"So you'll leave me here while you go back to the ranch in Arizona. You don't care that I might not want to stay here. You don't even care that I don't love Winter Wolf. My God, Nathan, I don't want to live with the Cheyennes the rest of my life. I swear to you, if you leave me here, I'll find a way to leave on my own. I don't care if I die trying to find my way home."

"You'll adjust, Anna."

"Don't!" she yelled angrily. "Don't tell me what I'll feel. I'm the one who has suffered, Nathan, not you. I was the one who was kidnapped and put on that horrible slave ship in San Francisco, I was the one who was taken by Roberto to Louisiana, and I was the one kidnapped by the Shoshonis. Don't you dare tell me how tired you are. It's been an effort for me to love you, Nathan. Did you forget that when I first fell in love with you, you lied to me about who you were? I didn't find out that you were Aeneva and Trenton's son until we were both at the ranch." She pounded her fist on the reed mat. "Damn you, Nathan. I won't accept the responsibility for this. I won't."

Nathan grabbed Anna's arm. "Anna, don't—"

"Don't what? What do you want me to do, Nathan? Do you want me to wish you good luck and pretend I never loved you?" Her eyes filled with tears. "Don't you know how much I love you, Nathan? Don't you know that if you leave, a part of me will die?" She bit her trembling lip to keep from crying. "But I won't beg you to stay if you want to go. I do have some pride left."

"I'm sorry, I don't want to hurt you."

"I don't think you know what you want. I think the only person you're concerned with is you. Just remember this, Nathan, when I leave here, and I *will* leave here, you'll never have the chance to love me again."

Nathan watched Anna as she left the lodge. He wasn't sure what his life would be like without her. They'd never had a chance to see what a life together would be like. He closed his eyes. He didn't want to think about Anna anymore. He just wanted to forget.

Chapter 10

Winter Wolf watched Anna as she slept. The robe
had fallen from her bare shoulder and her soft skin glis-
tened in the dim firelight. She was a beautiful woman
and he desired her more than he thought possible. He
had thought he could make her love him, but he could
see now the impossibility of that. Her heart was with
the white man and nothing, it seemed, could sever that
bond.

The white man. Try as he might, Winter Wolf
couldn't figure him out. Why had he given in so easily
and sent this woman back to him? Why would any man
give up on her like that? Something about this man
troubled him. Winter Wolf knew that the man was a
fighter; he could see it in everything he did. Yet, when
it came to Heva, he was willing to give her up without
a fight. Why would a man like this not fight for the
woman he loved?

He had talked with his father about Aenohe. Brave
Wolf was also troubled by Aenohe's change of heart.

"This does not sound like Aenohe. When he came
into this village, he would have done anything to win
Heva back."

"I know that, Father."

"Did you go against my wishes and argue with him,

Winter Wolf?"

"We had no argument. He talked of his time spent with our people when he was a boy and he spoke of his mother and our great grandmother, Sun Dancer. He seemed strange, Father, as if something had happened to him. He asked me if I would change my opinion of white people if he gave Heva to me."

"Aenohe would not give up so easily unless something was wrong, Winter Wolf. This disturbs me."

Winter Wolf recalled the look on his father's face. "This troubles me also, Father. This man makes me feel weak, for he will not fight. So I must find a way to make him fight."

Winter Wolf nodded to himself as he looked down at Anna. He now knew there was only one way to make Aenohe angry enough to fight for Heva. It was the only way.

Anna furiously swept out the dirt from the lodge floor, her anger at Nathan still driving her. She had been with Winter Wolf for two days and she hadn't seen Nathan at all. Winter Wolf had virtually ignored her, as if by coming back into the lodge before the seven days were up, she had interrupted something. He didn't want to know about anything that had happened with Nathan. In fact, he didn't even seem to want her around.

She walked over to their mats and straightened them, pulling the robes over them and pushing the backrests against the side of the lodge. Little Deer had told her there was talk among the men of leaving soon. Many of them felt there was a cold and hard winter ahead and they wanted to start south to their winter grounds. Anna knew she had to find a way to leave before that happened.

Today she was going to ride. Besides the Appaloosa

colt, Winter Wolf had also given her a beautiful mare, a good, strong buckskin. Anna wanted to start riding every day to make her body strong again so that she would be used to the constant traveling. She reached behind her backrest and pulled out a bundle wrapped in buckskin. It contained strips of dried meat, a small pouch of medicine that Little Deer had made up for her, and some cakes of pemmican. She needed to keep adding to the supply so that she had enough for at least a week in case she couldn't find food. She also wanted to get a rifle, a large hunting knife, and a water bag. She would take the heavy robe that covered her at night to use as a horse blanket, and then she would cover herself and Robert with it when the weather turned cold. She would be prepared this time. She quickly rolled the bundle back up and placed it behind the backrest, covering it with part of the mat. She heard the flap to the lodge, and she turned around. Winter Wolf was standing there, watching her.

"What were you doing?" His voice was angry.

"Nothing. I was cleaning the lodge."

"You were hiding something." He walked to the backrest, threw it aside, and uncovered Anna's hidden bundle. He held it in front of her face. "What is this, Heva? Were you planning to leave?"

Anna saw the look of anger in Winter Wolf's eyes and she felt the fear flood back. "I was saving it for our trip south. Little Deer said we would be leaving soon and—"

"Do not insult me with your words, woman," Winter Wolf said angrily. "You were planning to leave with the white man."

"No, I wasn't. He doesn't even want me, Winter Wolf."

"I do not believe you. I think this is a plan the two of you have." He stood up, his face a mask of rage. "Do you take me for a fool, Heva?" He yanked her forward.

229

"When were you planning to leave?"

"We didn't have any plan. He was going to leave without me. He doesn't want me. I planned to follow when I could."

"I knew I could never trust you. I am surprised you did not put a knife in my ribs when I slept."

"Winter Wolf, please listen to me. I didn't mean to hurt you. You have been kind to me, but I miss my home. I just want to go home."

"You just want to be with the white man." His hands squeezed her shoulders, his fingers digging into the skin.

Anna's anger wasn't enough to overcome the fear. She saw that look in his eyes again and she was afraid of what he might do. "I'm sorry."

"You are not sorry, white woman. You just wanted to be with the white man and lie down on the ground and spread your legs for him. Is that not right?"

"Please, don't." Anna tried to look away, but Winter Wolf's fingers jerked her chin up.

"What is it like to lie with this man? Is he like a rutting stag that—"

"Don't!" Anna screamed, pulling away from Winter Wolf and covering her ears with her hands. She dropped to her knees, unwilling and unable to listen to any more of Winter Wolf's insults. But Winter Wolf wasn't ready to stop. He knelt in front of her, squeezing her arms.

"Do you think that a few tears will stop my anger? I should have left you with the Shoshonis. I have given up too much for you, woman."

"No more than I have given up," Anna said angrily. His hand caught her off guard, hitting her so hard it knocked her to the ground. She put her hands to her face to protect herself, but he hit her again. When she began to scream, he put his hand over her mouth.

"Do you think someone will help you? Do you think

that anyone cares what happens to you, white woman?" He stood up and walked to his weapons and came back with a rope. He quickly made a noose and slipped it around Anna's neck. She tried to stop him, but he pushed her on her stomach and pulled her hands behind her. Tying the rope around her wrists, he pushed her down. "Do not struggle too much, woman, or you might choke yourself."

Anna watched in disbelief as Winter Wolf left the lodge. She tried to maneuver herself into a more comfortable position, but if she moved her arms, the rope tightened around her neck. For a fleeting moment, she thought of yelling for Nathan, but she couldn't. Her pride wouldn't permit it, just as it wouldn't permit her to seek out Little Deer or Brave Wolf for help. She got to her knees and managed to move to the robe. She lay down and pressed her face to the soft fur. Tears streamed down her aching face, but she stifled her cries in the robe. She didn't know what had made Winter Wolf so angry, but she would have to do everything in her power not to anger him further. She prayed that he didn't return soon. She needed time. She needed time to think of a way to escape.

Winter Wolf saw Nathan as he walked through the camp, and he knew the time was right. The Indian was with a group of young men who were bored and ready for some fun.

"Hey, *veho*, come here," Winter Wolf yelled to Nathan. When Nathan ignored him, Winter Wolf walked to him, standing in front of him to block his way. "Some of my friends have bet me that I cannot beat you in a kicking match. I say it would be easy to do."

"I'm not in the mood for games, Winter Wolf." Nathan started to walk away, but Winter Wolf put his hand on his chest.

"Are you afraid, *veho?*" he asked shoving Nathan backward.

"Don't do that."

Winter Wolf shoved Nathan again. "I want to know if you are afraid of me, *veho*. I say that you are." Winter Wolf put his hand on Nathan's chest again, but this time Nathan grabbed it, squeezing it tightly.

"Get out of my way, Winter Wolf." Nathan walked around his cousin.

"So you are afraid of me, *veho*," Winter Wolf shouted after Nathan. "Is it because you know that your woman prefers to share my robe at night?" Winter Wolf watched as Nathan turned around, the anger clear on his face. "She is like a wildcat, *veho*. I can see why you couldn't handle her." Nathan rushed at Winter Wolf, his head ramming into the Indian's stomach, knocking him backward onto the ground.

"You bastard!" Nathan yelled.

Winter Wolf realized he had made his point all too well. The white man was sufficiently angry to beat him to a pulp. Winter Wolf started to stand, but kicked out a leg, sweeping it in a wide arc toward both of Nathan's legs and knocking him to the ground. Winter Wolf got to his feet, watching Nathan as he tried to get up. "Come, *veho*, let us finish this. Let us see who is the better man." He kicked Nathan in the ribs, sending him to his knees. "You are not very skilled at this game, *veho*. It is good that your woman no longer depends on you for protection." His leg went out, but this time Nathan grabbed it, twisting Winter Wolf's foot and bringing him to the ground. Nathan jumped on top of Winter Wolf, slamming his fist into the Indian's face. Winter Wolf rolled to the side, holding on to Nathan. They rolled back and forth in the dirt, their hands and arms flailing uncontrollably. The men surrounding them

232

cheered frantically, wanting to see a fight to the death. But they didn't get their wish. Their chief pushed his way through the throng of men and stood for a moment, watching his son and his nephew trying to kill each other.

"Enough!" Brave Wolf's voice was full of anger and disappointment.

Winter Wolf and Nathan stopped, looking up at Brave Wolf as he strode forward.

"You both gave me your word that you would cause no trouble for this village. It seems that I cannot even trust my own family." He shook his head in disgust. "Clean yourselves off and come to my lodge."

Winter Wolf and Nathan exchanged angry looks and stood up, brushing themselves off. They followed Brave Wolf to his lodge, waiting as he walked to the center. They stood in silence, watching the old man, waiting for him to speak.

"What happened?"

"It was my fault, Father, I—"

"No, we were just wrestling and it got out of hand, Uncle. We were both to blame."

Winter Wolf glanced at Nathan, wondering why he was defending him. "Father—"

"Silence!" He walked back and forth in front of the two young men. "I did not want this to happen. I was hoping that during this time, you two would get to know each other and respect each other." He walked up to Winter Wolf, the disappointment written over his face. "My own son cannot find it in his heart to welcome my sister's son into this village."

Winter Wolf could barely look at his father. He couldn't stand to disappoint him. He wanted to tell him that he was trying to help his cousin, but he could not. He had to do this on his own. "I am sorry, Father."

"Sorry is not sufficient, Winter Wolf."

"Don't blame him, Uncle. It was as much my fault."

"And what have you done that is so wrong, Aenohe?" He glared angrily at Winter Wolf. "You rode hundreds of miles to get your wife back, only to find she was given to another man in marriage. You could have tried to take her then, but you respected my wishes and you did nothing. You even gave her back to my son. Why, Nephew? Why would you do such a thing?"

Nathan shook his head. "I cannot explain my reasons, Uncle. I just thought that Anna would be better off with my cousin."

"Your cousin?" Brave Wolf stepped forward, his anger growing. "You can call this man your cousin after all he has done to you?"

"He has done nothing to me, Uncle. His guilt lies only in the fact that he loves another man's wife. He didn't know I would come after her."

"What is wrong with you, Aenohe? Why do you give up so easily? At least today you fought."

Nathan looked at Winter Wolf. "I fought today only to save my pride, but I won't fight for Anna. Don't ask me to, Uncle, or I'll leave today."

"I will not ask you, Nephew, but know that I am disappointed in you as well. It is hard for me to believe the son of Aeneva, warrior woman, would not fight for the woman he loves." Brave Wolf looked at his son. "You and I will talk later, Winter Wolf. But know this— as long as Aenohe is in this village, he is under my protection. He is my nephew and I do not want anything to happen to him. I expect you to look after him as if he were your brother. Do you understand me?"

"I understand you, Father."

Winter Wolf started to leave, but Brave Wolf spoke again. "Do not leave until I say you can go."

Winter Wolf controlled his anger. "Yes, Father."

"And you, Aenohe, do not think that my anger toward you is any less. You came here like a man fighting for what he thought was his, and now you act like a boy who has had something taken away from him and he wants to cry. If you want this woman, truly want this woman, then you should fight for her. Our life on this earth is too short before we take the Hanging Road to Seyan. Do not waste your time on inconsequential things, Nephew.

Brave Wolf looked at both men again. "I will leave the lodge. I want you two to speak. Do not fail me in this."

Winter Wolf looked down at the floor of the lodge, wondering how he could make peace with this man when he was trying to make him angry enough to keep fighting. But he could not disappoint his father. He reached up and rubbed his jaw. "You are good with your fists, *veho*."

Nathan rubbed his ribs. "And you're good with your feet."

"Why did you try to defend me in front of my father? There was no need."

"I could have walked away, but I chose to fight. It was as much my fault as yours."

"What do we do now?"

"It doesn't really matter. I'll be leaving here soon. If we can just stay out of each other's way, we'll be fine."

"I still don't understand about Heva. Did she do something to displease you?"

"I don't need to explain anything to you, Winter Wolf. I'm giving her to you. What more do you want?"

"I want the truth."

Nathan squinted slightly, his pale eyes almost imperceptible in the dim light of the lodge. "The truth is that Anna is the kind of woman whom men will always be attracted to. I'm tired of fighting."

"I see," Winter Wolf said, nodding his head. "You

think if she stays here, no man will want her? She will live with me and have children and her life will be full?"

"Something like that."

"Ah, *veho*, you do not know this woman like you think you do. I feel sorry for you." Winter Wolf walked to the flap of the door.

"What do you mean?"

"Never mind, you will find out in your own time." Winter Wolf left his father's lodge and walked to Elk Horn's lodge. Elk Horn always had some of the white man's whiskey and he knew that he would need a lot of it in order to give him the courage to do what he knew he must. There was no other way.

Anna lay on her side, the rope rubbing her neck and wrists raw. The lodge was pitch-black. She could see the stars through the hole of the top of the lodge and she wished she were outside, away from this place. She heard a noise outside the lodge, and for a wishful moment, she thought it might be Nathan. But as soon as the flap opened and she heard the footfall, she knew it was Winter Wolf. She closed her eyes and pretended to be asleep. She didn't want to be beaten again. She just wanted to be left alone.

Winter Wolf walked to the fire ring and brought out two fire sticks. He twirled the upright greasewood stick on the lower cottonwood stick, which was sprinkled with dry buffalo-chips, until the fire ignited, then added a few pieces of kindling. He knew that Heva was pretending to be asleep. He had heard her move when he entered the lodge. He hated the way the whiskey made him feel, he even hated the taste, but he had had no other choice this night.

He walked to the water bag and took a long drink, dropping it on the floor when he was done. He stumbled slightly as he walked to his mat, falling heavily onto it. He steeled himself for what he was about to do.

He reached over and yanked the rope around Anna's neck. She cried out in pain. "Wake up, woman." He watched her eyes as they opened, full of pain and anger. He pulled the large knife from the sheath on his hip and held it behind her head. He could see her cringe in fear. He sliced through the rope that connected her hands and neck, then he cut it from her wrists. She rubbed her wrists, reaching up to slip the rope from around her neck. Both her neck and wrists were raw, and he could still see the knife scar he had given her when he had cut her arm. It seemed there was no end to the pain he would inflict on this woman. "Have you decided to tell me the truth about you and the white man?"

Her expression was one of weariness mixed with fear. "I have nothing to say."

"But you have many things to say to him, yes?"

She turned her head, not willing to argue. "I'm tired, Winter Wolf. I just want to sleep."

"You will not sleep until you answer my question. When were you and the white man planning to leave?"

"I told you before, we weren't planning anything. Why won't you believe me?"

He looked at the bruises on her face and longed to reach out to her, but he remained aloof. "I cannot believe you because you are a white woman who will do anything to save her own life."

"Say anything you want, Winter Wolf, but you can't do anything to me that you haven't already done."

"That is not true, woman. There are many things I can do to you." He watched as her arms went instinc-

237

tively around herself in a protective gesture. He reached up, his hand going around her neck. He pulled her forward, their faces barely apart. "I can make you suffer in ways that you have never dreamed of."

"Winter Wolf, please." Her voice quivered.

"What do you want, woman? Do you want me to let you go to the white man? Well, go, but he will not take you. He does not want you." He reached up and placed a hand on her breast, squeezing it hard. Her arms tightened around her, but he pried them apart. "Do not fight me or I will hurt you."

"Did you do this to Rain Woman also? Is this how much you loved her?"

Winter Wolf reacted without thinking, hitting Anna across the face again, hitting her so hard she fell backward onto the robe. He could hear her cry, but he didn't stop. He ran his hands up and down her legs. "You know nothing of how I loved Rain Woman. Do not ever speak her name again." He pushed her dress up above her knees.

Anna tried to pull away but he held on to her arm. "Don't do this, Winter Wolf. I know you don't mean to hurt me. This isn't you."

"Then you do not know me very well, woman. You do not know me at all." He pulled off his shirt, and while he was removing his pants, Anna tried to crawl away. He grabbed her ankle and yanked her back. "It will do you no good to try to get away from me, woman." He was only in his breechcloth and he towered above Anna, his bare chest and thighs shining in the firelight. "Do you think that I am made from stone, that I should lie next to you night after night and not have any desire for you? You are not the most beautiful woman, but you are pleasing to the eye at times." He watched her as he spoke, and the expression on her face tore at his heart. She was frightened and humiliated and that was how he needed her to feel. He ran his hand up the inside of her thighs. She tried to turn away, but he swung one leg over her, effectively pinning her to the ground. "Tell me something, woman. How do you act when you and the white man lie together? Do you fight him or do you willingly spread yourself for him?"

"No!" Anna said in an anguished voice.

"It will do you no good to cry out. I will do whatever I want with you and when I am through, I may give you to someone else. It depends on how much you please me." He shoved her dress up around her waist, climbing atop her, pinning her arms to the ground.

"Please stop, Winter Wolf. I'll do anything you ask of me. I'll be your slave, I'll work all day, every day, but don't do this."

"Do you not realize that you are already my slave, woman?" He looked into her eyes, and behind the fear he saw the hatred. He felt himself grow hard and he hated himself for it. He had always thought their love-making would be so gentle. He looked at her a moment longer, then plunged into her. He muffled her scream with his hand, watching her face as he penetrated her again and again. She fought him at first and then she just lay there, tears streaming from her vacant eyes. But he kept on hurting her until he finally spent himself. Then he rolled away, lying on his robe. He heard her sobs and he could do nothing to comfort her. He had defiled this woman in the worst possible way, something he had sworn he would never do to any woman. And she would never know that he had done it for her and for her husband. He threw his arm across his eyes, trying to blot out the memory of what had just occurred. But he would never forget the look in her eyes as he had rammed himself into her and after, as she lay there like a doll with no life in her. He had taken something precious from her; he had taken away her right to give herself freely to him. He didn't think he could ever forgive himself for that.

Anna opened her eyes, afraid she might find Winter Wolf next to her. He was gone. She sat up. She felt sore all over. She could tell her jaw was swollen just by touching it, but that was nothing compared to how she felt inside. What Winter Wolf had done to her the night before was brutal. He knew he was hurting her, yet he didn't stop. The man she thought she knew no longer existed. She tried to get up but sat back down. She felt sick to her stomach. She closed her eyes and lay back down on the robe. She wasn't going to leave the lodge today. Everyone would know what had happened. She heard laughter outside and she heard Winter Wolf's voice. She turned over, so that her back was to the flap, and she heard him enter. She closed her eyes tightly as she heard him go to the fire, and then she knew he was coming to the robe. She squeezed her eyes shut, praying that she looked as if she were asleep.

He lay next to her, his arm going across her waist. She cringed but forced herself to remain still. His hand went up to her breast and then traveled down her stomach to her thighs. She couldn't pretend any longer. She turned over, staring at him. "I'm surprised you'd want a woman again so soon that you had to take by force. I thought you were more of a man than that, Winter Wolf."

He sat up, his expression angry. "It sounds to me like you need another lesson. It seems that last night you did not learn that you cannot win with me. You do as I say, or you will suffer."

"I think I've already suffered enough at your hands," she replied as bravely as she could.

"You have not begun to suffer, woman. You do not know the meaning of the word." He put his hand around her neck and shoved her back down on the robe. His hand tightened around her throat and she felt as if she were going to choke. "Do not push me, woman. I will think nothing of killing you." His hand closed even tighter. "Do you understand?"

"Yes," Anna managed to say before he loosened his hold.

"Get up and collect some wood for the fire and make sure to check the traps. I am hungry."

Anna slipped on her dress and moccasins. It wouldn't do her any good to argue with him. Besides, she would be away from him if she went outside. She stopped, trying to still the fear in her voice. "Winter Wolf, where is Robert? I'd like to take him with me."

"Do not worry about the boy. He will stay with my mother until you can learn to be a good wife."

"But—"

"Do you wish to argue with me, woman?"

Anna knew better now. She grabbed her cloth sling from the ledge and slipped it over her shoulder, then picked up a blanket and wrapped it around her shoulders to keep out the chill. Quickly, she left the lodge, eager to get far away from Winter Wolf. She passed a few people. She heard them talk as she walked by and she lowered her head, unable to look at anyone.

When she got to the woods she walked to the place that Little Deer had shown her. She wondered how far she would get if she followed the woods all the way back, but the thought of bears and mountain lions kept her from looking. She remembered the traps and jumped to her feet. She didn't want to give Winter Wolf a reason to come after her.

She walked to the small trap by the edge of the woods and checked it. It was empty. She walked to all of the others they had set. They were empty as well. What would he do to her if she came back without any meat?

She bent and began gathering kindling, piling it in the sling until it was full. Maybe if she found some berries, he wouldn't be angry with her. She walked farther back into the woods and collected chokecherries and also some wild plums and currants. She felt elated. Surely he wouldn't punish her if she came back with these fresh fruits.

She walked out of the woods and stood by the edge of the river. It was a cloudy, cool morning, and the water reflected the dark sky. She thought about the day she had saved the young boy and how grateful Winter Wolf had been. Tears of sadness mixed with tears of rage filled her eyes as she thought of the times he had been so gentle with her, and of what he had done to her the night before. The memory of that terrified her so much that she decided to go back to camp before he came looking for her.

She walked along the trees behind the camp so she wouldn't run into any people. She saw Nathan's lodge sitting off by itself and she wanted to run to it and beg him to help her, but she couldn't do it. She was tired of depending on men and having them fail her.

She stumbled on a branch and fell forward, her twigs and fruit falling all over the ground. "No," she said, desperately trying to pick up everything. She crawled on her hands and knees, trying to retrieve every berry and twig she had dropped.

"Do you need help?"

She heard Nathan's voice behind her. She didn't want him to see her this way. She didn't need his pity. She lowered her head so that her hair hid her face. "No, I don't need your help." She continued to pick up her fallen fruit and twigs, trying to ignore Nathan. She saw his moccasins as he walked around and stood in front of her.

"Let me help you." He began picking up berries, but Anna roughly took them from him.

"I don't need your help. You made it clear how you feel about me. I want you to leave." She turned her head, trying to make sure her face was covered.

"Why don't you look at me, Anna?" Nathan asked.

Anna turned around, pretending to search the ground. She felt his hand on her arm and she jerked it away. "Leave me alone. I don't want to get in trouble."

"You won't get in trouble."

She scooped everything into her sling and hurried toward the camp, but Nathan blocked her way. She looked frantically toward the camp, praying that Winter Wolf didn't see them together. "I have to go." She tried to pull away, but Nathan swung her around to face him. His hand went up to her face, pushing the hair back. She heard him gasp as he saw the bruises covering her face. She turned away, feeling ashamed, and started toward the camp.

"Did he do this to you, Anna?"

She stopped, not knowing what to do. She was afraid that Nathan would go to Winter Wolf and confront him. Nathan wouldn't stand a chance against him. "I fell last night in the dark, I—" She felt his hands on her shoulders, gently holding her.

"Why did he do this to you?"

"It doesn't matter, Nathan." She turned to face him. "Just pack your things and leave."

He touched one of the bruises on her face. "I can't believe he would do this to you."

"He didn't . . ." She saw someone coming out of the camp and she turned, afraid it was Winter Wolf.

"Don't worry, it's not him. Let's go someplace where we can talk."

"No, I can't be seen with you. If he finds out I've

243

been with you, he'll . . ." She stopped, realizing she'd said too much.

"What will he do, Anna? Will he beat you?"

She looked into his clear blue eyes. She felt tears sting her own eyes, but she refused to cry. "It doesn't matter what he does to me, Nathan. I'm his wife. You gave me back to him. The best thing you can do for me now is to leave." She walked toward the camp.

"Anna, I want you to meet me later, here by the trees before the sun sets. If you don't, I'll go to his lodge."

Anna hurried into camp, keeping her head lowered, holding on to her precious bundle. She went into Winter Wolf's lodge, dumping the wood and fruit by the hearth. She stacked the wood neatly in a little pile and put the pieces of fruit into a basket, then took the water bag and poured water over to clean it. She ignored Winter Wolf, hoping that he was asleep.

"How many rabbits did you bring back?"

Anna tried to speak, but she couldn't find her voice. She knew how he would react when he found out there was no meat. "There were no rabbits. I checked all of the traps."

"There were no rabbits?" His voice seemed to echo inside the lodge.

"I will check again later."

"Later? I do not want rabbit later, I want it now. Come here."

Anna got up and walked to the robes. "Yes."

"Down here . . ." Winter Wolf patted the robe next to him. Anna sat, trying to quell the shaking of her body. "You do not understand me, woman. I am a man of many needs. Did you not learn that last night?"

Anna nodded silently, trying to put the picture of Winter Wolf's body on hers out of her mind.

"When I tell you I want meat, I want meat." He reached over and put his hand under her dress, rubbing her thigh. "When I tell you I want you to lie down for me, you will lie down for me. Do you understand?"

"Yes." She was afraid to look at him.

"Lie down for me, woman."

Anna couldn't move. She felt her body begin to shake all over. The thought of him hurting her like he had the night before made her sick. Her insides already ached from his intrusion. She closed her eyes. "I cannot," she said, her voice quivering.

"You cannot or you *will* not?" Winter Wolf's voice was like a knife that cut through her heart. "You will be punished for this."

"Haven't you punished me enough?" She looked at him, the tears streaming down her face. What had happened to the Winter Wolf she knew?

"I have not begun to punish you, woman. You will pay for everything you have ever done to me. You will pay for your lies. When I am through with you you will wish you had never been born."

Anna clenched her hands together, hoping to find some strength. "Do what you must, Winter Wolf." Her tear-filled eyes sought his out. "I have been punished enough for caring for you. No punishment could be worse that what I have seen you become." His hand lashed out and struck her on the jaw, crushing her lip against her teeth. She felt the blood ooze out of her mouth, but she didn't move. She wouldn't beg for mercy this time.

Winter Wolf raised his hand again to strike Anna, but he stopped when he saw the look on her face. He could see by the vacant expression in her eyes that she had given up. She didn't care what happened to her. She almost looked as if she wanted to die. He lowered his hand, not willing to inflict any more pain on her.

He wanted to take her in his arms, but knew he must continue the charade. He forced his eyes away from her. He didn't know how long he could do this. "You are not worth the effort," he said in a voice filled with contempt. "Leave me."

He watched her as she sat, staring motionlessly ahead. Perhaps he had hit her too hard. Perhaps he had injured her. "I have nowhere else to go."

He closed his eyes. He could not hurt her anymore. He reached out and pulled her to him, feeling her trembling body against his. He wrapped his arms around her, burying his face in her hair. Sobs wracked her body as he held her. It would be over now. If the white man would not fight for her, then he could do nothing about it. He would not cause her any more pain.

He felt her fall against him, her body exhausted from the pain and fear. He lay down, wrapping his arms around her as she cried. He was amazed that she could still trust him after what he had done to her. He stroked her hair. "Do not cry, Heva. It will be all right."

"I'm sorry," she said between sobs. "I didn't mean to make you angry."

"Do not worry. It is all right."

"I won't make you angry again, Winter Wolf. I promise you. I will be a good wife to you."

Winter Wolf shook his head. Her voice was so full of fear and anguish, and her will had virtually been shattered. He had done this to her. "Rest now, Heva." He felt her body soften and her sobs lessen. Soon there was little sound from her except an occasional whimper. She had fallen asleep in his arms, his hands stroking her hair. The same hands and arms that had held her down and forced her to give herself to him, the same hands and arms that had beaten her until she was bruised and bleeding. He rested his head against hers, closing his eyes. He would find a way to make this up to her. She would not suffer at his hands again.

Anna had slept for most of the afternoon. She awakened feeling exhausted and sore. She didn't understand why Winter Wolf had suddenly changed his mind and decided not to punish her further, but she was grateful that he hadn't. She would do everything she could to make sure she pleased him, even if it meant giving herself to him.

She reached up and touched her lip. It was swollen and sore. Her head throbbed. She longed to go to Little Deer for medicine for the ache in her head, but she would not. She would not risk Winter Wolf's wrath again.

She looked up through the hole in the lodge. The sky was a dark blue. The sun was beginning to set. "Nathan!" she said to herself, sitting up. He expected her to meet him at sunset. If she didn't show up, he would come for her here.

She struggled to her feet, feeling the effects of her ordeal. She wrapped a blanket around her shoulders and ran her fingers through her hair, pulling it down around her face. Nathan wouldn't be able to see how badly bruised she was at night. If she could just convince him that everything was all right, hopefully he'd leave and she wouldn't have to worry about him.

Again she thought about escape, but it frightened her now more than ever. How would she get all the things she needed and hide them from Winter Wolf? She had seen his rage when he'd found out she was planning to leave. If he found that she was planning to leave again, he might kill her. No, for now she would have to be content being his wife, doing whatever he wanted her to do. Her life depended on it.

Nathan waited by the edge of the trees. It was almost dark and Anna was nowhere in sight. He knew he was putting her in danger by making her meet him, but he had to know the truth. If Winter Wolf had beaten her, Nathan knew he couldn't leave her here. Even if he had to kill Winter Wolf, he'd take Anna away.

He saw her coming toward him, a slight figure wrapped in a blanket. Her long dark hair hung almost down to her waist. She walked with her head down. When she reached him, she turned to face the camp, looking to see if Winter Wolf was anywhere around.

"What do you want, Nathan?"

"I want to make sure you're all right."

"I already told you I'm fine. Aren't you about to leave here?"

"I won't leave until I'm sure you're safe."

"Safe?" Anna whirled around angrily. "Safe? How can I ever be safe in a place where I don't belong? Damn you! How dare you blame me for being here. If I'd never met you, maybe my life would be different."

When she turned, her hair swung out from her face. Nathan gently pushed back the dark mane. Her jaw was swollen and already horribly discolored. Her bottom lip was red and puffy. One cheek had a bruise on it. He lowered his eyes and saw the faint redness around her neck. She tried to move away, but he held on to her, shoving the blanket aside. The red welt around her neck was still visible from the rope, even in the waning daylight. "What did he do to you?" He tried to control his rage, but he felt his blood pumping furiously.

"I told you before, he didn't do anything to me."

"I swear to you, Anna, if you don't tell me the truth right now, I'll go to him. Is that what you want?" He could see the fear in her eyes.

"I made him angry. It wasn't his fault."

"It wasn't his fault!?"

Anna grabbed Nathan's shirt. "Please, Nathan, it doesn't matter. I'll be fine. Don't say anything to him. If he finds out that I've talked to you, there's no telling what he'll do."

"He won't do anything to you, Anna. I won't let him touch you."

"You can't stop him. I'm his wife. You gave me back to him, remember?" The hurt in her voice was so obvious, it tore at Nathan's heart.

"I'm sorry. I didn't do it to hurt you."

"Then why did you do it?"

Nathan shook his head. "I thought I was doing the right thing. I didn't know what I was doing. I guess I just didn't want to see you get torn apart by us."

"I'm already being torn apart, Nathan."

"Tell me what happened, Anna. If you tell me, maybe I can help."

"You can't help me. No one can help me."

He put his hands on her shoulders. "Please, Anna."

Anna glanced toward the camp. "He found a bundle of food I was hiding. I was going to escape. I was going to try to get home on my own."

"Oh, Anna," Nathan said gently, touching her shoulder.

Anna shook his hand off, remembering how easily Nathan had turned her away. "He was convinced that you and I had planned our escape together. I told him that wasn't true, that you had turned me away, but he didn't believe me."

"So he hit you?"

"I said some things to make him angry. I shouldn't have spoken."

"Since when can't a wife voice her opinion to her husband?"

"We're in a Cheyenne camp, Nathan. Things are different here, or haven't you noticed?" She pulled the blanket tighter around her shoulders, constantly looking toward camp.

"How many times did he hit you?"

"What does it matter?"

"I want to know."

"I don't remember, two or three."

"Or more?"

"Nathan, please, it doesn't matter. I can accept it."

"Until the next time you make him angry, you mean?" He brought Anna close to him. "Did he do anything else to hurt you?"

She looked toward the camp, her eyes darting back and forth. "No."

"I know you, Anna."

"No, you don't know me," she cried, backing away from him. "If you had known me, you would've known how much it hurt me when you told me you didn't want me anymore. I loved you, Nathan."

"Anna—"

"No, don't say anything more. It doesn't matter. You decided to leave me here and I've decided to survive any way I know how, and I mean *any way*."

"What does that mean?"

"It means I'll be his wife, I'll be his slave, I'll . . ." She stopped.

"Go on, what else does it mean?" Nathan put his hand on her bruised cheek, caressing it softly. "I love you, Anna. I never stopped loving you. When I came here, I expected to find you and take you away. When I found out you were another man's wife, I couldn't believe it. It was as if I began to believe we weren't meant to be together. But when I saw you this morning with those bruises on your face, I knew I couldn't leave without you. You are part of me, Anna. You always will be." He could see her lips tremble and he could feel her

250

tears on his hand as they rolled down her cheeks.

"This doesn't change anything, Nathan. I can't go with you."

He drew her into his arms, holding her as he would a precious doll which had been broken. "He hurt you in some other way, didn't he?" He could feel her body tense when he asked the question. She tried to pull away, but he held her close. "Talk to me, Anna. I can't help you unless you talk to me. I promise you, I'll never desert you again." He felt her go limp in his arms as she fell to the ground. He knelt and held her, rocking her back and forth as she cried. "I'm sorry, Anna, I'm so sorry I hurt you."

She looked up at him. "He'll kill me when he finds out I've been with you, and he'll kill you, too. You have to leave here, Nathan."

"I'm not afraid of him."

"You *should* be afraid of him. He frightens me more than any person I've ever known. He likes to hurt people."

"He won't hurt you anymore."

"He can do anything he wants to me, just like he did last night."

"What did he do last night? Tell me."

"After he hit me, he forced me down on the floor." She lowered her head. "You know what he did to me, Nathan. You know."

Nathan felt the rage rise in him like a gathering storm. He held Anna in his arms. She was a tall woman, but she was thin, and right now, she seemed so very frail. It wouldn't take anything for a man like Winter Wolf to overpower her. He stroked her hair, kissing the top of her had. "It's all right, Anna. It's all right."

She raised her face, her sobs choking off her words. "It hurt, Nathan. It hurt so badly."

He tightened his hold on her, closing his eyes, trying

to blot out the picture of Winter Wolf forcing himself on Anna. But no matter how hard he tried, a vivid picture of the Cheyenne raping Anna formed in his mind. He couldn't believe this was happening to her again. She had been through it once in San Francisco, when the captain of a slave boat bought her. It had taken her a long time to get over that, and now she had to face it all over again. He couldn't believe Winter Wolf would do this to Anna. He was sure the man cared for her. What had made him hurt her in such a way?

"I have to go back, Nathan. He'll come looking for me."

"You're not going back there. You're staying with me."

"I can't. Nathan, these are his people. They will listen to whatever he says. Please, I'll be all right as long as I know you aren't going to leave me here."

"You're not going back to him, Anna."

"Just for tonight, do as I say. He won't hurt me again."

"How do you know that?"

"I just know."

"What about tomorrow?"

"Tomorrow we'll decide what to do next." She put her face close to his. "I want our life back, Nathan."

"So do I." He kissed her very gently, then stood up, pulling her up with him. "Are you sure? You don't have to go back to him."

"I'm sure."

He watched her as she walked back to the camp. He couldn't stand the thought of her going back to Winter Wolf for another night, but he knew she was probably right. He just needed a little time to plan their escape and soon they would leave this place. But he had to be careful. He had to make Winter Wolf believe that he still wanted to leave, that he didn't care about Anna

252

anymore.

He had already found a way out. He would take his horses and tie them in the woods. From there, they would walk about a mile upstream and cross the river. No one would see them there, and if they left at night, they'd have a good start. If they traveled wisely, Winter Wolf would never find them.

Suddenly, there were no good memories for him here. The only good memories he had were of Anna and his family at the ranch. He couldn't wait until they went back home.

Chapter 11

Rachel looked at the clock. It was almost seven. Roberto would be here soon to pick her up. Since she had returned to working in her office, he was bound and determined to drive her in and pick her up at night. She had to admit that she was getting to enjoy it. Tonight he had promised to take her to the restaurant at the hotel. She'd never eaten there; it had always seemed too fancy for her, but she said she'd go.

During the day, she'd gone to the ladies' clothing store in town and shopped for a dress. She felt strange in her pants, shirt, and hat, but the owner, Miss Devereaux, had been very kind and helped her try on different outfits. They had decided on a deep green linen dress with puffed sleeves that went to the elbow. The neckline was rounded and a bit low for her, but the dress accentuated her petite figure. The short jacket that matched the dress was cut in at the waist and buttoned up to the bodice, looking very much like a long-sleeved vest. She had to admit that it looked very striking on her. Miss Devereaux had talked her into buying a cameo necklace and earrings, and she had even talked Rachel into doing her hair. She'd made her sit in one of the chairs by the hat counter, and she'd brushed her hair in an assortment of styles until she decided on one she liked. She had brushed back the top and sides and fastened them with a green bow in back. She'd brushed the rest of Rachel's soft brown hair so that it fell softly around her shoulders.

Now, as Rachel looked at the clock, she hurried into the examining room and changed. She refused to wear one of those ridiculous corsets with bones and stays, but she did buy a beautiful lace slip and underwear. She even bought herself a pair of stockings, which she hated to put on, but after she'd tied the dainty strings in her new boots and managed to zip herself into her new dress, she felt good. She put on her jacket and buttoned it up until only her bare neck and part of her chest showed. After she fastened the cameo necklace around her neck and slipped on the earrings, she went to the washbowl and turned up the lamp, staring into the mirror. She couldn't believe her eyes. She actually looked pretty. She smiled and scrutinized her teeth, making sure they were clean. She brushed her hair until it looked soft and shiny, then she slapped her cheeks to give them some color. Finally, she took a deep breath and walked out into the waiting room. Roberto was standing there, looking at a picture of the human skeleton, when she walked in.

He looked handsome in gray suit and boots. His dark skin and hair made him look rather exotic. The Indian in him stood out quite obviously. There was something darkly exciting about him.

"I'm ready," she said nervously, hoping that he'd approve of her appearance. She knew that he'd traveled a lot and that he'd probably been with lots of women. She also knew that she wasn't beautiful, and she wondered why Roberto showed such interest in her.

Roberto turned and stared at Rachel, his eyes registering his surprise. He smiled slowly, nodding his head. "You look great, Doc." He smirked and cocked his head. "Sorry. I mean Rachel."

"Thank you. You do, too. I mean, you look quite handsome." She couldn't believe she felt like such a young girl when she was with this man.

"Well, I have a table reserved for us at the hotel restaurant. Are you ready?"

"Yes." She turned down the lamps in the office and locked the door. She took Roberto's arm as they walked down the sidewalk, their feet making a pounding noise on the wooden planks. It felt good to be walking again without pain. And it felt good to be working. But what felt best of all was to be out with a man like Roberto, a man who genuinely liked her.

They walked into the lobby of the hotel and past the desk. They stopped at the entrance to the restaurant, where Roberto gave his name. The head waiter eyed Rachel suspiciously.

"Is that you, Dr. Foster?"

Rachel felt herself blush. "Yes, William, it's me."

"You look real pretty tonight, Doc. Can't remember the last time I saw you—"

"Thank you, William," Rachel interrupted him. "Could you show us to our table now?"

They followed behind William. Rachel was aware of the stares they drew. She wasn't sure if it was because she was dressed up or because Roberto was so handsome. William stopped in front of their table, ready to pull out Rachel's chair, but Roberto stepped in, seating Rachel himself. When they were both seated and William had handed them their menus, Rachel looked around the room. The round tables were set near the walls, each lit by a pair of candles in a silver holder. Snowy linen napkins lay beneath sparkling silver dinnerware. The rich, muted colors of the brocade that covered the walls formed a backdrop for the bright colors of the women's dresses. Each woman was like a flower in an evening meadow.

"Haven't you ever been in here before?"

Rachel shrugged her shoulders. "I don't have time to eat here. I always order food from the saloon. It's quicker, and I don't have to worry about how I look."

"You really do look lovely, Rachel. I can't believe you hide behind all those old clothes."

"I'm not hiding behind them. I told you before, it's just easier to dress up like a man when I'm riding around the countryside. I feel safer."

"But you're in town most of the time. Why don't you wear a dress when you're in your office?"

"I wasn't aware that wearing a dress would make me a better doctor," she snapped. She picked up her menu and opened it.

"You know I didn't mean that."

Rachel looked at him over the top of the menu. "What did you mean then?"

Roberto reached out and took her hand. She tried to pull it away, but he held on to it. "I think you're a beautiful woman and I don't understand why you try to hide it. You should be proud of yourself, Rachel."

Her eyes met Roberto's, and she felt as if she were drowning. She had never seen such beautiful brown eyes in her life. The touch of his hand frightened her. She felt things with Roberto that she'd never felt in her life. She looked around the room, trying to regain her composure. All around her, couples were laughing and talking, genuinely enjoying each other's company. Why couldn't she do the same thing?

"Would you like to order now, sir?"

Rachel quickly snatched her hand away when the waiter appeared. She looked at Roberto. He looked incredibly at ease.

"We haven't had a chance to look at the menu. What do you recommend?"

"The stuffed quail is excellent, sir."

"How does that sound, Rachel?"

"That would be fine, yes."

"We'd also like a bottle of your best champagne."

"You seem at home here," Rachel observed.

"I've traveled a bit. Lived in the South for a time. That's where I acquired my taste for champagne."

"You've done a lot of things, haven't you?"

"A lot of things I wish I'd never done."

"But at least you've done them. I feel as though I've just watched my life go by."

"I wouldn't call being a doctor watching life go by. You help to save lives, Rachel. That's very admirable."

"Sometimes I'd rather be more than admirable."

"It's never too late to change."

They watched in silence as the waiter came with the champagne bucket. He popped the cork and poured it into their glasses. Roberto held his glass up.

"A toast."

Rachel held her glass next to Roberto's. "To what?"

"To living life," he said, clanking his glass against hers.

Rachel watched Roberto as he drank from the champagne glass. She lifted hers to her mouth and felt the tiny bubbles burst against her nose. She sipped at the bubbling liquid, amazed at how good it tasted. She sipped again, feeling as if she were about to begin an exciting adventure.

"What do you think?"

"It's good."

"Just good?"

"Why, should it be more than good?"

"It's a very expensive bottle of champagne. I thought it would impress you more than that."

"I'm not used to champagne, Roberto. I don't know anything about it."

"Haven't you ever had it before?"

"No," she said, feeling slightly embarrassed.

"Well, I'm glad to be the first person you drink it with."

Rachel smiled. "Me, too." She finished her glass and set it down. "Would you pour me some more?"

"You should take it easy. It tastes so good you don't think it'll do much, but it'll make you as drunk as a half bottle of whiskey."

"A few glasses won't hurt me. I drink wine at home." She held her glass out, smiling at Roberto. She watched him as he deftly poured the liquid into her glass. His hands were dark and strong, the fingers long and slim. She wondered how his hands would feel on her body. She felt her face flush, shocked at her own wicked thoughts.

"Are you all right? You're cheeks are bright red."

258

Rachel looked around her, fanning herself with her hand. "It's just the champagne." She picked up the refilled glass and drank half of it.

"Take it easy, Rachel. You haven't even had dinner yet."

Rachel nodded, setting her glass down. "I guess I'm a little nervous about being here."

"Why should you be nervous? You could fit in anywhere."

"But I don't fit in anywhere, Roberto. I'm different."

"So am I. I don't let that stop me and neither do you."

"But I do."

"If you did, you wouldn't be a doctor today, would you?"

Rachel smiled gratefully. "I suppose not." She studied Roberto's handsome face, wondering if she could ask him something that had been on her mind for a long time. "Tell me about Anna."

Roberto looked up, obviously caught off guard. "Why do you want to know about Anna?"

"I'm curious what kind of woman gets two men like you and Nathan to fall in love with her."

"That's just it, she didn't get us to fall in love with her. We just did."

"Please tell me what she's like, Roberto."

Roberto stared past Rachel into some unknown place. "Anna is unlike any woman I've ever known. She's so pretty. She has dark hair and blue eyes, and she's so full of life." He shook his head. "She's the most unselfish person I know. When she loves, she loves with all her heart and soul. She'll do anything for the people she loves."

"How do you get over a love like that?"

"I suppose you never do," Roberto said absently. "There's probably a part of me that will always love Anna."

Rachel nodded to herself, staring into her champagne glass. "She's a lucky woman."

"No, she's not a lucky woman. She's had some horrible things happen to her, Rachel. If she's loved, it's because she deserves to be loved."

They were silent all through dinner and Rachel realized

that she had touched a raw nerve. Roberto was obviously still very much in love with Anna. When the waiter had cleared the table, Rachel finished her fifth glass of champagne. She realized that she felt very strange. She'd never drunk enough of any alcohol in her life to know what it was like to be drunk, but she was afraid she had passed that point tonight. Her body felt incredibly loose, and she almost felt giddy as she looked across the table at Roberto.

"Do you forgive me yet?" she asked boldly.

"Forgive you for what?"

"For asking you about Anna."

"There's nothing to forgive. You didn't do anything wrong."

"Are you sure?"

"I'm sure. Would you like some dessert?"

"No, if I have dessert, I think I'll be sick. Besides, I have that blackberry pie at home I made yesterday."

"Do you want to go home?"

"I suppose. Why, did you have something else in mind?"

"I thought we'd walk around the town. We can even walk past the saloon and look inside."

Rachel smiled. "I'd like that."

Roberto paid the bill and escorted Rachel out of the restaurant. She took his arm as they began to walk, and a peculiar sense of well-being came over her. She felt comfortable with him. They walked up and down both sides of the street. The town was growing. There were smaller restaurants, the general mercantile, the ladies' clothing and yard goods store, the barber shop with a carved wooden tooth on the sign, indicating that the barber also served the town as dentist. Rachel wanted to stop and look into the window of the shoe store, but she felt timid when Roberto didn't pause. They walked on past the bank, now dark and shuttered for the night. They crossed the street and started back toward the center of town, passing a lawyer's office, a millinery shop, a candy store, a bakery, the livery, the train station, her office, the telegraph office, and finally a decent distance from the other businesses, the saloon.

Roberto peeked over the doors and laughed.

"What is it?"

"There's a man dancing on one of the tables."

Rachel peeked over the lowest part of the swinging doors. "That's old Jeb McGiver. He's been married to the same woman for over thirty years. He has five daughters and numerous grandchildren, and he still comes to this saloon at least three times a week."

"Bet you could write a book about the people who frequent this place." Roberto gave a long, low whistle. "Who's that dark woman dressed in blue standing by the piano?"

"That's Yvette. She came here about a year ago from Louisiana. She's part Creole."

"She's a beauty."

Rachel watched Roberto's face as he stared at Yvette. He looked at her in a way that left nothing to the imagination. She looked over at Yvette again and understood why. She was a tall woman with a beautiful figure. Her skin was dark and her oval eyes were almost black. When she smiled, she revealed beautiful white teeth and a full, sensual mouth.

She had treated Yvette on several occasions. She had acute asthma. When the weather turned cold, she almost always had some serious attacks. But Yvette had never complained. Rachel had always liked her and admired her courage. She also liked her animated way of talking and gesturing, but right now, she envied her. She wished that just once she could know what it was like to have a man look at her the way Roberto was looking at Yvette.

Rachel watched as Yvette walked toward Jeb McGiver. She did her best to coax him down from the table. People were now enjoying watching the old man make a fool out of himself and they weren't about to let a saloon girl stop him.

One of the regulars, a man named Pete, grabbed Yvette by the arm and yanked her away. Yvette stood up to the man trying to reason with him. Rachel touched Roberto's arm. She knew what would happen if Yvette got overly ex-

261

cited.

"Why don't you go in and help her, Roberto?"

"She seems fine to me."

"She doesn't need this."

Roberto looked at Rachel. "Rachel, she's used to taking care of herself."

"Fine!" Rachel yelled, pushing through the swinging doors. She walked up to Pete, grabbing his arm as he was about to shove Yvette. "Leave her alone, Pete."

"Who the hell are . . ." He lowered his hand, narrowing his eyes under the brim of his hat. "Is that you, Doc?"

"It's me, Pete, and if you don't leave Yvette alone right now, I'll have to tell the good people of this town the reason you were in my office the last time." As small as she was, Rachel cast an imposing figure.

Pete let got of Yvette's arm. "Didn't mean no harm, Doc. We was just having fun with Jeb here."

"Well, the fun's over." Rachel walked over to the table. "Get down from there right now, Jeb McGiver. Isn't it about time you grew up? What would your grandchildren think if they saw you up there dancing like a fool?"

The old man sheepishly climbed down from the table. Ignoring Rachel, he walked over to the bar.

Rachel walked up to Yvette. She could see that her face was pale and her breathing was becoming raspy. "Come with me, Yvette."

Yvette shook her head. "I can't, Dr. Foster. I need the money."

"Don't argue with me." She took Yvette's arm and led her out of the saloon. She took her key out of her purse and handed it to Roberto. "Would you please run ahead and open my office. Turn up a lamp and turn on the stove so I can boil some water."

"Do you want me to carry her?"

"No, Roberto," Rachel answered sharply, "just please do as I ask."

"I don't need your help, Dr. Foster. If Miss Madeline finds out that I have a disease, she won't let me work."

"She won't find out from me, and how many times do I have to tell you, call me Rachel." She led Yvette into her office. Already the young woman was beginning to wheeze and Rachel could see the panic that was about to consume her. "I want you to relax, Yvette. We've made it through this every other time, haven't we?"

Yvette nodded her head, putting a hand to her throat.

"You must force yourself to relax." She led Yvette up the steps to her office. "Go on back to the examining room. I'll be right with you."

Rachel took off her jacket and put on her apron. She went to the stove in the corner and tested the water. She looked at Roberto, who had already taken off his jacket and rolled up his sleeves. He was ready to help. "There's a large bowl in the examining room. Would you please bring it here?" Rachel went to her cabinet and brought out a small bottle. She unscrewed the top and waited for Roberto to return. When he came back with the bowl, she poured half the bottle into it, then set it down on top of the stove. She poured the steaming water into the bowl and immediately a pungent and spicy odor filled the air.

"What the hell is that?"

"It's eucalyptus oil. It'll help Yvette to breathe. Grab one of the towels from the cupboard in the examining room. You might be able to help me."

Rachel could hear Yvette wheezing, gasping for air, as she entered the examining room. She was sitting on the edge of the table, her hands around her throat. Her eyes were large and filled with fear. Rachel went to her, moving her back on the table. She placed the large, steaming bowl between Yvette's legs. "I want you to relax, Yvette. You know this will help you. I'm right here." She took the towel from Roberto and put it over Yvette's head, forcing her to breathe in the pungent steam from the bowl. Rachel rubbed Yvette's back with a soothing hand. "It will be all right. I won't leave you." She looked up and caught Roberto's eye. There was something different there, a look she'd never seen before. She smiled, and when he smiled back,

263

she actually felt her heart flutter. She looked down at Yvette. "Keep breathing, Yvette Just relax." Rachel stood with Yvette for over an hour until the woman had begun to breathe more normally. She handed the bowl to Roberto and took the towel from Yvette's head, wiping the tear-streaked make-up from her face. She walked to the wash-bowl and dipped the towel in until it was wet, then walked back to Yvette. She kept wiping until Yvette's face was clear of all make-up. "There. You're so pretty without all that."

Yvette looked up at Rachel, her exotic eyes showing her fear. "Thank you, Rachel. I don't know what I'd do without you."

"Yvette, you have to get out of that saloon. I told you before that it's going to kill you. You have to stay away from situations that are going to excite you."

"But what can I do? I'm not like you. I'm not fit for anything else but this."

"I don't believe that. You're smart and you're attractive. There are lots of things you could do."

"Like what? You know no one's going to hire a woman like me." She shook her head. "My father always said I wasn't fit for anything."

Rachel put her arm around Yvette. "Listen to me, Yvette. I had a father who said the same thing to me. He only made me want to try harder. Don't let something that ignorant man said to you years ago make you miserable forever."

"But what do I do?"

"You can start by quitting that job at the saloon and working for me."

"What?"

"I'm starting to get very busy here. You can take care of the people who come in until I'm ready to treat them. I'll also train you to help me in the examining room. I assume that after all the fights you've seen in the saloon, blood won't bother you."

Yvette smiled for the first time. "No, blood doesn't

264

bother me. I can't believe you'd do that for me."

"I can't pay you very much right now. The people around here don't always pay me on time, but—"

"No, no, it doesn't matter," Yvette interrupted. "I've got some money saved. I'll get by." She reached over and hugged Rachel. "Thank you. I'll work very hard for you. You won't be sorry."

"I know I won't be sorry." She smiled as Roberto helped Yvette down from the table. "I want you to move out of that saloon and into the boardinghouse. It's real nice there. It even has a nice little salon with windows you can use when you need to sit in the sun."

"I don't think Mrs. Perkins will let me move in there. She only takes 'nice' ladies."

"You *are* a nice lady, Yvette. Don't worry about Mrs. Perkins. She'll let you take a room."

"Thank you, Rachel." She smiled at Roberto and left.

Rachel sat on the table, swinging her legs back and forth, feeling like a small girl. Roberto looked at her, a wide grin on his face. "What? Why are you smiling like that?" she asked.

"I don't think I've ever seen anyone as beautiful as you look right now."

Rachel felt her cheeks grow warm with the flush of embarrassment. "I don't compare to Yvette. She's a truly beautiful woman."

Roberto put his hands on either side of Rachel on the table. He leaned forward so that his face was very close to hers. "You're right. You don't compare to her. You're much better."

Rachel felt the sweet anticipation of Roberto's kiss, but it didn't come. She looked up at him. He was staring at her with his dark eyes. "What are you staring at?"

"I loved watching you work. You're a very competent woman. Smart, too. I like that."

"Most men don't like it."

"Most men aren't me."

"So I've noticed." She smiled, suddenly feeling pretty. "I

have a bottle of brandy in my cabinet. Would you like a glass?"

"I'm surprised at you, Doc."

"It's purely for medicinal purposes." Rachel hopped down from the table and went to the other room. She unlocked the cabinet and brought out the bottle of brandy. She took out two small glasses that she kept in her desk drawer and filled them with the brandy. When she got back in the other room, Roberto was sitting on the table. She sat next to him, handing him a glass. "To living life," she said, touching her glass to his.

Roberto nodded and sniffed the brandy. "I'd like to help you, Rachel."

"What do you mean?"

"I have a lot of money and I need to do something with it. What if I give you enough money so you can pay Yvette for a year?" He looked around him. "And this place could use some new furniture. In fact, the whole place could stand to be redone."

"That's very generous, Roberto, but I couldn't possibly accept money from you."

"I heard you say there are some new instruments you'd like to order from the East. You could order all of the latest equipment, Rachel. Just think of it. You'd not only be the only woman doctor around here, you'd be the most modern."

Rachel smiled slightly. The idea was very appealing. "And if I agree, what do you want in return?"

"I've already gotten enough from you. You saved my life and you've put up with me for the past couple of months. It's the least I can do."

"There are some things I saw in my medical catalogue that would be wonderful to have. I could treat people and not have to worry if they could pay me."

"I thought that's what you did anyway."

Rachel shrugged her shoulders. "That's the way it is out here, but you get paid in other ways. Sometimes I'll see a little baby that's healthy and I know it's because I was there

266

to deliver it, or I'll see someone that I performed surgery on and they've healed well. I suppose that's the real reason I went into medicine."

"Well, we'll go to the bank tomorrow and set up an account just for you and your practice. I'll have to wire my bank in Louisiana, but it shouldn't take too much time."

"I can't believe you're doing this. It's a wonderfully unselfish thing to do."

Roberto smiled roguishly. "It's not completely unselfish." He leaned forward and kissed Rachel.

Rachel closed her eyes and reveled in the feel of Roberto's lips against hers. The brandy glass tipped and the liqueur spilled on Roberto's lap. "Oh, I'm sorry. I didn't mean to . . ." She started to wipe up the liqueur from his legs, but pulled her hand back.

Roberto took her hand, laughing. "It's all right. I've never had a woman so lost in my kiss that she spilled her brandy on me." He took the glass from her hand and put it on the table. He put his hands on her face and drew it close, kissing her deeply.

Rachel held onto his arms. She couldn't believe this was happening to her. She couldn't believe that someone like Roberto would find her attractive. His mouth moved to her neck, caressing it softly, and she closed her eyes. "Maybe it's time to go home," she said, letting her head fall back as Roberto kissed her throat.

"I guess we should," he said, tracing the line of her jaw.

She put her hands on Roberto's face. "Uncle Zeb won't be there."

"Where is he?"

"He's gone off somewhere with Lyle. When he does that I don't see him for weeks sometimes." She brushed her fingers through his hair. "And tomorrow's Sunday. I won't come into the office unless someone needs me."

Roberto stood up, placing his hands on Rachel's waist and lifting her down from the table. "Let's go home."

Rachel locked her cabinet and turned down the lamps. She got her purse and medical bag and walked to the wagon while Roberto locked the office. Exchanging few words, they rode back to the ranch, enjoying the cool, clear night and the sounds of the creatures who lived in it. She heard an owl hoot in a tree as they drove by and the frantic yips of the coyotes in the hills as they stalked their prey. She put her arm through Roberto's and laid her head on his shoulder. She was surprised how comfortable she was with him. She was even more surprised at how attracted she was to him.

She closed her eyes and let herself relax as the jolting of the wagon rocked the seat. She tightened her hold on Roberto's arm, feeling the strength in it, yet knowing the gentleness that was there.

The ride to town usually took an hour by horse, an hour by wagon. But this night the hour seemed to fly by. Rachel couldn't believe it when they pulled into the yard. Roberto jumped down, lifting her from the wagon.

"I'll unhitch the horses and be right in."

Rachel nodded and hurried into the house. She walked upstairs to her room, turning up the lamp illuminating the staircase just enough to see. She opened her hope chest and dug down inside. She came out with a wrapped package. She took off the paper and held up a beautiful, white lace nightgown. It was something she had bought in Boston when she was going to school. She had always thought she would wear it on her wedding night, but she decided she would wear it tonight.

She quickly undressed and slipped on the gown, tying the delicate white ribbons on the front. She took off the cameo necklace and earrings and let down her hair and brushed it out. Then she sat down on the window seat that overlooked the woods, waiting nervously.

She heard Roberto as he came into the house and shut the door, then his footsteps on the stairs. She closed her eyes as he walked toward her room. She wanted to be beautiful for him. She didn't want to disappoint him.

"Rachel?"

She turned to look at him, realizing that in the dim

light, Roberto couldn't see her sitting on the window seat. "I'm over here." She watched him walk across the room, throwing his jacket on the bed as he crossed. He took her hands and pulled her up.

"Come into the light," he said.

Rachel walked into the light. She watched Roberto's eyes as he looked at her. He seemed pleased. She looked at him. "I don't want to disappoint you, Roberto."

"You won't."

"You don't understand, I've never done this before." She took her hands from his, wringing them in front of her. "I had more than a few chances in medical school, but I wanted to be with a man who I respected and loved." She closed her eyes, embarrassed at her slip of the tongue.

"I'm glad you waited." Roberto's voice was soft and caressing. He leaned down and kissed Rachel, wrapping his arms around her. "I think I'm in love with you, Doc."

Rachel thought she was going to cry. She wasn't sure she had ever felt such joy in her life. She looked up at Roberto. "No matter what happens, thank you for this. Thank you for making me feel wanted."

Roberto bent down and lifted Rachel into his arms. "You are wanted, Rachel." He carried her to the bed, lying her down.

Rachel watched as Roberto took off his shirt. He had a beautiful body, and it looked bronze in the dim light. He sat down on the bed and took off his boots, then his pants. She had seen his unclothed body before, but this time it was different. This time he wasn't her patient, this time he was her lover.

He lay down next to her, patiently untying the bows that held the nightgown's bodice together. He lowered his head to her breasts, and Rachel moaned with pleasure as he kissed and caressed her. His hands explored her body, and she found she wasn't afraid. His touch was gentle and exciting. She was ready for this. She wasn't a child; she was a woman. When Roberto pushed her nightgown up to her hips, she knew it was time. She didn't resist as he moved

269

atop her, resting most of his weight on his hands. His mouth sought hers in the darkness and she gave it to him, just as she gave herself to him when he finally entered her. She moved her body with his, unable to believe that this was what she had heard women complain about for so long. This didn't seem like a chore to her, something to be done because it was a duty. Instead, it seemed a pleasure. It was incredible to her that she could feel this close to another human being, that they could be feeling the same thing together. She wrapped her arms tightly around Roberto's neck as he moved faster inside her. The pleasure was so intense that she thought she would scream and, indeed, when the time finally came, she cried out, feeling him pull her body even closer to his until she heard him say her name. Their bodies were warm and wet and she delighted in the feel, still amazed that this was what it was all about. She was a doctor, yet she had had no idea that being with a man could be so wonderful.

Roberto rolled to the side, pulling her close to him. He kissed her forehead, pushing her damp hair away from her face. "Are you all right?"

Rachel laughed. "Yes."

"You're sure? I didn't hurt you?"

"No, Roberto, you didn't hurt me. It was wonderful. I never knew that it was supposed to be like that."

"It isn't always like that, Rachel."

"Oh," she said, embarrassed, realizing that Roberto had had many other women.

"Are you sure you've never been with a man before?"

"Of course I'm sure . . ." She stopped. "Why?"

"Because you seemed to enjoy it more than most women I've been with who get paid for it."

Rachel thought for a moment. "I'm not sure if that was a compliment or not."

"It was a compliment."

She reached up and ran her fingers through his hair. "So, where do we go from here?"

"There's only one place we can go."

Rachel wasn't sure she wanted to hear the answer. "Where?"

"To a church to get married."

"But we don't even know each other."

"Oh, I think we know each other real well."

Rachel felt herself blush. "Marriage? I've never even thought about marriage."

"Yes, you have. You just never thought you'd do it."

"But I want to keep practicing medicine."

"I know that. Why do you think I offered to help you? I'm sure I can start some kind of a business here, and this old house could use some real fixing up. We could build more rooms and I'm sure Zeb could do with a bigger barn."

"Let's not rush into anything. You may wake up tomorrow and be sorry that you ever said anything."

"I'll never be sorry where you're concerned, Doc." Roberto kissed her deeply.

Rachel closed her eyes and wrapped her arms around him. This man, this incredibly handsome and gentle man, loved her and wanted to marry her. She was afraid to ever open her eyes and leave this room again. She was afraid it was all a dream.

Anna hurried to the lodge. Winter Wolf and a few other men were sitting by the cook fire in front. She lowered her head, unable to look at them. She went inside. What would he do if he found out she was with Nathan? She wasn't sure she could take another beating. She thought about getting her small knife, but she knew that she wasn't quick or strong enough to use it against him. She had told Nathan that Winter Wolf wouldn't hurt her, but now that she was back in the lodge, she wasn't so sure. She sat on the mat, pulling her blanket around her shoulders. She rocked back and forth. The nights were so much cooler now. It seemed as if she was never warm anymore. She heard the voices and laughter from outside and she knew the men were getting ready to leave. She steeled herself for another confrontation with Winter Wolf. When he entered the lodge he was carrying a small bowl. He handed it to her.

"Drink this. It will warm you."

Silently, she took it from him. She sipped at the hot, bitter tea that she knew Little Deer had brewed for her. Winter Wolf knelt beside her, lifting the robe from the mat and draping it around her shoulders. It was heavy, but it was warm. "Thank you," she said softly, still holding the warm bowl between her cold hands. She felt the weight of his hands on her shoulders, and her heart sank. She didn't want him to force her again.

"What should I do with you, Heva?" His voice was gentle, with no edge of hardness to it.

She wondered if he expected an answer. "I told you I would be your wife, Winter Wolf. I will do as you ask."

"You would do anything to protect the white man, wouldn't you?" His hands gripped her shoulders through the heavy robe.

She closed her eyes. He knew. He knew that she had been with Nathan. "No, I just don't want to be punished again. I don't want to make you angry."

"If that is so, what were you doing in the woods with the white man, Heva? Were you planning your escape again?"

Anna felt a stabbing pain in her stomach. It was going to begin again. He would beat her senseless. "No, he wanted to know about the bruises on my face. I told him I fell down."

"Did he ask you to leave with him, Heva?"

"He said he would be leaving soon and if I needed his help I could go with him."

"And what did you say?"

"I told him I am your wife and I will stay here with you." Winter Wolf removed the robe and blanket from Anna's shoulders. She felt his fingers dig into her skin. She wanted to make him stop. "I told him that I would have your children," she lied, hoping to make him stop.

"You told the white man this?"

"Yes."

"Why would you tell him such a thing?"

"Because I am your wife. I told you I will do anything you ask of me, Winter Wolf. I just don't want you to be angry with me again."

Winter Wolf turned her face around. "You would have my children, Heva? You would stay with me willingly and have my children?"

"Yes," she said, her voice quavering. She didn't want to have his children, but if it meant that Nathan would go free, she would do anything he wanted her to do.

"And what of your plans to escape?"

"I can't leave on my own. I don't know the way. I don't even know how to hunt."

"But you were willing to try once before."

"I was angry at you and at Nathan."

"But you are no longer angry?"

"No, I just want to live in peace." She hesitated. "I want to please you."

"But you do please me, Heva. You please me very much."

Anna closed her eyes as she felt Winter Wolf's hands slip underneath her dress and touch her bare shoulders. This was something that would never change. She would have to endure his touch and his brutal manner of taking her. This man awakened nothing in her but fear. It was hard for her to remember when she cared for him, when his touch was gentle, when his voice was kind. She felt him pull her back against him and his arms go around her. He didn't hurt her, he just held her. She opened her eyes. What new game was this? Was he trying to frighten her even more?

"You must do something for me, Heva."

"What?" She was afraid to know the answer.

"I want to see for myself that you do not care for the white man. I want you to tell him that you no longer desire him. I want to hear you say it." His mouth was close to her ear. "I want you to make him believe it, Heva. I want no acting from you this time. If you do not convince him to

273

leave, I will kill him. If you think that my father will protect him, you are wrong. It would be very simple to kill the white man. All my warriors hate him as much as I do. We could take him into the woods at night and torture him. There are many things we could do to him. Have you heard of some of these things?"

"Yes," she answered, remembering the stories Aeneva had told her of the ways the Cheyennes and their enemies tortured each other.

"Do you understand that this is not a game to me? I have chosen you for my woman and I expect loyalty from you. Do you understand me, Heva?"

Anna tried to control the shaking of her body. Winter Wolf's arms were locked around her so tightly she felt as if she were imprisoned. "Yes, Winter Wolf, I understand. I will do as you say."

"Good. We will do it now."

"Now?"

"Yes, I want to know that you are truly mine, Heva." Winter Wolf stood up, helping Anna to her feet. He reached for the blanket and wrapped it around her shoulders. "When we return to this lodge tonight, I will make you mine forever."

Anna felt as if her heart had just been ripped out of her body. She had no choice. She had to make Nathan believe that she wanted to stay with Winter Wolf or he would be murdered. But how could she do it? She had just said she would go away with him. How could she make him believe that all she had said was a lie?

"Let us go to the white man, Heva."

Winter Wolf led her though the camp, lit only by an occasional campfire. They walked in the darkness to the edge of the trees. It was always curious and eerie to Anna how Winter Wolf seemed to be able to see in the dark. When they reached the front of the lodge, Winter Wolf shoved Anna forward. She prayed for some inner strength to guide her through this. She looked for Winter Wolf but couldn't see him. He was in the darkness somewhere, waiting, listening.

She stood next to the flap of the lodge. "Nathan, it's Anna. I have to talk to you."

There was movement inside the lodge and Nathan appeared at the flap. His chest was bare and he was wearing only buckskin pants. It was obvious that he didn't see Winter Wolf standing off to the side. "Anna, are you all right? Come."

"No, I can't. Just let me say what I've come to say."

"What is it? Did he hurt you again?"

"I can't go away with you, Nathan. I'm going to stay here with Winter Wolf."

"I know he's making you say that."

"He's not making me say it. I'm staying because I want to. He's been kind to me. He saved my life."

"He's beaten and raped you! Is this the kind of man you want to stay with?"

Anna cringed as he spoke. Winter Wolf would now know that she'd told Nathan the truth. But she couldn't worry about that now. She had to convince Nathan to leave. "He didn't rape me, Nathan."

"What? I saw you this evening. The man has hurt you."

"No, he hasn't. Last night wasn't the first time with him, Nathan," she lied.

Nathan was quiet. His tall, lean form was outlined in the entrance to the lodge. "He didn't rape you? What did he do then?"

"That's just it, he didn't do anything. He wanted to make love and at first I didn't want to. But then I did. He's my husband, Nathan." She couldn't see Nathan's face in the shadows of the lodge, but she could imagine his expression.

"You've been with him before?"

"Yes."

"How many times?" His voice was loud and angry.

"Nathan—"

"How many, Anna?" His voice grew louder in the quiet night.

"I don't know, but almost from the beginning. At first I

275

felt I owed it to him, and then I began to desire him."

"I don't believe you. You're lying. What about the bruises?"

"I got in a fight with one of the women. Her name is Bright Leaf. I found out she was sleeping with Winter Wolf. It made me angry."

"You were lying to me? Jesus, Anna, I was ready to kill that man. What's happened to you? I don't know you anymore."

Anna couldn't still the tears that rolled down her cheeks. She was thankful that it was dark and Nathan couldn't see her. "I don't know you either, Nathan. That's why you should go back to Arizona." She walked away, ignoring Winter Wolf who was still standing to the side in the darkness. She heard Nathan's footsteps and she felt his hand on her arm.

"Wait!" he said, his voice full of anger and frustration. "Anna, I know you. I heard what you said this evening. I heard the fear and anguish in your voice. You weren't lying."

She couldn't turn to face him. "I was angry at Winter Wolf. I knew if I came to you and he found out about it, he would be jealous. I had to make it seem real. He loves me Nathan. He'll take care of me."

Nathan shook his head. "He'll kill you, Anna. I know you're lying. You're lying because you're scared. If you think this is going to work, you're wrong. I'll stay here for as long as it takes, and I'll watch you. If I ever see that anything is wrong, I swear I'll kill him."

"Nathan, don't. You can't kill him. You can't get close enough to him." She had to be careful what she said. "I want to stay with him, Nathan. When I was hurt in the river, he saved my life. He was gentle with me. He's a good man."

"I'm not leaving, Anna. No matter what you say, I'm not leaving."

Anna turned around and looked toward the lodge. She couldn't see Winter Wolf in the darkness, but she knew he was there, listening to every word. "You don't have a choice anymore, Nathan. I'm going to have his child," she lied, knowing how much she had just hurt Nathan. How many times had they talked of having children together? Now he was going to leave thinking that she was having Winter Wolf's child.

"No," he protested, "I don't believe you. You wouldn't do that. You wouldn't have another man's child."

"But I am having another man's child, Nathan, and there's nothing you can do about it."

"Why, Anna? Why would you do this?"

"I needed him, Nathan. I was alone and I was frightened. You weren't there. Winter Wolf was."

"And that's supposed to make me feel better? I'm supposed to ride away from this godforsaken place and just forget that I ever loved you?" He pulled Anna to him, his face close to hers. "I know you love me, Anna. I don't know what you're trying to do here, but I do know that you love me."

"A part of me will always love you, Nathan. But you were right. Maybe we weren't meant to be together." She reached up and touched his cheek, trying to control her trembling voice. "Have a good life, Nathan. I want you to be happy." She walked back to Winter Wolf's lodge, never turning around to look at Nathan again. She didn't want to remember him angry. She wanted to remember him as she always had—with light hair and eyes the color of the sky.

She went into the lodge and walked around, unable to control her shaking body. She tried not to think about Nathan, but his anguished voice kept haunting her. She felt as if she were losing her mind. It was as if her life had been taken out of her hands and put into the hands of a man who was so powerful he could not be fought. She didn't look up as she heard Winter Wolf enter the lodge. She kept pacing back and forth.

"You did well, Heva. I think you convinced the white man. He still has questions, but I think he will leave soon when he realizes that you are truly my woman." He walked

277

to Anna. "It is time for us to sleep, Heva."

"I don't want to sleep." She shrugged off his hands. "Can't you just leave me alone?"

"So, you must really love the white man. You will say anything to save his life, won't you?"

"What do you want from me?" she screamed, pulling the blanket from her shoulders and throwing it on the ground. "I did what you asked me to do." She walked over to him, her head held high. "Do you want to beat me now, Winter Wolf? Or do you want to force yourself on me? You are so much stronger than I, why must you prove it all the time? If only you had been gentle with me, I might have cared for you. But you don't understand about kindness. I feel as if you've ripped my heart out of me. I feel as if there is no reason to live." She stood back and untied her dress, pulling it up over her head. "Is this what you want, Winter Wolf? I'll make it easy for you. I won't fight you anymore. I'll lie here and I'll let you hurt me. But every time you hurt me, I'll die a little bit more." She stood before him, naked, shaking from the cold and from her anger. She watched Winter Wolf as he walked forward, reaching down on the ground. He put her blanket around her and pulled her close to him.

"I will not force myself on you again, Heva. It is over."

Anna looked up at his face, not understanding his words. "You aren't going to punish me?"

Winter Wolf lifted his hand to rub it against Anna's cheek. "I will not punish you, Heva. There is nothing to punish you for. Come." He led her to the robes, covering her when she lay down. He stroked her long hair. "Rest now, Heva. Just rest."

Anna closed her eyes, her body feeling the strain of the last day. She was sore and bruised and unwilling to fight anymore. She just wanted it to be over. She would stay with Winter Wolf as long as he didn't hurt her. She moaned slightly, her face and jaw aching from the bruises. She felt Winter Wolf's hand on her forehead, rubbing it softly. She felt her body relax. She didn't think of Nathan.

278

She didn't think of Winter Wolf. She thought of freedom. That was the only thing that mattered to her now.

Winter Wolf watched Anna fall asleep as he stroked her head. He had inflicted so much pain on this woman and yet she was willing to stay with him. He knew it was because she loved the white man and wanted to protect him, but he also had the feeling that she would be content with him if he had never hurt her.

He did not understand why he had hurt her so badly. He had almost enjoyed it. Was it to make her pay for what had happened to Rain Woman? Was he going to make Heva pay forever because she had white blood in her veins? His father was right—his anger would be his undoing. He had to learn how to control it. If he could do that, perhaps he could make Heva fall in love with him.

She was here with him now, and she would remain here. He knew she would do anything to save the white man, even if it meant giving up her life with him. Now, all he had to do was be gentle with her. He had to show her some kindness. She had responded well to those things before. If he treated her well and with respect, perhaps there would come a time when she would give herself to him freely.

He closed his eyes, imagining what it would be like to have this woman without forcing her. He could see her long, lithe body on top of his, he could feel her smooth skin against his, he could hear her moans of pleasure, instead of her moans of pain. He could imagine her body growing round with child, smiling as she felt the life grow inside her. She would take his head and press it to her swollen belly, stroking his hair. He would love this woman and he would love the children she gave him. He realized in that moment that he would not, he could not, ever let her go.

He lay down beside her, his arm draped over her waist. She was a strong woman and she had endured much. But he did not know if she could live without the love of the

279

white man or if she could live in a place where she did not belong. He loved this woman, but he did not want to be the cause of her death.

Chapter 12

Nathan lay awake all night, wondering how to get Anna out of the camp. Even if it were true that she was carrying Winter Wolf's child, he knew that she still loved him. He knew that she could never love another man the way she loved him.

He had thought about going to his uncle but had decided against it. Brave Wolf had done enough already. Besides, this was between him and Winter Wolf.

He waited in his lodge until he saw Anna go to the river, then he went to Winter Wolf's lodge. He issued no formal greeting, merely opened the flap and went inside. Winter Wolf was lying on his robe, a bare flank exposed, his strong, muscular legs revealing his power. Nathan walked to the robe, standing above him.

"Wake up, Winter Wolf. It is your cousin, the white man."

Winter Wolf jerked awake. He turned to face Nathan, a knife in his hand. He was ready to fight. "What do you want, white man? Did you come to see my wife? Did she not tell you that she is carrying my child?" Winter Wolf smiled, slowly standing to face Nathan. "Do you know what it is like to lie with a woman like that, white man? Do you know that she will do anything that I ask her to do?"

Nathan showed no emotion, but his hand shot out, knocking the knife from Winter Wolf's hand. His fist went into Winter Wolf's rib cage, sending him reeling backward.

Winter Wolf didn't fall. He stumbled slightly and regained his balance. Slowly, a smile spread across his face.

"You want to fight, white man?"

"Yes, I want to fight, but I want to fight someplace where your father can't stop it." He moved forward, his face still showing no emotion but his voice filled with anger. "I want this to be a fight to the death, Winter Wolf. The winner takes Anna."

Winter Wolf laughed. "There is no need to fight, white man. Heva has made her choice. She wishes to remain with me. She wishes to lie with me. She wishes to have my children."

Nathan spit at Winter Wolf's feet. "You're no man. No man would ever do to a woman what you did to Anna." He shook his head. "You see, I know her, Winter Wolf. I know everything about her. I know when she's lying, and I know she was lying last night."

"You cannot bear to hear the truth, *veho*."

"No, I think *you're* the one who can't bear the truth. The truth is, she loves me and she'll do anything to save my life, including staying with you."

"If what you say is true, why is she so willing to lie down with me? Is that to save your life also?"

Nathan wanted to put his hands around Winter Wolf's throat and squeeze the life out of him. But he forced himself to be calm. "She will do whatever she must to survive. I understand that. What I don't understand is why the son of Brave Wolf would force a woman to try to love him." Nathan could see the expression on Winter Wolf's face change. "I grew up with my mother telling me stories of how honorable the Cheyennes were. When I knew I had to come here for Anna, part of me was happy to be with my mother's people again. But since I have been here and known you, I feel nothing but shame for my mother's people. You have dishonored your father, your tribe, and your people." Nathan anticipated Winter Wolf's anger, but he didn't anticipate that the man could move so fast. He lunged through the air, tackling Nathan to the hard floor.

His hands were around Nathan's throat, slamming his head to the ground. Nathan took the heel of his right hand and jammed it underneath Winter Wolf's chin, knocking him backward. Both men were up in a crouch, eyeing each other, circling each other as two animals do when ready to pounce on each other. A movement at the flap made them stop. Anna entered the lodge. She ran between the men.

"Stop it, please. You both promised Brave Wolf that you wouldn't fight."

Nathan looked at Anna. Her face was even more discolored today. She looked so tired. It frightened him. He stood up, not wanting to upset her.

Anna looked at Nathan. "Why are you here, Nathan? We have no more to say to each other."

Nathan watched as Winter Wolf stood. He moved close behind Anna, his hands on her shoulders. "My wife speaks the truth, *veho*. You should not be in this lodge."

"Anna, I know what he's doing. He's forcing you to stay here. I don't know how he's doing it, but I know he's forcing you." He watched as Anna leaned back against Winter Wolf, taking one of his arms and putting it around her.

"He is not forcing me, Nathan. I told you that last night. I want to be here with him."

Nathan looked into Anna's eyes, trying to see if she were lying. There were no tears, there was no sadness. She seemed to mean what she said. He couldn't believe it. "Look at what he's done to you. He beat and raped you, for godsakes."

"I already told you, he didn't rape me. I am his wife, Nathan."

Nathan shook his head. "I want to talk to you alone, away from him."

"No!" Winter Wolf objected.

"If she loves you so much, why are you afraid to let her talk to me alone?"

Winter Wolf eyed Nathan, then turned Anna around to face him. He put his face close to hers, his voice barely a whisper. "Talk to him, but remember what I said. He will die with great pain if you turn against me."

Anna put her arms around Winter Wolf's neck, and he, in turn, wrapped his arms around her. "I will not be long, my husband."

She walked past Nathan and out of the lodge. "This isn't over. Whether she stays with you or goes with me, I want to fight you, Winter Wolf. I want you, alone."

"I would be glad to fight you, *veho*. I would also be glad to kill you."

Nathan left the lodge. Anna was standing to one side, obviously perturbed by his presence. "What do you want?"

He took her hands and led her out of the circle of lodges, toward the trees. "Now, talk to me. He isn't anywhere around."

"I've said all I have to say. What do you want from me, Nathan? I want to be with Winter Wolf. I'm carrying his child. I can't and I won't go back with you. I don't love you anymore."

He wasn't prepared to hear those words. He thought he would be able to argue anything, but hearing Anna say she didn't love him was too much for him. He looked at her. Her eyes were calm and her face wore no expression. She meant what she said. "You just can't stop loving someone, Anna."

"We have nothing left, Nathan. I'm carrying another man's child. I want you to leave." Nathan watched her walk away, her head held high. He remembered the defiant look in her eyes. She was not the beaten woman he had seen the evening before. Maybe she had been lying, but he couldn't believe she would go to such lengths to make another man jealous. He felt angry and he felt hurt, but in his heart he knew that she still loved him. He just had to prove it.

Anna sat back on her heels, scraping the hair from the deerskin. It was tiring, tedious work. First, she had to scrape off the blood, fat, and flesh from the skin. Then she took the thresher and scraped it back and forth along the hide to thin it. The flesher was made from a piece of elk horn, and Anna felt her arms burn as she continued the monotonous process. Little Deer had already shown her how to mix the tanning mixture, which she would soon apply. The mixture was made from brains, liver, soapweed, and grease. Anna would apply the mixture to both sides of the hide and then fold it up, letting it sit overnight. The next day, she would unfold the hide and let it sit in the sun to dry. It would then be pulled across a knotted rope that was stretched from a tree branch to a peg in the ground. Anna dreaded the work. She knew she would be on her knees for hours, dragging the hide back and forth across the knotted rope until it was softened.

She wiped the sweat from her forehead and looked at the women around her. They were extremely hard-working people, who seldom complained, and certainly not in front of their husbands. Anna was still uncomfortable with the fact that the women did the majority of the work, while the men sat around and gambled and played games all day. But they worked hard to hunt and bring in food, and they put themselves in danger whenever they had to fight an enemy. Anna found herself shaking her head. She hated it here. She hated it even more since Nathan had gone. Her life seemed empty now that he was gone forever. It was easy for her to go on before because she had always lived with the belief that Nathan would come for her. Now he was gone and she would never see his face again. Tears filled her eyes and she closed them, arching her back and rubbing it with her hand.

"Are you all right, Heva?"

Anna quickly wiped the tears from her eyes when she heard Little Deer's voice. "I am well, thank you, Little Deer." She bent forward and continued to scrape the deer hide.

"I am troubled by something, Heva." Little Deer knelt next to Anna, taking the scraper from her hand. "How did you come by the bruises on your face?"

Anna felt the flush in her cheeks. She had already told

Little Deer the same story she had told Nathan. Why was she asking her again? "I already told you, Little Deer. I got into a fight with Bright Leaf. I was jealous of her. I thought Winter Wolf was lying with her in her lodge. She is a pretty woman." Anna reached for the scraper, but Little Deer held it to her.

"I do not believe you, Heva."

"Why would I lie, Little Deer?"

"Why, indeed?"

Anna averted her gaze, watching some of the women as they helped each other with the hides. "I must finish scraping this hide, Little Deer. My other hides are dry, and I want to soften them."

"I spoke with Bright Leaf, Heva. She says Winter Wolf has never been near her lodge."

"Bright Leaf would not tell Winter Wolf's mother if her son had been with her."

"I have known Bright Leaf since she was born. She would not lie to me. She says you and she have never even spoken."

Anna moved the hide, gently taking the scraper from Little Deer. She continued scraping. "I told you what happened, Little Deer."

"Look at me, Heva." Little Deer's voice held a note of contempt that Anna had never heard before. "Did my son do this to you?"

Anna looked at her. She wanted desperately to tell Little Deer the truth, but if she did, she knew that Little Deer would tell Brave Wolf. When Winter Wolf found out he would kill her, she had no doubt. "No, he did not, Little Deer. Your son has been good to me."

"Ah, that is good to hear, Heva. So, if Winter Wolf did not do this to you, that leaves only one person. Aenohe, the white man."

"No!" Anna exclaimed before she could stop herself. She held the scraper in her hands, oblivious to the pieces of flesh and hide that were on it. "Nathan would never hurt a woman. He is too gentle." She felt her resolve begin to

286

crumble.

Little Deer put an arm around Anna's shoulders. "If I were ever taken captive by a white man, I do not think I would ever survive. I have heard the stories, the way Indian women are treated in the white world. I would not have the strength to live without my people." Her hand rubbed Anna's shoulder. "Yet you live in a world that is alien to you and you do not seem to mind. You do not even seem to mind when the man you have loved with all of your heart rides away. Tell me why that is, Heva?"

"Sometimes we have no choice in what happens in our lives, Little Deer."

"Yes, and sometimes we live with the knowledge that the people we love are not always what we wish them to be."

Anna looked up. "What do you mean?"

"I have known about Winter Wolf for a long time. He is my son and I love him, but I know that he has a cruel streak in him. He had it even as a child. When he was married to Rain Woman, I thought he would change. He seemed to be much more gentle, especially after his son was born. But there came a time when he thought that Rain Woman was interested in another man. She was not, but he believed it to be true. She could not prove otherwise. He beat her badly and she lost the child she was carrying. When she was well enough, she took their son and ran away. I know he told you that white men killed his family, but his family would not have been alone if he had not forced them away from him."

Anna felt a chill in her spine. "I can't believe it, Little Deer. He loved Rain Woman and his son. I can't believe he would have done anything to hurt them."

"He loved his family, Heva, this anyone could see. But his anger has always run so deep, it frightened even me. Do not lie to me any longer, Heva. Did Winter Wolf do this to you?"

Anna dropped the scraper on the ground. She rubbed her hands along her thighs in a nervous gesture, not able to look at Little Deer. She nodded slightly, feeling as if she were putting a knife through Little Deer's heart.

"Come here, child," Little Deer said gently, putting her arms around Anna.

Anna buried her face in Little Deer's shoulder, feeling the security of the older woman's arms around her. It had been so long since Aeneva had died. She had not had a mother's arms around her in a long time. She felt the tears begin to flow and they would not stop.

"It is all right, Heva. I will help you."

Anna lifted her head from Little Deer's shoulder, wiping the tears from her eyes. "You cannot help me, Little Deer. I will not come between you and your son."

"I will not have a son who beats his woman because he cannot control his anger. I am much stronger than you think, Heva. I am still his mother."

"But there is nothing that you can do. We will soon break camp and leave for the winter camp. No one can take me back to my people."

"What of Aenohe? Will he not come back for you?"

"He will never come back for me, Little Deer. I had to convince him that I didn't love him. That's the only way he would leave."

"He did not have to leave, Heva. He had Brave Wolf's protection."

"That was not enough. Winter Wolf swore that if he stayed here, he would kill him. He said he and some of his men would take him into the woods and torture him. I couldn't go to you or Brave Wolf. I couldn't take the chance with Nathan's life."

Little Deer reached out and took Anna's hand. "My heart aches for you, Heva. I am sorry that my son has done this to you. He has dishonored his father and me."

"Don't be angry with him, Little Deer. I know that he is a good man. I have seen it many times. There is a gentle side to Winter Wolf, but he is afraid to show it. Maybe I can help him."

"You cannot heal my son, Heva. Do you understand me? It is not up to you. My son must heal himself." She pursed her lips in anger. "He will not get away with this."

"You can't say anything to Brave Wolf, Little Deer. Promise me you won't say anything." Anna was squeezing Little Deer's hands so tightly the woman pulled them from Anna's grasp.

"Did he also threaten you again, Heva?"

"I just don't want to anger him, Little Deer. If he finds out I talked to you, I don't know what he'll do."

"Do you trust me, Heva?"

"Yes."

"Then you must believe in me to do the right thing. I will not endanger you any further. You say nothing to Winter Wolf of our talk and I will take care of the rest." Little Deer smiled reassuringly and left.

Anna watched Little Deer walk away, but somehow she wasn't reassured. Although she trusted Little Deer, she still had reminders of how strong Winter Wolf really was. She didn't want to face his wrath still another time.

Little Deer walked with her basket, picking berries as she went along. It was late in the season and there were few berries left. She walked with a quick step, enjoying the afternoon sun as it danced in and out of the blanket of treetops. She walked to her favorite place, the place she had taken Heva, and she stopped. She looked behind her, making sure she wasn't being followed, then she walked farther into the woods. She came to a place that was so dark it almost seemed like it was night. But Little Deer was not frightened, for she knew that soon she would come into the light.

She walked still farther until she made her way through the trees. The light was beginning to shine through in spots and she could hear the river, already beginning to flow harder because of the newly melted snow from the mountains. She came out onto a narrow embankment and she waited patiently, watching the water as it coursed by.

"I am here, Little Deer."

Little Deer turned and followed the voice back into the trees. "Are you well, Aenohe?"

"Yes, Little Deer, I am well," Nathan replied. "Have you spoken with Anna?"

"Yes. It was as you thought. She still loves you, but my son has threatened her. He told her that if she did not make you believe that she loved him, he and his men would torture and murder you. She had no choice, Aenohe."

"I am sorry, Little Deer. I know this is difficult for you. I didn't want to come between you and your son."

"You did not come between us, Aenohe. What my son did, he did on his own." She reached up and touched Nathan's cheek, smiling as she did so. "I can remember how proud Aeneva was of you. You would sit in her lap and she would rock you back and forth. She would stroke your yellow hair and she would kiss the top of your head. You would cry whenever she left you."

"She was my mother, Little Deer. I loved her very much."

"She did not fail you as I have failed my son. You have turned out to be an honorable man."

"You did not fail Winter Wolf. You and Brave Wolf are fine, honorable people, and I know that Winter Wolf is also honorable."

"You are too generous, Aenohe."

"No, I have many reasons to hate him, Little Deer, but Winter Wolf saved Anna's life twice. He didn't have to. He could have let her stay with the Shoshonis, but something in him couldn't leave a helpless woman. Anna sees it, too. She told me that she's seen a gentle side to him."

"Thank you, Aenohe. You are truly Aeneva's son."

"How is she, Little Deer? Is she well?"

"Well enough. There is a sadness about Heva, a very heavy sadness. Her young eyes have seen too much, her mind has endured too much. I worry for her."

"Is she ill?"

"No, but she is weak in spirit. This frightens me even more. You cannot wait much longer, Aenohe."

"What if you bring her into the woods with you? Winter Wolf trusts you. He will not question it if she goes berry-picking with you."

"I have thought of this. I have also thought of another way. I can tell Brave Wolf, and he can send Winter Wolf out to scout, to make sure the way is safe for our people when we break camp."

"I don't know if I like getting Brave Wolf involved in this."

"You do not trust him?"

"I trust him, Little Deer, but this has been very hard on him. He has tried to be so fair to both me and Winter Wolf. I'm not sure he would send his son away so that I could take Anna."

Little Deer thought for a moment. "You are right. Brave Wolf loves his son so much, it is hard for him to see that Winter Wolf has any faults. Let me think on this. I will find a way. Meet me here in two days."

"All right."

"You have enough food?"

"I'm fine. There are berries and dried meat, and there's plenty of water."

Little Deer reached into her basket. "Just in case that's not sufficient . . ." She handed Nathan a bundle. "Take care of yourself, Aenohe. I would never forgive myself if something happened to you."

"I don't know how to thank you, Little Deer."

"There is no need to thank me. I want you to take Heva and go back to your home. Love each other and be happy. Do all the things that Aeneva would have wanted you to do."

Nathan led Little Deer through the darkness of the trees until Little Deer could manage on her own. She turned to wave. As she looked at Nathan standing there, his long golden hair shining in the sunlight, his skin bronzed, she thought he resembled a god. But she knew that he was simply a man, a very good and honorable man who wanted to be with the woman he loved. And now she had to figure

291

out a way to help this man take the woman he loved away from her only son.

Winter Wolf held Anna's hands in his, gently rubbing them with bear grease. "I told you to stop, but you would not listen. Your hands are not suited to this type of work."

Anna rested her hands in her lap. "They will soon toughen."

"My mother tells me you have done many hides in the past few days. You will be the envy of the women."

"I don't do it to have the women envy me," she replied curtly. She found it difficult to look at Winter Wolf. Whenever she met his gaze, she found that she remembered her brutal humiliation and her beatings.

"Why do you work yourself so hard, Heva?"

"I don't want anyone in this camp saying that the white woman is lazy and cannot work."

"No one says that."

"They are quiet around you, but when I am alone, I hear the things they say. I will work hard. I will not embarrass you in front of your people." She reached out to hold the bowl of broth, but her hands shook.

"Finish your broth," Winter Wolf commanded.

Anna did as he said. He had that tone to his voice, and she didn't want to anger him. When she was finished, she set her bowl down and reached for his, but he took her hand. "I want to clean the bowls."

"The bowls do not matter. Take off your dress and lie on the robes."

Anna stared at him. Surely he didn't want to have her, not now. "But . . ."

"Do as I say, Heva."

Anna got to her feet and walked to the robes. She dropped to her knees, quickly slipping off her dress, then lay on her back, covering herself with her hands. The night was cold and she began to shiver.

"Turn on your stomach, Heva."

Anna heard his voice from across the lodge as he rummaged through the baskets. On her stomach? What was he planning to do? She had heard of these things. Her mind reeled. She turned her head away from him, afraid to see what he was doing. She heard him walk across the lodge and drop to his knees. She felt the softness of one of the robes as he pulled it to cover her legs and buttocks. He squatted over her, his knees on either side. She felt her body tense. She prayed that she would faint and never know what he was about to do.

She felt something cold on her shoulders and then his hands as he rubbed the mixture into her aching muscles. She recognized the mint smell of Little Deer's soothing balm and she felt ashamed that she had thought he was going to hurt her. His strong hands moved over her neck and shoulders, kneading the muscles, working out the soreness. His hands moved down her back, his thumbs running down her spine. She began to relax as his fingers moved up and down her spine, working out the soreness that seemed to be everywhere. As his fingers moved they lightly brushed the sides of her breasts and she felt a shiver run through her. Was he doing this to her on purpose? Was he trying to excite her?

His hands moved to the small of her back and gently worked around the muscles. She felt his hands on either side of her waist and it made her feel so small. His hands moved back up to her shoulders and he leaned forward so that his chest was on her back. He stretched her arms, covering them with his, massaging them gently. His body was heavy on hers. She felt his knees on either side of her and his mouth by her ear. She felt his breath on her and she closed her eyes. She would never want him, not after what he had done to her.

He rolled to his back, pulling her on top of him. She felt her breasts against his chest and the length of her body on his. His eyes stared into hers, wondering. "Are you a witch, Heva? Why do you have such power over me?"

His hands were behind her head, forcing it down until it

293

met his mouth. She tried to push away from him, but his mouth begged her not to go. He moved his lips against hers in a gentle caress.

Anna felt her body respond to his kiss, but her mind would not. She remembered how he had taken her before; she would never forget it. She remembered the times she and Nathan had made love and how good and sweet it had been. She moved her head, resting it on his shoulder. She didn't want to anger him, but she was afraid to encourage him. "I am tired, Winter Wolf. My body aches." She felt his large hands move up and down her back.

"You say you will have my children, Heva. Were you lying to me?"

"No, I was not lying." She rolled away from him, lying on her back on the robes. She knew she couldn't delay it any longer. "I am your wife. I will not fight you."

Winter Wolf lay on his side, looking at her. She tried to look away, but his eyes commanded her to look at him. "I want you to give yourself to me, Heva. I do not want to have to force you. I could do that every night if I wanted to, but I do not wish to hurt you again. I want to please you. I want to awaken the desire in you."

Anna felt his hand on her breast and she closed her eyes, trying to calm herself. Maybe if she gave herself willingly to him, he would be gentle.

"Are you thinking of me or the white man?" His voice sounded ominous.

Anna opened her eyes. "You are my husband, Winter Wolf. I think only of you," she lied.

"Those are nice words, Heva, but I do not believe you." He sat up. "Perhaps it is time for me to look elsewhere for another wife." He looked at her, his eyes dark and angry. "I will keep you, Heva. You will continue to do the work, but I will take another wife to quell the fire that burns within me. I will not force you again."

Anna sat up, holding the robe against her. "You would take another wife?" She couldn't imagine another woman living in the lodge, lying next to Winter Wolf. Where would he make her sleep?

"I am a man with needs, Heva. If you cannot meet those needs, I will find another woman who will lie with me and have my children."

"Would I remain in your lodge?"

"Women are jealous. Perhaps my new wife would not want another wife around, or perhaps she would like someone to do her work for her. I cannot tell you what will happen, Heva. I might have to sell you to someone else."

Anna's heart sank. As badly as Winter Wolf had treated her, at least she was familiar with him, at least she had seen a gentle side to him. She had observed many of the men in the camp and it was hard to believe that any of *them* had a gentle side to them. She sat up, hugging Winter Wolf from behind, resting her face against his muscular shoulder. "I don't want to be a wife to anyone else, Winter Wolf. I am your wife." She had no choice. Her only chance of survival lay in staying married to Winter Wolf.

Winter Wolf turned slightly, wrapping his arms around Anna. "You are the only woman I desire, Heva. I do not want another woman."

Anna nodded, pressing her face into his chest. If only she could forget Nathan . . . His hands moved to her breasts and he pushed her down on the robes. She closed her eyes, trying to tell herself that this was the only thing she could do, but she hated herself for believing it. She couldn't imagine Aeneva giving herself willingly to any man but Trenton. His hands were all over her, his mouth on her breasts. She forced herself to think of other things, but his hands deftly moved over her body. Soon, he was between her legs and again she felt him inside her. She squeezed her eyes tightly, trying to stop the tears that came. She felt her fingers dig into his shoulders; she didn't want to scream like she had done before. She hated herself for her weakness. She wondered where her strength of will had gone and when it had deserted her. All the while, Winter Wolf continued to drive himself into her. At one point she cried out from pain, not from desire. But Winter Wolf mistook it for desire and went faster and harder until he was spent. Anna didn't look at him as he rolled away from her. She couldn't look at him. She was afraid she would see herself in his eyes.

She felt his hand on her breast and she didn't move. "You are so beautiful, Heva. You make me feel stronger when I am inside you." He moved closer, putting a leg across her body. "Tonight you carry the seed of my son."

Anna thought she was going to be sick. She wanted to scream. She remained quiet, though her mind was frantic. What if it was true? What if after tonight she was carrying Winter Wolf's child? If that was so, then she could never leave him, and he knew it. She heard his deep voice in her ear.

"Do not worry, Heva. I will put my seed into you every night so that I am sure you will soon be carrying my son."

Anna knew as soon as he spoke the words that she couldn't go on like this. She couldn't live like an animal, without any love or kindness. Even when Winter Wolf was kind, it was because he wanted something from her. She was glad she couldn't see herself right now, because she was sure if she could, she would be sick at the sight.

Anna smiled wanly as Robert ran with the other small children. He had become such a part of these people that it was frightening. When he spoke, he spoke in Cheyenne, and when he wanted something, he reached out for Winter Wolf or Brave Wolf. It was as if she no longer existed. She had failed Roberto. She had tried to keep his son alive, but all she had managed to do was turn him into a Cheyenne.

She dropped her root-digger. She felt worthless. She had willingly given herself to Winter Wolf and soon she would be carrying his child. She would rather die than bear his child and have him raise it to be like him.

She stood up and walked down the bank. She looked back to make sure Robert was safe. He seldom ventured far from camp and he was always under the watchful eye of an old one. She looked for Little Deer. They were to go picking berries in the woods today, but Anna couldn't find her. She had to get away, if only for a little while.

She walked downstream, looking at the river that had almost taken her life once before. She felt someone watching her and she looked up. One of the camp guards observed her every move. Winter Wolf would never let her go.

She walked down to where the river was rushing, near the place where she and the boy had almost drowned. Winter Wolf had saved her life that day and she had been grateful. She had seen a kind side to him then, but it had disappeared somewhere.

"Heva!"

Anna heard Winter Wolf's voice and she turned. He was rushing toward her. Why didn't he leave her alone? God, she hated him. She turned around and looked at the embankment. It was a steep drop into the river, but she didn't care. She wanted to be away from Winter Wolf. She backed up almost to the edge. "Stay away from me, Winter Wolf."

"Heva, you are too close to the edge. Come away."

"No," she said, her eyes wild. "I have found a way to be free of you."

Winter Wolf stepped forward and Anna felt herself lose her balance and begin to fall, but Winter Wolf grabbed her. "Heva, what is the matter with you? Were you trying to kill yourself?"

Anna stared at him, her eyes angry and frustrated. "I would rather be dead than be with you. I hate you." Anna felt his arms relax around her and she pulled away, losing her footing and falling over the side and into the rocks. She felt the rush of water in her mouth and around her head and the shock of the rocks as her body slammed against them. But this time she didn't care. She had no will to fight. She couldn't live with Winter Wolf any longer, and what was worse, she couldn't live with herself. She closed her eyes and let the rushing torrent of water take her into its dark, cold blackness.

Winter Wolf watched Anna as she struggled to breathe. Every weak breath she took made him ache inside. The fall into the rocks had broken many bones and bruised others. When he had finally gotten to her, he wasn't sure she was alive. Now, watching her shallow, raspy breathing, he still wasn't sure she would live. He watched his mother minister over her with another woman from the band until he could watch no more. He went outside, ignoring his father. He walked to the river and watched its seemingly peaceful waters flow by. He had never wanted this to happen. He had never meant to hurt her in this way. He heard footsteps behind him and knew it was his father. He was not in the mood to hear one of his lectures. He turned to confront him, but saw his mother instead. Little Deer's face held an expression he had not seen before. Was it contempt?

"How is she, Mother?"

"She is fighting for her life, Winter Wolf."

He watched as his mother folded her hands gracefully in front of her, trying to calm herself. He could never remember his mother being truly angry with him. "She is strong, Mother. She will survive."

"Is that what you think? Is that how you are able to live with yourself, Winter Wolf?"

"Mother, I—"

"Stop!" Little Deer put up her hand. "Do not insult me with your excuses. I am not a feeble old woman. You have insulted and dishonored your father and me with your treatment of this woman. I cannot believe you are my son. I cannot believe that I bore you, that I raised you."

"She is my wife," Winter Wolf replied defensively. "I have treated her better than most men treat their wives in this camp."

"You are not most men, Winter Wolf. You are the son of Brave Wolf, the great grandson of Stalking Horse and Sun Dancer. You were never raised to treat a woman in such a manner. Have you ever seen your father raise his hand to me?"

"It is different with Heva and me. She has many things to learn about becoming a Cheyenne."

Little Deer grabbed her son's arm. "You are not listening to me, Winter Wolf. She does not want to become a Cheyenne. This woman would rather die than be your wife and live in this camp. Do you not understand that?"

"It was an accident. She slipped and fell into the river."

"Do you truly believe that?"

Winter Wolf turned away from his mother, ashamed that she knew the truth. "I want her to love me, Mother. That is all I want."

"You cannot make a person love you, Winter Wolf. You knew from the beginning that she loved Aenohe, but still you fought it. Did you think that would change because you had saved her life? Do you think that I would forget about your father and fall in love with a white man just because he saved my life?"

Winter Wolf met his mother's gentle but angry eyes. "She cares for me, I know she does."

"Yes, I believe she does care for you. That is not the same thing as loving a person with all of your heart." Little Deer took her son's chin in her hand. "It is not the same love that makes a woman do anything she has to do to save the life of the man she truly loves. Are you listening to me, Winter Wolf? Do you hear my words? This woman was willing to stay with you, to lie with you, to submit to your beatings, so that Aenohe could live. But her love for him is so strong that she cannot live without it."

Winter Wolf shook his head. "I do not believe that. She has given herself willingly to me. Would she do that if she did not care for me?"

"Would she give herself to you if she were not threatened?" Little Deer's angry voice rose. "Rain Woman came to me many times. I knew of the beatings, and I did nothing to help her. I will not let it happen again, Winter Wolf. You will not drive this woman to her death also."

Winter Wolf looked at his mother. He had never seen such resolve or strength in her face before. He felt ashamed. "I have always felt such anger. I know not why. I feel it rise in me like some bad spirit and I am unable to control it."

"You must do the right thing, Winter Wolf."

"What is the right thing, Mother? I do not know anymore."

"You must let Heva go back to her people and to Aenohe. If she stays here she will die. Is that what you want?"

"I do not want her to die, Mother. She is a good woman. She has tried to help me, and I have shamed her in the worst possible way."

"You can still do the honorable thing, my son. There is such goodness in you."

"I do not know anymore, Mother. I feel as if the goodness is being eaten up by the evil inside me."

"No, there is much good in you. Do not be afraid to let it come out."

Winter Wolf looked at the small, gentle woman who stood in front of him. He had never seen her look more beautiful. He had never admired her more. She had such courage. He did not want to dishonor her further. "When Heva is well, I will take her back to her people."

"You do not have to take her back. Aenohe is waiting for her."

Winter Wolf felt the anger rise in him. "He is here?" he demanded angrily.

"He is nearby. Did you think that he would leave so easily, Winter Wolf? He loves this woman as much as she loves him. He did not believe her lies."

"And you have helped him? My own mother has helped my enemy?"

"He is not your enemy, Winter Wolf, and he is not my enemy. He is the son of a woman I loved like a sister. Sometimes I believe he is more Cheyenne than you, my son. He knows the meaning of honor."

Winter Wolf lowered his head. "I do not want him to win, Mother."

"This is not about winning, my son. This is about saving the life of a woman you say you love. If she stays with you, she will surely die. If you let her go to Aenohe, she will live."

"I cannot give her to him, Mother. I cannot."

"Can you live with yourself if another woman dies because of you? I will not let it happen, Winter Wolf. I will not."

Winter Wolf watched his mother as she walked away, a wry smile on his face. He was proud she was his mother. He wished that she could be as proud of him.

Nathan paced anxiously up and down the riverbank. Where was Little Deer? She was supposed to be here hours ago. Something had happened. He had thought about going back to the camp, but he was afraid that it would be too dangerous for Anna. He made himself wait. He heard a noise in the trees and thought of running into the woods, but he didn't. He was tired of hiding out.

"Aenohe?"

Nathan hurried to the trees to meet Little Deer, holding branches for her as she walked out to the embankment. "Are you all right, Little Deer? I was worried that something had happened."

"I am well, Aenohe. It is Heva. She is ill."

"Did he hurt her again?"

"No, she fell from the riverbank and hit the rocks below. She broke some bones and swallowed much water. I was afraid she would die."

"When did this happen?"

"Yesterday."

"How did it happen, Little Deer?"

"I do not know for sure." She stared out at the water. "I believe she was trying to kill herself."

"What?" Nathan shook his head. "Anna wouldn't do

that."

"She felt she had lost you, and she knew she could not live with Winter Wolf any longer. I believe she felt it was the only way for her."

"No," Nathan said, walking back and forth. "Anna wouldn't try to kill herself."

"It does not matter why, Aenohe. What is most important now is making sure she lives. As soon as she is well, you will take her from this camp."

"I want to see her."

"No, you must not come to the camp. I have talked to Winter Wolf. I believe he will let her go, but if he sees you, he might change his mind. He needs time to think. You must be patient, Aenohe."

"You are asking too much of me, Little Deer."

"I am asking no more than I think you can give."

Nathan closed his eyes. "This shouldn't be happening to her. I sometimes feel we will never be together." He felt tears in his eyes and he was ashamed.

Little Deer reached up and gently wiped the tears from Nathan's eyes. "You will be together, Aenohe. I know this to be so. I had a dream. In the dream I saw Aeneva. She and I talked of you and Heva. We pointed to your children and we laughed because they were all fair except for one. Aeneva said that one would be a troublemaker."

Nathan couldn't resist a smile. "You have dream visions? I remember Aeneva telling me of Sun Dancer's dream visions. Sometimes they were frightening, but sometimes they were happy. They were always true."

"I have had only four. Two of them have come true. One I hope will never come true."

"What is it, Little Deer?"

She looked at Nathan, her eyes weary and sad. "It is Winter Wolf. I have seen him die."

"You're sure it's Winter Wolf that you saw?"

"I am not sure. It is frightening, Aenohe."

"It means nothing. You're just angry with him. Winter Wolf is a strong warrior. He will not die young."

"He will die, and there is nothing I can do to prevent it. All I can do is help him to die with honor." She smiled wanly. "Have patience, Aenohe. I will care for Heva. And I will return soon."

Nathan walked Little Deer as far as he could without being seen and then returned to his place in the woods. He sat, calming himself, knowing there was nothing he could do for Anna. He wanted only to love her and take her away from this place. He prayed it would be soon.

Anna ran along the trail, feeling better than she had in a long time. Her laughter rang out, and she felt her long hair flow out behind her. She felt light, as if she were walking on air. She looked below her and saw there was no ground. It appeared she was walking on a cloud. She stopped, confused. Where was she? She heard laughter behind her and saw Aeneva, followed by another woman. She ran to Aeneva, overjoyed at seeing her again.

"Aeneva, I thought I would never see you again." She wrapped her arms around her. "I love you so."

"And I love you, child. I have missed you." Her hand caressed Anna's cheek. "You are more beautiful than I remembered."

Anna smiled. She looked past Aeneva to the tall Cheyenne woman who was standing behind her. She was the most beautiful thing Anna had ever seen, her face so incredibly serene and gentle. "You are Sun Dancer," she sad.

"Yes, my child." Sun Dancer stepped forward. "You are a good girl, generous of heart and strong of spirit."

Anna looked in awe from one woman to the other. "You are both so beautiful and yet so strong. I yearn to be like you, but I am much weaker."

Sun Dancer took Anna's hand in hers. "You are not weak, *nexahe*, my grandchild. You are being tested, just as I and your mother were tested."

"But you two never gave up. I have." Anna looked around her. "If I hadn't given up, why would I be here?"

"You are only visiting, Anna," Aeneva said gently. "It is up to you to be strong. You must find the will to live so you can be with Nathan. He needs you."

"You have seen Nathan, Mother?"

"Yes, he is close. He is waiting for you."

Anna hugged her mother, tears coming to her eyes. "I will make myself be strong. I don't want to dishonor you or Grandmother."

"You could never dishonor us, *nexahe*," Sun Dancer said. She looked down the white, cloudy road. "It is time for you to return. But remember this: the strength which you seek is already inside of you." She hugged the girl and kissed her on the top of the head. "Tell Nathan that I miss him. Tell him I will always remember his smile."

Anna kissed Sun Dancer on the cheek, then looked at Aeneva, feeling an enormous weight on her heart. "I don't want to leave, Mother. I miss you so."

"Do not be sad, *nahtona*, my daughter. We are happy here in Seyan. You have a long life to live yet. You must be strong and you must be true to yourself. If you do those things, you will have a good life."

Anna wrapped her arms around Aeneva, feeling the tears stream down her face. "I love you, Mother."

"You must do something for me, Anna."

"Anything."

"You must tell Nathan not to grieve for us. Tell him there was nothing he could do to save us. It was our time to go. Tell him that my heart is full of love for him."

"I will tell him, Mother." Anna thought for a moment. "Mother, did you know that Roberto is alive?"

"Yes, I knew when I did not see him here. Is he a good man?"

"Yes, he's a very good man, Mother. He misses you and Trenton." She smiled. "He looks like you. He's very handsome."

"Tell him that we love him and that someday we will meet again in Seyan."

Anna nodded, knowing that it was time to go but not

willing to leave. "How is Trenton?"

"He is well, Anna."

"I want to see him, Mother."

"You cannot, Anna. It is time for you to go back. Trenton will always be with you, just as I will always be with you. Go now."

Aeneva's voice seemed to disappear. She and Sun Dancer were enveloped by a fog and Anna couldn't see them anymore. "Mother!" Anna screamed. "Don't leave, Mother." Anna began to cry. She felt lonely, but she remembered what Aeneva had told her—Nathan was nearby, waiting for her. She ran down the cloudy road, not knowing where it led, wanting only to be with Nathan again. Suddenly she felt light-hearted and happy again. She felt renewed. Somehow she would find the strength within herself, as Sun Dancer had said she would. She was ready to live again.

Chapter 13

"Little Deer, come quickly."

Little Deer hurried from the cook fire when she heard old Elk Woman's voice from inside the lodge. She knelt next to Anna's sleeping form. "What is it, Elk Woman?"

"There . . ." Elk Woman pointed to Anna's face. "Tears."

Little Deer reached up and touched the warm droplets that came from Anna's closed eyes. How was it possible, she wondered. She had never seen anyone cry when they were sick. "Has she spoken?"

"She moaned and said words in the white man's tongue. I did not understand her."

Little Deer patted Elk Woman's shoulder. "Thank you for your help, my friend. Go back to your lodge and rest. I will sit with her." She touched Anna's forehead. She was no longer burning with the fever. "Mother!" Anna screamed, and Little Deer pressed Anna down to the robes with gentle, sure hands. "It is all right, Heva. Sleep now." Little Deer nodded to herself. Heva was going to live. She could see that something had happened. Perhaps she had been visited in her sleep by friendly spirits, but more likely, Aeneva had visited her and given her strength. She smiled. She knew that Aeneva would not let her daughter die.

Winter Wolf entered the lodge, but Little Deer didn't

look up. She was fascinated by Anna, wondering just what she had seen in her sleep. These dream visions were something that happened to only a very few in the band. She herself had had only four, and she had told no one but Aenohe of them. People were too curious and she did not wish them to know about her life or her dreams. Sun Dancer had become famous for her dream visions. She had had many, and all of them had come true. While the dream visions were a good thing, they could sometimes be a heavy burden to bear.

She looked up at her son, and suddenly her heart felt as if it would break. As angry as she had been at him, she did not want him to die. He had been a good son to her.

"Mother, are you all right?" Winter Wolf asked.

Little Deer nodded, patting the place next to her. "Come, sit next to me, Winter Wolf." She looked at his face, so handsome in peace, so ugly in anger. "You have not slept."

"I worry for Heva. Will she live, Mother?"

Little Deer looked at Anna. "I believe she will. The fever seems to have left her body."

"Thank you, Mother. You have healed her."

"I have done nothing. Heva has healed herself."

"How do you know this?"

"I just know." She reached out and took Winter Wolf's hand in hers. He resisted at first. She looked at the hand that was almost twice as big as hers. The palm was callused, but the fingers were long and graceful. It was hard to believe that this man had been a baby with tiny fingers. When she had borne him in the birthing lodge and found that he was healthy, she had taken each of his fingers and kissed them. She took his hand and lifted it to her cheek. "I love you, my son. I do not tell you that enough."

Winter Wolf was confused by this display of emotion from his mother. "What is it, Mother? What is wrong?"

"Nothing is wrong. I have given you much criticism

lately and have taken little time to tell you that I love you. You have been a good son."

"Are you ill, Mother?"

Little Deer was touched by the concern in Winter Wolf's voice. "No, I am well." Anna groaned again, and she looked at her. "You have not changed your mind about Heva?"

There was a long silence before Winter Wolf spoke. "I do not want to take her back and give her to the white man, Mother." He took Little Deer's hands in his. "But I will do it because I do not wish to further dishonor you and Father."

Little Deer breathed a sigh of relief. "If you do this thing, Winter Wolf, you will also be honoring yourself."

"I can never make up for the pain I have caused her, but I *can* set her free."

"That is enough." Little Deer sat up, rubbing her back. "Will you sit with her while I walk. I want to check on your father and Hahkota."

"Thank you, Mother."

"I have done nothing, Winter Wolf."

"You have done everything. You have helped me to see clearly again."

Little Deer pressed her cheek to her son's and left the lodge, feeling better than she had in days.

Winter Wolf watched his mother walk out of the lodge. She was truly a good and honorable person. He looked at Anna. She, too, was a good woman, a woman who had suffered too much because of him. He placed his hand on her forehead. His mother was right—the fever was gone. She seemed to be sleeping peacefully. He stroked her hair, taking in every detail of her face so that he would never forget it.

"Nathan?" Her voice sounded very weak.

"No, Heva, it is I, Winter Wolf."

"No!" Anna screamed, throwing the robe from her. She opened her eyes. "Don't touch me. I won't let you touch me again."

"I will not touch you, Heva. I want you to lie down. You need to rest. You have been ill." His voice was calm and reassuring.

"You won't hurt me?" she asked.

"I will not hurt you, Heva. I will never hurt you again." He rubbed her forehead. "Sleep."

Anna closed her eyes. "I am sorry for you, Winter Wolf," she said, her voice barely audible.

"Do not be so, Heva. It is I who should be sorry for everything I have put you through."

Anna's eyes opened slightly. "I am cold, Winter Wolf. Will you lie with me one more time?"

Winter Wolf was confused. Did she know that he was taking her to the white man, or was she giving up. He leaned close to her. "You must not give up, Heva. I will take you back to Aenohe. Do you hear me?"

Anna smiled weakly. "I knew you had a good heart, Winter Wolf. You were just afraid to let it show." Her teeth chattered and she began to shake.

Winter Wolf lay down next to Anna, pulling the robe over them both. He put his arm across her body, reveling in the feel of her against him. There was no tenseness in her body now. She trusted him and he could not betray that trust. As much as it pained him, he had to take her back to the white man.

Nathan was getting impatient. He'd been in his wooded hideout for over two weeks. But it would be over soon. Little Deer had told him that Anna was recovering quickly and that she would bring her to him when she was well.

It seemed as if he and Anna had known each other all their lives, yet they had been allowed so little time to be together. They had sacrificed too much, and Anna had lost a good part of her innocence. But he would make it up to her somehow.

He cocked his head to one side, looking through the

trees. He heard a sound, different from any he had heard before. A movement across the river caught his eye. More than likely it was a deer, or even a bear foraging for berries.

The noise continued and he thought he heard voices. He made sure he was well hidden as he crept forward on his hands and knees. He stayed in the trees but was able to see across the river. There were people, Indians, but they didn't look Cheyenne. He squinted his eyes, trying to get a better look. He saw two of them come out onto the riverbank. They pointed toward the woods on the other side where Nathan was hiding. He tried to look at their hair ornaments and their quillwork. From what he could see, they looked like Shoshonis. They were planning to raid the village! There were no Cheyenne guards this far upstream because there was a clearing at the end of the woods. Anyone approaching the camp would be seen by the guard who stood watch.

Nathan observed as the two men gestured rapidly toward the village. One seemed to be arguing that they should cross farther downstream, while the other kept pointing toward the dense woods. Nathan couldn't tell if there were any more Indians, but he knew if there were, they would be close behind. It would be dark soon. They would wait until the camp was asleep and then they would attack.

He crept silently back through the woods until he was sure the Shoshonis couldn't hear him, then he ran. It was almost a mile to the village. If he could get there quickly, they might have time to prepare for the attack. He ran as fast as he could through the trees, knocking branches out of his way with his hands and arms. He didn't want these people to be murdered. He wanted to warn them.

He finally reached the clearing and ran as fast as he could, pumping his arms up and down. He saw the guard turn and point a rifle at him. Nathan stopped, holding his hands up in front of him. "Shoshonis," he said, pointing back through the woods. The man looked at him, not knowing whether or not to believe him. "I want to see Brave Wolf," he said in Cheyenne.

The man regarded him for a moment, then pointed to the camp with the rifle, pressing the barrel in Nathan's back. He gestured him in the direction of Winter Wolf's lodge. Nathan started to protest but decided it didn't matter. Even if Winter Wolf hated him, he wouldn't endanger his people.

"*Haahe*, Winter Wolf," the guard said as he stood in front of the lodge, his rifle still pressed in Nathan's back.

Winter Wolf soon appeared at the lodge flap. He started to say something to the guard but stopped when he saw Nathan. His eyes seethed with anger. "What is it you want here, *veho?*"

"Listen to me, Winter Wolf. I saw two Shoshonis upstream about a mile. I don't know if they were hunting or if they were scouts, but I think you should be prepared."

Winter Wolf narrowed his eyes, looking into Nathan's, as if in that way he could determine whether or not he was telling the truth. "You will show me," he ordered, stopping to tell the guard to get all the men of the village ready for an attack.

Nathan led the way through the dense growth of trees, ever mindful of Winter Wolf at his back.

"So, you did not leave at all. You were here all the time."

Nathan stopped abruptly. "Yes, I was here. I never intended to leave without Anna. But that's not why I came to you now. Let's leave our differences aside until we find out if there are only two Shoshonis or two hundred."

Winter Wolf didn't hesitate. "I agree with you on this, *veho*. Lead the way."

Nathan pushed his way through the trees until he was fairly close to the place where he had observed the Indians, then he slowed down. "We should be quiet. They may have crossed the river." He motioned for Winter Wolf to get down on the ground, and they continued on their hands and knees. When they got to the edge of the trees, they could hear voices. Across the river was a group of Shoshonis, talking and gesturing. Some were even laughing.

"How many do you count?" Nathan asked.

"Ten that I can see. We do not know how many are back in the trees."

"Why are they sitting there laughing? Don't they know they might be found?"

"They are arrogant. They have sent out a scout who has seen that we do not come this far upstream. They will just rest until it is dark and then they will attack."

"You think there are more?"

Winter Wolf nodded. "If they have discovered we are here, there are more. They would not take the risk of having so few attack such a large band."

"How did they find the camp without you seeing them?"

"We can only guard so many places, *veho*. We try to pick our camps for safety as well as convenience, but sometimes it is impossible to keep out intruders." He looked back across the river and shook his head. "It seems the Great Spirit smiles down on us in the form of a white man. Perhaps it is my punishment."

Nathan couldn't resist a smile. "Or maybe we were meant to be on the same side, Cousin."

Winter Wolf looked at Nathan. "I must talk now, for I may not have time later," he said, his voice low. "I do not give Heva up willingly. She is my wife, but that is not enough for her. It seems she need to be free of this world and back in her own. It also seems that she cannot exist without you, *veho*."

"She can exist without me, Winter Wolf. She just couldn't exist with your brutality." Nathan expected Winter Wolf's anger, but it didn't come.

"It is true. Perhaps if I had not let my anger overpower me, Heva would be staying with me."

"Anna is convinced you are a good man, Winter Wolf. So am I."

"Why is this, *veho*?"

"You saved her from the Shoshonis. You didn't have to do that."

"I had no choice. She set me free. I had to take her with me."

"No, you didn't."

"What is this, are you becoming my defender, *veho?*"

"No, I am telling the truth. Part of me hates you for what you did to Anna, but if she's willing to forgive you, then I am, too. I'm just sorry about one thing. I'm sorry you and I couldn't have gotten to know each other better. I think we might have liked each other."

"Now you ask too much of us both."

"I don't think so. I saw pride in your eyes that I could break that horse."

"It was only that I did not want to be humiliated in front of my people." He looked back across the river. "Look, there are more of them. It is not a hunting party."

"How do you know?"

"Look at their weapons. Those are not used for hunting deer and elk."

Nathan studied the Shoshonis. Some carried lances, others carried war clubs and knives, while still others carried rifles. "Shouldn't we get the women and children out of the camp?"

"Yes, we will move them to a safer place. The men will remain and fight." Winter Wolf turned around. "Let us go."

"Wait," Nathan said, his voice devoid of anger. "I have something else to say to you."

"What is it, *veho?*"

"I am proud that I am part of the Cheyenne people. My mother always told me it was an honor, and now I understand why."

Winter Wolf's eyes softened. "You say this even after what I did to Heva and you?"

"Yes. I know your father and mother. They are good and honorable people. It is not possible for their son to be anything less." For a moment Nathan thought that Winter

Wolf would speak, but he didn't. He merely nodded and started forward. But he could tell that his words of kindness had made an impression on his cousin.

They hurried through the trees until they reached the clearing, then ran to the camp. Winter Wolf barked orders to the men, while Nathan went to Brave Wolf. He had already heard the news from the guard and was awaiting their return.

"*Haahe*, Aenohe. It gladdens my heart to see you again."

"And mine, Uncle."

"You have seen the Shoshonis?"

"Yes. Winter Wolf and I counted almost twenty of them. He thinks there are probably more of them on the way."

"They have scouted us then. They know how many strong we are."

"Without the women and children and old ones, how many are we, Uncle?"

Brave Wolf thought for a moment. "Perhaps fifty. I do not count the young inexperienced ones."

"Can we hold them off?"

"It depends how many strong they are. We are blessed that you were there, Aenohe. With your hawk eyes, you have given us an advantage."

"What can I do, Uncle?"

"We must begin to get the women, children, and the old ones together. We will leave the lodges and take only a few horses for the ones who cannot walk far. There is a place to the north that has many rocks. They can hide there until it is over."

"Do you want me to lead them there?"

"No, Aenohe, I will need you here. I will place one of the younger ones in charge to care for our band. Make sure everyone gets together quietly. We do not need to arouse the Shoshonis' suspicions."

"What of the people who are ill or injured?" Nathan was thinking specifically of Anna.

"We will put them on travois, and the horses will pull

314

them. Make sure some of the younger men have weapons, especially some rifles. When you are finished, look for me or Winter Wolf."

"Yes, Uncle." Nathan hurried from the lodge, telling every woman he saw what Brave Wolf had said. He saw panic in their eyes, but they managed to stay calm. He explained everything to Little Deer and she said she would gather everyone together. She told him to bring Anna outside to one of the travois because she was too weak to walk.

Nathan went to Winter Wolf's lodge. Anna was sleeping peacefully. He bent down and kissed her on the forehead and lifted her into his arms, covering her with one of the robes. Then he carried her outside, looking for one of the travois. He found Little Deer, and she led him to one of the travois and Nathan laid her down. She didn't awaken. Again he kissed her, lingering for a moment to look at her.

"Do not worry, Aenohe. I gave her some tea to make her sleep."

"Maybe it's better she doesn't know what's going on." He grasped Little Deer's shoulders. "Are you sure you have weapons?"

"Do not worry, Aenohe. Brave Wolf will send some of the younger men to guard us." She took his hand and brought it to her cheek. "It seems that you are here to protect us. Walk safely, Aenohe. You have become like a son to me."

Nathan stepped forward and hugged the petite woman. "Thank you, Little Deer, for everything." He watched her walk away, leading the horse that pulled the travois on which Anna lay, then went back to the center of the camp. There was already a large circle of men. Brave Wolf motioned for Nathan to sit on one side of him. Winter Wolf sat on the other.

"It seems we have Aenohe, my nephew, to thank for our good fortune."

Some of the men nodded begrudgingly, but most ig-

315

nored his presence.

"If my cousin had not been in the woods and had not had the eyes of an eagle," Winter Wolf spoke calmly, his voice commanding attention, "we would have been killed in our sleep." He looked at Nathan. *"Ne-aoh-oheshe, na-vese-sone.* Thank you, my cousin."

Nathan nodded, realizing what it took for Winter Wolf to acknowledge him in front of his band.

"The women, children, and old ones should soon be safe. We should talk of a plan."

"We need no plan!" One of the young ones spoke out.

"Yes, let us cross the river and attack them," another concurred. He tapped his chest. "I am not afraid of the Shoshonis."

"You would be foolish not to be afraid of them," Winter Wolf said calmly. "They are cunning like the fox. They would hear us coming and be ready to fight."

"Are you afraid to fight, Winter Wolf?" one of the younger ones asked.

Winter Wolf's eyes hardened. "I have never been afraid to fight, Spotted Elk, but I respect the abilities of my enemy. It would be foolish to think the Shoshonis are not prepared to fight us. Have you forgotten already that they stole some of our women and children from beneath our noses? Have you forgotten that I went after them and they took me captive? They are fierce enemies and you would do well to respect them."

"I agree with my son," Brave Wolf said proudly. "They will probably attack after dark, thinking that we are asleep. This camp must look as usual. We must have some fires burning outside lodges."

"Where do we hide?" Spotted Elk asked.

"Some could hide in the lodges, others along the river. We could become part of the night." Nathan looked at Brave Wolf, realizing that he had not asked for permission to speak. "I am sorry, Uncle. I did not mean to speak out of turn."

"No, you are right, Aenohe. We should be waiting for

them in different places. We will divide into groups. Use the weapons you are most suited for." He looked around at some of the men. "I know the young ones like the rifles. I have long objected to these death weapons of the white man, but tonight I will voice no objections. Use them if you wish."

"We should have some warning, Father," Winter Wolf said, then looked at Nathan. "Aenohe and I will go back into the woods. When they are ready to attack, I will howl like the wolf that is my medicine and my protector."

"It will be dangerous for you both, Winter Wolf."

"It does not matter, Father. We must save as many people as possible."

"I agree, Brave Wolf. I will gladly go with my cousin."

"You waste time, Winter Wolf. Why not take a rifle and fire it into the air when you see them coming? That would be a much more suitable warning," Spotted Wolf said impatiently.

Nathan looked at Winter Wolf. Though he was maybe only a few years younger than himself, his face possessed the wisdom and experience of a man twice his years. Winter Wolf remained calm, fixing his steady gaze on the young, inexperienced warrior. "It seems to be a good idea, Spotted Elk," Winter Wolf replied calmly, taking in Spotted Elk's smug expression. "But what if the Shoshonis are all around us? A signal like that could bring them riding into the camp. We do not know how many strong they are. What if they number in the hundreds? Do we let the shot warn them as well?"

Spotted Elk hesitated. "I thought—"

"No, you did not think, Spotted Elk. You are too young to remember when we were attacked by the Crows. They rode into our camp, set our lodges on fire, and killed our people as they ran from the lodges. I do not wish to see that sight ever again."

"I agree with Winter Wolf," one of the elders said. "We should let him and," he hesitated, trying to find the right word, "his *cousin* go into the woods and warn us. We will

317

at least have a few moments to prepare ourselves."

"Uncle, what if they ride into the camp farther downstream, by the village?"

"We must have guards along the river."

"They will be too easily seen, Father."

"What if we are down in the water?"

"What do you mean, Cousin?" Winter Wolf asked, a bemused expression on his face.

"My father once told me that he and part of the band were attacked by Crows. He said what saved them was hiding along the riverbank, covering their bodies with the mud so they couldn't be seen or sitting in the water. They were able to attack many of the Crows as they rode across the river."

"It is good." Winter Wolf nodded his approval. "Spotted Elk, perhaps that is something you could do. Can you shoot your rifle well at night?"

"I can shoot it with my eyes closed, Winter Wolf."

"What about the water? Will it damage the weapons?"

"We will keep the rifles out of the water for as long as we have to, Winter Wolf. I would like to lead some men in this," Spotted Elk said eagerly.

Winter Wolf looked at his father. "What do you think, Father?"

"Yes, it is a good idea. You take fifteen men, Spotted Elk. We are counting on you and that white man's weapon."

"We will not fail you, Brave Wolf."

Brave Wolf nodded. "Buffalo Bull, you take your men and hide in some of the lodges. Make sure you are not together. Loosen the stakes that hold down the lodge. If they try to burn you out, you can escape underneath." He looked at another man. "Red Fox, take some of your men and hide near the trees and on the other side of the camp. We don't want them getting through the camp and riding up into the rocks. They will soon discover there are no women and children here and they will begin to look for them." Brave Wolf looked at all of the men. "You are all brave men and good warriors. If tonight is your time to die, die with honor. Always remember, you are Cheyenne."

The men quickly scattered to various places in the camp. Nathan walked over to Brave Wolf. "If you don't mind, I'd like one of those white man's weapons. I'm better with a rifle than with a knife."

"Go to my lodge. I have many there. I keep them because I do not want the young ones to get too wild and forget how to fight with their hands."

"Thank you, Uncle. Good luck."

"You also, my nephew." He put his hands on Nathan's shoulders. "Thank you for having the eyes of a hawk. Tonight you have proven that you are a Cheyenne."

Nathan nodded, moved by his uncle's words. "I will meet you at your father's lodge, Winter Wolf," Nathan said, knowing that the father and son would want to speak to each other alone.

"Ah, my son. How many times have we fought together?"

"Many times, Father."

"Yes, many times."

"Father, I want to say something and I want you to hear me. I am sorry that I have dishonored you and my mother by my treatment of Heva and Rain Woman. I have no excuses for what I have done. I only know that I do not wish to live with that kind of anger any longer. No matter what happens this night, know that I love you and my mother. You have both taught me the true meaning of honor. Tonight, I will try to make you proud of me."

Brave Wolf's eyes filled with tears. "You need to prove nothing to me, my son. I know what kind of man you are."

"You are being too generous, Father, but thank you. Walk safely on this night. *Ne-mehotatse tsehe-heto.* I love you, my father."

Brave Wolf nodded his head. "*Ne-mehotatse tsehe-eoh-ohha-heto.* I love you, my son. *Ne-sta-va-hose-voomatse.* I will see

319

you again."

Winter Wolf smiled. He hugged his father, holding him tightly, then he walked away, hurrying toward Brave Wolf's lodge. Nathan was waiting for him. "You are ready, Cousin?"

"I think so. What about your weapons?"

"We will stop in my lodge. I do not use the rifle so well. I will use my own weapons."

Nathan walked with Winter Wolf to his lodge, waiting outside until he emerged. The long, gracefully bent Osage orange wood bow hung over one shoulder, a brightly decorated quill filled with arrows hung down his back. A large hunting knife was strapped to his thigh, and he carried a lance in his hand. "Are we ready?"

"Let us go, Cousin."

They hurried back to the woods, this time skirting the outside of the trees closest to the camp. They ran silently. Winter Wolf stopped, listening for any sounds. Nathan faced the woods, hearing the random rustle of wind in the branches, the calls of night birds. A rustling close by startled him. "Raccoon," Winter Wolf breathed. Nathan felt his taut muscles loosen, and an instant later they were running again. Through the dense growth on their left Nathan heard the sound of the river. Winter Wolf clasped Nathan's shoulder, gesturing to a tall cottonwood. "Wait here, Cousin. Listen. I will circle through the woods and return. If you hear my signal, do not wait for me. Go to the village."

Nathan watched as Winter Wolf disappeared into the shadows. He looked upward into the branches and chose a low, sturdy limb to climb. The rough bark tore at his hands as he worked his way upward. He looked back toward the village. The flickering of night fires lit the lodges from within. Other than the unnatural silence, the village was peaceful, deceptively welcoming. Facing the dark woods, he strained his eyes and ears, trying to distinguish the normal rustlings of the forest from the ominous sound of the enemy. They would be nearly silent, he knew that.

He might have no more warning than the single careless snapping of a twig or the sound of leaves as they brushed past. He wondered how Winter Wolf would manage to elude the Shoshonis, but he knew that his cousin was a skilled hunter and warrior, used to the ways of the woods. A scraping sound on the trunk of the tree shattered his thoughts. He aimed his rifle downward and felt the tenseness in his shoulders give way as he heard Winter Wolf's voice.

"I did not frighten you, did I, Cousin?" Winter Wolf settled himself on a nearby branch

Nathan could detect the amusement in Winter Wolf's voice. "I'd be lying if I said you didn't. Did you see anything?"

"I worked my way around in a circle, going to the edge of the woods. I did not hear or see them. If they are there, they have not yet crossed the river."

"Or they're crossing farther downstream near the village. Why don't I go there?"

"No, Spotted Elk and his men are there. We must stay here." Winter Wolf leaned slightly forward. "It is strange that I can sit here with you, my enemy. I have always feared and hated the white man," Winter Wolf whispered, "and yet so many of our wars are with other Indians. Do your people make war so often?"

Nathan strained to hear. Winter Wolf's words had been so faint that he barely heard them. "I understand your hatred of the white man. There is much to hate. Yes, we've had wars. Too many wars."

"When we fight your people, all we want is our freedom. We want to be left alone on our own land."

"It won't happen, Winter Wolf. There is a certain greed which runs among my people. They think they have the right to own everything. They don't understand that this land belongs to you and your people."

"You sound sad, Aenohe."

"I am a white man, Winter Wolf. That will not change. But part of me is with the Cheyenne people and I understand their need to be left alone."

"Perhaps you could talk to your chiefs and tell them what you have told me."

"It won't do any good. Our chiefs don't listen to anyone. They do as they please. They are afraid of you and your people because you're different."

"I do not . . ." Winter Wolf stopped abruptly, reaching out to Nathan. The sudden pressure on his arm was a warning.

There was a crackling of leaves as someone or something walked through the woods. The sound was close, coming closer. Nathan held his breath as the Shoshonis passed underneath them. Nathan tried to tell how many there were, but it was impossible to see through the branches of the trees down into the darkness of the woods. There was suddenly complete silence; even the natural night sounds of the woods were stilled. Nathan realized that it was this silence that had alerted Winter Wolf before they could hear the first rustlings.

Winter Wolf cupped his hands around his mouth. An instant later, the high, eerie lingering howl of a wolf shattered the silence. Nathan started down the tree, but Winter Wolf grabbed his arm. "Wait."

He looked out at the camp. Nathan tried to see beyond the camp to the rocks where the women and children had been taken, but it was too dark. He hoped that Anna was all right. "Look . . ." he said to Winter Wolf, noticing movement in the clearing.

"It is time," Winter Wolf said, descending the tree.

Nathan followed, trailing behind Winter Wolf. By the time they reached the clearing, shots rang out. Shoshonis on horseback were riding into camp. Nathan raised his rifle. There were more of them than they had thought.

"Fight well, Cousin. One of us must live to take care of Heva."

Anna heard the shots. Instinctively, she clutched Robert

to her. She looked out over the rocks and down on the village. She could see the fires burning and she could hear the war cries of the men as they fought. Her body still ached as she leaned against the rock.

"Do you have a knife, Heva?" Little Deer whispered to Anna.

"Yes."

"Good. If the Shoshonis make it through our men, we must defend ourselves." She ran her fingers through Robert's hair. "It would be best to find a place for Hahkota to hide. Some of the older children can watch him." She held her arms out for the boy.

Anna nodded, kissing Robert on the head. "Go with Little Deer and be very quiet." She watched as Robert followed Little Deer. He was silent; all the children were silent. They had been taught from infancy that silence could mean the difference between life and death.

She struggled to her knees, grimacing from the pain. She peered over the rocks again. It was hard to see what was happening. Somewhere in the darkness Winter Wolf was facing death with the rest of the braves. *But at least Nathan is safe,* she thought. Her hand went to the knife strapped to her thigh. She wasn't sure what use she would be if a Shoshoni came into the rocks, but she knew she didn't want to be taken captive by them again.

She looked around her. The young men, boys really, stood guard over them all, backed up by the old men. Older girls watched the children and babies, while the women sat tensely, their hands on their weapons. *They are as afraid as I am to be caught,* she thought.

"Waiting is the hardest part," Little Deer said, kneeling next to Anna. "I cannot count the number of times I have waited for my men to come back from a raid."

"Brave Wolf and Winter Wolf are fine warriors, Little Deer. They will fight well."

"I know this to be true, but I do not know the numbers of the enemy. This frightens me, Heva."

Anna put her arm around Little Deer. The woman had

done so much to help her. "How many times have I heard the men say they are the bravest of all warriors, that one Cheyenne warrior is stronger than five of any other?"

"You make me smile even while I tremble, Heva. Thank you."

"We have to believe they will be all right, Little Deer. And if the Shoshonis do come up here, we'll fight as bravely as the men. That's what my mother would have done."

"I wish Aeneva were here now."

"She is with us in spirit, Little Deer. Perhaps we can draw strength from that."

"Look!" Little Deer called out as some of the lodges went up in flames.

Anna felt a sadness in her heart. They were the Indian's homes, like any other homes. They contained furniture, weapons, medicines, clothing, blankets, everything that white people kept in their homes. Anna thought about the baskets, bowls, blankets, robes, and jewelry that had been handed down in families from mother to daughter to granddaughter. She felt Little Deer's hand on hers and she squeezed it. She had no words of comfort for Little Deer now. All she could do was wait and hope that they would be safe.

Nathan raised his rifle and fired at the Shoshoni who was silhouetted against a burning lodge. For a moment he thought he had missed because the horse kept coming toward him. He started to fire again, but the Shoshoni fell from the horse as it galloped by. They seemed to be everywhere, riding in from all directions. He had to find cover. Another shot rang out near his feet and he hit the ground, rolling to one side. He fired off two quick shots, knocking the Indian from his horse. Avoiding the flickering lights of the burning lodges, he ran across the clearing and found cover in the dark end of the village. While he reloaded the rifle, he looked out. Across the clearing, war cries and muted screams of pain rang out. Now that the Shoshonis were in the clearing and fighting hand-to-hand with the Cheyennes, it was hard to distinguish the enemy. For a fleeting moment, he admired the courage of men who fought their wars close enough to see the fear in each other's eyes and wondered if he was capable of the same kind of courage. A second wave of mounted Shoshoni warriors ended his thoughts, and he knew the best way to help the Cheyennes was to fight his own way. At least he might be able to narrow the odds.

He took aim and fired at the Shoshonis in the clearing, reloaded, and fired again. He put his sights on another warrior, but the closing thunder of hoofbeats spun him around to face the Shoshoni warrior who was riding toward him. Nathan fired a useless shot, cursing himself for not changing his position sooner. The fire had spread and most of the clearing was lit. Nathan saw the Shoshoni warrior lift his rifle an instant before bullets hit the ground around him, throwing dirt and rocks into his face. He rolled against the lodge. Unless he could reload, he was dead. But there was not time. The Shoshoni leapt from his horse, his war cry freezing Nathan for a crucial instant. Almost too late, he raised his rifle to deflect the blow of the Indian's war club. The Shoshoni stepped back and raised the club again, but Nathan smashed the butt of his rifle into the man's knees, knocking him down. Nathan was on top of him, the butt of the gun jammed into the man's throat. *You can,* Nathan thought. *You can see the fear in their eyes.*

He heard a cry from behind him, and turned to see one of the Shoshonis fall from his horse, a lance in his stomach. Winter Wolf ran to the man and pulled out the lance. Nathan reloaded the rifle and ran to join his cousin. A war cry sounded to their right, and Nathan looked to see a Shoshoni ride toward them. He raised the rifle and pulled the trigger, but it jammed. The Shoshoni was poised to throw his lance, but was stilled by Winter Wolf's weapon. Nathan looked at his cousin, running to pick up the dead man's rifle. He looked around him. Bodies lay everywhere, lodges burned brightly in the night, and still, the enemy kept coming.

Nathan and Winter Wolf fought side-by-side until almost dawn, when the last of the Shoshonis rode away. Twice more, Nathan knew he owed his cousin his life. Twice more Shoshonis got close enough to see the fear in his eyes. When the last of the Shoshonis withdrew, Nathan dropped his rifle, his hands and arms were numb with exhaustion.

More than half the lodges were burnt to the ground and bodies lay across the clearing and beyond, where the fighting had spilled over into the woods. It would be hard to tell how many Cheyennes were still alive. Single file, the women and children made their way back into the village. Piercing cries of grief rang out as women found their husbands and sons. Winter Wolf went to Little Deer, gently leading her into what was left of their village.

Nathan saw Anna, Robert clutched in her arms. As he watched her, she faltered, but she had seen him. Joy flickered across her face for a moment but disappeared as she made her way through the fallen bodies. Without speaking, he pulled her into his arms, lightly kissing the top of Robert's head. For a moment they stood, man, woman, and child swaying slightly, comforted by each other's presence. Little Deer's wailing sound of grief shattered the moment of simple closeness.

"Brave Wolf," Anna whispered. "God, no."

Across the clearing, Little Deer knelt beside the man she had loved all her life. Rocking, crying, lost in grief, she tore her clothes. Nathan started toward her but Anna caught her arm.

"No, not now. Leave them alone."

Beside his mother, Winter Wolf stood rigid and silent, the marks of the battle still visible even at this distance. But Nathan knew he wasn't feeling the pain of his wounds. The invincible warrior who had fought beside him all night was gone. The man who stood in the clearing by Little Deer was far from invincible. The battle hadn't frightened him, but the death of his father clearly had.

Chapter 14

Winter Wolf waited in front of Nathan's lodge, calling for him to come out. *"Hahee,* Cousin," he said when Nathan appeared.

"How is Little Deer?"

"She is grieving still. It will be a sad time for her. I have come to ask a favor of you."

"Anything," Nathan replied.

"I would like you to help me erect the scaffolding for my father."

Nathan hesitated before answering. "I am honored, Winter Wolf, but shouldn't a Cheyenne help you?"

"You are Cheyenne, Aenohe, you proved that last night. It is also my mother's wish that you help."

"I will help then."

Nathan followed Winter Wolf to a place in the clearing where long saplings had already been cut. "This is where the scaffolding will be erected, in this tree. It is a good place."

Nathan nodded, picking up some of the long poles and following Winter Wolf to the tree. A thin ladder rested against the trunk of the tree and Winter Wolf easily climbed it, long strands of rawhide hanging over his shoulder. Nathan followed him up the ladder, carrying as many of the poles as he could. He waited until Winter Wolf had selected a good spot and then handed him a pole.

Winter Wolf laid the pole across two branches three feet apart from each other. He secured the pole on his end by wrapping the rawhide around it and the branch. He reached for another pole, doing the same thing until he had tied ten poles about an inch apart on one side. Then he crossed to the other side and secured them all to the other branch. He leaned on the platform, making sure it was sturdy enough to hold his father's body.

Nathan watched Winter Wolf, remembering when he had built the scaffoldings for his parents. He remembered asking Aeneva once why the Cheyennes were buried on scaffoldings, and sometimes left on the prairie covered in robes. She had told him that they wanted to be buried under the sky, not under the earth. They wanted the animals to eat their flesh and scatter it far and wide over the land so that they would always be a part of it. He hadn't understood it as a boy, but he understood it now.

Winter Wolf nodded his head. "It is good."

Nathan climbed down the tree and waited for Winter Wolf. He looked up at the scaffolding. "You've done fine work, Cousin. Your father would be proud."

"Yes, he liked this place. He liked the river and the trees. It is good that he will be buried here." He looked at Nathan. "You told me you buried your parents on your land. Is it comforting to have them nearby?"

"I haven't been back there since they died, but one of the first things I'll do is go up to the hill and talk with them. It's a peaceful place."

"I will look forward to coming back here so that I, too, may speak with my father." He picked up the other pieces of wood and tossed them aside. "It is time to get my mother. This will not be easy on her."

"She has you, Winter Wolf. She will get her strength from you."

Winter Wolf nodded slightly. "It is not the same as having my father."

Winter Wolf's eyes met Anna's as he entered the lodge.

He nodded a silent thank-you to her for staying with his mother. Earlier in the morning, Winter Wolf had assisted Little Deer in preparing his father's body for burial. They had dressed him in his finest clothes and moccasins and his long feather headress, earned through many battles. His body, with his hands at his sides, had been placed on his favorite robe. They had folded the robe over him, lashing it to his body with numerous ropes.

Winter Wolf bent down, placing his hands gently on his mother's shoulders. "Come, Mother. It is time."

Little Deer looked up at Winter Wolf, nodding slightly. "The travois. We will need to put him on the travois."

Winter Wolf shook his head. "We will need no travois on this day, Mother." He walked to Nathan. "Please, Aenohe, carry my father's things for me."

Nathan nodded, picking up the bundle that lay next to the body. He also picked up the shield and lance. He exchanged a brief glance with Anna and waited.

Winter Wolf led Little Deer to Anna and then went back to his father, kneeling to lift his body into his arms. Nathan knew this was breaking with tradition. The body of the fallen warrior was always pulled on a travois for all to see, but Winter Wolf wouldn't allow that. He would carry his father to his burial scaffolding.

Nathan followed the procession of people as they walked with Little Deer and Winter Wolf to the scaffolding. Women cried and chanted, men were stoic, grieving in their own way. Nathan watched Winter Wolf as he walked, carrying his father's body. He held his head high, his expression never betraying the fact that his father's body was weighted down by heavy robes. When he got to the tree, he turned, his eyes seeking out Nathan.

Nathan quickly climbed the ladder to the edge of the scaffolding and waited for Winter Wolf. He put Brave Wolf's weapons and his possessions on the scaffolding. He waited as Winter Wolf began the precarious climb up the ladder, holding his father's body. Winter Wolf climbed the ladder as if he had nothing in his arms, finding the rungs of the ladder without looking. He braced his father with one arm, and held on to the trunk with the other. As he neared the top, Nathan reached for Brave Wolf's body, holding him until Winter Wolf reached the edge of the scaffolding. Before Nathan handed Brave Wolf's body to Winter Wolf, he looked down at the covered figure, remembering Brave Wolf's distinguished and wise face.

"Good-bye, my uncle. May you have a good trip to Seyan. Thank you for all that you have given me." He looked at Winter Wolf and handed Brave Wolf to his cousin.

Winter Wolf gently laid his father's body along the scaffolding, lashing the body to the wood. He took his father's shield and lance from Nathan and laid them alongside him. He unwrapped the bundle that Nathan had carried and hung his medicine bag, his pipe, his favorite necklace, and the rest of his personal possessions on the scaffolding. He knelt next to his father, his head on Brave Wolf's chest. "Thank you, my father, for all that you have given me. Thank you for the life that you gave me and the many lessons that you taught me. Thank you for the wisdom that I ignored for so long but that I will now try to honor. Have a safe journey along the Hanging Road where the footprints all point the same way. Live happily in Seyan. *Ne-sta-va-hose-voomatse, tsehe-heto. Ne-mehotatse.* I will see you, again, my father. I love you." Winter Wolf embraced Brave Wolf one last time, then nodded to Nathan. They climbed down the tree and Winter Wolf went to Little Deer, putting his arm around her. "Do you wish to say good-bye, Mother?"

Little Deer shook her head, her tear-filled eyes looking up at the high scaffolding. "No, my son, we said our good-byes this morning. It is good."

Nathan watched as Winter Wolf and Little Deer

331

walked back to the camp, followed by the other people of the tribe. He looked out over the partially destroyed camp. Half-blackened lodges still stood, others were totally destroyed. There were still many men to be buried and, after that, the band would soon pack what was left on their horses and travois and start the long journey southward to their winter home.

He looked at Anna, still bruised and obviously in pain from her fall into the river, sadness masking her face. He walked to her. Silently, he put his arm around her and led her and Robert back to camp. He didn't know what their future would be together. He didn't even know if she still wanted to leave with him. But now was not the time to ask. Now was the time to help others deal with their grief.

Anna walked into the clearing and found Winter Wolf sitting next to his father's scaffolding. She knew it would take him time to get over his loss and she wasn't quite sure what to say to him. She and Nathan hadn't even had a chance to talk. But it was important, she knew, to speak with Winter Wolf first.

Tentatively, she walked up to him, respecting his grief. When he looked up at her, she saw the sadness in his eyes for the first time. "I don't wish to disturb you, Winter Wolf."

"You do not, Heva. Sit."

Anna sat down next to him. "This is a peaceful place."

"Yes, I wish we were not leaving for our winter home so soon. I would like to spend more time here."

"I visited my parents where they are buried. I feel close to them there." Anna felt Winter Wolf's eyes on her and she looked at him. "How can I help you, Winter Wolf?"

"You have helped me, Heva. It is I who can help you now."

"What do you mean?"

332

"I want you to go back to your world with Aenohe. He is a good man."

Anna knew how hard this was for him to say. "I'm sorry if I hurt you, Winter Wolf. I wanted to help you."

"I am the only person who can help me, Heva. I am not your worry."

"But you are. I have come to grow fond of you."

Anna winced as Winter Wolf reached out and pushed on her ribs. "Even after I did this to you?"

"You didn't do this to me, I did this to myself. I had grown weak. I am ashamed that I could have given up so easily."

Winter Wolf shook his head. "You make excuses to help me retain my honor, Heva. It is not necessary. We both know that I treated you very badly." He looked at her, his dark eyes full of sadness. "I beat and raped you, Heva. I did everything I knew how to frighten you." He looked away from her and up at the scaffolding. "It shames me to say this in front of my father."

"Don't be ashamed, Winter Wolf. I'm sure Brave Wolf is proud of you right now."

"And my mother?"

"Little Deer loves you very much. She has always known that there was a true and honorable man inside you."

"You are a good woman, Heva. I will never forget what I did to you."

"You must forget it and start your life over, Winter Wolf. There is a woman for you. You can be a good husband and father. You have already learned to let go of some of your anger. Do not dwell on mistakes of the past. If I did that, I could never move forward again."

"Perhaps you are right, Heva."

Anna reached out and took his large hand in hers, running her fingers over the bruises and cuts. "Perhaps we will meet another time, Winter Wolf."

"Perhaps, Heva."

"I would like to stay for a while to make sure that

333

Little Deer is all right. She has become like a mother to me."

"No, I think it is best for you and Aenohe to leave as soon as possible."

"Don't be angry."

"I am not angry, Heva. I think it would be less painful if you leave now."

"All right." Anna started to get up, but stopped, reaching over and wrapping her arms around Winter Wolf. "I have learned from you, and I thank you for that. Have a good life, Winter Wolf." She kissed him on the cheek and then walked away, trying to still the tears that stung her eyes. She didn't know why she felt like crying. Winter Wolf had hurt her in many ways and yet she still couldn't hate him. Perhaps she had understood part of what had driven him and felt sorry for him. She hoped that he would someday find the kind of love he was hoping for.

Anna went to Little Deer's lodge, calling out to her and then entering. She was surrounded by many of the women, but when she saw Anna, she held out her arms to her.

"Come here, Heva."

Anna sat next to her, her hand on Little Deer's. "Nathan and I will leave soon. I wanted to say good-bye."

"Yes, I knew it would be soon. I will miss you."

"And I you, Little Deer. You have been like a mother to me."

"Yes, I am sad, but Aeneva is smiling. She is with her brother again and she is looking down on us, happy that we have grown to care for each other."

"I wish I could stay, Little Deer. I want to be here to help you."

"There is nothing you can do, Heva. Do not be sad for me. I had a good life with Brave Wolf and my heart soars to see my son become the man I knew he could be."

"I just talked with Winter Wolf."

"Did it go well?"

"Yes, it went very well. We have parted as friends."

"That is good. That is how it should be." She turned to Anna, taking her face in her hands. "You are like a daughter to me. I shall not forget what you have brought to us all."

Anna wrapped her arms around Little Deer, holding her for a long while. "Thank you, Little Deer. We will say good-bye before we go." Anna rose and left the lodge, walking slowly and hesitantly toward Nathan's.

Nathan tied their packs to their horses. He was riding the stallion that Winter Wolf had given him, and they would be leading the Appaloosa colt that Winter Wolf had given Anna. Little Deer had given them each a parfleche filled with food, medicine, and little gifts that she had made for them. She had also given them each a blanket and robe to keep them warm for their journey south. He took two rifles with extra ammunition and water bags. Little Deer was coming toward him, carrying something else with her. He smiled.

"We have enough already, Little Deer. You are also going on a long journey. Think of yourselves."

"We are fine. Nothing was damaged in our lodge. Take these." She handed two wooden flutes to him. "These were Brave Wolf's, handed down to him from his grandfather, Stalking Horse. He would want you to have them."

"I cannot take them, Little Deer. They should be given to Winter Wolf."

"It was Winter Wolf who said I should give them to you."

Nathan stared at the intricate carving on the delicate wood, and he nodded his head. "Thank you, Little Deer. I shall give one to my brother." He packed them in the parfleche. "I wish I had something to give to you," he said sadly.

"You have already given much, Aenohe. You have been like the sun to me and my family. You shined on us and you made things better."

Nathan looked away. Little Deer reminded him so much of Aeneva, it made him want to cry. "You are too generous, Little Deer. You and Brave Wolf have shown me much, and when I fought with Winter Wolf, I saw what a truly brave warrior he is. I owe my life to him many times over."

"So, we are like a real family, are we not?"

"Yes. I feel as if my tie with my mother's people has been renewed through you and your family. Thank you for that."

"Come here to me, Aenohe. Hug this old woman."

Nathan smiled as he stepped forward and took Little Deer into his arms. She was so small yet so full of strength. "I feel as if through you I have seen my mother again, Little Deer." He bent and kissed her on the cheek. "You are not an old woman. You are a beautiful, strong woman who has made me a better man."

Little Deer smiled, shaking her finger at him. "Just like your father. Aeneva said your father could weave a magical web with his words. Be happy, Aenohe. May the Great Father always smile on you."

Nathan felt the tears sting his eyes as he watched Little Deer walk away. He would miss her. He went back to his horse and rummaged through his saddlebag. He gently pulled out a wooden box and opened it. It contained Sun Dancer's silver necklace and his father's pocketwatch, which had belonged to his grandfather. He held the items in his hands, knowing it was time to give them up.

"Do you need help, Cousin?" Winter Wolf walked up to Nathan.

Nathan turned around. "No, I'm packed. Do you remember the necklace I told you about, Winter Wolf? The one that Sun Dancer gave to my grandfather?"

"Yes, I remember the story well."

Nathan took the necklace and held it up for Winter Wolf to see. "This is it."

Winter Wolf's eyes widened as he took the silver-and-turquoise necklace in his hands. "It is a beautiful piece of work. Our people have not worked much with silver and turquoise, but I am impressed by this."

"I want you to have it," Nathan said solemnly.

Winter Wolf handed the necklace back to Nathan. "I cannot take it. It was entrusted to your father by Sun Dancer. She wanted *you* to have it."

"She wanted it to stay in this family. What better person to have it than her great-grandson?"

"You also are her great-grandson."

"Not by blood."

"Is blood so important, Aenohe?"

"You told me once that it was."

"But you have taught me differently. I have fought side-by-side with you. You helped me to bury my father. No blood brother could have done more."

"Then that is why you should take the necklace. Save it for your son or daughter. Please."

Winter Wolf hesitated for a moment but finally took the necklace. "I am honored, Aenohe. You have taught me that not all white men are to be feared. You have also taught me about forgiveness."

"I'm glad we are able to part friends, Winter Wolf. Thank you for saving my life. It would have been easy for you to let me be killed. You could have had Anna to yourself."

"I could never have truly possessed Heva. I know that now. Her heart was always with you." He reached out and firmly grasped Nathan's shoulder. *"Ne-aoh-oheshe, na-vesesone.* Thank you, my cousin."

Nathan reached out and grasped Winter Wolf's opposite shoulder. *"Ne-sta-va-hose-voomatse, na-vesesone.* I will see you again, Cousin." Winter Wolf nodded and walked away. "Winter Wolf—wait. I have something for Little Deer." He held the watch up for him to see.

337

Winter Wolf smiled. "I will not argue with you, Cousin. I know how much pleasure this will give my mother. Thank you."

"Tell her to remember that each time she hears it chime Aenohe loves her."

Nathan watched Winter Wolf walk away and he felt as if he had resolved some things. Now, he was ready to continue to live his life. He hoped that he and Anna could put the shattered pieces of their love back together again.

It had been over a week since Anna and Nathan had left the Cheyennes, and each carried their own scars. Anna had spoken very little on their ride. She wasn't sure how she felt anymore. She had been through so much and yet she was sad to leave Winter Wolf and Little Deer. She was also frightened to be alone with Nathan, knowing that she would be forced to confront the fears she now had about their future together.

They had run into an early snow, and Nathan had decided to stop and find shelter. He found a small cave that would make suitable shelter, and he unpacked the horses and laid out the blankets and robes for Anna and Robert. Anna made sure that Robert ate, and she watched Nathan as he unpacked the horses. Something had gone wrong between them. She couldn't talk to him. When he came into the cave, she handed him a piece of pemmican.

Nathan nodded his thanks. "Do you want me to start a fire?" he asked.

"I'm not that cold," Anna answered. "The robe keeps me warm." She pulled it up around her legs, making sure that Robert was covered. "Are you still hungry? There's some meat and dried fruit."

"No thank you," Nathan replied curtly. "I'm tired." He lay down on his robe and wrapped himself up in it.

Anna watched him as he slept, and part of her wanted

to reach out and touch him. But she felt too distant. She wasn't sure how to approach him. So much had happened between them. He knew that Winter Wolf had raped her, but he didn't know that she had been with him willingly. Could he ever forgive her for that? She wasn't sure she could ever forgive herself for being so weak. She lay down on the robe, gently pushing Robert down. She patted his back, helping him to sleep. She closed her eyes, not wanting to think anymore. All she wanted to do was sleep.

Nathan woke to the howls of wolves. They sounded as if they were right outside the cave, but he knew they were farther away than that. The night was totally dark, without even a touch of moon. He tried to see Anna and Robert in the darkness, but he couldn't. He wanted to reach out to Anna, but neither of them was ready for that yet.

He stood up and walked outside, carefully finding his way to the horses. He checked to make sure they were all right, then went back to the entrance of the cave. He looked up at the sky. It was amazingly clear. The storm had passed, and there was little snow on the ground. He saw the cluster of stars that Aeneva called the Hanging Road and he smiled to himself. He liked the Cheyenne belief that a person would follow the Hanging Road where all footprints pointed in the same direction to Seyan, the place where a person would meet all his friends and relatives, where there were endless herds of buffalo and deer, and where the water ran clear and the land was unending.

"Nathan?"

He heard Anna's voice from the mouth of the cave and he walked to her. "Are you all right?"

"Yes, I just wondered where you were."

"I was just looking up at the stars and thinking about Seyan. It must be a beautiful place."

"I had a dream when I was sick. I was on the Hanging Road. I was running and laughing and I felt so happy. Then I met Aeneva and Sun Dancer. They spoke to me. They told me to be brave."

"You saw Mother and Sun Dancer? You had a dream vision?"

"I don't know. Maybe I just wanted to see them."

"But they spoke to you?"

"Yes, Mother told me not to be afraid, that you were near."

"I'm glad you saw them."

"Aeneva had a message for you, Nathan. She told you not to grieve for her and your father. She said there was nothing you could have done for them, that it was their time to go."

Nathan could barely speak. "She said that to you? You heard her words, Anna?"

"Yes, as clearly as if she were standing here beside me."

"I feel as if a weight has been lifted from my shoulders."

"She wanted to tell you something else. She said to tell you that her heart was still full of love for you."

Nathan nodded in the darkness, unable to speak. Even if it had been a dream, he felt as if he had been forgiven. It was more than he could have asked for.

"Sun Dancer said she would always remember your smile."

Nathan laughed, recalling the many times he had sat in Sun Dancer's lap while she had told him a story with her hands. "Was she still beautiful?"

"Yes. She and Mother were still the most beautiful women I have ever seen. I'm convinced they came into my dream to make me live."

"I'm glad of that, but I'm sorry I wasn't there to help you."

"There was nothing you could have done, Nathan."

"But you thought I had gone. If I had been there—"

"Stop it, it's over now. We can't live in the past anymore. If I keep remembering everything that's happened to me, I'm afraid I'll go mad. Instead, I have to think about the future."

"And have you thought about the future, Anna?"

"A little."

"Have you decided anything?"

"Not really. I just want to get Robert back to Roberto and then I want to go back home and rest. I want to be where I feel I belong."

"I know."

"But at least we have a home to go to. I keep thinking about the Cheyennes and wondering what they will do. They have so little now."

"They'll survive. Winter Wolf will lead them."

"But it won't be long until their land is taken from them, though Winter Wolf will fight before allowing that to happen."

"Winter Wolf will keep finding places for them to live that the whites won't be able to find. It'll be a while before their land is taken from them."

"You grew to like him, didn't you?"

"I didn't think it was possible after what he did to you, but I saw something different in him the night we fought. He showed no fear and he never gave up. He proved what a true warrior he is."

"The wind is picking up. I'm going back inside."

Nathan followed Anna into the dark cave, lying down on his robe and covering himself. He wanted to reach out to her, to hold her, to feel the closeness of another human body next to his, but he couldn't do it yet. They had so far to go to find their way back to each other, and neither one was willing to take the first step.

Roberto pounded in another nail, his arm burning from all the strenuous work. He and the ten men he'd hired had already begun to enlarge Rachel's office. She

341

had ordered new examining tables, instruments, and real beds instead of cots. She wanted an area where people could stay if they were badly hurt, similar to a hospital but not as large. Yvette fit in perfectly. She already knew everyone in town and they eagerly told her their medical problems while she listened patiently. It seemed everything was working out well for him, except for one thing. He still didn't know if his son was alive. He had already decided that he was going to talk to Lyle and see if he'd heard anything new. If he hadn't, he was going to try to find the Cheyennes' winter camp.

"Aren't you hungry?"

He heard Rachel's voice, and looked down at her. She stood with her hands on her hips, her hair pulled back in a thick braid. She was wearing a dark-blue dress, and he wasn't sure he'd ever seen her look more lovely. He didn't think it was possible, but he fell more in love with her every day. She was unlike any woman he'd ever known. She was bright, funny, competent, and extremely passionate. He couldn't wait until Nathan, Anna, and Robert came back so he could marry her.

"You're going to freeze up there," Rachel said.

Roberto put down his hammer and moved to the ladder, climbing down. He ordered the men to take some time for lunch and he went inside. He took Rachel's hand in his. "Have I told you lately that you're beautiful and I love you?"

Rachel blushed but smiled. "Have I told you that you can freeze to death in this kind of weather if you insist on staying out in it too long?"

He saw Yvette smile as she pretended to be busy at her desk.

"Why don't you get yourself some lunch, Yvette. I know your boss is a slave-driver, but I'll let you go."

"I was just going to tell her to go," Rachel said indignantly.

"Do you want me to bring anything back?"

"No, Yvette, you go on ahead. Take your coat. This

weather's not good for you."

"You worry about me too much, Rachel."

"She likes you a lot," Roberto said, sitting in one of the chairs and pulling Rachel into his lap.

"I like her, too. She's been a great help to me." She put an arm around Roberto's neck. "What would people think if they walked in here and found their doctor sitting in a strange man's lap?"

"Let them think anything they want," he answered, kissing her deeply.

Rachel put her hand over his mouth. "Wait, please. I want to say something."

"This sounds serious."

"It *is* serious. No one has ever believed in me the way you have, Roberto. You've done so much for me, I'm not sure how I can ever repay you."

"You don't have to repay me, Rachel. I already told you that."

"But you've not only helped me, you've helped this town. Do you realize how much you've given them by rebuilding this office?"

"It doesn't matter. What matters is that *you're* happy and *I'm* doing something useful with my money."

Rachel wrapped her arms around his neck. "I do love you."

"I know," Roberto said, kissing her. "I've been thinking about something myself, Rachel."

"Now *you* sound serious."

"If I don't hear from Nate soon, I'm going to look for Robert. I couldn't live with myself if I didn't try to find him."

"I understand. I'll wait for you, no matter how long it takes."

"Thank you." He held her against him, never tiring of how she felt in his arms. He closed his eyes, wishing that they were already married.

"Rachel! Rachel!" Zeb's voice sounded frantic from outside the door.

Roberto exchanged glances with Rachel and they both stood up, hurrying to the door. Zeb slid from his horse, almost falling on the ground. Rachel ran to him.

"Uncle Zeb, have you been at the saloon already?"

"Rachel, it's Nathan and the woman. They're back." He looked at Roberto. "They have your son. He's fine."

"Thank God," Roberto muttered. "I'm going out there."

"You better bring your bag and come too, Rachel," Zeb suggested. "The woman don't look too good. Nathan's not at his best, neither."

Rachel grabbed her bag and jacket. "Uncle Zeb, would you please wait here until Yvette gets back. Explain to her what happened. If there are any emergencies, I can be reached at the ranch."

"I'll be here," Zeb said, standing on the steps.

Roberto untethered his horse and mounted, pulling Rachel up behind him. He was happy that Robert and Nathan were all right, but he was afraid for Anna. He knew only too well what she had suffered and felt he had contributed to it.

He rode his horse hard, not even feeling the cold against his face. Rachel's arms were wrapped tightly around his waist. He urged the horse faster, hoping to gain precious seconds. He tried to keep from thinking while he rode, but his mind kept coming back to Anna. If he hadn't kidnapped her and taken her to New Orleans, maybe none of this would have happened. Maybe she'd be safe today. But thanks to Anna, he'd found out about the son he never knew he had.

The rolling pastures that led up to the ranch were on either side of them and Roberto still didn't let up. When they reached the yard, he gave Rachel his hand and helped her down, then slipped a leg over the saddle horn and jumped down. They hurried across the yard and up the front steps. He threw open the door and went inside. Nathan was sitting in front of the fire, Robert on his lap. He turned when he saw Roberto and Rachel, a weak smile on his face. Roberto rushed to him, taking

Robert and crushing him in his arms. He kissed his son over and over and then looked at him, making sure he was all right.

"God, I can't believe he's here."

"Where is Anna?" Rachel asked Nathan.

"She's in the bedroom where Roberto and I stayed. She's pretty weak."

Rachel sat on the arm of the chair, looking into Nathan's eyes and feeling his forehead. "You're a little warm. Roberto, get him some soup and bread. Make sure the boy gets some of the broth." She picked up her bag and hurried across the room.

Roberto pulled the other chair next to Nathan. If Robert seemed uncomfortable with his father after not having seen him for so long, he didn't show it. He sat contentedly in Roberto's lap, playing with his belt buckle. Roberto touched Nathan's arm. "Are you all right, Nate?"

Nathan stared at the fire. "I'm all right, I guess. I'm tired, Berto. I just want to go home."

"You can't go home, not for a while at least. The weather's bad right now. Soon there'll be storms. It's not good traveling weather."

Nathan nodded slightly, as if he really weren't paying attention. "Do you remember that hill you and I used to ride up when we were kids? I beat you all the time and mother always told me to let you win once in a while."

"I remember."

"I'd give anything to go back to that time."

"What's the matter, Nate?"

Nathan looked at Roberto, his eyes vacant and tired. "I've lost Anna and I can't get her back."

"You haven't lost her, Nate. She's right here."

"You don't understand. She's been through too much. She doesn't want to be reminded of the last few years, and all I do is remind her."

"Did she tell you that?"

"In so many words."

"Nate, you're just tired. Let me get you something to eat, and then you rest. Sleep for as long as you need to. Don't worry about Anna, Rachel will take good care of her."

Nathan nodded. "Yeah, maybe I need some sleep." He looked over at Robert. "He's a good boy, Berto. He's strong, just like you."

Roberto stood up, taking Nathan's arm. "Come on, Nate. Let me get you something to eat, then I'll show you where to sleep."

"I'm not really hungry."

"You better eat or Rachel will force it down you. I promise, you can sleep afterward." Roberto helped Nathan to the table, his heart going out to his brother. He had never seen him look so weak or disheartened. Nathan had never let him down; he'd almost gotten killed trying to save his life. Now it was his turn. Whatever it took, he would help Nathan and Anna see that they belonged together.

Rachel finished washing Anna and carefully slipped a clean nightgown over her head. There was redness and swelling around Anna's rib cage, and Rachel was sure she'd broken some ribs. While Anna had slept, Rachel had taken several wide pieces of gauze and wrapped them tightly around Anna's rib cage. It would be difficult for her to breathe for a time, but it was the only way Rachel knew to let the ribs heal.

She cleaned the various cuts and bandaged them. When Anna awakened, Rachel had spoken to her, explaining to her who she was, and then had given her something to make her sleep through the night.

She took the dirty clothes and placed them in a pile in the corner. She stood at the foot of the bed, watching Anna, making sure she was breathing evenly. She heard the click of the door handle and nodded to Roberto when he looked around the door. He stood by Rachel.

"How is she?"

"Very weak. She's so thin it looks like she's barely eaten in weeks. I think some of her ribs are broken, and she has bruises and cuts all over her. I don't know what happened, but it's clear she's been through a lot."

"Will she be all right?"

"I think so. She'll need a lot of rest and she'll need someone to check on her every day for a while.

"I'll do it. I don't think Nate is up to it."

"Did he tell you what happened?"

"No, he just said he'd lost Anna."

"They must have been through a terrible time up there. We have to be as patient as we can with them, Roberto."

"I feel terrible, Rachel. If Nathan hadn't gone up there alone . . ."

"There was nothing you could do about it. You know that. Even if Robert hadn't been up there, Nathan would've gone for Anna. Whatever happened, they're the ones who have to work it out. All we can do is help them by being their friends." She looked toward the half-open door. "Where's your son? I'd like to meet him."

"He's at the table eating. So is Nate."

"I'd better check on him." Rachel made sure that Anna was covered. She picked up her bag and went to the kitchen, kneeling next to the chair where Robert was sitting. "Hello, Robert."

Robert was busy stuffing a piece of bread into his mouth and didn't seem too interested in Rachel at the moment. She smiled and playfully rubbed his head. She stood up and pulled a chair next to Nathan. He sat, his elbows propped on the table, playing with a piece of bread. "Nathan, look at me," she ordered.

Nathan glanced up at Rachel. "Don't lecture me, Rachel. I'm not in the mood."

"Well, that's too bad, because you're going to get one," she said curtly. She took the bread from his hands and turned his face, forcing him to look at her. "Listen to

347

me, Nathan. I don't know what happened between you and Anna, and frankly, I don't care. I just want to help you both. But I can't help you if you won't let me."

"I never said I wanted your help."

"You don't have a choice, Nathan."

"Leave me alone, Rachel." Nathan pushed his chair away from the table and stood up. "Maybe the best thing would be if I get on a train and head back for Arizona."

"What's in Arizona without Anna?" Rachel demanded.

Nathan stopped, his eyes reflecting his weariness. "Maybe there's nothing for me there, but there's nothing for me here, either."

Rachel walked up to him. "Is this the real you, Nathan? Do you always give up when things get too tough? Roberto told me you almost died trying to save his life once. Why are you giving up so easily on the woman you love?"

"Too much has happened. I'm not sure either of us can forget."

"Then give yourself time, Nathan. Stay here with us. Be with Roberto. He's missed you. Let me take care of Anna. See how things are when you're feeling a little stronger. Please."

"I don't know, Rachel. There's so much to be done at the ranch. I haven't been there in so long . . ."

"I can keep you real busy. Roberto is building me a new office. You can help. It'll take your mind off things."

Nathan shook his head. "I bet you always get your way, don't you?"

"No, only when I know I'm right. There's another reason you can't leave, Nathan."

"What is it?"

"Roberto and I are going to be married. We wanted to wait until you and Anna came back."

Nathan took Rachel's hands in his. "I'm glad for you both, Rachel. You'll be good for each other."

"You'll stay then? Roberto won't get married without you here. If you leave, I may never have a husband."

Nathan couldn't resist a small smile. "All right, I'll stay until after the wedding. I can't promise you anything after that."

"Thank you, Nathan. You won't regret it."

Chapter 15

Anna sat by the window, staring out at the yard. She could see part of the Rockies even from the back of the house. They were covered with snow. She pulled the heavy blanket up around her waist. She wasn't sure why she felt so alone. Nathan and Roberto were here, and Rachel was very sweet, but still she felt as if she didn't belong.

There was a knock on the door, and she knew it was Rachel. She smiled as Rachel came into the room, carrying a tray filled with food and a small pot of tea. Anna liked her very much and she was happy that she and Roberto were getting married. "Hello. Shouldn't you be in town?"

"I'll leave in a bit. I wanted to check on you first." Rachel set the tray down next to Anna. "I want you to eat. You need to build your strength back up."

"You shouldn't be doing this, Rachel. You have more important things to do than take care of me."

"You're going to be part of my family, Anna. No one is more important than my family." She looked into Anna's eyes and checked her breathing, then pulled down the blanket. "Lift up your nightgown. I want to check that wrap." She put her hands around Anna's rib cage, making sure the wrap was secure. "You seem to be breathing better."

"It's not as painful. I think I'm healing."

"In spite of yourself."

"Please don't, Rachel. I'm not up to talking about my problems with Nathan."

"You're going to have to talk about them sometime, Anna. You can't keep things inside forever."

"It doesn't do any good to talk. He and I have been through too much, seen too much, to ever make it right again."

"What about Roberto?"

"What does he have to do with us?"

"He went through a terrible time when he was put on that ship as a boy. He was a slave for almost ten years. He told me that he was bitter and full of hatred. But look at him now."

"Did he also tell you that he forced me to marry him and go away with him, that if I didn't, he'd kill Nathan?" she said angrily, staring out the window.

"Yes, and he also told me that you're the one who helped him to change. He said your patience and kindness helped him to see that life was worth living."

Anna refused to look at Rachel. "I don't really care what Roberto says. Could you just leave me alone?"

"I'll leave you alone if you'll look at me for a minute."

Begrudgingly, Anna turned her head.

"I've been waiting a long time to meet you, Anna. I had heard so much about you from Nathan before he went to search for you. He's in love with you. I've never seen a man so in love with a woman."

"Rachel, please . . ."

"Just listen to me, Anna. I don't know what happened between you two, and I don't know what happened to you up there with the Cheyennes. All I know is what Nathan told me and what Roberto keeps telling me. You and Nathan are bound together by something very strong. Even though you've been torn apart, you can still manage to be pulled back together. Don't give up so easily on something that's so precious, Anna. You could regret it for the rest of your life."

Anna looked away from Rachel. She heard the door close as Rachel left the room. She rested her head on her arm, feeling the tears roll down her cheeks. It was true, she had never loved any man more than she loved Nathan, but she now knew that love wasn't enough.

"That's enough, Nate. You're going to kill yourself if you don't take a break."

Nathan stopped for a moment, looking down from the roof of Rachel's office. He'd been working since early that morning. It felt good to be busy. It helped to keep his mind off Anna. "I'm fine. I just want to put a few more boards in place."

Roberto climbed up the ladder. "You're as stubborn as a damned mule. Do you know how cold it is out here? Your fingers could fall off from frostbite."

"I'm all right. I'll take a break in a while."

"Why don't you just jump from the roof. It'll make things a lot easier."

Nathan put the hammer down, blowing on his hands as he rubbed them together. "What do you want from me?"

"Anything. Why don't you push me off this ladder because I messed up your life by taking Anna away from you."

"You did what you had to do."

"So, that makes it all right? We both know if I hadn't forced Anna to go to New Orleans with me, she would never have been taken from that train. Your lives would have been so different. Why aren't you angry with me, Nate? I deserve your anger."

"I don't know, Berto. I guess because it doesn't serve any purpose." He picked up the hammer again, but Roberto grabbed it and threw it down on the ground.

"Listen to me, damnit! I owe you so much, Nate. I owe you my life and my son's life. I'm going to do everything I can to pay you back."

"Stop it, Berto. You don't owe me anything. You would have done the same thing for me."

"Have you forgotten already that I almost let you die? Think about it, Nate. I wasn't such a nice guy when I came back."

"But you *didn't* let me die, did you? As much as you hated me, you couldn't let me die."

"Do you remember telling me I had to let go of my anger? Do you remember that?"

"I'm not angry, I'm just—"

"Giving up. That's worse."

"Just leave it alone," Nathan said angrily, moving to the ladder. "Get down, would you?"

"I don't think so, Nate." Roberto held on to the edge of the roof and kicked the ladder out from underneath him. It fell to the ground with a crash. "Unless you want me to follow that ladder down, you better help me up."

"Goddamn you," Nathan muttered, pulling Roberto's arms and dragging him onto the roof. "What are we going to do now?"

"I'm sure someone will be along soon."

"And in the meantime we'll freeze to death."

"I didn't think the cold was bothering you."

"You know, I think I liked you a lot better when you were mean."

"Sorry to disappoint you, big brother, but thanks to Anna and Rachel, I don't have much meanness left in me."

"I ought to beat the tar out of you, Berto."

"Go ahead. Maybe it'll make you feel better."

"It's not going to work, you know."

"What's not going to work?"

"You think you're going to get me alone up here and I'll tell you all about me and Anna. I don't have anything to say on the subject so just leave it alone."

"Whatever you say."

"When are you and Rachel getting married anyway?

353

I'd like to get the hell out of this godforsaken place."

"I think it's real pretty up here."

"When are you getting married?"

"Rachel wants to get married in the spring. She wants to have the ceremony in the pasture with the wildflowers blooming."

"I'm not waiting until spring. If you two don't get married real soon, I'm leaving."

"It would break Rachel's heart. She's never had much of a family. She already considers you and Anna like a family."

"Would you stop it. We're not kids anymore, Berto, and this isn't a game. Anna and I have been through too much. Instead of bringing us closer together, it's pushed us farther apart. So, no matter what you or Rachel say, I'm not staying here."

"Would you really let some stranger stand up with me when I get married?"

Nathan shook his head in disgust. "I can take the train back up here in the spring. Besides, I can't stay away from the ranch any longer."

"I've been in constant contact with Jake. I've sent him money to pay the men, and he says everything is fine. There's no hurry, Nate."

Nathan turned his head, staring off into the magnificent mountains that dominated the horizon. "Have you talked to her?"

Roberto moved closer to his brother. "No, not yet. I thought I'd give her some time. Time can heal a lot of things, Nate."

"I don't know, Berto. I always thought our love was so strong that nothing could destroy it. Now I realize that no love is that strong."

"You're wrong. Listen to me, Nate," Roberto said, putting his hand on Nathan's shoulder. "Don't expect so much of yourself or of Anna. Just take it slowly."

"When did you become such an expert?"

"When I met Anna. She taught me all about forgiveness. Now she has to forgive herself, just like you do."

Nathan nodded. "We'll just have to see, Berto. We'll just have to see."

Anna rocked back and forth in Zeb's creaky old chair on the porch. She smiled as Robert tried without success to catch a chicken in the yard. It was a cold day, but the sun was shining and the clouds that usually hung over the mountains had partially cleared. She pulled the blanket tighter around her. Nathan had left early in the morning, as usual, to work on Rachel's office. Roberto had remained behind to spend the day with Robert. She knew it was only a matter of time before Roberto tried to get her to talk. She heard his footsteps across the hardwood floor and the doors opened.

He handed a steaming cup to her. "A hot cup of coffee with sugar and cream," he announced.

Anna smiled. "You remembered."

"How could I forget? You drank a lot of coffee in New Orleans."

Anna held the cup in her hands. "New Orleans seems like a hundred years ago."

"But it wasn't, Anna."

Anna ignored Roberto's obvious attempt to get her to talk. "How's Rachel's office coming along?"

"Why don't you come see for yourself?"

"No, I don't think so."

"Why, because you might have to talk to Nate?"

"If you're going to lecture me, too, Berto, don't bother. I've heard enough."

Roberto bent down in front of the rocking chair, placing his hands on the arms to stop Anna from rocking. "This is me, remember? I'm the one who took you away from Nathan. I remember how much you wanted to be with him. When I saw you two together, I didn't think any two people could be so much in love."

"Things change."

"What could have changed that much, Anna?"

"I don't want to talk about it, Berto."

"Did he hurt you in some way? Was he the one who beat you?"

"No, he didn't hurt me. He tried everything he could to protect me, but he couldn't." She looked past Roberto, purposely ignoring him.

"Did someone else hurt you?"

"I don't want to talk about it, Roberto."

Roberto held his hands up in the air. "All right. I won't bother you any more. Will you just answer one question?"

Anna shrugged her shoulders. "Depends on the question."

"Do you still love Nate?"

Anna patted Roberto's hand. "I'm tired, Roberto. Do you mind if I go inside?"

Roberto stood, holding Anna's blanket while she got up from the chair. He called for Robert, and they followed Anna into the house. He went into her room and laid the blanket across her lap. "I'll leave you alone for now, Anna, but I'll find out what's wrong with you and Nate. And when I do, I'll find a way to fix it."

Anna looked out the window. She knew there was no way anyone could fix what was wrong with her and Nathan. It wasn't any specific thing; it was an accumulation. They were both tired of trying to love each other. They were tired of fate always getting in the way. Anna leaned her head against the wall and closed her eyes. Right now, it seemed better and easier not to love at all.

Nathan was growing agitated. He and Anna had been here less than two weeks and he'd only seen her a few times. Tonight Rachel had talked her into sitting at the table with them, but she refused to be cordial. No matter how much Rachel and Roberto tried to get her to talk, she refused.

"Don't you think so, Nate?"

"What?" Nathan asked his brother absently.

"I was just saying to the ladies that I think Rachel should get herself a partner. After all, she's going to have children to look after someday. She won't have the time to be a doctor to everyone."

"He's probably right, Rachel. You'll be so busy raising babies, you won't have time to look after other people."

"I'll always have time to look after other people. It's what I do. What do you think, Anna?"

Anna shrugged her shoulders. "You should do what you want to do," she said simply.

Nathan dropped his spoon into his bowl. It made a loud, clanking noise. "If you don't mind, I think I'll get some air."

"If you're leaving on my account, don't. I'm going to my room," Anna said, getting to her feet.

"Well, that's a surprise. You've barely left that room since we got here. You know, Anna, if you're so heartbroken, I can take you back to Winter Wolf." He watched her lips tremble and her eyes tear up.

"I used to think you knew me so well, but you really don't know me at all. At least Winter Wolf treated me with respect."

"He treated you with respect, all right. He beat and raped you and treated you like a slave. If that's what you're used to, then why don't you go back to him, Anna." Nathan threw his napkin on the table and stomped out of the house.

Anna lowered her head. "I'm sorry, I didn't mean to ruin your dinner." She ran to her room.

Rachel shook her head. "I feel so sorry for them. I wish there was something we could do."

"Maybe I should beat some sense into my brother."

"Anna isn't trying, either, Roberto. It's as if they're afraid to admit they need each other."

"Then maybe we need to force them to need each other. Let's stay in town Saturday. We'll get a room at the hotel and we'll go to dinner. I'm sure Yvette wouldn't mind watching Robert."

"And what about Uncle Zeb? What if he comes back?"

"He said he'd stay with Lyle for a few weeks to let Anna mend. He won't be back."

"Are you sure we should do this, Roberto? What if we just make things worse?"

"How can things be any worse, Rachel? Did you hear the way they spoke to each other? If we're not around, they'll be forced to talk to each other."

"Anna might just stay in her room all night and never come out."

"There's always that possibility, but we won't know unless we try."

"All right. We'll do it your way and pray they don't wind up killing each other."

Nathan put his tools away, said good-bye to the other men, and went inside Rachel's office to clean up. He knew that Rachel and Roberto thought he'd run right back to the ranch when they told him they were staying in town, but he would be damned if he'd do it. He'd brought a change of clothes. He was tired of the ranch. He needed to get out and be with people. He washed up, changing into a clean shirt, then brushed his hair, which grew well over his collar. He looked like a blond-haired Indian. It was time for a haircut.

He turned around to leave and walked right into Yvette, catching her by the arms. "I'm sorry, Yvette. I didn't see you."

"It's all right." Yvette stared at him.

"Is something wrong?"

"You don't look very much like your brother."

"We aren't much the same, I guess." He sat on the

chair to clean off his boots.

"You are going to the saloon tonight?"

"How'd you guess?"

"I can tell when a man is trying to impress a woman."

"All I did was change my shirt and clean my boots. I just want to have a few shots of whiskey."

"You are looking for trouble, Mr. Hawkins."

"How would you know, Yvette?"

"Because I worked in that saloon for many years before Rachel brought me to work here. I've seen many men like you, men who have had their hearts broken but who are too stubborn to do anything about it."

"I get a lecture everywhere I go!"

"Rachel tells me that you have a woman at home. Why not go to her, Mr. Hawkins? The women in the saloon are not what you want."

"Thanks anyway, Yvette, but I'm a grown man. I think I can decide for myself." He walked out of the office and onto the plank sidewalk that led to the saloon. He tipped his hat to women he passed, and tried to ignore the stares of strangers who wondered about him.

He heard the sounds of the saloon before he reached it. A piano player pounded the keys in an off-note tune, and the voices of men and women laughing made him realize how lonely he really was. He pushed open the doors and walked in. He stood for a moment, getting used to the multicolored bright lamps, then he walked to the bar. Round tables were set around the saloon, some filled with card players, others with lonely men and women trying to pass a long winter's night. The shiny bar was lined with men talking about the weather, the price of beef, or their wives.

He ordered two whiskeys and drank them quickly. He leaned on the bar, looking at the people. He already recognized many faces. Many of these men were married, yet they were here, drinking and dancing and doing whatever else to all hours of the morning. The women were dressed in brightly colored, low-cut dresses, their faces painted with make up to make them look more beautiful. In reality, he thought they all looked like they were playing at being happy. Suddenly, he didn't want to be here. This place held nothing for him. He put some coins on the bar and walked out and back to Rachel's office. Yvette was sitting at the desk, writing. He knocked on the door and walked in.

"Mr. Hawkins. Did you forget something?"

"No, I just wanted to thank you. You were right. I'm going home."

"Good. Have a safe trip."

Nathan smiled and left the office. He pulled the jacket from his saddlebag and put it on. It was a cold night, too cold to be riding, but he didn't have much choice. He had to get back to the ranch, to Anna. It was time to start seeing if their love still existed or if it was just a sweet memory.

Anna sat in front of the fire, wrapped up in her blanket trying to read a book. But she hadn't read more than two pages. It was lonely at night. Where was Nathan? She was sure he would be here, knowing that she was alone. But she couldn't blame him if he didn't want to be with her. She'd been so moody lately. She had never been so unsure of herself in her life.

The large window shuttered back and forth as the wind blew against it. She could feel the cold through the thin glass. She put the book down and pulled the blanket up around her neck. She stared into the deep orange flames of the fire. She thought about the times she had sat before the fire in Winter Wolf's lodge and prayed to be away from him. Now, here she was, in a safe place with Nathan, but unable to really be with him.

She heard the hoofbeats of a horse as it came into the yard. She thought it might be Nathan, but perhaps it was Zeb. Or perhaps Roberto had come back for some reason. She picked up her book and held it in front of her, pretending to read. She heard the footsteps on the porch and the doors open. She forced herself to keep reading.

"Good book?"

Nathan's voice sent a shudder up her spine. She lowered the book slightly. She watched him as he stood in front of the fire, rubbing his hands to get them warm. He took off his jacket and threw it on the chair. He looked so tall and lean, leaner than before, and his hair was long. She liked it that way.

"It's cold out there. I think we'll be getting the first snow anytime soon."

Anna looked toward the window. "Yes, I think so, too. I've been watching the window shake back and forth. If a really strong wind comes, it'll blow it out."

"I'll have to get the wood out and nail it up. Rachel says Zeb is crazy about that window. As soon as winter's here, he covers the window with a board to make sure it doesn't get broken."

"Did you see Rachel and Roberto in town?"

"I saw them earlier. They were looking forward to an evening alone. Is Robert all right?"

"Fine. He went right to bed." She held the book against her chest. "I feel bad that I've been here so long. Rachel doesn't need another patient."

"She loves to take care of people."

"You like her don't you?"

"Yes. I think she's the best thing to happen to my brother."

"I've never seen Berto so happy. He's like a different person."

"He says love made him that way."

Anna lowered the book to her lap. Absently, she fiddled with the pages. "He's lucky."

"It doesn't have anything to do with luck. He made it happen."

"It *does* have to do with luck. If we'd never been on that train and Roberto had never been hurt, Rachel would never have met him and taken care of him."

"He still made it happen. Rachel was scared to death of him when they met, but Berto was determined to make her fall in love with him."

"Then she was lucky that he was so determined."

"God, you're a stubborn woman."

"How is Rachel's office?"

"Rachel's office is fine. Would you like to know how I am?" Nathan waited, pacing back and forth in front of the fire. "Well, actually, I feel like hell. I've been chasing around after the woman I love for almost three years, and when I finally think we have a chance for a future together, she decides she doesn't want me."

Anna couldn't meet Nathan's eyes. "Don't be angry, Nathan."

"Don't be angry? How can I not be, Anna? Am I supposed to be happy that you've decided you don't love me anymore? You tell me. Just what am I supposed to do?"

"I don't know. I don't know myself what to do, how can I tell you?"

"Can you at least tell me how you feel? Can you do that, Anna? Be honest with me for a change?"

Anna closed the book, running her fingers over the fine leather cover. "I don't know how I feel, Nathan. I'm scared, I know that, and I'm confused. I feel as if I've had no say in my life for the last three years. I always thought I was strong, but now I know I'm not. I'm weak, and I'm not sure I can live with that." She closed her eyes, not wanting to cry in front of Nathan. She felt his hands on her knees as he knelt in front of her.

"Look at me, Anna."

Anna shook her head, afraid to look into his clear, honest eyes.

"Look at me."

His voice was gentle but commanding. She opened

her eyes. Nathan looked the same. He was still the same person he had always been. But why did everything seem so different?

"Do you want to go back to Winter Wolf?"

His words startled her. She hadn't expected them from him. She'd thought a lot about Winter Wolf, and she was sorry for his loss, but she knew that she could never stay with him. What was it then? "No, I don't want to go back to Winter Wolf. I never loved him, Nathan."

"What about me? Do you love me, Anna?"

Anna couldn't meet his eyes. She stared down at the book in her lap. She wasn't sure if she was capable of love anymore. She felt as if she'd been stripped of all her emotions.

"Never mind, I think you just answered my question," Nathan said angrily, standing up and walking back to the fire.

"No, I didn't answer your question."

"You didn't have to. It's all right, Anna. As soon as I can get on a train, I'm leaving and going back to the ranch. I'm going to live there. I don't know what you want to do, but I'll make sure you get a portion of the money Mother and Father left."

"Nathan . . ."

"I have that land in California. Maybe you could move out there. At least you'd be near Garrett and Molly."

"Nathan, please be patient with me."

"I've tried to be patient with you, Anna, but I've run out of patience. Maybe you're right about luck—maybe we just don't have any."

Anna watched him as he walked up the stairs to his room, slamming the door behind him. She put her hands over her face, trying to stifle the sobs that wracked her body. She was so afraid. She began to shake all over. She stood up to get closer to the fire, but the shaking grew worse. Then she heard Nathan's door open as he came back down the stairs. She didn't want to hear his angry words again. She turned toward the fire.

"Don't worry, I won't bother you for long. I just need something to read."

She heard him rummage through the bookcase. He was so close, yet she couldn't reach out to him. She closed her eyes, trying to make the shaking stop.

"Anna, what's the matter?"

She couldn't answer. She felt Nathan's hands lead her back to the chair. He knelt in front of her and covered her with the blanket. He took her hands and rubbed them. She watched him as if he were a stranger. She didn't know how to reach out to him.

"Are you feeling sick again, Anna?"

Anna shook her head. "No, I'm not sick. I'm not sick," she repeated, trying to force the fear from her mind. She felt Nathan gently pull her up from the chair and place her in his lap. She felt comforted with his arms around her, and she laid her head against his shoulder.

"It's all right, Anna, I'm not going to leave you again."

"Don't say that, Nathan. Every time you say that, something terrible happens."

"That's what this is all about, isn't it? You're afraid something will happen to keep us apart again."

"I don't know what I think. I'm just tired of being afraid."

Nathan held her tightly. "I want to help you, Anna. Please."

"I don't think you can help me, Nathan."

"Just rest now, don't worry about anything. I'll take care of you."

"I don't know what's the matter." She closed her eyes and soon she was asleep.

Nathan rested his head against Anna's, holding her as he would a frightened child. He knew now that she still loved him but was afraid of losing him again. He didn't know how to help her, but he would find a way. Now that they were finally together, he wouldn't lose her again.

"I've looked through my books and there aren't many things that relate to Anna's type of illness."

"What do you mean her 'type of illness?' "

"She's not physically ill, Nathan. She should be up and around. Nothing is preventing her from doing that except her mind."

"Are you saying she's insane?"

"Of course I'm not saying that. What I am saying is that Anna has suffered a lot in her young lifetime. A person can't endure that kind of suffering and not have scars. And she does have scars, Nathan. They may not be visible to any of us, but they're there."

"Can she be helped?"

"I think so. She's young and she's strong and she has a man who loves her very much. But she needs to learn how to trust again. She needs to learn how to love."

"I can't believe this. I always thought she was so strong."

"She *is* strong, Nathan. If she weren't an incredibly strong woman, she would never have survived the things she's been through. I can't believe everything you've told me. Even if you don't count the last three years, think about her early childhood. Her mother died when she was small and her father was a drunk who took her from town to town while he drank and gambled. Even though your parents gave her love and security, that all disappeared when she was kidnapped by Driscoll. And it kept getting worse. I'm surprised Winter Wolf didn't completely break her."

"He almost did. She tried to kill herself."

"But she didn't, did she? She's strong, Nathan, but you have to be patient with her."

"I feel so helpless, Rachel."

"She knows you're here. She let you hold her, didn't she?"

"God, I couldn't stand it if I lost her this way."

"It's your turn to be strong, Nathan. Be loving and patient. Anna will come back to you in time."

Nathan paced around the room. "How do I get her to come out of her room?"

"You don't. You let her decide when she's ready. But you also let her know that you're not going to stop living because she won't come out of her room."

"Thank you, Rachel. I think I'll go in and see her now."

"Why don't you wait. I'd like to talk to her first."

Nathan simply nodded.

Rachel knocked on Anna's door, not waiting for an answer to open it. Anna was sitting in the window seat staring out at the mountains. "How are you, Anna?" Rachel sat down next to Anna.

"I'm all right."

"Would you like to go for a short walk with me? I have something I'd like to show you."

"No, I don't think so."

"Please, it won't take very long. I think you'll like it."

"All I have is this dress that you bought me. I won't be warm enough."

"Sure you'll be warm enough." Rachel pulled the blanket up around Anna's shoulders. "Now, just slip your boots on and we'll go."

Rachel stood by the door as Anna pulled on her boots. "Rachel, I . . ."

Rachel gently took her arm. "Come on, you'll like this place." Rachel led Anna through the house, past a silent Nathan, and out around the back to her favorite place. She and Anna sat down on the stone bench. The stream was already full and the rosebushes had already died.

"This is my favorite place. I like to come here and sit, especially in the spring and summer when my roses are blooming."

"But they look dead."

"They are, but when the snow melts, I'll plant new bushes and they'll bloom. It's the most wondrous thing. Uncle Zeb says I'm a witch. He says rosebushes aren't supposed to bloom that quickly after being planted, but they always do."

"Why do you bother, Rachel, especially when you know they're going to die?"

"Because they bring me such joy while they're here. When I come out here and see the first flower beginning to bloom, its petals just starting to open and its fragrance floating in the air, I feel alive. I feel as if I understand what life is all about."

Anna stared at the barren brown branches of the rosebushes. "It makes me sad. They bloom once and then they die."

"It's rather like humans, don't you think, Anna?"

Anna looked at her, her eyes puzzled.

"We are only alive for a short time, but what matters the most is how meaningful we make our lives. If we take from life what we can, then we are also blooming. Don't you think it's worth it, Anna?"

"I don't know anymore, Rachel," she replied sadly. Tears streamed down her cheeks

Rachel reached over and took a tear on her finger. "Look at this Anna. This tear proves you're alive. Don't you see? As long as you're breathing, you have a chance. You can do anything you want. You're a strong woman. You've been through so much and still you're fighting."

"I don't know how to fight anymore."

"But you do. If you didn't, you'd be dead right now."

Anna looked at Rachel. She wiped the tears from her face. "I want to comfort Nathan, but I don't know how."

"Don't worry about Nathan right now, worry about

you."

"I'm afraid."

"We're all afraid, Anna. Do you know that before I met Roberto, I'd never had a man in my life. Never. I never wanted one because I was afraid. I was sure if I showed any interest in a man he'd laugh at me. Roberto helped me not to be afraid, but I found the real courage inside me. It's in you, too, Anna. I know it is."

Anna thought back to her dream. What had Sun Dancer said? The strength she sought was already inside her. "What if I lose Nathan again?"

"There are no guarantees, Anna. You might lose him again, but you might have a wonderful life together. Can you risk losing what you might have together because you're afraid?"

"So much has happened, Rachel. I was with another man. I don't know if Nathan can forget that."

"I don't think Nathan is the one who will have trouble forgetting it."

"This man raped me, he beat me, he made me cower like a frightened lamb, and still I had feelings for him. That's not normal, Rachel."

"I don't understand how you can be so hard on yourself, Anna. This man may have treated you badly, but he also saved your life and, in some strange way, he cared for you. There's nothing wrong about caring for someone who saved your life."

"I hate myself. I hate myself for being so weak and cowardly that I let him do whatever he wanted to me," Anna said, her voice choked with sobs.

Rachel put her arm around Anna. "You didn't do anything wrong, Anna. You have to forgive yourself and be proud that you were strong enough to survive."

Anna nodded, staring at the dead rosebushes. "I'd like to see the roses when they bloom."

"If you stay, you will. Roberto and I don't want to get married until spring. We'd love it if you stayed with us."

"Roberto's lucky to have you."

"Luck had nothing to do with it," Rachel said with a big smile. "I wanted him as much as he wanted me. I wasn't about to let him go."

"Then I suppose if I want Nathan back, I'll have to work at it."

"Yes, you will, but I don't think you'll have to work too hard. Come on, we should be going in now."

"I'm going to sit out here for a while longer."

"All right, but not too long."

"Rachel."

"Yes?"

"Thank you."

"There's nothing to thank me for. Just get well, Anna."

Anna continued to stare at the dead rosebush, and instead of making her sad, it somehow gave her strength. Perhaps there was hope after all.

Nathan narrowed his eyes. "I think you're bluffing," he said, his voice cold.

"There's only one way to tell," Anna replied, her face expressionless.

"I'll see your two dollars and I'll raise you another two dollars."

Anna threw the money into the middle of the table, much to the delight of Rachel and Roberto. She raised Nathan another two dollars.

"You'd better be careful, Nate. Don't forget, Pa taught her how to play."

"Yeah, I know." Nathan stared at Anna, realizing that her eyes sparkled for the first time in weeks. "I call."

Anna spread out her cards. "Three jacks, two kings. A full house, Nathan."

"I know what a full house is, Anna," he replied curtly as he spread his cards out on the table. Anna laughed. "Two pair, threes and fives? That was your hand? You've lost your touch, Nathan." Anna brought the money over toward her. "Twenty dollars. I could buy myself a new dress and hat with this."

"I can't believe you had a full house. I thought for sure you were bluffing."

"I guess you don't know me as well as you think you do."

Nathan grinned. "You palmed a jack, didn't you?"

"I did not. I don't even know how to do that."

"Pa taught Berto and me how to do that when we were just kids. If he taught us, he taught you."

"I didn't palm a jack, Nathan."

"I don't trust you."

"You don't have a choice. This hand is over."

"Come on, Nate. She won fair and square. You always were a bad loser."

Nathan shook his finger at Anna. "I know you did it."

"You can't prove it."

"How about some pie and coffee?" Rachel offered.

Roberto moved closer to Nathan. "Why were you accusing her like that? She's just now beginning to act like her old self."

"I know she palmed the jack, Berto, and she knows I know."

"So, what does it matter?"

"It matters because she's showing some of her old spirit. I haven't seen her like this since we left New Orleans."

"She even looks better. I forgot what a beautiful woman she is."

"I've never forgotten how beautiful she is," Nathan said in an absentminded tone.

"How about if Rachel and I take our pie upstairs and leave you two alone?"

"No, she likes you two. Besides, she may leave if she's left alone with me. I have to take it real slow, Berto."

"Here we go," Rachel said, setting down plates of apple pie. Anna brought over mugs of coffee for each of them.

"So," Nathan said as he looked across the table at Anna, "you want to tell us how you palmed that jack? I have to admit it was good. I never saw you do it."

"That's because I didn't do it, Nathan. If you're so upset over your money, I'll give it back."

"No, that's all right."

"You just bet on a lousy hand."

"Two pair isn't lousy."

"It is when the pairs are threes and fives. Trenton taught me never to bet high on two pair low, especially when the other person keeps raising you."

Nathan nodded. "Did he also teach you to palm a card as you were dealing in case you might need it?"

"I don't know what you're talking about." Anna looked at Rachel. "This is wonderful pie, Rachel. Is there anything you can't do?"

"I can't play cards very well."

"Playing cards well won't get you very far in life," Anna replied. "What was the matter with you tonight, Berto? I saw you play cards on a riverboat. You're a pretty good player yourself."

"I'm nothing compared to you. You know, Anna, Pa did teach us how to do that. We used to play with the ranchhands all the time. They couldn't tell when we palmed a card."

Anna shook her head. "I wouldn't cheat you or Nathan."

"I know better," Nathan said

"That's enough about cards," Rachel said with finality. "We have more important things to talk about. We have those fences to mend in the far pasture. We're going to have to do it before it freezes."

"It's already frozen, Rachel and 'we're' not doing anything. Nate and I will do it."

"For heaven sakes, Roberto. I've done it every other year. Uncle Zeb and I were the only ones around to do it."

"Well, we're here this year and you won't have to do

371

it."

"He's right, Rachel. Besides, you don't need to be out there in this cold. I've seen the way you've been limping lately."

"All right, I won't argue with you. Just be careful. It's miles from the ranch. If you get caught out there, you'll freeze to death."

"She doesn't think much of us, does she, Berto?"

"I guess not."

"I don't know how Aeneva put up with you two," Anna said. "You must've driven her crazy."

"On more than a few occasions." Berto looked at Nathan and laughed.

"At least she had you to love," Nathan said, his voice gentle.

Anna's eyes met his. "Thank you," she said simply.

Roberto stood up suddenly. "Well, I'm tired. How about you, Rachel?"

"I'm not—"

Roberto walked to Rachel's chair and helped her out. "Of course you are. You need to rest that leg of yours. Good night, you two."

"Night."

"Good night, Rachel. Good night, Roberto."

"Roberto never was very good at being subtle," Nathan said.

"He's so happy he just wants us to be happy too. He feels responsible."

"I know. I've talked to him about that. I told him not to blame himself."

"I'm proud of you. You've forgiven Roberto. I know it must have been hard for you."

"It wasn't all that hard when I reminded myself what he'd been through. In fact, I don't have much of a problem forgiving people. You're the one who doesn't do such a good job at it."

"What are you talking about?" Anna was clearly upset.

"You seem to be able to forgive everybody, even Winter Wolf, but you can't forgive yourself. Why, Anna?"

"Don't, Nathan. I don't want to talk about it."

"But you're going to have to talk about it one of these days. You keep hiding away in this house, hoping that you won't have to face yourself. But some day you will have to face yourself, Anna."

Anna stood up, slamming her hands on the table. "Why is it everyone around here has an opinion about me? Can't I just be left alone?"

Nathan stood up, facing her across the table. "No, because we all care about you."

"Just because you all care about me doesn't give you the right to interfere in my life!" She pushed her chair back and walked around the table. Nathan grabbed her and pulled her to him.

"I think I have more of a right than anyone else."

"What gives you any right to me?"

Nathan's eyes bored into Anna's. "The fact that I've loved you more deeply than I've ever loved another human being." He lowered his mouth to hers, but Anna turned her head.

"Nathan, don't," she said.

"You can't hide forever, Anna." He took her head between his hands and stared at her. "I love you. Nothing will ever change that. I don't care what Winter Wolf did to you. I know it wasn't your fault. Why won't you let me love you, Anna?"

Anna pushed Nathan away, running into her room. She stood against the closed door, shutting her eyes. Nathan was still able to get to her. He knew her so well. She walked over to the window and stared out at the darkness beyond. She could feel the wind blowing in through the thin glass of the window. She shivered. The door opened and light suddenly illuminated the dark room. Nathan walked to her, pulling her into his arms.

"Keep running from me, Anna, but I'll always be right behind you. I'll never give you up. Never." He touched his mouth to hers, barely pressing his lips against hers. He caressed her cheek, then left the room.

Anna touched her trembling lips. She loved the feel of his mouth against hers, the familiarity of his body next to hers. She didn't want to drive him away, she wanted to love him. But she was afraid she had forgotten how to love.

Chapter 16

Anna sat while Rachel brushed her long dark hair and pulled it back with a blue ribbon. She squirmed in the blue wool dress that Rachel had bought for her. "I don't know why I let you talk me into this."

"You're going to have fun." She stood back and looked at Anna's reflection in the mirror. "You're so pretty, Anna. I always wanted to be pretty like you."

Anna looked at Rachel in astonishment. "You *are* pretty, Rachel. More than that, you're smart. You've done something important with your life, something you wanted to do. I wanted to go to college. I wanted to write for a newspaper."

"Why didn't you?"

"I met Nathan and my whole life changed." She looked at herself in the mirror. "If I'd never met him, maybe my life would have been different."

"And you might never have known the kind of love you've known with Nathan. Come on, they'll be waiting for us." Rachel picked up a dark wool cloak with a hood and handed it to Anna. "Don't forget this. You'll need it."

"I can't believe people have parties when it's this cold outside."

"It's not cold in the barn. We have a little stove and when we get all of the bodies inside it gets nice and warm."

"How far is this barn?"

"Only about a mile from here."

"Far enough for all of us to freeze to death."

"Come on, Anna. You'll have fun."

Anna put the cloak over her shoulders and followed Rachel out of the room. Nathan and Roberto were waiting in the front room by the fire. Robert was already asleep.

"You both look lovely, ladies." Roberto kissed Rachel on the cheek as she walked to him.

Nathan nodded his head in agreement, staring at Anna. "You look beautiful."

Anna thanked him, then walked to Zeb, who was sitting in his chair smoking his pipe. "It's good to have you back, Zeb. I want to thank you for being so nice to me that first day."

"Wasn't nothing, girl. Someone as pretty as you deserves all the attention she can get."

Anna felt herself blush. "Are you sure you don't want to come to the dance. A man like you should be out dancing with the women."

"Someone has to stay here with the young'un. Besides, I'm too old to be dancin' anyway."

"I don't believe that for one minute." Anna bent and kissed Zeb on the cheek.

"Why, Anna, I do believe you've made Uncle Zeb blush."

"Git on outta here before I lose my temper," Zeb railed.

"We shouldn't be too late, Uncle Zeb. Thank you." Rachel kissed her uncle on the cheek and followed the others out the door.

Roberto had rented a covered buggy for the night from the livery, and he had it parked in front of the porch. "Well, what do you all think?"

"I haven't been in a carriage since I lived in the East," Rachel said enthusiastically, letting Roberto help her inside.

"You sure know how to impress the ladies, little brother."

"I learned everything from you, Nate." Roberto helped Anna up into the carriage. "Go ahead, Nate. I'll drive."

"No, why don't you ride inside. I doubt if I'll be welcome inside." Nathan climbed up onto the seat and headed the carriage out of the yard.

Anna talked with Rachel and Roberto on the way. She was beginning to feel a little better, but still, the cloud of doom continued to hang over her.

"I think we're here," Rachel said, unable to contain her excitement. She held Roberto's arm. "Before I met you, I used to come to these dances and stand off by myself in the corner. I always wanted to dance in the worst way, but no one would ask me."

"Well, you're going to dance so much tonight, your feet will never be the same."

Anna looked at the two lovers and she envied them. She had never seen two people more in love or more suited to each other.

The carriage stopped, and Nathan jumped down and opened the door. He helped Anna down, then Rachel. Rachel and Roberto walked on ahead leaving Anna to herself, unsure of what to do. Nathan took her elbow and led her to the barn. There was a lot of noise from inside. Fiddlers played and people sang. The sound of laughter filled the night air. As Nathan opened the door, the bright light from inside shone outside on the yard. Anna couldn't keep from smiling as she walked inside. Women and men clapped their hands, dancing around in circles as a caller told them what to do. The center of the barn was cleaned out except for the bales of hay which served as seats. There was a tablecloth thrown over several bales, and punch, coffee, cookies, and little cakes were laid out. Some of the men stood in the corner, sipping from a flask, acting as if no one could see what they were doing. There was an infectious gaiety, and Anna smiled as she watched the people.

"Would you like to dance?" Nathan asked.

"No, I don't think so. I'd rather watch." Anna continued to observe the people, unaware that Nathan had walked away from her and over to Yvette. She watched as Roberto and Rachel square-danced, laughing as they missed the steps and ran into each other. She envied their simple, uncomplicated love.

The music changed suddenly. A man with a guitar played a slow, haunting melody. Men took women in their arms and danced closely together. She knew that Nathan would soon ask her to dance, and she took a deep breath. She didn't feel like dancing. She turned to tell him so, but she couldn't find him. She looked around the barn until she saw him dancing with Yvette. She was such a beautiful girl and it was obvious that she enjoyed Nathan's attention. Anna pulled her cloak closer around her, suddenly feeling like a spinster. She was the only female, except for a few elderly women, who wasn't dancing. She wished she hadn't come.

She noticed that Yvette had her hand on the back of Nathan's neck and was playing with his hair. It made her angry that another woman would be so familiar with him. Nathan had his hand firmly around Yvette's tiny waist and their bodies were very close. Feeling self-conscious, she stepped backward, sitting down on a bale of hay. She remembered the first time she had ever danced with Nathan. She had felt like a princess at that ball in San Francisco and when he had asked her to dance, she was sure she would faint. But she didn't. Instead, she fell in love.

When the song ended, Roberto walked toward her. "Will you dance with me, little sister?"

Anna smiled. He had called her that but a few times. "I haven't danced this way in a long time."

"Quit making excuses, Anna. Dance with me."

Anna dropped her cloak on the hay bale and took

Roberto's extended hand. She followed him to the circle of people and waited as the caller told them what to do. She had always enjoyed this kind of dancing. She and Garrett had danced many times late into the night when his family had parties.

When the music began, Roberto put his arm around Anna and twirled her around in a small circle. Then he took her hands in his and skipped sideways around the large circle, following the other people. By the time they got back to their place, the caller told the men to move to the right one person, and Anna had a new partner. She found herself laughing, dancing around the large circle each time with a new partner, until, finally, Nathan was her partner. When he put his arm around her and danced her around, she felt as if she were dancing on a cloud. She looked at him as they skipped around the circle, and she realized she was having fun. When they returned to their original spots, the caller told the men to take their ladies and "squeeze them real tight." Nathan held onto Anna until the next song began. Again, the guitar player strummed a slow, beautiful tune. This time, she didn't resist his arms. She held onto his hand and put her other hand on his shoulder, absently rubbing it.

"This is nice," Nathan said. "Do you remember the first time we danced?"

"Of course."

"I thought I was dreaming when I saw you. You were so young and fresh and beautiful."

Anna suddenly felt angry. Her body became tense. "I don't think I want to dance anymore."

"You don't have a choice." Nathan held her waist tightly. "I think you're even more beautiful tonight than the first time I saw you."

"Don't," Anna said, staring over Nathan's shoulder, avoiding his eyes.

"I'm glad you're not that innocent girl I first met."

"Why, you like your women with more experience?"

she asked angrily, trying to pull away.

"You're going to cause a scene, Anna. Do you want to embarrass Rachel and Roberto? These are their friends."

"Then let me go."

"I'll let you go as soon as you listen to me."

"I don't want to hear anything you have to say."

"I don't care about any other men, Anna. You were forced. It wasn't your fault."

"Please, don't," Anna pleaded, trying to pull away.

"No, I won't stop until you listen to me. I don't think anything less of you because of what happened. How could I? I admire your courage. You're the bravest woman I've ever known."

"Nathan . . ." Anna said softly, burying her face in his chest.

"It's all right, Annie," Nathan said, his mouth close to Anna's ear. "I love you, don't you know that."

"What if something happens and I lose you again?"

"At least we will have been together and had the chance to love each other. I think it's a risk worth taking."

"I don't know. I need more time."

"I won't push you."

Anna looked up, a slight smile on her face. "You always push me."

Nathan shrugged. "I'm not perfect."

"But you are so sweet."

"Does that mean you'll dance with me all night tonight?"

"I don't know. Maybe this would be a good time for you to see if there are any other women who you might be interested in."

"What are you talking about?"

"There are some attractive women here. You might have better luck with them than you did with me."

"Never." He lowered his mouth to her ear. "Why don't we take the carriage and go home early? I'm sure Rachel and Roberto wouldn't mind."

"No! I couldn't do that."

"Why not?"

"Because." She pulled away and walked back to the hay bale, pulling the cloak around her shoulders. "I just want to sit for a while."

"I thought we were having fun."

"Ask someone else to dance, Nathan," she said brusquely. She watched him walk away without saying a word, the anger evident on his face. She sighed. It was only going to get worse.

"Why did you stop dancing? You two looked like you were having fun." Rachel sat down next to Anna, sipping at a cup of punch.

"I need to talk to you, Rachel."

"Of course. We can talk tomorrow."

"No, this can't wait."

"What is it? Are you feeling ill again?"

"No, that's not it." Anna looked down at the cloak, pulling the cloth between her fingers. She looked around to make sure no one could overhear her. She leaned closer to Rachel. "I think I'm going to have a baby."

Rachel set the cup of punch down. "Anna, are you sure?"

"I think so. I don't know. I've been miserable about it ever since we left the Cheyennes. It's possible that I'm carrying Winter Wolf's child. Nathan could never live with that."

"You don't know that for sure, Anna."

"I know Nathan. He can forgive a lot of things but not another man's child."

"His father forgave Aeneva, and he raised Roberto as his own."

"This is different, Rachel. I gave myself to the man willingly. He didn't force me."

"He raped you, Anna. How much more force do you need?"

381

"He raped me the first time, the second time I gave in to him. I feel so ashamed."

"When was your last cycle?"

"In the camp."

"And you've been here two months."

"See!" Anna said anxiously. "I know I am, Rachel. I know it."

"Have you been feeling ill in the mornings?"

"No."

"Have your breasts been swollen?"

"Not really."

"And you don't look like you've put on any weight. That's good."

"So you think there's a possibility I'm not going to have a baby?"

"I don't think so, Anna. You're probably worrying for no reason."

"I hope so."

"I'll examine you in the morning. We should be able to tell for sure after that."

"I don't know what I'll do if I am."

"Don't worry about it now. Try to have a good time."

Anna nodded as Rachel kissed her on the cheek and walked away. Nathan had said she was the bravest woman he'd ever known. If he knew how scared she was right now, he would never have said that.

She was suddenly feeling warm. She saw Nathan talking to Yvette again and she walked to the door. Quietly, she opened it a fraction and slipped out. She pulled the hood of the cloak up over her head and pulled the cloak around her. She walked out into the yard and into the still night. The noise and gaiety from the barn seemed to be hundreds of miles away. She looked up at the stars, wondering where Aeneva and Trenton were. She missed them so much. She would give anything to see them again.

"Are you looking for the Hanging Road?"

Nathan startled her. "I was just wishing I could see

Aeneva and Trenton again. They had a way of making everything seem so clear . . . I'm sorry about earlier, Nathan. I'm still trying to get used to the idea that I don't live with the Cheyennes anymore. I'm surprised no one around here has said anything to me."

"They wouldn't. Rachel is too well respected."

"It must have been hard for you working in town. I'm sure people have talked."

"I don't care if they talk, Anna. I don't give a damn what anyone says. The only thing that matters is that you're back with me and you're safe." He put his hands on her shoulders. "I know I'm pushing again, but I just want to tell you how much I love you. I want to marry you and I want you to have my children."

Anna turned away, covering her mouth with her hand. "What if I couldn't have children. Would you still want me, Nathan?"

Nathan was quiet for a moment. "I've always dreamed what our children would be like. We'd have two sons, one with light hair, one with dark hair, and we'd have a little girl who'd look just like you."

"Nathan, stop it! Some things just aren't meant to be."

"We're meant to be, Anna. I know it."

"I don't think so, Nathan. Not anymore."

"Why? What suddenly changed? You were beginning to feel good again."

"Could you forgive me anything, Nathan?"

"Of course I could."

"Could you forgive me carrying another man's child?" Even in the dim light of the yard, Anna saw the look of pain in Nathan's eyes.

"No, you're not—"

"I think I'm carrying Winter Wolf's child. Could you raise another man's child, Nathan? Could you love it as you would your own?"

Nathan turned around, staring out into the dark night. "When did you find out?"

"I've suspected for some time now."

"That's what's been bothering you."

"I knew you could never accept it."

"You're not giving me much of a chance to answer for myself."

"Well, could you raise another man's son?"

Nathan shrugged. "I don't know, Anna. I'd be afraid that every time I looked at the child, I'd think of Winter Wolf."

"So will I, but I won't have a choice. I have to raise this child because I'm the mother. You have a choice."

"Well, this does change things a little, doesn't it?" Nathan shook his head. "I should have known that things couldn't work out for us."

"I'm sorry, Nathan. I don't know what to say."

"There is nothing to say." He walked back into the barn.

Anna walked to the carriage, climbing up and shutting the door. She pulled her cloak tightly around her and huddled in the corner. After her examination, she would get on the first train and head west. She'd go to San Francisco and stay with Molly and Garrett. She'd have her baby and raise it where no one would know that its father was an Indian. She would love it and take care of it. She would never let it find out that it was created out of hatred. It would know only love.

"I hate this place!" Nathan yelled, shaking his hand up and down.

"Why don't you go on back to the ranch? You've been in a foul mood ever since we got here this morning."

"I told you I'd help mend fences and that's what I'm going to do."

"What's the matter with you today?"

"Doesn't matter."

"What is it with you and Anna? I've never seen two

384

people enjoy making each other as miserable as you two do."

"I guess we were never meant to be together."

Roberto threw the hammer into the snow. "I've heard enough of your self-pity."

"Me? What about Anna?"

"Anna has a reason to feel sorry for herself, but she was beginning to come out of it. What did you do, tell her you didn't want the baby?"

"You know about the baby?"

"Rachel told me last night."

"I should have known."

"I'm not going to tell anyone, Nate. But God, what did you say to her?"

"I said I didn't know if I could raise another man's child."

Roberto walked over to the hammer and pulled it out of the snow. "That's interesting, Nate. Just think how different our lives would've been if your father had felt the same way."

Nathan looked like a guilty young boy. "I'm sorry, Berto. I wasn't thinking."

"Don't you think it ever entered Pa's mind that he didn't want to raise me, that I might remind him of my father? But it didn't stop him from loving me as if I were his real son. Just like Mother loved you as if *you* were her real son."

"I'm not Pa, Berto. I don't know if I can do what he did."

"Of course you can. Why blame an innocent baby for something its father did? If you give it a chance, that baby will only know you as a father. Did you care any less for Robert because he was your nephew?"

"Of course I didn't, but he was your son. This is a lot different."

"It'll be easier, Nate. You won't have the father around to worry about." He shifted from one foot to the other. "Now, you want to help me mend these fences before we freeze. Besides, I'd like to finish up here and get into town before the storm hits. Rachel and I will be staying there tonight."

"Why don't you go ahead, I'll finish up. I like it here. Nobody can bother me."

"I hate to leave you by yourself."

Nathan cocked an eyebrow. "But you will, won't you?"

"Of course I will, big brother. I always was the smarter of the two brothers." He flashed Nathan a brilliant grin. "See you tomorrow."

Anna buttoned her dress, waiting for Rachel to come into the room. She'd never had an examination like that and it had embarrassed her. She was glad it had been Rachel and not a man. Rachel came back into the room, looking at some papers.

"Well?" Anna asked anxiously.

"I don't think you're going to have a baby, Anna. I think you've been worrying so much about everything that happened to you that it has affected your body. There's also something else I want to talk to you about."

"What?"

"Tell me again about when you fell into the water."

"I already told you. I slipped off the bank and hit the rocks."

"You cracked some ribs, but do you remember your stomach being sore? Did you bleed at all?"

"I don't know. I was unconscious for a few days."

"What about the other time, the time you saved the boy in the river? You said you were slammed up against some rocks? Where exactly did the rocks hit your body?"

"Rachel—"

"Please, Anna, it will help me to know more."

"I remember being thrown forward and my chest and stomach hitting the rocks several times. I was turned awround in the water and my sides hit, too."

Rachel wrote as Anna talked.

"What is it, Rachel?"

"I don't know. I think it's possible that you may have injured your insides during one of those falls."

"What do you mean?"

"You might not be able to have children, Anna."

Anna stared at Rachel, shaking her head. "No! How can you be sure of something like that?"

"I can't be completely sure, Anna. But there are tests that can be done."

"Tests? What kind of tests?"

"There are different ways to find out for sure. I have the name of an excellent specialist in San Francisco. I interned with him. He's very good, Anna."

"No," Anna replied adamantly.

"Anna, this may not be as bad as it seems."

"And I should just continue to live life, is that what you're going to tell me, Rachel?" Anna slid down from the table. "No, thank you. I don't want any more lectures or any more opinions. I just want to get out of here." She walked out of the examining room and took her cloak from the rack in the waiting room and pulled it around herself.

"Anna, please wait."

"There's nothing more to say, Rachel." Anna walked outside. The sky was dark. A storm was fast approaching. She mounted her horse and rode hard, ignoring the piercing cold wind that blew into her face. She was so angry she could barely keep from screaming. There was no use feeling sorry for herself. It wouldn't do any good. It had never done any good.

As she rode, she tried to think of what she would do. She couldn't stay with Nathan. He'd already talked of the children they would have together. How could she tell him she couldn't have any? As she neared the yard, she decided to ride up into the pasture. She loved the view at the top of the hill. It overlooked a valley and beyond, the Rockies.

She walked the horse up the hill, patting his neck with her gloved hand. She could see the breath from his nostrils, and it finally occurred to her how cold it was. When she reached the top of the hill she leaned over the horse's neck, feeling the heat from his body. "It's all right, boy. It's all right."

She looked down the valley to the fence at the end of the pasture and saw movement. She walked the horse farther down the sloping hill until she got close enough to see Nathan. She felt like turning and riding back to the house, but she walked the horse up to him.

"What are you doing out here, Anna? You're going to freeze to death!" Nathan said.

"I'm not a child. I've been in snow many times before when I used to travel with my father." Anna edged her horse closer. "Can I talk to you for a moment, Nathan?"

Nathan stopped, wrapping his arms around himself. He looked up at the sky. "It's going to start snowing soon. You should get back."

"I'm not carrying Winter Wolf's child, Nathan."

Nathan stared at her, his eyes seeming unnaturally pale. "That's good, isn't it?"

"No, it's not good."

"You wanted his child?"

"I didn't say that."

"What then?"

"I'm going to be leaving as soon as I can get a train out of here. There's no future for us. Sometimes I can't even remember a time when we got along. There's always going to be some obstacle thrown our way. We'll never make it, Nathan."

Nathan nodded his head, an angry expression on his face. "Do whatever you have to. I don't care anymore, Anna."

Anna hesitated. She wanted to tell him the reason why she was leaving, but she knew it didn't matter. "I did love you, Nathan," she said softly, riding slowly up the hill. She turned once to look back at him, and could see him pounding furiously on a rail. A gust of wind blew the hood from her face and she felt moisture. She held out her hand. It was snowing. She pulled her hood back up and started toward the house. There was nothing left for her here. It was time to leave. As soon as the storm cleared, she'd be gone.

Nathan pounded the nails in a fury, taking a new one out of his pocket and hammering it into the stiff wood. He drove the nail in with one quick blow and then started on another. He looked up at the mountains. They looked almost black against the gray sky. It was beginning to snow. He walked farther down the fence, shook it, and nailed it in the loose places. The wind was rising. He pulled the collar of his sheepskin jacket up, but the cold still seeped in. He couldn't wait to sit in front of the fire. A few more nails and he'd be finished.

There was a sudden gust of wind that took his hat and sailed it toward his horse. The startled animal leapt back, breaking its reins. Nathan dropped the hammer and ran toward the horse, but it was too late. Sensing the coming storm, the animal trotted uncertainly for a few steps, then broke into a gallop toward the ranch house. For a moment, Nathan stood with his hands on his hips, watching the horse. Then he picked up his hat, slapping it against his leg before he angrily pushed it back onto his head. The ranch house was a little over two miles away and his hands and feet were already numb. Nathan glanced up at the sky. The clouds were getting lower, but the snow wasn't falling very hard yet. He turned back to the fence and hammered in four more nails before he started to walk.

The slick leather soles of his boots slid on the frozen ground, and his numb feet made him clumsy. The snowfall thickened, small white flakes driven in the wind. Nathan squinted, lowering his head. The snow was beginning to stick now, outlining the rocks. He shoved his hands into his pockets and hunched his shoulders.

He shook his head, angry with himself for being so stubborn. Roberto had warned him not to stay out here too long. What luck if after all he'd been through, he'd die just two miles from home. He kept wanting to laugh, realizing the absurdity of the situation. He was a tracker, part Indian, but still he lacked enough common sense to guide him through a situation his emotions had ruled. If his horse made it back to the ranch, Roberto would come looking for him, but the way his luck was running today, the animal would probably fall and break a leg on the way.

The snowfall became thicker and thicker, the small, stinging flakes nearly blinding him. He kept walking uphill facing directly into the wind until he felt the land begin to slope downward. Squinting he could barely make out the shapes of the naked cottonwoods that lined the road. He shifted direction, heading for the trees.

The wind gusted and swirled. The ground was nearly white now, and Nathan walked slowly, unable to feel his feet. Snow crusted his eyelashes and rimmed his jacket. He freed one hand from his pocket and rubbed at his eyes. A flash of fear as tangible as an ache went through him as he realized he could no longer see the trees. Without thinking, he turned quickly, trying to scan the horizon. Just as quickly he turned back, realizing that the driving whiteness of the snow had obliterated the landscape. He walked uncertainly forward, then stopped. Had he changed direction? The wind seemed to come from every direction, blinding his vision. He started walking but stopped again. How was he supposed to know what direction to go? But if he stayed where he was, he'd freeze to death.

Nathan squeezed his eyes shut and thought about his father. Trenton had always talked about the innate sense of direction that guided migratory animals through storm and darkness. He tried to find that ability within himself, and after a moment, started walking. He had been less than a half a mile from the road. He counted his steps, and by the time he had counted to a thousand, the muscles in his legs were trembling and he had lost all feeling in his face and hands. It would be easier just to sit down and wait until the storm was over. Roberto would come and find him. Besides, he was tired.

Nathan shook his head fiercely. He hadn't grown up in snow country, but his father had. He could almost hear Trenton's voice telling stories of how men had frozen to death. "It feels like falling asleep, Nate. That's why men don't fight it. It doesn't hurt and it catches up with you slowly."

With his father's voice ringing in his ears, Nathan forced himself to walk again. He cocked his head to one side, noticing a difference in the sound of the wind. Had it shifted? His thoughts moved slowly, as though the cold had somehow seeped into his skull. The urge to sit down and rest was very nearly irresistible. The wind hadn't shifted but it sounded different. Trees, Nathan realized. That was the sound of wind through tree branches. He rubbed at his eyes again with numb fingers. Then he saw it. The ghostly outline of cottonwoods drew him forward. He had found the road and his sleepiness receded. He had a chance. On the road he had a chance.

"Nathan!" The sound of his name pierced the wind. "Nathan!" Anna's voice pulled him forward into a stumbling run. Her cloaked figure appeared in the whiteness, leading his horse. He slowly mounted it and followed Anna back to the house. They rode the horses into the barn. Anna quickly dismounted and took Nathan's arm, leading him into the house. Nathan didn't argue. When they got inside, Anna latched both doors shut. Nathan went to the fire, rubbing his gloved hands together. Anna walked to him, taking off his gloves, hat, and jacket.

"Sit down," she ordered. Nathan did as he was told. Anna pulled off his boots and his wet socks. She rubbed his feet with her hands. "Move the chair closer to the fire and take off the rest of your clothes. I'll be right back."

Nathan curled his toes, reaching down to rub his numb feet. He took off his pants and his flannel shirt, and sat in his long underwear. He closed his eyes for a moment, leaning close to the fire, letting it warm his body. He opened his eyes when he heard Anna's footsteps. She dropped a small tub on the floor in front of him and returned a moment later with a large pot of boiling water, pouring it into the tub.

"Try that," she ordered.

Nathan gingerly touched the water, resting his feet on the sides of the tub. "It's hot," he said in reply to Anna's tapping foot.

"Of course it's hot. It won't do you any good if it's cold."

"Just give me a minute. I'll get them in there."

Anna left with a disgusted look and returned holding two glasses filled with whiskey. "Here, maybe this will help build your nerve." She took a blanket from one of the chairs and put it around his shoulders. She pulled the other chair close to the fire and sat sipping at the whiskey.

Nathan thanked her gratefully for the whiskey and felt it wind a fiery path to his stomach. He looked at Anna, put down his drink, and slowly stuck his toes in the water.

"You're worse than a child."

"All right," he said, gingerly easing his feet into the steaming water. He gripped the arms of the chair as the water burned his feet, but soon he began to relax, feeling the warmth spread throughout his body. He leaned his head back against the chair, closing his eyes. His toes and the bottoms of his feet began to feel prickly. Feeling was returning to them.

"Better?"

Nathan opened his eyes. "Yes."

"Good. Are you hungry?"

"Not really. I just want to sit here. I never knew a house with a fire and a tub of hot water could feel so good."

"Why did you stay out there, Nathan? You knew that storm was coming."

"I was angry with you."

"You were angry with me so you were going to freeze to death? What was that going to prove?"

"I wasn't trying to freeze to death. I was just going to work for a while longer."

"It's not like you to have so little respect for nature. You know how quickly those things can hit."

"All right, so I wasn't thinking. I've learned my lesson. If I ever work on a fence in the snow again, I'll be sure to leave as soon as clouds appear. Satisfied?" Nathan picked up his glass and sipped at the whiskey. "I'm happy to be alive, if that's what you mean."

Anna got up and reached for the blanket on her chair. She laid it across Nathan's lap, tucking it in around him. "Are you warmer?"

"A lot warmer than I was an hour ago."

Anna sat back down. "When I saw your horse come back, I knew something had gone wrong."

"Where is Berto? And why is it so quiet here?"

"He and Rachel had plans to stay in town. He told me that you knew."

Nathan nodded his head. "He told me. I just wasn't thinking." He looked up at Anna. "If you hadn't been here, chances are, I'd be dead right now."

"I don't think so. You would have found your way back here eventually."

"I doubt it. I couldn't see a thing. It was the damndest thing. How did you see where you were going?"

"I didn't. The horse instinctively went down the road. I thought I'd look there first and then ride up into the pasture."

"You could have been lost in that storm."

"I could have, but I wasn't."

Nathan stretched his feet out from the water. "The feeling's coming back. They're starting to hurt."

"Why don't I rub them for you," Anna offered.

Anna moved her chair around until she could easily put Nathan's foot in her lap. She vigorously rubbed it, then slowly massaged it. When she was done with one foot, she did the other. "How does that feel?"

"I think I'm in Seyan," Nathan joked.

Anna smiled. "If you were in Seyan, you would never have been in a storm. You would have been walking in a beautiful meadow in spring, there would be wildflowers all over the hills, and a small stream would be flowing through the meadow."

"And what would I be doing there?"

"You would be lying on your back, feeling the warm sun on your chest and face, chewing on a piece of wild grass."

"Am I alone there?"

"I don't know."

Nathan shook his head. "I'm not. There's a woman lying next to me. She's beautiful, with long dark hair and deep blue eyes. She has her eyes closed. Do you know what I do then? I lean over and tickle her nose with the wild grass. She twitches her nose but doesn't wake up. She's dreaming."

"What is she dreaming about?"

"Me," Nathan said calmly, putting both feet on the floor. He wiggled his toes. "I think I'm going to live, thanks to you."

"Now you should get into bed and get some sleep." Anna started to get up, but Nathan held onto her

394

wrist.

"No, stay with me a little longer. Remember, I was a dying man only a short time ago."

Anna smiled. "All right, I'll stay for a while."

"I *am* in Seyan." Nathan sighed deeply. "Are you sad that you're not carrying Winter Wolf's child?" he asked.

"It wasn't meant to be."

"But if you *had* been carrying it, you would have had it."

"Of course I would have. Whatever mistakes I've made, an innocent child shouldn't be made to pay for them."

"I know, and I'm sorry I didn't react very well. That's not how Pa reacted to raising Berto."

"You don't know how he reacted when he found out Aeneva was going to have another man's child. He could have been angry, for all you know."

"Not Pa. He was too good."

"He told me once that he was ready to leave Aeneva, Nathan. He said that he had always been ashamed of the way he'd reacted when he saw her with the baby. You reacted like any man would have. I understand that."

"So, where do we go from here?"

"We don't," Anna said uneasily.

"Don't you think it's time we stopped running away from each other, Anna? I know you love me, no matter what you say, and I love you. So what's to stop us from finally building a life together?"

"There'll always be something, Nathan. The Great Spirit has never smiled kindly on us."

"But he *has*, Anna. If I had never met you, I would never have known how deeply I can love someone. I wouldn't go back for anything. Everything we've been through has led us to this moment."

"I can't believe that."

"But you do or you wouldn't be here."

"I won't be here for long."

395

"Don't run away, Anna."

"I can't stay here any longer, Nathan. You and I are always fighting. I don't want to remember you that way."

"Are you planning to find yourself another man, get married, and have children?"

"No, I don't ever want to have children," Anna said angrily.

"Why not? You're wonderful with children."

"I don't want any of my own."

"What has changed so suddenly, Anna? You were prepared to raise a child on your own and now you don't even want children."

Anna stood up. "I'm going to go to bed. If you need anything, call me."

Nathan grabbed Anna's arm as she walked by, pulling her into his lap. "Talk to me, Anna. What's wrong?" His hand went up to stroke her soft hair.

Anna didn't fight Nathan. She looked down at her hands clenching and unclenching them. "I can't have children, Nathan." She looked at him, tears rolling down her cheeks. "I can't have your children."

Nathan heard her words, but he wasn't as shocked by them as he thought he would be. He reached up and wiped the tears from her cheeks. "I don't care. I love you, Anna."

"But you *will* care. You'll want someone who can give you lots of children."

"I want you. We can adopt children. Do you think Aeneva loved you or me any less because we weren't her blood children? Or my father—did he spoil you or love you any less because you weren't his blood daughter?"

Anna smiled. "No, he used to say I was his daughter because I reminded him so much of Aeneva. Both your parents loved me as if I had been their own."

"Don't you think we can do the same? We can adopt as many children as you like. What matters the most is

396

that we love them and care for them the way my parents cared for us."

Anna nodded, biting her lip. "You are like your father, Nathan. He would be so proud of you right now."

"I'm not doing this for my father, Anna. I'm doing this for us. I know we can be happy as long as we have each other. If I lose you I'll have nothing."

"But—"

"No more buts. If I die tomorrow, at least we will have had today." He kissed Anna gently. "Aren't you at least going to argue?"

"No," she said gratefully, wrapping her arms around his neck and leaning her head against his. "It's been so long since you've held me."

"Can I ask you something, Anna?" Nathan's voice was grave. "I want you to be honest with me."

"All right."

"Did you palm that jack?"

Anna lifted her head from Nathan's, a smile on her face. "What do you think?"

"I think you did."

"You're right."

"I knew it. Pa taught you real good."

"Now, can I ask you something?"

"Yes."

"Will you marry me?"

Nathan looked up at the ceiling, then shook his head. "I don't see how I could possibly marry a woman who cheats."

Anna hit him in the chest. "Be serious."

"You already know what my answer is. I want to marry you, and I want to marry you as soon as possible."

"Are you sure, Nathan? I don't want to push you into anything?"

Nathan laughed, pulling Anna closer into his arms. "God, I love you, Kathleen Anna O'Leary." He kissed Anna, savoring the sweetness of her mouth. Finally, their time had come. As he held her in his arms, he knew in his heart that they would be together for a long time. The Great Spirit was indeed smiling on them.

Chapter 17

"Will you stand still?" Roberto pinned a small white flower to Nathan's lapel, then brushed off the collar of his suit. "You look good, Nate. Can't believe you even got a haircut."

Nathan wriggled his neck, pulling at the constraining collar. "Why do people wear these things? They're not made for humans."

"Quit complaining. Here . . ." He handed Nathan a glass of whiskey. "Here's to you, big brother. It's about time."

Nathan downed the contents, shutting his eyes for a moment. "Me, a married man, who would ever have thought?"

"I'm happy for you, Nate. I tried to think what I could give you for a wedding present, but I figured you didn't need anything with Anna as your wife." He smiled and handed him a piece of paper. "But I thought of something anyway."

Nathan opened the piece of paper. Roberto had renounced all claims to the Arizona ranch and had given Nathan twenty-five percent ownership in Driscoll Shipping. "Berto, you didn't have to do this."

"I know I didn't have to. It was the least I could do for all the trouble I caused. Besides, I won't be going back to the ranch. I'll be staying here."

"Half of that ranch is yours."

"No, Nate. You've always loved that ranch and it's fitting that you should have it."

"I don't need to own part of your company."

"I know you don't need to, but if something should happen to you, at least you'll have money coming in. You can save it for your children."

Nathan folded the piece of paper and wrapped his arms around his brother. "Thank you, Berto. I don't know what to say."

"You don't have to say anything. Just have a good life . . . But there's something else. I've been in touch with LeBeau. He's found Anna's sister."

"I don't believe it. This is the best present she could have."

"LeBeau says he's been in contact with the sister and she'll write Anna."

"That's wonderful. What about Garrett and Molly?"

"They arrived last night, I already checked. They'll be out here real soon."

"Then everything's set."

"No, not everything." Roberto reached into his pocket and brought out a folded handkerchief. He handed it to Nathan. "Open it."

Nathan opened the handkerchief. He stared in puzzlement at the small gold band.

"Look at the inside."

Nathan held up the ring to the light. "Love, J.H.," Nathan said slowly. He looked at Roberto. "This belonged to my grandfather."

Roberto nodded. "He gave it to your grandmother on their wedding day. She gave it to your father and he gave it to Aeneva."

"How did you get it?"

"Remember the letters Mother left for us? She left the ring for me, saying you had Sun Dancer's silver necklace and she wanted me to have something, too. I got to thinking that this ring should be yours. Jim Hawkins was your grandfather, not mine. You should give it to

Anna."

"No," Nathan refused. "Mother gave it to you. She wanted you to have it."

"She also would have wanted you to have it if she'd known you gave the necklace back to her family. It's right, Nate."

"But what do you have of Mother's?"

Roberto smiled. "I have everything of Mother's. Right here," he said, patting his chest.

"And what ring will you give to Rachel?"

"I don't know, I'll buy her something."

Nathan reached into his pocket. He handed Roberto a small box. "We'll start our own tradition. You gave me the ring for *my* wife—now I'll give you the ring for *yours*."

Roberto whistled as he held up the diamond ring. "This is a beauty. Are you sure you want me to have it?"

"Of course I'm sure. Will Rachel like it?"

"She'll like it." Roberto smiled. "Thanks, Nate."

Nate looked toward the bedroom. "Shouldn't they be ready by now?" he asked.

"Hell, the minister, Zeb, Molly, and Garrett aren't even here yet. You can't get married without your friends around."

"Pour me another whiskey, will you?"

"What do you think?" Anna stood up, the white lace dress falling softly around her slim body.

"I think you're the most beautiful bride I've ever seen." Rachel hugged Anna. "I am so happy for you. But Anna, I have something else to say. I wrote to my colleague in San Francisco, and he thinks there's a good possibility you may be fine. He thinks your injuries from your fall into the river might just need time to heal. If you aren't able to have children within the next year, then he wants you to visit him. Will you do that?"

Anna nodded her head. "All right, Rachel, I'll do it."

Rachel turned toward the door. "Your friends must be

here. I hear a lot of laughing."

"You'll love Molly and Garrett. Garrett was my first love."

"Then I definitely want to meet him."

"Anna!" There was a frantic knocking on the door.

Anna flew to the door and pulled it open, quickly yanking Molly inside. "I can't believe you're here," she said, hugging Molly to her. "I've missed you so much."

"You look beautiful, Anna." Molly kissed her on the cheek.

"Come here, I want you to meet someone." She brought Molly to Rachel. "Molly, this is Rachel. Rachel saved my life."

"I'm real pleased to meet you, Rachel. So, you're the lucky woman who's going to marry Roberto?"

Rachel smiled. "I guess so."

"In the spring," Anna said. "Come over here and sit down. We have so much to talk about."

"Anna, you're about to get married, or did you forget that?"

"I haven't forgotten. Let them wait. They'll be drinking whiskey anyway. So, how is Garrett?"

"He's fine, just fine. He loves California and the ranch. We've happy there."

"And you're wearing a ring, I see. When did you two get married?"

"Right after we got there." Molly took Anna's hands in hers. "I have to tell you something, Anna. Something real important."

"What is it?" Anna asked, her face going pale.

"Why don't I leave you two alone?" Rachel started for the door.

"No, please stay, Rachel," Molly said. She motioned to the bed. Come over here and sit by us." Molly waited until Rachel was sitting on the bed. "Do you remember when you asked Roberto to look for your real sister?"

"Yes, but he didn't find anything out."

"He had LeBeau working on it all this time and he's

402

found your sister, Anna."

"He found her?" Anna looked from Molly to Rachel. "Where is she? If I'd known, I would have written her so she could be here."

"She is here, Annie. I'm your sister," Molly said, tears filling her eyes.

Anna stared wide-eyed at Molly. "You're my sister? How can that be? You had two sisters of your own."

"Remember your father left you that letter saying that you had a sister who was about five years older than you?"

"Yes, her name was Megan O'Leary and she lived with her mother in San Francisco. Her mother's family name was Foster." She stared at Molly. "My father also said my sister had blue eyes and light hair. You have brown eyes, Molly."

"Just listen to me . . . My mother went a little bit crazy, from our father leaving and from the death of Rosie, our sister. She couldn't handle the responsibility of raising a daughter on her own. Her mother talked her into giving me away to another family. Her mother had friends in the East who knew people who had a nice home and two small daughters but very little money. My mother paid them to take me in and pretend I was their oldest daughter. Their last name was O'Brien."

"But your eyes. . . ?"

"LeBeau found a woman who had worked for my mother. My eyes were always a very dark blue, but eventually they turned brown."

"My God, I can't believe it."

"For the longest time I had a memory of a man sitting in my room telling stories. I know I was just a baby, but I remember his voice. I even remember Rosie. She was so pale, and I remember that she always coughed. Poor Rosie."

"Molly . . ." Anna said, pulling her sister into her arms. "I can't believe it. I always told you I felt as if you were my sister. It's so hard to believe."

403

"I know. When LeBeau first sent the report to us, I couldn't believe it, but it all fits. He even found my mother and talked to her."

"What did she say?"

"He said that she was angry at first and tried to have him kicked out, but when he told her that he'd met me, she softened and wanted to know all about me. She confirmed everything he'd found out. She told LeBeau she gave me away because she didn't want any reminders of Mr. O'Leary."

Anna squeezed Molly's hand. "I feel sorry for your mother, Molly. She must be a lonely woman."

"She never married again. She's still alone."

"You could go to see her."

"Not right now, Anna. Maybe someday."

"Well, this day is a double celebration," Rachel said, taking both women's hands in hers. "I am so very happy for you both. You are very much alike, you know. You're both strong. Look how well you've both turned out."

Anna looked at Molly, a wide grin spreading across her face. "Do you remember when we climbed down that rope to get out of Thornston's doll room? You said we were crazy."

Molly started laughing. "I also said I wished I had a sister like you. I still can't believe it. I've thought about it for so long. God's given us a gift, Anna."

There was a knock on the door, and Anna ran to answer it.

Garrett walked into the room, looking lean and healthy. He smiled when he saw Anna, picking her up in his arms and swinging her around. "I don't think I've ever seen you look so beautiful, Annie."

"I can't believe you're here, Garrett. Thank you." Anna wrapped her arms around him, closing her eyes as she nestled against his chest. There was a familiarity about Garrett that she had with no one, not even with Nathan. No one could take Garrett's place in her heart.

"So, you finally decided to give in and marry the poor man. He's as nervous as a treed bobcat. Roberto and I practically had to tie him to a chair to make him stay."

Anna hit Garrett's arm. "I might have believed that a few weeks ago but not now."

Garrett looked over at Molly. "What did I tell you? I knew being taken captive by Indians wouldn't slow her down any." His eyes rested on Rachel. "Sorry, ma'am. I'm Garrett McReynolds."

"I'm pleased to meet you, Garrett. I'm Rachel. I'm going to go on out and tell them you'll be out soon, Anna."

"I think I'll go on out, too," Molly said. "Give you two a few minutes alone. You don't need my help anymore, Annie. You couldn't look any more beautiful if you tried." Molly kissed her sister on the cheek and left the room.

"Are you happy, Annie?"

"Yes, I am, Garrett, but it took me a long time to get there. I never felt so frightened or so alone as I have the past few months."

"With all these people here who love you?"

"It didn't matter. There were problems only *I* could solve." She looked at Garrett. "The man who took me captive raped me. I was so frightened of him, I gave into him willingly another time. I couldn't live with myself for doing that. I kept thinking I should've been stronger."

"You are strong, Annie. I don't think I've ever known a woman as strong as you, except for your mother. Remember what I told you when Driscoll sold you to that bastard captain? I told you that no person, no man or woman, could take away the most important part of you. That's your heart, Annie." Garrett pulled her into his arms. "God, I love you. If only things had been different."

"I know," Anna said, feeling the tears well up in her eyes. She loved this man so much—he had been her first

405

real friend, her first real love. "You have always been so honest and open, Garrett. I'll always be grateful for that. I love you, too."

Garrett lifted Anna's chin, barely touching it with his fingers. He kissed her very softly, lingering for a time, then pulled back. "If I'm going to give you away, I'd better get out there and you'd better hurry. Your groom is going to be real anxious to see you."

Anna smiled as she watched him leave the room. She hurried to the mirror, fixing her hair and adjusting the small lace veil that hung down her back. She took a deep breath and opened the door. Garrett was waiting. He held out his arm to her and she took it, flashing him a brilliant smile. They walked slowly into the middle of the living room. Zeb and Rachel stood off to one side. Rachel held a squirming Robert. Nathan stood by the fireplace, resplendent in a gray suit and shiny black boots. He'd even cut his hair. Roberto stood next to him, dark and handsome. Molly stood opposite the men, smiling broadly at Anna. In the middle stood the minister.

Anna let Garrett lead her to Nathan. She stopped and kissed Garrett, then took Nathan's arm. They stood together in front of the minister. Anna didn't really hear what the man said. She couldn't believe she and Nathan were finally getting married. She looked up at him while the minister spoke, realizing that he would soon be her husband.

"Mr. Hawkins, will you have this woman?"

Nathan stared at Anna, love written on his face. "I will have her for eternity."

"And you Miss O'Leary, will you have this man for your husband?"

Anna stared at Nathan, a smile spreading across her face.

"Did you hear me, miss?"

Anna looked at the minister. "I'm sorry. What did you say?"

"I asked you if you'll have this man?"

"Of course I will," Anna replied without hesitation.

"The ring then, sir."

Roberto handed Nathan the small gold band and he placed it on Anna's finger.

"I now pronounce you man and wife. You may kiss the bride."

Nathan smiled at Anna, lowering his mouth to hers. He kissed her softly at first, then more passionately, until everyone in the room began to clap. "We'll finish this later," Nathan said, smiling.

Anna turned to give Molly a hug. "I'm so glad you were here."

"I wouldn't have missed it for anything. Besides, it's not every day I can attend the wedding of a sister I never knew I had."

Anna then directed her attention to Roberto, hugging him, too. "Thank you for everything. You've been such a good friend and brother. I don't know what I would have done these past few weeks without you and Rachel."

"It's the least I could do, Anna. I'll never be able to make up for what I did to you and Nate before—"

Anna pressed her fingers to Roberto's lips. "You already have. You found my sister." She kissed him on the cheek. "Thank you for that." She walked to Rachel and took Robert in her arms, hugging him tightly. "Hello, little Hahkota. You're such a good boy." She kissed him on the cheek and put him on the floor. "Thank you, Rachel. I'm ashamed of the way I've behaved."

"Don't say anymore, Anna. You know how I feel. I know what you've been through, and I'm just glad you're well and happy."

Anna hugged Rachel. She walked to Zeb and kissed him on the cheek. "And thank you, Zeb."

"For what? I didn't do nothin'."

"Yes, you did. You made it possible for Nathan to find me."

"Aw, I didn't do nothin', but I'm real glad that boy

found you. Woulda been a real shame if you'd been left with them Injuns."

Anna nodded. She felt an arm go around her, and saw Nathan smiling at her, offering her a glass of champagne. "Are you trying to get me drunk?" she asked.

"No, I want you wide-awake when we get upstairs." He kissed her.

"How about a toast to the bride and groom?" Roberto held up his glass. "Here's to my big brother and his lovely new bride. I wish you all the happiness in the world. I wish you lots of healthy children. My final wish for you is that your love grows stronger every day." They all drank from their glasses and Roberto held up his hand. "I have one other little surprise for Nathan and Anna." He walked forward. "You won't be spending your honeymoon night here."

"And where will we be spending it, Berto?"

"On a private train car heading south to Arizona. You're both homesick. It's time."

"But what about your wedding? And Molly?" Anna asked.

"Garrett and Molly can stay here for a few extra days, then take the train to Arizona and spend some time with you. Don't worry, they already know about it."

Anna looked at Nathan.

"I can't think of a better idea," he answered her unspoken question.

Anna nodded. "We accept, Berto, but we'll be back in the spring for your wedding." She looked at Molly and Garrett. "You will stay with us for a while?"

"Yes, Annie. Besides, I'd like to stop by and see my folks," Garrett replied.

"It's settled then," Nathan said, his arm around Anna. "My wife and I will honeymoon on the train."

Anna sat on the edge of the small bed, nervously shaking her bare foot. She was wearing a pink satin nightgown that was cut in at the shoulders and fairly low across the breasts. She felt as nervous as a schoolgirl anticipating her first kiss. She and Nathan had made love before, but it had been a long time since they had been together and so much had happened.

She got up and started walking around the room, wondering where Nathan was. He said he was going to the dining car for a drink and would give her time to change. That was an hour ago. She walked to the window and looked out at the dark countryside. She couldn't see anything. The clack of the tracks soothed her somehow. She turned away from the window and looked around. Roberto had spared no expense. The car had a bed, a couch and chairs, a desk with writing materials, a small table for dining, complete with vase of fresh flowers, and a closet for their clothes. She heard a click, then Nathan opened the door and walked in carrying a tray.

"What do you have?" Anna asked excitedly.

"Just sit down and I'll show you." Anna sat at the table and watched as Nathan set out a bucket with ice and a bottle of champagne, two glasses, two sandwiches, and two pieces of pie.

Anna took a bite from the sandwich, staring across the table at Nathan. "I can't believe we're going home."

"It's going to be so good to be there. Maybe it's what we both need."

Anna nodded, sipping at her champagne. "I can't believe I have a sister. Just think, if my father had never written me that letter, I would never have found out about Molly."

"He really loved you, Anna."

"I know that now."

"I need to ask you something. I know you might get angry, but it's something I've wanted to ask you for a long time . . . If I'd never come back to the camp and you recovered, would you have stayed with Winter Wolf?"

Anna set down her glass, twirling it between her two hands. It occurred to her how strange Winter Wolf would find all this, as strange as she had found *his* world. "I don't know what I would have done, Nathan. I cared for him." She met Nathan's blue eyes. "Yes, I probably would have stayed. I don't think I would have tried to take my own life again."

Nathan nodded, staring into his glass. "I thought that would be your answer."

"Does it make a difference?"

"I don't think so."

"Nathan, you aren't jealous of him, are you?"

"No, I can't explain it. After I got to see the kind of man he really was, I could understand why you would have wanted to stay with him."

"That's in the past. Now I want to think about our future."

Nathan clinked his glass against Anna's. "To our future."

Anna drank her champagne. "I'm not really too hungry right now." She stood up, the nightgown clinging to her body. "Why don't we go to bed?"

Nathan stood up. He took off his jacket and unbuttoned his shirt. He walked over to Anna, cupping her face in his hands. "You are so beautiful, you take my breath away." Anna felt his mouth cover hers. He ran his hands up and down the smooth satin of her nightgown, feeling the curves of her body. She put her hands around his neck, then he bent down and lifted her up, carrying her to the bed. He set her down on the edge, kneeling on the floor in front of her. He took off his shirt, and Anna ran her hands over his chest and up to his face, kissing him passionately. She felt him lower the straps on the nightgown, so that her shoulders were bare. He kissed her throat and slowly, very slowly, moved his mouth down to her breasts. He pushed the nightgown down until her breasts were exposed, then kissed the curve of them, lightly touching them with his tongue.

She felt him run his hands up her legs until he had pushed her nightgown almost to her waist. He ran his hands up and down her thighs, tickling the insides with his fingertips. Anna watched as Nathan stood up, pulling off his boots, then his pants. She felt like smiling as he stood before her in his long underwear, but when he took them off, her smile faded. He had an extraordinary body, lean and long and muscled. He came to her, kneeling on the bed next to her. Anna lay back and let Nathan pull the nightgown completely off her. She closed her eyes as his hands moved gently and seductively over her. His mouth covered hers, his tongue lightly probing her mouth. His hand moved between her thighs. She was embarrassed yet excited by his boldness. She had forgotten what it was like to be this comfortable with a man.

"Look at me, Anna. Look at me."

Anna's mind raced. "Look at me, Heva. Look at me!" She was suddenly afraid. Slowly, she opened her eyes, fear making them large. This was not Nathan who was making love to her. It was Winter Wolf raping her.

"Anna." Nathan's voice was gentle. "Look at me, please."

Anna looked into the light-blue depths of Nathan's eyes. "I'm not him, Anna. I won't hurt you."

Anna closed her eyes again. "I'm afraid, Nathan."

"So am I. I'm afraid it won't be like before. But I don't want us to wait. I want us to know each other just like we knew each other the first time. I want you to hold onto me like you did the first time." Nathan buried his face in Anna's neck, kissing her.

Anna wrapped her arms around Nathan's neck, running her fingers through his silky hair. "I want you to love me, Nathan. Please, love me." Anna's mouth met his, and she felt herself being drawn into something from which she couldn't return. His body lay against hers, one arm wrapped around her, the other touching her body, loving it. Anna felt her excitement rise. She wanted him

411

in a way that a woman was meant to want a man's body—with the consent and desire of both. She felt his fingers between her legs and she began to moan slightly, throwing her head back. She felt Nathan shift his weight until he was between her legs, his hands by her shoulders.

"I love you, Anna," he said, lowering his mouth to hers, kissing her softly, teasing her.

Anna felt him enter her, and at first she was frightened. She expected the sharp, jabbing pain of Winter Wolf, but instead, Nathan entered her slowly, gently, almost teasingly, until she started to respond. She found her hips moving against his. Nathan pulled her legs up until they were on his back and he rocked back and forth. Anna moaned loudly, calling out Nathan's name. He moved faster inside her, all the while making sure he wasn't hurting her. Anna ran her fingers up and down his back, feeling the soft skin under her fingertips. Nathan moved faster still, putting his hands under her hips and holding her up to him. Anna felt herself begin to lose control. She shut her eyes, reveling in the feel of this man whom she loved beyond all else. She called out his name and he moved so fast that she thought she would scream, but Nathan kissed her, taking her scream into him as he exploded and gave himself to her. They moved against each other for a while longer until Nathan relaxed, resting his head on Anna's breasts, kissing each of them.

"You are incredible," he said breathlessly. "I don't ever want to have to wait that long to make love to you."

"You make me feel so loved." She closed her eyes, running her fingers through his hair. "Thank you for the most wonderful honeymoon a woman could have."

"You must be talking about the sandwiches," Nathan said glibly.

"Those sandwiches are nothing compared to you, my love," Anna said with a smile. "I will only make you one promise tonight, Nathan. I won't promise you that I'll

412

never leave you, because we both know that can happen. But I promise you that no matter where I am, no matter how old I get, I'll love you with all my heart."

Nathan raised his head, looking into Anna's eyes. "I'll make you the same promise. *Ne-mehotatse, na-htseoh-oheme.* I love you, my wife."

Anna sat on the rocks overlooking the valley. A warm breeze blew her hair and she threw her head back, enjoying the feel of the sun on her face. She looked over at the scaffoldings of Aeneva and Trenton and she smiled. *"Pave-voonaoh-oho, tsehe-shketo. Heeheoh-ohe, tsehe-heto.* Good morning, my mother. Good morning, my father. It is a good day to be alive. I feel as if I were in Seyan with you." She saw the dark horse riding up the slope to the rocks and Nathan dismounted, greeting his parents as he always did, and climbing the rocks next to Anna.

"I thought I'd find you here." He kissed her on the cheek. "You look beautiful this morning."

Nathan reached over and gently rubbed Anna's rounded belly. "I can't believe we've been married four months, and in six months we're going to have a baby."

"I didn't think it was possible."

"The Great Spirit was smiling on us."

"It was probably Aeneva and Sun Dancer mixing some magic medicine."

"I don't care what it was." Nathan put his arm around Anna. "I don't think I've ever been this content in my life. I have you, a child on the way, and land that I love." He shook his head. "I keep thinking about Winter Wolf. He told me once that all his people wanted was to be left alone on their own land. I don't think I fully understood what he meant until I came back here."

"I like to think that Winter Wolf and his band will find a place where no one can uproot them."

"Let's hope so." Nathan kissed Anna again. "I do love you, Anna. Do you know that?"

"Yes." She patted her stomach. "I have proof."

Nathan smiled, pulling her to him. "We're lucky, Anna. I know neither of us felt that way six months ago, but I suppose it was a road we had to travel just to get here."

"You sound like Aeneva."

"Maybe after all this time I've finally learned from her. She taught me to be patient and she said if I was honorable and true of heart, that which I wished for most would come to me. She was right."

"I love you, Nathan. You are what I wished for most in this world, and you came to me. Thank you for my life." She put her arms around Nathan's neck, secure in the knowledge that whatever happened, Nathan's love would always surround her.

HEART SOARING ROMANCE BY LA REE BRYANT

FORBIDDEN PARADISE   (2744-3, $3.75/$4.95)

Jordan St. Clair had come to South America to find her fiance and break her engagement, but the handsome and arrogant guide refused to a woman through the steamy and dangerous jungles. Finally, he relented, on one condition: She would do exactly as he said. Beautiful Jordan had never been ruled in her life, yet there was something about Patrick Castle that set her heart on fire. Patrick ached to possess the body and soul of the tempting vixen, to lead her from the lush, tropical jungle into a FORBIDDEN PARADISE of their very own.

ARIZONA VIXEN   (2642-0, $3.75/$4.95)

As soon as their eyes met, Sabra Powers knew she had to have the handsome stranger she saw in the park. But Sterling Hawkins was a tormented man caught between two worlds: As a halfbreed, he was a successful businessman with a seething Indian's soul which could not rest until he had revenge for his parents' death. Sabra was willing to risk anything to experience this loner's fiery embrace and seering kiss. Sterling vowed to capture this ARIZONA VIXEN and make her his own . . . if only for one night!

TEXAS GLORY   (2222-1, $3.75/$4.95)

When enchanting Glory Westbrook was banished to a two-year finishing school for dallying with Yankee Slade Hunter, she thought she'd die of a broken heart; when father announced she would marry his business associate who smothered her with insolent stares, she thought she'd die of horror and shock.

For two years devastatingly handsome Slade Hunter had been denied the embrace of the only woman he had ever loved. He thought this was the best thing for Glory, yet when he saw her again after two years, all resolve melted away with one passionate kiss. She *had* to be his, surrendering her heart and mind to his powerful arms and strong embrace.